CASSIE EDWARDS

THE SAVAGE SERIES

Winner of the *Romantic Times*

Lifetime Achievement Award for Best Indian Series!

"Cassie Edwards writes action-packed, sexy reads! Romance fans will be more than satisfied!"

—Romantic Times

SAVAGE EMBERS

Falcon Hawk ran a finger slowly up the column of her neck, making a sensual shiver soar through her. "Here stands a flawless white throat," he said admiringly. "Your arms are dainty, and your legs are long and tapered beautifully. Once the child is gone from inside you, you will be small again. When we make love, I will be holding someone delicate."

"When we...make love?" Maggie stammered.

"It is certain that we will make love after you have your child," Falcon Hawk said. "You will stay. You will be my *h-isei.* The child will be reared as mine."

"It will?" Maggie gulped. Then she placed a hand on his arm. "How can you be so generous after I kept the truth from you?"

"There were good reasons, were there not?" Falcon Hawk said, taking her hand and holding it to his lips, kissing her fingertips.

"I feared telling you for many reasons, but mainly because I did not want to lose your love," Maggie murmured. "I do love you so, Falcon Hawk. I have from almost the moment I first saw you."

Other *Leisure Books* by Cassie Edwards:
TOUCH THE WILD WIND
ROSES AFTER RAIN
WHEN PASSION CALLS
EDEN'S PROMISE
ISLAND RAPTURE
SECRETS OF MY HEART

The *Savage* Series:
SAVAGE ILLUSION
SAVAGE SUNRISE
SAVAGE MISTS
SAVAGE PROMISE
SAVAGE PERSUASION

SAVAGE EMBERS

CASSIE EDWARDS

LEISURE BOOKS  NEW YORK CITY

Savage Embers is dedicated to a special fan—
Donna Lorkowski, this one is for you!

A LEISURE BOOK®

February 1994

Published by

Dorchester Publishing Co., Inc.
276 Fifth Avenue
New York, NY 10001

Cover Art by John Ennis

Printed in the United States of America.

Love is not forever,
Never has it been!
Only can it be
If one should look within.

The heart, if pierced,
Love shall never leak and drain.
The kiss of love shall tell
And erase the pain.

Budding in its beauty,
Love shall never die.
Troubled not by hate
Nor blemished by a lie.

Love can be forever,
Only if it's true,
So look into my eyes
And tell me—
"I love you."

—Helen Bowden

SAVAGE EMBERS

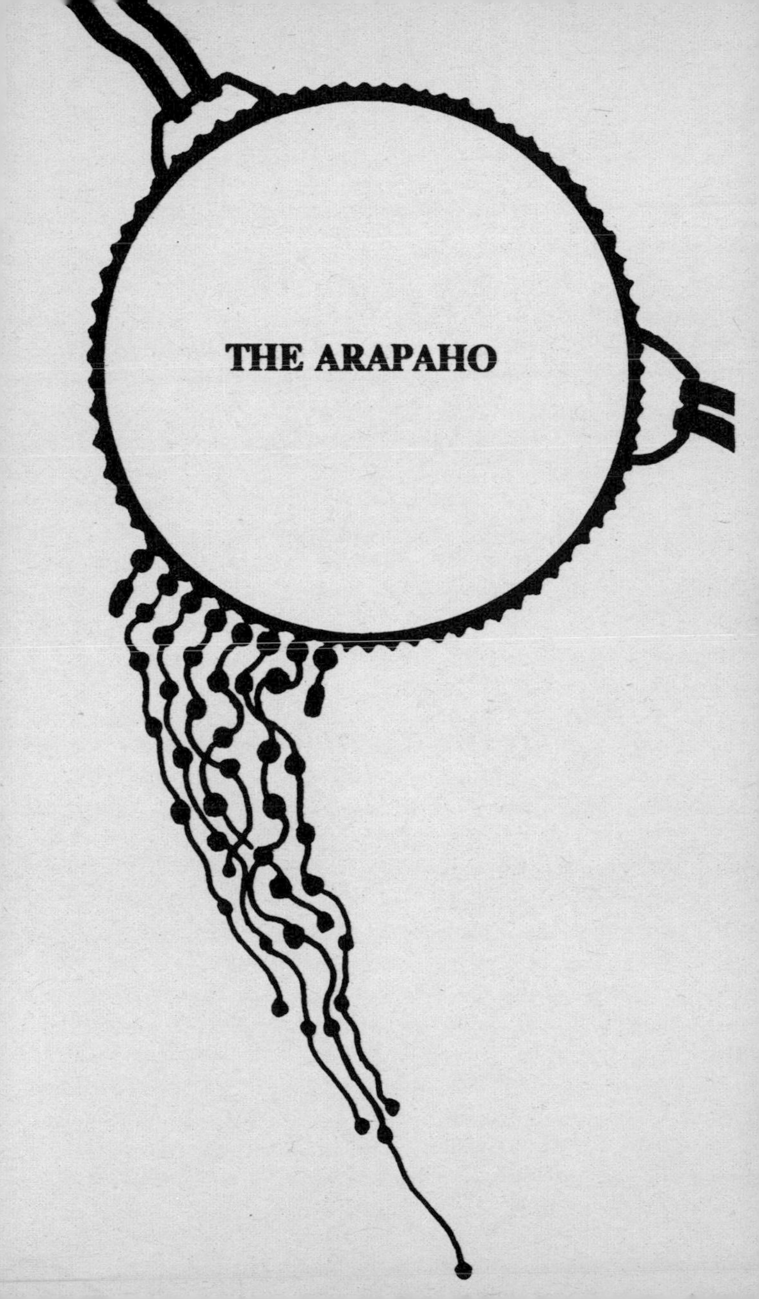
THE ARAPAHO

Prologue

Kansas City, Missouri—1889

A candle glowed softly in the dark, wavering as the woman carried it toward a safe. She placed the brass candle holder on the floor while her trembling fingers worked the combination. When the door of the safe finally squeaked open, piles of neatly stacked money were revealed.

Without hesitation, she lifted the money into an open satchel, until only one lone bill was left behind, as a final insult to the man to whom it belonged.

Tears streamed down her cheeks as Margaret June Hill blew the candle out and fled from the office, the bulging satchel heavy at her right side. Although she had just taken back money that was rightfully hers, nothing could ever return her virginity to her. Tonight she was escaping the man who had stolen her innocence; she prayed that she was severing her ties with him, forever.

Chapter One

Wyoming—1890

With the first thin line of pink on the horizon, the coyotes near the Wind River Indian Reservation began their salutations to the dawn. Joining the cry of the coyote were the chants of the Arapaho Indians as they performed a rain dance in an effort to end a lengthy dry spell. One spark of fire in the wrong place could wipe out the herds of buffalo that the Arapaho hunted for their livelihood.

Long Hair, an elderly Arapaho, who had been at one time the proud chief of his people, sat with his arms folded across his massive bare chest within the circle of his people as the younger warriors danced before them, among them Long Hair's pride and joy—his grandson, Chief Falcon Hawk.

Long Hair's old face crinkled into a smile as

he singled Falcon Hawk out, his faded eyes watching his grandson's every movement. He was envisioning himself participating in the rain dance at the age of thirty winters, as his grandson was now.

Long Hair lifted his chin proudly. He had been just as handsome in his youth as his grandson. His hair had been as perfectly black, sleek, long and flowing. His body had been as tall, slender, thin of flank, and sinewy of muscle. His arms had showed the same rippling bands of muscles as Falcon Hawk's.

Although much had changed about Long Hair as he had aged, he knew that he still boasted the same bold cheekbones as his grandson, a jaw that was square and firm, and eyes as black as midnight. Both men shared the same alert expression and an aura of strength and confidence.

Just watching his grandson took Long Hair back to his own youth. As he tapped a fan made from an eagle wing against his bare knee, his mind wandered. He recalled when he had been agile enough to join in the rain dance, and how proud he had been to wear the elaborate belt of his people that represented the thunder-bird—the red and yellow ribbons at the base of the eagle feather symbolized flashes of lightning; the bells represented thunder and hail.

Lost in thoughts of his past, Long Hair was not even aware that the dance had ended and that the people were disbanding around him. Of late, he could allow his past life almost to encompass his present.

"Old grandfather?" Falcon Hawk said, gently

placing a hand on his grandfather's lean shoulder. "The dance is over. The sky has heard. Soon there will be rain. *Naba-ciba,* come forth from your thoughts and bid this grandson farewell. It is time for me to wander on my horse, to be alone as I commune with the Great Unseen Power. This, also, is needed to bring our people rain."

Long Hair blinked his eyes, then gazed up at Falcon Hawk and gave him an embarrassed smile, realizing that once again he had entered a place that no one but he could go. This sign of aging was not one that he should boast about, even though he received much pleasure from his memories.

What else did he have? He could no longer join the warriors on the hunt. He could no longer bed a woman. And there were no more wars between tribes, or even with the white man!

When his people had been forced onto the reservation, all of the ideals and challenges had been taken away, as one might remove a child from the breast of its mother, denying it the milk of sustenance. Long Hair had found that it was better to escape into his own private world of memories than to sit and watch the world change from Indian to white.

Long Hair slowly pushed himself up from his blanket on the ground. Falcon Hawk's hand was quickly at his elbow, assisting him. "The dance was good," he said, nodding, his voice deep. "Soon there will be rain. *Haa,* my grandson, there will be much rain to fill the rivers and streams."

"You will be all right while I am gone, *Naba-ciba?*" Falcon Hawk asked, removing his rain belt and handing it to his grandfather for him to place in Falcon Hawk's tepee. Falcon Hawk had readied his white stallion for travel before the rain dance. He was anxious to be alone. He was tired of the pestering of a young widow who made herself known to him more than he desired.

He had not been able to dissuade her from believing that she would one day be his wife.

He had not even taken her to his blankets with him. Such a denial was usually enough to prove to a woman that she was not desired by a certain man. But even this had not proved how wrong she was to fill her mind with thoughts of him.

Today it would be good to ride free and alone in the wind without the bother of women. He hoped that while he was gone, Soft Voice would find another warrior with whom to become enamored.

But he doubted that. She was not sweet and adoring as her name would lead one to believe. She was cunning and spiteful.

"Old grandfather, while this grandson is gone, will you eat well and get plenty of rest?" Falcon Hawk asked, placing an arm around his grandfather's shoulders as they walked toward Falcon Hawk's horse.

Falcon Hawk frowned with worry as he cast his grandfather a sidelong glance. The wise one was nearing eighty winters now, and each day he seemed slower in his actions and speech.

It hurt Falcon Hawk to see the stoop to his grandfather's shoulders. In his time, Long Hair had been a powerful, aggressive leader of the Arapaho, winning many wars with the Ute, their longtime enemy.

Today his grandfather was just a shadow of that man.

Falcon Hawk stepped up to his horse and patted its rump, still awaiting Long Hair's response. He realized, though, that once again his grandfather's mind was elsewhere, dwelling on another time, another place.

Falcon Hawk gazed at length on his grandfather, his eyes stopping at the old man's hair. He was noted far and wide for his long hair. Long Hair had been told in a dream long ago to preserve all of his hair as he combed it out. In consequence, he had braided together all that he had saved until the rope made from it reached a length of thirty feet, with a thickness of about half an inch. He wore his remaining hair drawn up in a bunch over his forehead, sticky and matted.

Falcon Hawk shifted his gaze again. Always his grandfather wore a necklace consisting of an iron chain to which were attached several red, pearl-shaped stones, two iron rings, and an arrowhead. The stones were shaped much like small medicine bags, and were used as medicine when rubbed over the body. The iron rings, because they were hard and indestructible, preserved the wearer's sound health. The arrowhead symbolized long life. Normally Long Hair wore long, flowing buckskin robes. Today, like Falcon Hawk, he wore only a breechclout and moccasins.

"*Haa,* this *naba-ciba* will eat well and get enough sleep while his grandson is gone," Long Hair said suddenly, as though the question had just been asked. "Soft Voice will see to my needs.

She is attentive to this old man as though he were virile and young."

Wrinkling his leathery face, Long Hair grinned up at Falcon Hawk when he saw his grandson's annoyance at the mention of Soft Voice. "This grandfather realizes that Soft Voice is attentive to this old man only because of his grandson," he said. "Falcon Hawk, when will you take her as your wife? She would be a feisty one between the blankets, do you not think so?"

Falcon Hawk realized that his grandfather was teasing him, for Long Hair knew that Soft Voice was nothing but an annoyance to his grandson.

Falcon Hawk quietly mounted his horse. He smiled down at his grandfather. "When I return, I will bring a *real* woman with me to warm my blankets," he teased back, though of course that was not his plan at all. He did not even want to think about women.

Long Hair tapped his eagle-wing fan on his stomach. "Bring home woman that can cook well, my grandson," he said, chuckling.

When Soft Voice came running toward Falcon Hawk, he gave her an annoyed stare, then sank his moccasined heels into the flanks of his horse and rode off at a hard gallop. "Take me quickly away from that woman, Pronto," he said, patting his stallion's white neck. "If she could be gone when I return, I would forever be grateful to the Great Unseen Power."

Chapter Two

Although it was still early morning, the air in the hen house was stiflingly hot. It was so close that Margaret June could scarcely catch her breath as she went from nest to nest, gathering eggs from the straw. She smiled as the hens clucked at her, seemingly angry at her for stealing their eggs.

"Stop that fussing," Maggie said, loving the nickname her husband had given her. She laughed softly. "I learned the art of stealing too well nine months ago to let a few hen's squawks stop me now."

She almost tripped over the rooster as he came strutting into the hen house. His bright tail feathers swayed proudly as he walked past Margaret June.

"And as for you, young man," Maggie said, giving the rooster a soft smile. "Just you keep up your good work so that I can have the pleasure of stealing every morning. My husband's adding wood to the fire even now for a fine breakfast of eggs."

Her basket filled to the brim, Maggie stepped out into the brightness of the morning. The sun was already sending its burning rays across the scorched land. The young corn plants in the garden were limp from its heat.

Would it ever rain? she complained to herself, wiping her free hand across her damp brow. Surely, once it did, the temperatures would be more pleasant.

She shifted her hand to the round ball of her stomach. "I dread bringing my child into this heat," she whispered. She stared down at the proof of her pregnancy.

It had taken a long time for her to accept that she was pregnant with the child of a man she loathed. Frank Harper had taken her to her room on the pretense of comforting her after her father's funeral, but had forced himself upon her instead.

"But I love you, anyway," she whispered to her child as she lovingly stroked her stomach where the gingham dress clung to it. "You aren't to blame."

She began walking slowly toward the one-room cabin that had been built on the bank of a stream, envisioning her husband preparing the cooking fire for her.

It gave her a warm feeling inside to know that she had Melvin. He was a man of strength, utter kindness, and gentleness. How had she been so lucky to find a man who would care for her and her unborn child? He had pampered her during her pregnancy as though the child were his.

Her thoughts wandered to the first time they had met. After she had stolen the money from Frank's safe, she had rushed out into the night and had taken refuge inside the first covered wagon she saw, huddled in the back among the supplies. She had prayed that the owner of the wagon would take pity on her when he discovered her. All that she had known was that she had to get away from Frank, and this wagon train preparing to leave for Wyoming on the morrow had been the only way to escape.

The wagon train had not been on the trail for half a day when Maggie was discovered. By chance there had been a can of pepper close by where she had been hiding. Valiantly she had stifled the urge to sneeze. And then she had let out one of the loudest sneezes ever heard, alerting the driver to her presence.

She smiled as she remembered the shocked look on Melvin Daniel's face when he saw her there, a stowaway.

She had made sure her satchel of money was well hidden beneath a layer of blankets and then crawled up front and sat down beside the driver. Melvin, she soon learned, was a widower, a man going on in years, yet gentle as a lamb as he spoke to her.

Before long, she had spilled out her life history to him, explaining how both of her parents had died and how Frank, her father's business partner, had swindled her father out of all of his money.

The two things that she had left out of her story

were the confession that she had stolen all of her father's money back before she fled into the night and, of course, the rape.

She doubted, at that time, that she could ever find the words to tell anyone that she had been defiled. She had decided that would be her secret. It was too shameful to tell anyone.

But that all changed. Only three weeks out on the journey, she began having dreadful bouts of morning sickness and realized that she had missed her monthly flow.

Knowing that she had been with only one man, Maggie had burst out crying, horrified at the thought of being pregnant with Frank's child. She then had no choice but to admit the awful truth to Melvin.

He had listened. He had sympathized. He had taken her under his wing.

A preacher had been sought out among those on the wagon train. Melvin had married her right there on the spot, without having so much as taken the liberty of kissing her.

From that time on, she had idolized this man, but she had never experienced passion while making love with him. She had never felt anything while she had performed her nightly "duty" with her husband. She always felt like an empty shell. She was afraid that Frank had killed her ability to feel that kind of pleasure.

After Melvin and Maggie found their land and set up farming, their lives had been simple, yet peaceful. Maggie would not have traded that sweet simplicity for all of the lovely homes that she had seen in Saint Louis on a visit there with her parents. A cabin with a man who adored her was worth far more than wealth and luxury.

Her free hand went to her hair. Since her arrival in Wyoming, she had let it grow. Reddish-brown and thick, it hung to her waist now.

She laughed softly when she recalled how Melvin always complimented her as he hugged her to him while sitting cozily beside the fire. He said that he loved her wide, green eyes that were fringed in thick, dark lashes. He said that her face was always sunny, sweet, and pleasant. He had even told her that her pregnancy caused her to be more radiant and vivacious.

He often remarked that he should be ashamed of himself for marrying a young woman of nineteen, while he himself was fifty.

Maggie was the one who felt truly ashamed, but for different reasons. Never once had she told Melvin about the satchel of money, not even knowing that it could pay for more comforts in their cabin. She felt as though the money was tainted. The only important thing about it was to make sure that Frank Harper never got his hands on any of it.

She cast her eyes over her shoulder again at the hen house. She had dug a hole in the dirt floor and had buried the satchel there, then covered the hole with a thick cushion of straw.

Someday she might surprise the pants off her husband when she decided it was time to dig up the money and give it to him. She giggled at the thought of how his gray eyes would widen at the sight. The money could buy him a fancy saddle, a stallion and . . .

The sound of her name followed by a loud groan of agony made Maggie's heart skip a beat. She paled and dropped her basket of eggs, then ran as fast as she could to the cabin.

Breathless, clutching her stomach, she pushed the cowhide covering aside. She died a slow death inside when she found Melvin stretched out on his back on the floor. His gray eyes were open, locked lifelessly in a death stare at the ceiling of the cabin. The fingers of his one hand seemed frozen in a clutching position over his heart. Spittle was rolling from the corners of his mouth.

Maggie covered her mouth with her hands, stifling a scream behind them as tears streamed from her eyes. She could tell that Melvin's death had been one of terrible agony, for his face was marked with distortion.

Sobbing, Maggie hurried to Melvin and fell to her knees beside him. She lifted his head and cradled it in her lap. As she stroked his cheek, the many sweet times that she had shared with him swept through her memory.

Now they were all gone.

Then stark fear entered her heart. She was alone. Out in this forsaken land that had just entered the union as the forty-sixth state, she was alone. There were no neighbors.

She glanced down at her stomach, a sob lodging in her throat when she remembered that her child was due any day now. She had depended on Melvin knowing what to do when she began her labor pains. He could do anything he set his mind to.

Now it was all up to her!

"Melvin," she sobbed. "What am I to do? What . . . am I . . . to do . . . ?"

In her mind's eye she saw the Indians she feared, even though none had bothered her or Melvin. Most were confined to reservations, tamed by the hand of the white man.

But she knew there could be a few ready to draw a white man's blood for vengeance.

"Even a woman's?" she whispered, shuddering at the thought of being abducted and held captive.

"And what of my child?" she despaired aloud, sobbing again as she clung a while longer to the man whose heart had given out before its time.

A dust cloud rose as a rider set spur to his horse and moved on at a gallop, riding even more determinedly now that he was in Wyoming. Frank Harper had discovered the money missing from the safe the day after he had found pleasure in the arms of Margaret June—and then had discovered her gone also.

He had quickly put two and two together. He had not been hasty enough in changing the combination of the safe in which he kept his money, which at one time had been her father's safe. She had taken the money and had fled to parts unknown.

"Except for one lousy, damn dollar," Frank hissed out between tight lips. She had left it to humiliate and enrage him. He laughed a low, devilish laugh. "Bitch, I'll show you that Frank Harper ain't one to mess with, *or* to steal from.

I'll show you what true rage is once I get my hands on you."

By asking around, Frank had heard about a wagon train headed for Wyoming. He guessed that was how she had escaped. Business commitments prevented him from being able to up and leave just then, but he knew that he would find Margaret June later.

Now was later. He had appointed trusted men in charge of his various businesses in Kansas City and had set out with vengeance as his guide.

He was going to get his money back. And he was going to have Margaret June's neck. Never had he hated anyone as much as he hated that thieving bitch.

Spying a small cabin up ahead, where smoke spiraled peacefully from a stone chimney at one side of the dwelling, Frank smiled crookedly and swung his horse in its direction. As he approached, he saw a man and woman come out onto the porch, awaiting his arrival.

Never knowing who might be friend or foe, instinct made Frank's right hand move to the six-shooter holstered at his waist. He rode a compact, classy chestnut, sitting tall and square-shouldered in his heavily embossed saddle with its silver concho decorations. His silver spurs jangled as he came to a shuddering halt before the two wary strangers, whose eyes roamed slowly over him.

He knew that he made a magnificent sight in his close-cut leather trousers, neat boots, tidy gloves, and broad black hat of felted beaver. He had admired himself in mirrors often enough to know that he had clean-cut features with narrow, close-set, piercing blue eyes. He regretted his hollow cheeks and long nose, and he knew that his face was hard and tough-looking when he wasn't smiling, revealing that he was less than strong of soul and character. So he forced a generous smile, tipping his hat to the gentleman and lady.

"Good morning, ma'am," Frank said in a purposely quiet voice. "Good morning, sir."

The couple said nothing, just kept eyeing the newcomer suspiciously. Then the man offered Frank his ungloved, callused hand.

"Mornin'," the man said in a Kentuckian accent. "What brings you to these parts?"

"Wyoming itself. It's a brand-new state," Frank said, shaking the man's hand. "Thought I'd get a look at it."

"What's your business besides just lookin'?" the man asked, taking his hand back and placing his arm possessively around his wife's waist.

"Nothin' special," Frank said, idly shrugging. "Long trail's in my blood, I guess. Just can't settle down."

"Days are long on a horse," the woman said politely. "Why don't you come in and sit a spell? Share a cup of coffee with us?"

"Not much time for that," Frank said, a shadow coming over his face. He glanced over his shoulder, his eyes scanning the land. "Any close neighbors?"

"None," the man said, shuffling his feet uneasily. "Why'd you ask?"

"There was this young lady I once knew. I had my heart set on her, and one day she just up and disappeared on me," Frank said. "Perhaps you've heard her name spoken when you go for your supplies at the trading posts in these parts? Margaret June Hill. That's her name. Heard of her?"

"No, cain't say that we have," the man said.

"You're sure of that?" Frank said, his fingers kneading the handle of the six-shooter.

"Margaret June. That's a fine, pretty name," the woman said, smiling up at Frank. "I'd never forget it if I'd heard it."

The man drew his wife closer to his side. "You never told us your name," he said warily.

"You never asked," Frank said, grinning wryly.

"Where did you say you were from?" the man prodded.

"I didn't say," Frank said, spurring his snorting horse and driving him onward. He had wasted enough time questioning these settlers. They had proven useless.

He sank his spurs into the horse's flanks, hell-bent on finding Margaret June, no matter how long it took or how many people he would have to ask to find her!

Chapter Three

Tears rolled from Maggie's eyes as she took one last sorrowful look at Melvin, then laid his head gently on the braided rug that she had lovingly made for their cabin. Placing a hand at the crook of her back, she slowly pushed herself up from the floor. Her mind was working frantically as to what she must do.

She took a step away from Melvin and looked around her, knowing that she had no choice but to leave the house that had become special to her. This was her haven from all that was evil in the world. To leave it was to place all security behind her, yet she must. Her baby was due soon, and she did not want to have it alone. She must get to a trading post.

She and Melvin had traded at two posts, one to the north and one to the south. The one south of her settlement had burned down recently. She was forced to go north. This trading post was two days distant by wagon, and on Arapaho and Shoshone reservation land. If she was lucky, she could get there before being accosted by hostile Indians and before she had her child. She prayed that someone at the post might know of a doctor who lived close by, or someone who could assist in delivering her child.

But even that thought saddened her. She had learned to trust everything that Melvin did. But could she trust a total stranger? A man with crude hands who cared nothing for her or the child she was soon to deliver?

"I can't concentrate on all of the negatives," Maggie whispered to herself. "I'll find someone who will help me. I know that I will."

Through a renewed veil of tears, she went to the bed and took a blanket from it. Lovingly, she spread the soft covering over Melvin. It was tearing at her very soul to know that due to her pregnancy she did not have the strength or the muscles to dig a grave, even a shallow one, for her husband. Above all else she was thinking of the welfare of her child. She could not chance going into labor from having dug in ground that was as hard as rock due to the lack of rain.

"Dear husband, the good Lord will look after you when I can't," she whispered, covering his face.

Sobbing, she rose back to her feet. Everything seemed so unreal as she walked around in a daze, preparing herself for her departure. One thing was certain—she knew that it was best to look the role of a man in this godforsaken land where women were scarce. She grabbed

Melvin's floor-length buckskin poncho and swung it around her shoulders. Its looseness was surely enough to hide the fact that she was a pregnant woman traveling alone, should Indian renegades or outlaws happen along on the trail. She had gained only fifteen pounds through her pregnancy and was therefore scarcely heavy enough to make anyone suspicious of her being with child. With her loose gingham dress and buckskin poncho on, she didn't show her pregnancy at all.

Taking her husband's wide-brimmed felt hat, she plopped it onto her head and pushed her hair beneath it. She gazed into a full length mirror and nodded her approval.

Her gaze shifted and stopped as she stared at her husband's Winchester that lay across antlers above the fireplace mantel. Determinedly, she yanked the rifle from the antlers and placed it beside the door.

Then she began gathering up some of her clothes and other things that she planned to place in the covered wagon that had brought her and Melvin from Kansas City to Wyoming. For her survival these next two days, she placed a jar of jam, freshly baked bread, and freshly churned butter in a wicker basket, along with bacon, flour and sugar. She also placed an assortment of other cooking materials in a box. This, too, she placed beside the door, then took a final look around the room. Her gaze stopped at a small pile of tiny baby clothes that she had sewn for her child.

Tears splashed anew from her eyes as she folded and laid the clothes in a small chest made of cedar that Melvin had finished making for her only yesterday. He had labored over the chest with soft words about this child that he was treating as his own. She had kissed him softly and had promised that she would soon become pregnant again with a child that would really be his.

He had drawn her into his arms and held her close, making her feel needed, safe and grateful. Again she regretted with every fiber of her being that she had not felt passion for this wonderful man. When they had made love, she felt nothing.

Knowing it was best not to dwell on old regrets, and wanting to get several miles up the trail before nightfall, Maggie hurried outside and loaded her wagon with her belongings.

The squawking of the hens drew Maggie's eyes to the hen house. She couldn't just leave the hens and the rooster there to die of starvation and neglect. Some had become like pets to her.

"I must take them with me," she whispered, swinging away from the wagon.

The stench of the hen house and the closeness of the air, combined with the heat of the heavy poncho weighing down against Maggie's shoulders, made catching the hens and rooster and placing them in separate wire cages a chore that she wished that she could have done without.

But soon she had the cages tied to the sides of her wagon and enough food for them in a bucket that hung close beside them. She tied her one cow to the back and went one last time inside the hen house.

Taking a pitchfork she swept the loose straw aside on the floor, uncovering the small grave she had made all those months ago. It did not take much effort or strength to uncover the satchel of money that she had hidden there.

Bending, Maggie swept the rest of the dirt aside with her hands and lifted the satchel into her arms.

She stared down at the soiled bag for a moment, wondering what Melvin would have thought if he had known that such an amount of money had been so close at hand to buy more provisions for his ranch.

Guilt flooded Maggie's heart for not telling her husband about this small fortune that she had taken from the safe in Kansas City. Then she brushed such feelings aside. It was too late to worry about what might have been. There was only now and the next hours of her life.

So much depended on her being levelheaded and brave. . . .

Going outside again, she secured the satchel of money at the back of the wagon with the rest of her meager belongings, then hitched up her team of oxen. Melvin had told her that if Indians approached a wagon being drawn by oxen, they would not steal these particular animals. They saw oxen as worthless. The thought made her feel safer.

But what of her cow? What of her chickens? What if she were stopped for them?

Again forcing herself not to worry about such things, she climbed onto the wagon, lifted her reins, pointed her wagon tongue north, and headed out without looking back, and with no roads to guide her.

Always she had heard about the safety in numbers while traveling, and here she was totally alone, except for her unborn child that was kicking up a storm inside her, untouched by the stress of the moment. She placed a hand over her stomach, smiling as she felt the twitching of the child within her womb. Although a child of rape, it was *her* child, nourished by *her* body. Never would she ever think of the child being partly Frank's.

Never!

Yes, she was alone, except for her memories of times long past, of Mama and Papa, and there would always be Melvin, God rest his soul. He had made her believe in men again, but she wondered if she ever could truly love a man, or feel passion when a man held her. She prayed that she would. And one day she hoped to finally block Frank from her mind, heart and soul—the damn, thieving rogue that he was!

But she must get past one problem before facing another. She had to get to the trading post before her labor pains began. Could she make it on time? Until the death of her parents, her life had been spent within a day's journey of her home. Her father's land had lain about thirty miles to the southwest of Kansas City, and there she had been born and raised. There she had lived until she had said a sad farewell first to her mother, then her father. She had been left alone to fend for herself, and that she had done well enough until now.

Her worst fear was having the child alone. What if both she and her baby died?

The slow swaying of her oxen team went on, the iron wheels rolling, clanking and wobbling in the dust. Maggie shuddered when she spied several buffalo skulls bleached white by the sun lying along the trail.

She lifted her eyes to the sky. She could hear Melvin's words even now as they made their way into Wyoming in this very same wagon.

"Here the sky is half a man's world," he had said as he had stared upward, then slowly moved his eyes around him at land scarcely touched by any civilization besides Indians, a wild and free land where the ceaseless wind swept grass into a continuous, undulating surface, silver-crested.

Her husband had told her that Wyoming came from an Indian word, meaning "big river flats," because the state straddled the Continental Divide with a series of dry basin floors.

She had seen, as had her husband, that God had been the architect of Wyoming, with his cathedral mountains and awesome, endless prairies, dwarfing all human refinements.

"Husband, today it's still as beautiful, the skies are as fresh and blue as that day you gloried over it all," Maggie whispered. "The sky is unspeakably blue, darlin'."

She was startled when up ahead a band of antelope suddenly appeared and swept ghostlike across a ridge and was as quickly gone. A gray wolf stood near a hillock, gazing back at her, then also disappeared, as though he had been only an apparition.

"This wilderness, husband, is rude, bold, yet in so many ways sweet," Maggie whispered again, as though Melvin were with her. "The front door to the outdoors, didn't you call Wyoming, darlin'?"

Talking to Melvin seemed a respite from Maggie's loneliness, although she knew that if anyone saw her talking to herself, they would think that she had lost her senses.

Clearing her throat, feeling suddenly foolish and as though eyes were watching her, Maggie straightened her back and focused on traveling onward, determined to get to the trading post on time. An unsmiling gravity marked her when the dusky velvet of the prairie night began settling around her. The sun was so low that its light struck but the topmost branches of the trees and left all below in gray twilight.

It brought a general feeling of anxiety, dread, and uneasiness to know that she would be spending her first full night alone, without the protection of a husband or the four walls of her house to keep out intruders of the night.

She traveled a while longer, then stopped and made camp close to a bluff, feeling that at least she had protection on one side. She hugged herself as she stared around her, shivering. She was too afraid to build a fire. She feared this might attract Indians or outlaws to her. She could see the Wind River Mountains in the distance and suspected that she might have entered land that was marked off for the Wind River Reservation. If she was approached as an intruder on land that belonged to Indians, what danger might she be in?

Wanting to busy herself, to cast all of these doubts and worries aside, Maggie proceeded to milk her cow. She had not had her required amount of milk today. And how wonderful fresh milk would taste with her bread, butter, and jam. Her stomach was aching unmercifully from hunger. It was grumbling and growling, sounding strange in the still evening air.

After filling her tin cup with milk, Maggie sat down beside her wagon and had a small feast. Just before it became totally dark, she spread a blanket under her wagon and crawled beneath it, her Winchester beside her. She didn't chance removing her poncho. She feared being caught without it, so she snuggled up into it as she stretched out on the blanket to settle in for what she hoped would be undisturbed sleep.

When a coyote lifted its voice in a long and mournful howl somewhere in the distance, Maggie shuddered. Tears pooled in her eyes when, in answer, another coyote in the grass raised a high, quavering cry, wild, and desolate—the voice of the wilderness.

Unable to sleep, Maggie climbed from beneath the wagon and sat down beside it, resting her back against a wheel. She looked heavenward and sighed. The Great Dipper showed clear and close that night, as though she could reach up and touch it. Overhead countless brilliant points of light pierced the mantle of the night. The wind blew soft and low. The night on the prairie was solemn, evoking a brooding melancholy.

Suddenly Maggie had a strange feeling, as though she were being watched. She had felt it for some time but had seen nothing as she scanned the velvet darkness with her eyes.

Her hand sought out the Winchester that she kept at her side. It was cold and impersonal, compounding her loss tonight, the first night away from Melvin's bed and his warm, protectively comforting arms. She had adored his sweetness, his caring ways, and his honesty. How she would miss him. She already did!

Maggie had always heard that when one was tired, disheartened and frightened, music was good. She began singing softly to herself, unaware that she had an audience.

Falcon Hawk had seen the wagon through a break in the trees as he had been riding along on Pronto, just inside the boundary of the reservation. Curious to see who the travelers were, he had dismounted far from the wagon and had left Pronto tethered to a tree.

Stealthily, he had crept close to the campsite, puzzled as to why these travelers had not built a fire. Anyone knew that a fire was good not only for cooking food and for warmth, but also kept animals away from the campsite.

As Falcon Hawk got close enough to see better, he soon realized that there was only one traveler. The stranger was sitting on the ground, leaning against a wheel of the wagon.

Falcon Hawk crouched low and hid behind a thick stand of bushes and studied the lone traveler. The moon's light was all that he had to see by, and as far as he could tell, the stranger was a man and of white skin.

Yet, as the voice of this person wafted towards Falcon Hawk, in a soft, lilting sound of singing, he forked an eyebrow. This was not the voice of a man!

When the wind suddenly picked up, and a gust

brushed against the traveler's wide-brimmed hat and lifted it into the air, and the stranger moved quickly to make chase, Falcon Hawk's breath caught in his throat. This stranger was most definitely a woman. Her hair had tumbled free, long and wavy down her back.

Falcon Hawk leaned closer, able to make out the color of the hair in the spill of the moonlight. It was a beautiful reddish-brown, and the skin of the woman's face was as fair as the soft, white clouds of spring.

His gaze raked over her. The bulkiness of her poncho showed that she was a healthy woman.

When Maggie stopped only a few feet from where Falcon Hawk was hiding to finally retrieve her hat, he got a much better look at her face.

His heart leapt and his throat grew dry, for to him she was a vision.

She was beautiful.

She looked so innocent and alone!

His heart fluttered, and his loins grew warm at the thought of stepping out and letting himself be known to her. Yet he was wary of such a hasty decision.

Where was her man?

Why was she traveling alone?

After Maggie rescued her hat and secured it on her head again, then sat back down and resumed singing, Falcon Hawk became even more entranced by her, touched deeply by her voice. There was such a sadness in it!

A strange spell slowly fell on the soul of Falcon Hawk, one that he could not cast aside as foolish or dangerous. Something compelled him to assign himself to this young, beautiful thing, to watch out for her safety through the night, yet to keep himself unknown to her. Tomorrow he would follow her, perhaps find the answers as to why she was alone and perhaps discover her destination. He wanted to know more about her. He would find a way to make her acquaintance, but only after he discovered if she already belonged to another man.

Something deep inside his gut told him that she was nothing like Soft Voice, that here was a woman whose soft voice actually matched her personality.

One thing he absolutely knew about her. She was a woman of courage to be traveling alone in the wilds of Wyoming.

He settled down onto the ground, resting his back against a tree, and continued watching the woman, even after she climbed beneath the wagon and seemed to have fallen into a deep sleep.

"*Haa,*" he whispered to himself. "She is most brave. She is most *beautiful.*"

He could not help himself. He desired to know her, to touch her, to kiss her.

Chapter Four

The next morning, after Maggie had eaten some more bread, butter, and jam and had drunk her fill of fresh milk, she fed her chickens and rooster and climbed aboard her wagon, hoping to reach her destination before another night fell on her journey.

Her first night without Melvin had been a restless one, not only because she missed his comforting arms, but because she had awakened many times, still feeling as though she were not alone.

Her skin had crawled with the strange feeling that someone was near, watching her every movement. The morbid sounds of the howling and snarling of gray wolves, with an accompanying chorus of coyote, had stayed with her the entire night.

Because of these many disturbances, she had not dared to take the time for a quick bath in the nearby river when she awoke.

Now her restless eyes constantly swept the landscape in every direction. Not a movement in the grass escaped her.

Yet she still felt as though she were being watched!

Wiping a bead of perspiration from her brow with the back of a hand, Maggie wished now that she had taken the time to at least bathe her face, to rid it of the sweat, dirt, and grime that made her itch. It was another hot day to be endured, and only sheer willpower sent her relentlessly onward.

She looked ahead into the distance, forever hoping for a glimpse of the trading post, yet still seeing nothing but miles of golden-brown grass bending in the wind. High crimson rock walls stood to the west, and limestone cliffs lay north, opposite the mountain crests.

There was only a slight stirring of wind today. Everything was so very dry, the land broken only by a few islands of low, pine-dotted hills and rivers that were for the most part only trickles. Bands of antelope sometimes appeared on the still horizon. The barking of prairie dogs ofttimes broke through the silence that surrounded Maggie.

"I shouldn't have taken the time to sleep," she fretted to herself. "I could've been so much closer to the trading post by now."

She placed a hand over her abdomen, sighing with relief when her unborn child did a flip-flop within her womb. She had heard that just prior to the birthing of a child it lay quietly still in its warm cocoon. Today, at least, she did not believe that she would be giving birth.

Yet there was always tomorrow. Would she be in any better a position then to have this child?

She feared not. The circumstances were never going to be pleasant. Without Melvin, she had nothing at all to look forward to.

Falcon Hawk pressed his mount forward, making sure that he stayed far enough back from the covered wagon so that the white woman would not see him. To him, the ox-drawn wagon was only a dot on the horizon, yet he was close enough that if the woman became threatened by man or beast, he could reach her quickly on his fast steed. Pronto had not gotten his name just by chance. He had deserved it after winning many races in Falcon Hawk's Arapaho village.

Falcon Hawk leaned over and patted his white stallion on the neck, then sat straight in his saddle again, his chest bare, the sun warming his smooth, copper flesh. Otherwise he wore moccasins, fringed breeches and leggings which were tailored to fit snugly to the leg and were decorated with painted stripes, panels of quillwork along the seam, and a fringe of horsehair at the base.

Falcon Hawk's coal-black, straight hair blew in the wind as he nudged his horse into a harder gallop when he noticed that the wagon had made a turn into a thick stand of cottonwood trees and was now hidden from his sight.

His heart leapt at the thought of what lay among those trees—a small stream that was tainted. To drink from it caused a quick fever, one that lasted for many days. He had not yet seen the woman stop to drink or bathe. Surely that was her intention now.

Slapping his reins back and forth against his horse's neck, Falcon Hawk leaned low over the stallion and rode at a gallop onward, hoping to get to the woman in time.

The sight of the water up ahead through a break in the trees, sparkling and mirroring the keen blue of the sky, elated Maggie. The cow's milk had not quenched her thirst today. She was in dire need of water. She might even take the time to bathe. She did not relish the thought of arriving at the trading post stinking worse than a skunk.

She dismissed her previous foreboding about being watched. She had traveled for many miles today, and no one had yet accosted her. Indeed, being alone was causing her to imagine all sorts of things.

Having reached the banks of the small stream, Maggie jumped with a start when a bird she could not readily identify darted out across the water, just clearing the tops of rocks which broke the surface, and then was gone into the towering treetops.

"Lordie," Maggie whispered, drawing her oxen to a halt close to the stream. "Why must everything startle me? I must get a grip on myself." If not for herself, for her child. It wasn't good to allow it to feel so many of her tumultuous emotions. It should come into this world feeling safe and secure and very, very loved.

Securing her reins, Maggie climbed from the wagon, groaning with the effort. Then she waddled to the banks of the stream and knelt beside the crystal clear water. Thirstily, she cupped water into her hands and began drawing it toward her mouth, but spilled it all over herself when out of the blue came the most bloodcurdling scream that she had ever heard!

"E-e-e-ya-ya-ya-ya!" Falcon Hawk again shouted as he thundered on his horse through the trees toward the stream.

Maggie's heartbeat quickened, and a fearful wave of heat swept over her. The skin at the back of her neck and shoulders prickled as though with a chill when again she heard the terrible sound. She scrambled quickly to her feet to see who or what was the cause.

Her hair stiffened on her scalp when she caught sight of an approaching Indian on horseback, riding quickly toward her. She fought against feeling faint, knowing that she must stay alert, to save not only herself, but her unborn child.

Above all else, this Indian must not realize that she was pregnant! A woman alone was one thing. A pregnant woman was another.

Up this close, though, she would surely not be able to disguise her female identity. What this might mean to this Indian made her knees grow wobbly.

Yet she held her chin firm, her jaw tight with a keen determination to fend for herself. Never again would she allow anyone to take advantage of her, as had happened in Kansas City all those months ago.

Falcon Hawk wheeled his horse to a shuddering halt a short distance from Maggie. In his eyes came a deep relief when he realized that he had succeeded in stopping her from drinking the tainted water.

For a time, they stared across the waving grass at one another, and neither moved or spoke. Time seemed to stand still, Maggie's knees as weak as water, her fear of the Indian intense. At that moment her first impulse was to run, but in her condition, she knew that the Indian would catch up with her before she had gone two paces.

She knew that she could not avoid him by retreating, so she resolved to continue putting on a bold front.

The Indian was not hard to look at. Maggie felt his midnight-dark eyes soon holding her as if by a spell. His face was handsome, his body well-muscled. The only flaw that she could see about his smooth, bronze body was the scars on each side of his chest, as though at one time he had been terribly tortured.

Through her fears she found pity for the Indian, to have suffered in such a way. Somehow she did not see this man as one who was evil. There was a gentleness in his eyes as he looked at her.

Yet she knew to be wary, for he *was* an Indian, and she knew that she was most definitely not fooling him into believing she was a man. He was studying her face too closely not to know that she was a woman.

Boldly, and without further thought, Maggie

yanked the hat from her head and allowed her hair to spill out and tumble free across her shoulders and down her back. With a lifted chin, she gave the Indian an unwavering stare.

"Why have you come like this to frighten me in such a way?" Maggie blurted out. "I have done nothing to you. I am minding my business, causing you no harm at all."

A squirrel broke the silence, barking in a thicket to their left, unnerving Maggie. Yet she stood her ground under the continued close scrutiny of the handsome Indian.

Falcon Hawk eyed her steadily for a moment longer before speaking. Up this close, he could see the perfect shape of her lips and nose and the soft contours of her face. He stared at the large poncho, wishing to see what lay beneath it, and knowing that in time, he would. He would not only see her, he would touch her as well.

He dismounted, tethered his horse's reins to a low branch of a tree, and stepped forward.

"Woman in men's clothes, you have been saved from illness brought on by drinking tainted water," he said in careful English. One hand rested on a knife sheathed at his left side.

Maggie became pale as she turned to stare at the water. "Tainted?" she gasped. "Why, it looks quite decent enough to me. It is so clear, it is almost the same as looking into a mirror."

"Looks are deceiving," Falcon Hawk said, going to the edge of the water. He knelt beside it and let the water trickle through his fingers. "One drink and you would not be refreshed. Instead, your skin would burn with a quick, searing fever."

"Good Lord," Maggie said, placing a hand to her throat, knowing how close she had come to swallowing the water in great gulps.

She looked quickly down at him, marveling at his kindness at stopping her. Her child could have been the most affected by the water. This close to delivery, the child was susceptible to anything that harmed its mother.

"*Ethete,* it is good, that I stopped you?" Falcon Hawk said, moving back to his feet. He towered over her, as he gazed down into eyes that mystified and intrigued him. They were the color of the great cat that stalked through the dark night—the eyes of a panther!

"Yes, very good," Maggie said, laughing clumsily. "And I thank you. Yes, from the bottom of my heart, I thank you."

Falçon Hawk smiled. His smile was like molasses, sweet and clinging, making her blush at her reaction to it.

"It is said that the rainbow is the fishing line of the thunder," Falcon Hawk said, quite pleased to find this woman as polite as she was beautiful. "Lightning is generally thought to strike in these tainted waters, aiming at a monster that lives in its depths. This spring is inhabited by such beasts. The spring issues from the monster's mouth. Near this spring numerous snakes can be seen. Clothes and offerings are frequently tied to a nearby tree. The flashing of the eye of the monster can be seen especially in the morning or evening. Its tongue brings forth many poisons which taint the water."

"My goodness," Maggie said, her eyes innocently wide. "How fortunate I am that you came along."

She reached out a hand from the slit in her poncho. "My name is Margaret June Daniel," she murmured. "But you can call me Maggie."

Falcon Hawk stared at her proffered hand for a moment. He had never liked the white people's way of sealing friendships by the shake of a hand, for most had been falsely offered.

Yet this white woman seemed sincere enough. She was very visibly grateful for having been saved by a man with red skin.

"Falcon Hawk," he said, greedily wrapping his hand around hers, enjoying the softness of her flesh against his. "I am called Falcon Hawk. I am Arapaho. You are traveling on land of my people, now called the Wind River Reservation."

"Yes, I thought that I might be," Maggie said. She also knew that she should have reached the trading post by now and was convinced that she had been traveling in the wrong direction—away from the trading post instead of toward it.

She glanced down, noticing how he clung to her hand much longer than she had expected.

Then something sensual seemed to fill her entire being when she saw a look in his eyes that seemed similar to the way she felt about him.

He was attracted to her.

Even in her large garb and with dirt on her face, he found her attractive.

She did not know why realizing this did not frighten her. Their sudden feelings for one another seemed as natural as going to sleep at night and waking up in the morning.

And then she felt foolish for allowing her thoughts to drift to anything so farfetched as this Indian seeing anything before him but a fat woman in dire need of a bath.

She quickly withdrew her hand and clasped her fingers together behind her.

"This Arapaho, and those of my close acquaintance, have ties of peace with all white people," Falcon Hawk quickly interjected. "You have nothing to fear from me, or my people, ever."

"How could you ever think that I would fear you after you just saved me from a terrible dilemma?" Maggie said, finding her hand going to his arm, to rest gently on it, without much forethought. Yet finding it so natural to be at ease with him somewhat frightened her.

But she was deeply relieved that it was an Arapaho who had found her, instead of a member of one of the other tribes of Indians who were more warlike by nature. The Arapahos' reputation was of being friendly, contemplative, and religious, yet renowned for their past accomplishments in war—before the era of the reservation.

Contemplatively, Falcon Hawk eyed her hand resting on his arm. "This Arapaho has questions for the white woman," he said, lifting his gaze and looking into her lovely face. "Why do you travel alone?"

A sudden sadness entered Maggie's eyes, a look Falcon Hawk recognized. "Because I no longer have anyone to travel with me," was her only explanation. It hurt to the depths of her heart to have to say more to anyone.

She lowered her eyes to hide the tears that were suddenly there. She did not like being reminded of her husband's death and how she had been forced to leave him without a proper burial, and without proper words spoken over a grave. The sorrow she felt was so deep, it felt as if someone was pricking her with needles through and through!

"You do not have a man?" Falcon Hawk asked, placing a finger to her chin, bringing her eyes up to meet the question in his.

"No," she murmured. "I . . . don't have a man. I belong to no one."

She could see how this pleased Falcon Hawk by the way his eyes suddenly lit up. But just as quickly they became shadowed by other questions obviously bothering him.

"You dress in man's clothes," he said, sweeping his gaze over her. "Why is this?"

Not yet entirely trusting the Indian, a complete stranger to her, Maggie's insides stiffened. She just could not find within herself the courage to tell him the truth—that she was with child, a child that could be born any day.

"My husband died suddenly yesterday," Maggie explained softly. "When I was forced by his death to travel alone, I thought I would be safer if I traveled in the guise of a man. I was hoping to reach the trading post without mishap. But it seems I have taken a wrong turn somewhere. Just how far am I from the trading post? One day? Two?"

"You are three sunrises from the nearest trading post," Falcon Hawk said, seeing the sudden fear that entered Maggie's eyes with the knowledge.

"This makes you afraid?" he said. "Did not Falcon Hawk say that you had nothing to fear from the Arapaho?

"Come. Come and meet my people," he went on, warming inside at the thought of her going with him to his village. "Rest. Eat. Then Falcon Hawk will accompany you to the trading post."

Having so feared not being able to get to the trading post before her child was born, and now knowing for certain that she had no other choice but go to the Indian village with Falcon Hawk, in order not to have her child alone in this vast wilderness, Maggie smiled weakly up at him.

"That will be so kind of you," she murmured, yet fearing the unknown. She knew no customs of the Arapaho, or of any Indian, for that matter. She grew cold inside at the realization that she would be having her child among a people who were foreign to her in every way.

The only good thing about her situation was Falcon Hawk. In such a very short time, she was beginning to feel the closeness to him that she had felt for Melvin that very first day of their acquaintance.

Suddenly Falcon Hawk's hand was at Maggie's elbow. "You came to the stream for water," he said, guiding her toward his horse. "You shall have your fill from my buckskin flask."

She gazed up at him, in awe of this man whose gentleness was making her come alive deeply within, as never before in her life.

"Could it be?" she wondered to herself. "This

man? This Indian?" Was it meant to be that *he* would teach her the meaning of passion . . . ?

She lowered her eyes bashfully, blushing. Here she was very pregnant and as dirty as sin, and thinking about passion.

How utterly ridiculous of her!

She accepted the flask of water and tipped it to her lips, for the moment relishing only this quenching of her thirst.

But that satisfaction was short-lived. She shivered sensually when she felt Falcon Hawk's long, lean fingers stroking her hair.

"Your hair is soft and pretty," Falcon Hawk said softly.

Maggie closed her eyes, slowly melting inside, allowing herself the pleasure of these feelings that until now were foreign to her.

Chapter Five

Maggie broke from her trance when she no longer felt Falcon Hawk's hands on her hair. She blinked her eyes open and slowly turned around, finding him looking studiously at the caged chickens and rooster. When he began stroking the cow with his strong, commanding hands, as though testing its worth, she was completely catapulted back to reality with the realization that this total stranger might know the game of pulling one into trust and taking later by force what he desired.

Firming her jaw, she went and stood stiffly at Falcon Hawk's side. His interest in the cow was no less keen than moments ago, and she feared he saw the animal more as a source of meat than of the milk she needed.

"She gives very sweet milk," Maggie hurried to explain. "Would you like to have a taste? Her udders are quite filled, even now."

"Udders? Milk?" Falcon Hawk said, turning

quizzical eyes to Maggie, yet showing a quiet amusement in them that she did not understand.

Maggie reached inside her wagon for her small stool and a bucket, then positioned herself beside her cow and began pulling rhythmically at the animal's teats, directing the spurts of milk directly into the bucket.

"Do you see, Falcon Hawk?" she said, continuing to milk the cow. "The milk is fresh and unspoiled as it comes from the cow."

Falcon Hawk nodded, continuing to pretend his ignorance about cows, although he had a large herd of livestock of his own. "I see," he said, nodding. "And when do you eat the cow? After you milk it?"

He knew that this question would bring quick alarm to the beautiful woman's eyes, yet he could not help but play this game of "ignorance" with her. He had done it many times before when he came across white people who were not familiar with the ways of the Arapaho.

At first it had angered him to be looked at as stupid. But to be able to tolerate such behavior on the part of the white people, he had forced himself to find a humorous side to their ignorance.

In her shock at what Falcon Hawk had said and fearing for her cow, Maggie dropped her hands from the animal's teats so quickly that she overturned the bucket of milk.

She scampered to her feet as fast as her clumsy stomach would allow. "No," she said, her eyes wild. "Never would I eat my cow. As I said, I keep her only for milking."

She eagerly awaited his response.

"*Nyuh*, so be it," Falcon Hawk said, shrugging. He gave her a devilish smile as he bent to one knee and picked up the bucket and placed it inside her wagon. "Come, woman. I will take you to fresh water. There you can drink something besides your cow's milk. There we can water our animals. *All* of them." He smiled at her over his shoulder as he walked toward his horse. "Even your cow. It will taste even more delicious after it is refreshed with drinks of water."

When he saw how she paled at the thought of eating the cow, he decided to stop teasing her. He would much rather make her see him in a more favorable light so that she might one day even consider loving him.

He hurried back to her and tilted her chin with a finger so that her wide green eyes looked directly into his. "Falcon Hawk owns many cows and never has he eaten one that gives milk," he said seriously. "Nor will Falcon Hawk eat yours. It is your property to do with as you please."

Maggie emitted a quavering breath of relief. She smiled broadly up at him, not even caring that he had been playing games with her. The fact that her cow was safe was all that mattered.

With the discovery that Falcon Hawk could be lighthearted, carefree, and amusing, she even felt safer—and much more at ease with this handsome Indian.

"Thank you," she murmured.

"It is wrong of Falcon Hawk to play with your feelings in such a way," he said, his heart pounding as he felt this woman drawing him into wanting her.

It was wrong to approach her, even with a kiss, so soon after she had lost her husband.

He would wait. *Haa*—he would wait. And then he would discover the sweetness of her lips.

His gaze lowered to her stained poncho. Then his eyes shifted to the dirt and grime on her face. Upon his first look at her, he had been able to see through the filth, seeing her as no less than beautiful.

But even beautiful women needed bathing. He would suggest this upon their arrival at their campsite for the night.

Falcon Hawk walked Maggie to the side of her wagon, intending to help her into it, but gave her a quiet stare when she jerked her elbow free and pulled herself up onto her seat without his assistance, even though she had to struggle to do so.

He took a step away from the wagon, finding her not only attractive, but strong-willed as well. He liked this in women. He was discovering many things to admire in this particular woman, more than ever before when he had been drawn into an attraction to a particular *h-isei.*

"We will travel until the sun begins going to bed, covering the sky with his red blanket," he said, as Maggie took her reins in her hands, nodding in silent acquiescence.

With that, Falcon Hawk went to Pronto and swung himself into his Spanish saddle. He gave Maggie a signal with his hand, and she understood that this meant she was to follow him.

Snapping her reins, Maggie urged her oxen to draw the wagon around, then rode along the grass that was bent from Falcon Hawk's horse's hooves.

She could not help but stare at the Arapaho brave's back, with its rippling of muscles and its copper sheen beneath the bright rays of the sun. She allowed herself the leisure of admiring him, knowing that he would not be aware of her eyes on him.

His body was long and sinewy of muscle and thin of flank. She watched his brilliantly black hair whip in the wind as he rode in a steady gait toward the distant mountains. There was so much majesty about him, so much nobility. He had all of the attributes of a great leader. Perhaps he was even a chief.

Just being near him caused a sensual thrill to flow through Maggie's veins. Never had any man caused her to feel weak at the thought of him kissing her.

Then she dropped her gaze to her stomach when her child gave her a swift kick within the cocoon of her womb. It was a reminder of who she was, the condition she was in, and what lay before her. It was most certainly not the time to be allowing herself fantasies of a handsome man, and not just any man—an Indian.

She looked at the filth of her poncho and reached a hand to her face. She shuddered at the thought of what he must think about her appearance.

Lordy, how she wanted to take a bath. But while Falcon Hawk accompanied her on her journey, how could she ever take the chance of disrobing long enough to cleanse herself? She wanted to postpone telling him she was pregnant until it was necessary. If he knew of her pregnancy he just might change his mind about assisting her. It might not only offend him to think of helping a pregnant woman bring another white child into this world, but perhaps it was a thing of taboo to deliver a white baby in the village of the Arapaho.

Perhaps she should even turn away from him and take her chances of finding the trading post in time!

But she quickly shook that thought from her mind. She had a better chance of surviving in the Indian village. Alone, she might get lost again in this wilderness.

She lifted her eyes to the sky and prayed to the Almighty that the Arapaho would sympathize with her plight. If not, what then would be her future? Her child's?

A frown creased her brow as she lowered her eyes to follow Falcon Hawk's movements, cursing Frank Harper. He was to blame for her whole world being turned upside down. She would always hate him. Always. If by some draw of fate she ran into him again, it would not take much for her to lift a revolver and place it over his heart. She would delight in pulling the trigger!

They traveled onward until the purple mantle of the mountain twilight was dropping onto the hills. They neither rested nor ate until they reached the side of a clear stream that watered the valley. There they stopped, and soon Falcon Hawk had a comforting fire built within a circle of rocks.

"The black night will soon be upon us," Falcon Hawk said, taking his horse's reins. "It is best to get our animals watered and then ourselves. It is best also to bathe before the cooler sting of night creeps upon us. Tomorrow we may only find dried-out rivers and creek beds again. This drought makes life hard and uncertain."

Maggie had been untying her cow from her wagon when the word 'bath' came to her like a clap of thunder. "A bath?" she stammered out, turning to gaze up into Falcon Hawk's deep, dark eyes as he stared down at her.

Maggie realized more than anyone her need of a bath, but again she felt that it was best to postpone it until Falcon Hawk was not there to discover the truth of her condition.

"Do you not know the meaning of the word 'bath'?" Falcon Hawk asked, puzzled over her reaction to his suggestion.

Was it not the custom for white women to bathe? Arapaho women bathed daily! How could it be any different for white women? Did they not also want to smell fresh and pure for their lovers or husbands?

Maggie laughed nervously. "Most certainly I know the meaning of the word," she said, trying to dismiss it as something trivial instead of threatening. "But, sir, ladies do not bathe in the presence of gentlemen. I shall wait until I have privacy. Can I be assured of such privacy at your village?"

Falcon Hawk was instantly relieved to see that she did practice taking baths. And it was easy enough to see why she balked at the suggestion now. She was bashful.

Shyness in a woman was acceptable in his

mind. After being forced to tolerate Soft Voice and her personality that knew not the meaning of 'shy', Falcon Hawk welcomed a woman who was the exact opposite of that immodest creature who shamefully chased him.

A warm glimmer came into his eyes, thinking that when the time came for him to make love to this shy white woman, it would be he who led the way. He would kiss away her shyness and teach her to never be bashful around him again.

"Such privacy will be provided," Falcon Hawk said, smiling down at her. He reached a hand to her face and ran his thumb beneath her chin. "One does not have to take a full bath to remove dirt from a face."

Without thought, she leaned into his hand, almost breathless at his touch, then jerked away and nodded quickly. "Yes, my face," she said, still nodding, so greatly relieved that her reason had been convincing. "I shall wash my face. It will not only make me more presentable, but I shall feel refreshed."

"That is so," Falcon Hawk said, then went on to the stream with Pronto.

Maggie followed close behind him, her cow trailing beside her. The oxen had been loosened and had ambled on their own to the water and were getting their fill. Fresh water had been placed in the chickens' and rooster's cages.

At the water's edge, as her cow lapped up long, grateful tonguefuls, Maggie admired Falcon Hawk's horse. It was glistening white, with a black patch on its rump. After its thirst was quenched, it began dunking its muzzle and blowing into the water with what appeared to be sensuous enjoyment.

"He is quite beautiful," Maggie said, breaking the silence between herself and Falcon Hawk. "I'm sure you are very proud of your stallion."

"A man is not a man without a dutiful horse," Falcon Hawk said, drawing Pronto away from the water. "And yes, Falcon Hawk is proud to be the owner of such a steed as this."

As Falcon Hawk lifted his Spanish saddle from Pronto, Maggie scurried about, securing her oxen by tying their ropes to stakes that she had struggled to drive into the ground. She tied her cow to the wagon, making sure it was tethered where it could feast on long, thick grass.

Watching the shadows of evening stealing higher and higher on the trees, Maggie went back to the stream and bent low over it, relishing the feel of the water as she splashed it onto her face and into her mouth. After drinking her fill, she scrubbed her face until she could see by the reflection in the water that she finally looked like herself again.

Pleased, she made her way back to her wagon and took her wicker basket of food from it, then went to the fire where Falcon Hawk was spreading two blankets. It had grown dark rapidly. The night was ghostly, with a kind of queer luminous light. It was like velvet, soft and heavy, yet cool and penetrating.

Welcoming the warmth of the campfire, Maggie was glad to sit down on one of the blankets after Falcon Hawk gestured with a hand for her to do so. Placing her feet close to the embers of the fire, she began unfolding and laying back the linen cloth that covered her food.

Out of the corner of her eye, as she began lifting her jam, jelly, and bread from the basket, she watched what Falcon Hawk was doing. He was opening a drawstring buckskin pouch containing his own kind of food. She wondered what it could possibly be. The pouch was small and looked weightless.

"Would you like me to prepare you a piece of bread, butter, and jam?" Maggie blurted out, thinking that she was coming to his rescue by the offering.

Falcon Hawk shook his head silently as he sprinkled a light-colored powder into the palm of his hand, then held his hand out for her, nodding toward it. "Take. Eat. It will fill you more readily than white woman's food," Falcon Hawk said, again motioning toward her with the hand that held the offering.

Maggie laid her bread aside and leaned closer to get a better look at the strange powder. "What on earth is that?" she asked. "How can that make anyone feel as though they have eaten anything?"

"Take. You will soon see," Falcon Hawk said, his lips curving into an amused smile.

Curiosity caused Maggie to allow him to pour the powder into the palm of one of her hands.

"Eat. It is used to break hunger quickly," Falcon Hawk said, shaking more powder into his hand from his pouch, then into his mouth.

Maggie noticed that he took a long swallow of water from his buckskin flask soon after. She stared down at the powder in her hand for a moment longer. The quantity was so small that she thought she might as well have gone without it. But she followed Falcon Hawk's lead and slipped it into her mouth, soon swallowing it.

Falcon Hawk forced the buckskin water flask into her hand. "Take a large drink," he flatly ordered. "Now. It is part of this meal of powder that is important. Very soon you will feel as though you have eaten a huge meal of corn and venison," Falcon Hawk said, pulling the drawstrings closed on his pouch.

"That is all you and I will be eating of it?" Maggie said, amazed that he could think it was enough to make a meal of. "Falcon Hawk, I'm going to eat my own food from now on, thank you." She proceeded to pick up her bread, which he just as quickly took away from her.

"It is not wise to eat anything else after eating the powder," he explained, laying the bread aside. "It is not good to eat more than just a little of this powder, for after it becomes wet, it swells, so that one might better eat none at all than too much."

"What on earth is this powder?" Maggie asked, already beginning to feel as though she had eaten a huge meal.

"It is Indian maize," Falcon Hawk said matter-of-factly. "Or corn, however you choose to call this plant. It has been finely ground and sweetened a little with the brown sugar from the maple. It is the custom to take some of it in the mouth and then drink water. In a short time one's hunger will have disappeared. It is carried on long journeys and eaten when there is no luck in the hunting, or when there is no time for the hunt."

"It works," Maggie said, laughing. "I couldn't eat another bite if I wanted to." She placed her food back inside her basket, covered it, then shivered when a chill breeze ran through her.

Falcon Hawk saw her discomfort. He went to his saddlebag and withdrew a bear robe, offering it to her.

Maggie smiled a thank-you. She wrapped it around her shoulders and scooted closer to the fire, curling her legs up beneath the robe. She jumped with alarm and looked quickly over her shoulder when a screech owl broke the night's silence.

"What you heard is an owl—yet in truth, is not," Falcon Hawk said, sitting beside her and stretching one long, lean leg out before him so that the fire warmed the soles of his feet through his moccasins.

"In our culture, we look to the owls as the ghosts of past lives who have not settled things before dying. They are the quiet or timid people who never spoke their minds while alive. Now they fill the air with their noise."

Maggie drew the bear robe more snugly around her shoulders, shivering. "I didn't need that tale tonight," she murmured, smiling weakly at Falcon Hawk. "I'd much rather talk about the stars." She looked quickly into the star-speckled heavens. "Yes. Let's talk about stars. Have you ever counted them? I have. One, two, three . . ."

A sudden hand closing over Maggie's mouth made her start with alarm. She looked wildly over Falcon Hawk's hand into angry, determined eyes.

"Do not count the stars—ever," he said, his voice flat and emotionless. "This causes misfortune."

Suddenly frightened of him, Maggie yanked her mouth free and eased away, then stretched out on the blanket, drawing the bear robe over her. She eyed Falcon Hawk suspiciously as he began making another sort of bedding from the boughs of an evergreen tree. She watched him guardedly as he came toward her.

"Come, Panther Eyes. Bring your blanket and bear robe," he softly encouraged her. "The bed of green boughs will give you a much better rest."

"Panther Eyes?" Maggie whispered, gazing at him questioningly.

"Your eyes are like the panther's," Falcon Hawk said, smiling. "The name Panther Eyes fits you well."

"I see," Maggie said.

"Come," Falcon Hawk again said, motioning toward her.

Not wanting to argue with him about anything and anxious to get her badly needed rest, Maggie did as he asked.

She eyed him suspiciously as he settled down only a few feet away from her. Although she had found herself becoming intrigued by this man and his beliefs, she was afraid to allow herself to totally trust an Indian. When he had fallen asleep, she moved quietly to her wagon and grabbed her Winchester, which she took back with her and placed beneath the bear robe at her side.

Her hand clutching the rifle, she fell asleep, then a short while later awakened with a jolt from a nightmare. She had dreamed of Melvin and how she had left him without a proper burial.

When Falcon Hawk's eyes opened and he saw her crying, he wanted to go to her and comfort her, yet he felt that if she had the need to cry, as women were wont to do, he should not interfere. It did not please him, though, to think that she might be thinking of her husband who had recently died. If she loved this man so much, was there room left in her heart for Falcon Hawk? He turned his back to her.

Her sobs seemed to wrench the very heart from his breast. He closed his eyes and forced himself not to hear.

Chapter Six

The next morning came, crisp and gray, with a leaden curtain of fog. Falcon Hawk told Maggie that ofttimes when there was a fog, if one drew the figure of a turtle in the soft earth and then beat it with a stick, the fog would be killed and would clear off.

She smiled when he did not venture to follow through with this. She had begun to see the amusing side of this man. It was good to know that he had a sense of humor. When he discovered that she was pregnant and that she had kept this secret from him, he would need all his sense of humor to keep from hating her. She could tell by the way he looked at her, and occasionally briefly touched her, that he was falling in love with her.

Would he have allowed himself such freedom with his feelings if he had known that she was huge with child?

No. She thought not.

Soon, when he discovered the truth, he might even feel betrayed. This weighed heavily on her mind. Yet, because of her fear of his not only hating her, but possibly abandoning her, she could not tell him.

The hot sun was finally burning away the blue haze of morning as Maggie snapped her reins, urging her oxen onward as Falcon Hawk led the way on his white stallion. The sight of lightning flashing across the purple sky in the distance helped her throw off her web of languor and the thoughts that troubled her.

Never had she seen such lurid lightning. Never had she heard such loud, fierce growls of thunder, seemingly rolling forever until they faded away, to be followed by another round of the same.

She shivered as the storm came closer. On the western horizon, a low, dark bank of clouds lay for miles, steadily rising and moving closer and closer.

As the storm gathered its forces, the breeze around Maggie grew steadily stronger.

Falcon Hawk fell back and rode close beside the wagon. "Do not be afraid," he cautioned Maggie. "Soon it will pass. It might not even come this far. The storms in Wyoming are spotty. It might be raining only a few feet from you, yet where you stand it could be dry."

"Shouldn't we find some sort of shelter just in case?" Maggie asked, her voice rising in pitch as her fears mounted. "I so fear storms. I—I am frightened of lightning."

Falcon Hawk gestured with his hand toward the tall, weaving grass that surrounded them. "Do you see shelter?" he shouted above the ever growing howling of the wind. "If the storm comes over us, it is in truth a blessing. The drought will end. Hold tightly to your reins. Do not let the oxen become spooked."

"I'm not used to being in command of these animals," Maggie cried. "My husband always led them, not me! What if I don't have the strength to hold them at bay?"

"If need be, I shall come aboard with you and take command," Falcon Hawk said, giving her a smile.

Maggie smiled weakly up at him, hating to sound so helpless. Under any other conditions, she could handle any situation, especially a team of dumb oxen! But now, because she needed to protect her child from harm, everything about her had changed.

Except for her determination to get to safety.

The sky blackened overhead. The wind died, and for a moment the world seemed to stand still. Everything was strangely still. A scattering of drops fell on Maggie's upturned face.

Then the rains came down, starting with a few big pattering drops, but steadily increasing to a downpour.

The wind started blowing in great gusts, then a blanketing rush of wind and rain fell. Sheets of lightning played visibly, with ripping zigzag flames across the sky, accompanied by steady, loud rolls of thunder.

The wind threw water against Maggie in great

sheets and lashed the grass about her into a fury. She clung to her reins as the oxen began pawing nervously at the wet ground beneath their hooves. The storm seemed to be at its height, the air so filled with the stinging rain that the world seemed blotted out.

Maggie looked anxiously around for Falcon Hawk, unable to see him in this crazed downpour. "Falcon Hawk!" she screamed. "Where are you? Oh, Lord, where . . . are . . . you?"

The next thing she knew, the oxen had spooked and were lumbering off blindly through the rain. In the excitement of trying to stop them, Maggie dropped the reins and found herself clinging to the seat of the wagon for her life, believing that this was the end for herself and her unborn child.

Then she heard another set of thundering hooves. The rain had died down enough so that she could see Falcon Hawk riding alongside the wagon, his eyes intent on the oxen. She flinched with alarm when Falcon Hawk daringly jumped into the wagon beside her and soon had the reins in his mighty, powerful hands. Then, as though he had waved a magic wand over the oxen, they stopped.

The storm ceased just as quickly, the clouds rolling away in great gusts of black, taking with them the incessant lightning and claps of thunder.

"Thank you," Maggie said, wiping water from her face with her hands. "How can I ever thank you enough?"

Falcon Hawk gazed intensely into her eyes, fighting back the urge to gather her into his arms to comfort her. Respect for the recent death of her husband caused him still not to reveal his deep feelings to her. He reached a hand to her hair and brushed the wet strands from her brow.

"*Hahou* is not necessary," he said. "It is blessing enough that you are all right."

Maggie's eyes widened and she swallowed hard, her insides melting from his touch and the way he looked at her and spoke to her. She knew now that she was right to suspect that he had strong feelings for her, just as she had for him.

Yet how sad that she could not act upon her feelings. It was hard to hold back, to not fling herself into his arms and confess her love to him. And she so badly wanted to thank him for bringing out these feelings within her, which she had thought dead.

Without conscious thought, one of her hands went to her abdomen. Then she tightened, realizing that the rain had all but plastered the poncho against the bulge which could very easily reveal her condition to Falcon Hawk. Quickly she pulled the poncho out away from her, so the shapeless bulk concealed her secret again.

Luckily, Falcon Hawk's eyes had not wandered from her face, or he would surely have discovered her secret.

She was beginning to feel trapped. The deeper their feelings grew for one another, the worse it would be to reveal the truth of her condition to him. How could she ever tell him?

Yet, how could she not?

"The word you just spoke in Arapaho—*hahou,*" she murmured, trying to draw their thoughts to a more innocent topic, to something safer for *her*.

"In Arapaho I said 'thank you'," Falcon Hawk said, fighting his feelings when he recognized the look of want in her eyes.

He was finding it hard to understand how she could lose a husband such a short time ago, yet show feelings for another man so soon. In his thirty winters, he had experienced enough women to know when one fell under his spell.

Until this woman with the eyes of a panther and the smile of innocence, he had ignored such looks in other women. Soon he must find a way to talk with her about her feelings.

But these delicate matters took time. He was not the sort of man who rushed a woman into anything.

"Falcon Hawk, look yonder!" Maggie cried, pointing to the distant sky, where a rainbow was painting its colorful arch across the heavens above the mountains. "Isn't it lovely? And the drought. Surely at least for now, it is over!"

"*Haa,* is it not pretty, where the bow of promise lies like a vast painted mist across the sky?" Falcon Hawk said, reaching his hand heavenward, as though tracing the line of the rainbow with his outstretched fingers.

"A bow of promise," Maggie said, shifting her gaze to Falcon Hawk. "What a beautiful way to describe it. It's like an Indian's powerful bow that sends the arrow into the air."

Falcon Hawk lowered his hand, smiled at her,

and nodded, pleased at how quickly she comprehended Indian ideas. Then, seeing the danger in staying so close to her, he slipped from his seat and into his saddle again when Pronto stepped closer to the wagon, as though a silent command had led him to such obedience.

"We shall now ride onward," Falcon Hawk said, lifting his reins into his hands. "The sun will soon dry us both. We will ride until dusk again. Then we shall stop and eat and sleep. Tomorrow, at sunrise, we will reach my village."

"Tomorrow?" Maggie said weakly, wincing at the thought of having to travel another full day. The child within her womb was quiet today. Even through the excitement of the storm, it had not made one turn inside her. The cow had bawled, the chickens had squawked, and the rooster had crowed frighteningly during the tumultuous moments through the storm, but her babe had remained still.

Maggie feared that her child might be ready to be born. She feared that she might not make it to the village in time.

What a dilemma it would be if Falcon Hawk not only discovered that she was pregnant too soon, but also had to deliver the baby himself!

Again her fears mounted that he might not want to touch her or the child once he realized that she was pregnant. She did not even want to think about having to deliver her own child! She would surely bleed to death, or harm the child in some way.

"*Haa,* one more day," Falcon Hawk said, arching an eyebrow. "What can one more day matter?

Falcon Hawk is with you, protecting you. Nothing can harm you."

Maggie swallowed hard and pulled her eyes away from his, seeing too much question in their depths. "One more day is just fine," she said, lifting her reins. "Just fine."

Falcon Hawk nudged his stallion in the sides with his knees and rode on ahead of the oxen team, Maggie stiffly following, her heart thundering within her chest as she prayed to feel some movement from her abdomen.

"Please, God," she whispered. "Let me last one more day before giving birth to this child. Oh, God, please."

They traveled onward. Many hours passed. Falcon Hawk had been right to say that their clothes would dry fast beneath the hot rays of the sun. Maggie's poncho was not only dry, it was now stiff and even more uncomfortable than before it had been rained upon.

She peered across the waving grass, seeing that it was also dry. In fact, there were no signs whatsoever that a storm had touched this area. When she looked downward at the earth as the wind parted the grass, she could see wide-open gaps in this ground that seemed parched and turned to stone. The rain had not been enough, after all. At least here, where she and Falcon Hawk were traveling, the drought was still upon them.

Something drew Maggie's attention. Falcon Hawk's horse's ears had become even more pointed, and the stallion revealed his unease in the way he shook his head and snorted and occasionally stamped his foot. She knew enough about horses to know that when a horse behaved in this fashion, it was sometimes from foreknowledge of danger.

But what danger? They had already faced one peril today. Surely nothing more could again endanger her child or slow down her journey to the Indian village!

Yet she realized that Falcon Hawk also sensed his horse's behavior. He leaned low and patted Pronto affectionately and whispered something in his ear, but even this did not calm the horse entirely.

Falcon Hawk straightened his back and gave Maggie a somber look. "I must ride ahead to see what lies over that hill," he said. He did not wait for her response, but rode off in a hard gallop toward the hill. When he reached it, he grew numb inside. Far off, lying like a pale blue cloud over the ground, was smoke! It rose, fell, and rode with the wind.

Then he saw the red, dull gleam beneath the veil of smoke.

Fire!

It was a prairie fire advancing toward him, surely caused by the lightning. The fire had not been put out by the rain, because the rain clouds had drifted onward, away from that particular spot.

Fear gripping his heart, knowing what it meant to be caught in a raging prairie fire, Falcon Hawk wheeled his horse around and raced back toward Maggie. When he drew his horse to a shuddering halt beside her, he quickly explained what he had seen.

Already, even before his explanation was finished, Maggie could smell the faint odor of smoke and could hear a mysterious low humming in the air.

"Fire?" she said in an almost strangled whisper, becoming pale and weak at the thought of dying midst the flames.

"Turn your wagon around!" Falcon Hawk shouted. "There are ways to stop the fire. That Falcon Hawk will do. *You* will ride away from me until I come for you. Do you understand?"

Maggie reached a hand out toward him, tears stinging the corners of her eyes. "But you could be killed," she said, drawing her hand back and firmly gripping the reins when she saw the tight, determined set of his jaw.

"Ride from me and the fire," Falcon Hawk commanded. "Now!"

Before Maggie could get her wagon turned around, Falcon Hawk was already riding away from her, his long black hair flying in the wind, his smooth muscles rippling, his copper skin glistening with sweat.

Guiding his horse with a jaw rope of twisted hair, Falcon Hawk rode swiftly and silently toward the hill, his steed making long, reaching, low-headed plunges, as though seeking its own freedom and safety in that way. She watched until Pronto charged over the crest of the hill, leaping and jumping.

Then, fear gripping her, Maggie did as she was told. She fought back tears as she got her oxen finally turned around and they were lumbering as fast as they could over the crushed grass that they had just traveled across.

Maggie screamed when vast numbers of small, gray prairie hares came by, hurtling through the silence. Band after band of antelope followed them, running, looking back. Broken bands of white-tailed deer bounded irregularly past her, terror chasing them in the wings of the wind and smoke.

She looked back over her shoulder, then gasped and felt faint when she saw that the smoke was now a mile-wide cloud spinning, black as ink, across the sky. She did not see how Falcon Hawk could survive the ravages of such a fire.

Something compelled her to turn back. She could not leave Falcon Hawk alone, to die in such a way. She must find a way to encourage him to retreat with her.

Her pulse racing, she slapped her reins, sending the oxen again toward the danger they had just left behind. She realized that they too could react badly to the scare of the fire.

But for Falcon Hawk, she had to risk everything. It was not fair that he should be left alone to fight the fire. He was only one man. It would be best if they both retreated to the river. There the fire would be halted and they would be safe as they waited for the fire to die to savage embers!

The closer she came to the crest of the hill, beyond which the fire raged, Maggie felt a rush of hot, surging air on her face. When she reached the summit of the hill, she drew her oxen to a halt and watched, petrified, as Falcon Hawk kept just ahead of the flames, starting a dozen smaller fires. It was amazing to see the harsh prairie fire advance until it was halted by the fires that Falcon Hawk had set.

His face streaked with smoke, Falcon Hawk rode away from the smoldering ashes. When he found Maggie there, so close to the dangers of the fire, he gave her a stern, angry glare. "You did not obey my command," he growled. "You stayed."

"I left, then came back," Maggie said. "I could not leave you to die in the fire."

"And what would you have done to save me?" Falcon Hawk said, still in a scolding fashion.

"I was going to encourage you to ride with me to the river," Maggie said, squaring her shoulders against his angry scolding. "There we could have both waited out the fire."

"Do you not know that as fires advance, they grow in strength?" Falcon Hawk said, leaning down into Maggie's face. "We would not have reached the river."

"Truly?" Maggie said weakly.

"Truly," Falcon Hawk said. Then he took her reins from her and took it upon himself to turn her oxen around, toward the river. Then he threw the reins back at Maggie. "Now you will go to the river. It is safe for us both. There we will spend the night."

Maggie nodded eagerly and followed him. She watched him as he rode ahead of her, so relieved that he was all right and admiring his courage for fighting the savage fire.

It made her insides glow with gladness to watch him, realizing that she really did love him. This had been proven to her when she risked her own life, and that of her unborn child, to return for him, to see him safely from the fire.

How wonderful it was, to finally know the true feeling of love!

But what an unfortunate time to love. And loving an Indian was not going to be as easy as loving a white man. This sort of love was forbidden in the white community. Perhaps it was even forbidden in the Indian community for an Indian brave to choose to give his heart to a white woman.

Unless that brave was important and could do as he pleased. She could not help seeing Falcon Hawk as masterful in every way, as a chief might behave.

She smiled as she turned from him, thinking that he was most certainly a leader, if not a chief!

They rode onward until they reached the river and took their animals into a shielding fringe of cottonwoods. Scattered calls came from each side of the river as the birds settled in for the night. In the distance, a wolf howled.

Falcon Hawk dismounted and tethered Pronto to a low cottonwood branch. He then went to Maggie's oxen and began untying them as Maggie slipped down from the wagon. She sighed and held the small of her back as she stretched. Never had she been as exhausted as she felt now. Her eyelids were so heavy, it was hard to keep them open.

Going to the river, she bent low over it and splashed water onto her face. Soon she became aware of the smell of smoke behind her.

Startled, she rose to her feet and turned around, afraid that perhaps the fire had followed them after all. She smiled with relief when she caught sight of the campfire that Falcon Hawk had built within the protective wall of a circling of rocks.

When he turned and smiled at her, his eyes twinkled and gave way to the warmth he felt for her. "Panther Eyes, come and sit by the fire with me," he said. "Or would you rather take a bath? I shall give you all the privacy that you wish for a bath."

"You . . . will?" Maggie said, seizing the opportunity to get the stench off her body and now totally trusting him.

"Whatever time is needed for your bath, Falcon Hawk will keep his back to you," he said, nodding.

"How I would love to get into the water and relax a mite," Maggie said, running her fingers through her grimy hair.

Falcon Hawk took his saddle from his horse and set it down close to the fire, then lay down on the ground, his head resting on the saddle, his back to Maggie. "Now, before it gets too dark, take your bath," he said. "Then I will take mine."

Maggie blushed at the thought of him undressing near her, then cast that worry aside and hurried to her wagon. She took from it a fresh dress, underthings, and a towel, washcloth, and scented soap. She went to the river and was soon standing on the pebbled bottom, relishing the feel of the water against her flesh. Every once in a while she gave Falcon Hawk a quick glance, always relieved to find that his concentration was on something besides herself.

After she was finally clean, her hair squeaky as

she ran her fingers through it, she walked from the river and hurriedly dressed. She groaned as she looked at the stiff poncho, dreading having to wear it again.

But she had no other choice. Perhaps, though, later tonight, she might find the courage to tell Falcon Hawk the truth. If he truly loved her, *truly* loved her, he would understand. His heart seemed large enough to understand anything.

The poncho drawn over her head and her dirty clothes back inside her wagon, Maggie went to the fire and sat down. She cleared her throat, to draw Falcon Hawk's attention. "Falcon Hawk? I'm through with my bath," she finally said. "Now it is your turn. I promise not to watch."

When he turned her way, anxious to see her without the filthy poncho, and with her hair luxuriously clean across her shoulders, a keen disappointment entered his eyes when he discovered that she still wore the large garment that hid her body beneath it.

He tried to understand. Surely it was because she had recently been widowed. She did not want to flaunt her womanly figure in front of another man.

Perhaps soon she would be more willing to reveal herself.

He had this to look forward to, for he wanted nothing more than to run his hands over her firm breasts, to taste her flesh.

He wanted to show her how to forget that other man.

He rushed to the river and took a quick bath,

then returned to the fire and started to offer Maggie a strip of dried meat from his pouch. But he found her fast asleep, a bear robe drawn over her where she lay on a blanket close to the fire.

Disappointed, having wanted to spend the evening talking to her about the events of the day, Falcon Hawk sat down on the blanket close to Maggie. As he watched her sleep, he bit off a piece of the meat and chewed it slowly, his eyes devouring the sweet loveliness of Maggie's face.

Suddenly he had an urge to touch her. He moved closer to her and softly ran his fingers over the contours of her face and then her lips. His heart pounded as he thought of moving his hands beneath the bear robe, to gather her breasts within his trembling fingers. It would be so easy. She would never know.

But he did not venture to do such a dishonorable thing. Instead, with a fire raging in his loins, he tossed the dried meat aside and stretched out on his own blanket and closed his eyes, to force sleep upon himself.

Yet sleep would not come.

His eyes would not stay closed for long. He kept wanting to take another look at the white woman.

Then he would look away, realizing that his mind was traveling a dangerous path.

Chapter Seven

Maggie and Falcon Hawk awakened to the soft pink of the sky at morning. The sun bathed the hills in a wondrous glow as they traveled on reservation land toward Falcon Hawk's village.

Maggie's eyes followed a squadron of birds flying across land where deer loped. She looked into the distance at the vast plains that ended in rugged mountains, the dazzling red rock contrasting with the flowing carpet of green grass. She had seen enough to know that the domain of the Arapaho was populated by the grizzly bear, buffalo, elk, deer, mountain lion, and numerous smaller animals. In the streams and rivers beaver and all sorts of fish were found aplenty.

Maggie could relax while enjoying the scenery now, for in the not-so-far distance she could make out an Indian camp nestled in a grove of cottonwood trees on the bank of Wind River. Finally they would reach Falcon Hawk's home. She did not have to fear having the child as much now.

There would be women near. Surely they would take pity on a very pregnant woman and assist in the delivery, even if she was white of skin.

The one thing that still worried her was Falcon Hawk's attitude when he discovered that she was heavy with child. He could keep the women from assisting her. He could banish her from his village.

Her thoughts were diverted when several braves on horseback came bounding from the village. They sent a welcome to Falcon Hawk, waving, shouting, and whooping as their horses' pounding hooves stirred up the dust.

Maggie watched as the braves stopped and greeted Falcon Hawk in their Arapaho language. She was thankful that Falcon Hawk had known English well enough that she had been able to converse intelligently with him during their time together.

Then there was a strained silence as all eyes, including Falcon Hawk's, moved to Maggie, studying her. She stiffened her back and very consciously drew the poncho out away from her stomach, hoping that none of these eyes closely scrutinizing her could guess her secret, although she would soon have no choice but to reveal it to Falcon Hawk. Hardly any time was left for secrets between her and this man she silently adored.

Then Falcon Hawk inched his horse backward, gently placing a hand on Maggie's shoulder as he again conversed in Arapaho with his many friends.

"Is she not beautiful and ripe for loving?" Falcon Hawk said in Arapaho, after explaining to his friends how he felt about her.

Maggie smiled weakly up at him, wishing she knew how he was introducing her—as a stranger seeking shelter? Or as a woman for whom he had special feelings?

When she could see a quiet amusement lighting up several faces, her curiosity became even more aroused over what might have been said to the braves.

She jumped as several of them began laughing and patting Falcon Hawk on the back, as though congratulating him about something. She blushed, thinking that somehow these congratulations included her. This made her pregnancy weigh even more heavily on her mind. If Falcon Hawk was bragging about her as though she would soon be his conquest, or perhaps already was, he would have even more cause to hate her once her condition was revealed to him.

What an embarrassment she could be to Falcon Hawk then!

When the braves began riding hard back toward their village, and Falcon Hawk stayed behind to accompany Maggie there, she looked up at him guardedly, fearing the next hours.

"Panther Eyes, come with me now into my village," Falcon Hawk said, wheeling his horse around in the right direction. "My braves will spread the word of our coming."

"They did not seem to mind that I am with you," Maggie said, nervously twining and untwining the reins around her fingers. "What did you say to them?"

"Falcon Hawk explained that you had been

recently widowed," he said, smiling down at her. "I also told them that when I look into your panther-green eyes, I see more than a woman who is widowed. I see a woman who stirs feelings within this chief that no other woman has created. I told them that it is the belief of this Arapaho that this beautiful white woman also shares the feelings of their chief."

Maggie's heart was pounding like a sledgehammer within her chest, almost taking her breath away as she listened to what he was saying. She felt more and more trapped by the minute. He had cause to believe that she had feelings for him, even enough to brag about.

Yes, she loved him! There was no doubt about it! But it was all useless. When he found out about her unborn child, it would change everything.

Suddenly his words caused Maggie's eyes to widen and her lips to part as she whispered, "Chief?"

Then she spoke aloud. "You are a chief?" she said, yet she was not all that surprised. She had seen the nobleness of his carriage and the command of his very being. Almost the minute they had met, she had known that he was a great person.

"*Haa,* chief," Falcon Hawk said, squaring his muscled shoulders with pride.

Then he nodded toward his village. "Now we go," he said, sending his horse into a soft trot beside Maggie's wagon as she snapped her reins and the oxen moved onward in their slow, swaying fashion.

"The Arapaho live in small bands," Falcon

Hawk explained as he gazed down at Maggie. "Each camp is made up of about twenty tepees. Each band is led by a respected chief, selected for his generosity and clear judgment. Upon the death of *neisa-na,* my beloved father, I was appointed chief of my band of Arapaho. I carry on the tradition of my father and his father before him, searching for peace and harmony, even with the white people who force us to live on reservations. The Great Unseen Power has blessed me well as a leader."

She did not have the time to respond. Many children and dogs were running from the village, excited at the sight of their young chief. They came to him, touching him, smiling adoringly up at him. Some ran lightly beside Maggie's wagon, some pointing out the chickens, some patting and admiring the cow.

Others were looking at her quizzically, distrust in the depths of their dark eyes.

Maggie smiled at each of them, then looked forward again as she moved into the village. Her eyes darted around as her pulse raced, realizing that she was entering into an existence which was beyond her wildest dreams. Up until these past two days, all that she had known about Indians was what she had read in reference books or cheap novels that had portrayed them as terribly savage and bloodthirsty.

Now she was seeing an Indian village firsthand, and so far nothing seemed savage. Strange to her eyes, but most definitely not savage. These people seemed to live a simple existence. Their love of animals was quite evident. Various small forest animals were either caged or running free throughout the village, obviously as pets. The dogs of the village were making a clamor around the legs of her oxen with their snarling and snapping.

As she rode farther into the village beside Falcon Hawk, she caught sight of some old men standing or sitting in groups. There were few women to be seen.

From what she could observe, the clothing, homes, and horses were decorated with natural materials—horn from elk, quills from porcupines, hair from the moose, feathers from the eagle, claws from the bear, and shells found along the riverbanks.

Tiny fires were scattered everywhere, twinkling into the dusky evening, casting weird shadows among the tepees. The odor of the food cooking at the fires came to Maggie with a change of wind, and she realized just how hungry she was. Although Falcon Hawk had said that they would arrive at his village earlier, it had taken much of the day and they had not stopped once to feed their hunger. The ache in her stomach gnawed as she came closer to the cook fires.

Yet, all thoughts of food fled from her mind when Falcon Hawk stopped at a much larger tepee that stood in the center of the village on a slight rise of land. Scarcely breathing, she studied the elaborate designs painted on the skins that made up the outside of the dwelling. They were beautifully done in many bright colors.

Something else drew her quick attention. She gasped slightly when she discovered a beautiful eagle resting on a perch built high above the entrance flap of the tepee. It was secured with a rope around one leg and seemed to come to life when Falcon Hawk approached it with pieces of meat that he had taken from a buckskin bag hanging on a high tripod close to the bird.

As the bird consumed this offering of meat from Falcon Hawk's hand, Falcon Hawk stroked the eagle's beautiful head with his free hand.

The sight of this obvious love between man and bird made Maggie's heart warm. This man, this Arapaho chief, was indeed special.

A sadness crept then into her heart, fearing that soon she would be certain that she was never to see him again.

Once he knew the truth. . . .

Falcon Hawk wiped his hands on a cloth that hung from the bird's perch, then gave his full attention to Maggie. Afraid that he was going to assist her from the wagon and might thus discover that she was much heavier than she should be, she climbed down before he reached her.

She met his approach, smiling up at him, yet dying a slow death inside to know that the very next moments might change everything for them, forever. Her heart pounded when he motioned toward his entrance flap.

"Enter," he said softly. "Share this lodge with Chief Falcon Hawk."

"Do you mean this is where . . . I will spend the night?" she asked, unable to stop the quavering of her voice.

"If that is what you desire, then so be it, that is how it should be," Falcon Hawk said, lifting the entrance flap. "Go inside. Water for a bath, fresh clothes, and food will be offered to you. We will then talk about our feelings."

"Bath?" Maggie said, her voice guarded as she stepped inside the tepee.

"You will bathe, as will Falcon Hawk," he said nonchalantly. "The dust from the trail sticks like honey to faces when mixed with perspiration." He laughed throatily. "But it does not smell as good as honey, nor taste as good on the lips."

Maggie tried to see the humor in what he had said, but her fears of the next moments ruined all that might have been wonderful under any other circumstances.

Falcon Hawk came after her, directing her to the fire that was burning just forward of the center of his lodge, set in a little depression in the ground and outlined with cobblestones. Food was simmering in a pot, low over the flames.

Maggie's eyebrows rose when she discovered the food that smelled so tantalizingly delicious, and she was impressed at how neat his lodge was. Without even asking, she knew that he didn't have a wife. It seemed that it was his intention that she would fill that void in his life.

Then who kept his lodge fire burning? she wondered. Who kept food cooking in the large kettle? And who kept his dwelling so neat and clean?

She gazed around her. The interior resembled a hollow cone. The lodge poles were covered with a lining of leather, painted with picture writing. Along the inside, on the ground, were laid some twigs and rushes on which quilts and blankets were thrown. She concluded that these must be seats during the day and beds at night.

Near the opening which served as a door, cooking utensils were neatly kept—a frying pan, coffee boiler, bucket for water, and some tin plates and cups. Behind these were stored a little stock of groceries—coffee, sugar, flour.

Cords were strung between the lodge poles of the dwelling, weighed down by all manners of skins, weapons, baskets, and woven grass. Along the walls were piles of skins.

Then, as her eyes grew more accustomed to the dim lighting inside the tepee, she noticed that on the north side of the lodge was a true bed. It had a headpiece made from willow rods woven together. She could see that the bed was padded beneath with dry grass and pelts, and upon these rested a thick pad of blankets. The pillows looked thick and comfortable, more than likely stuffed with hair or feathers.

Along another wall she noticed a war bonnet. She had read in books that such a bonnet was the emblem of a warrior's achievements. Every feather represented a major exploit, and when worn, it was regarded as a mighty charm, protecting its wearer and sending up his prayer to the Great Unseen Power.

"You are looking upon my father's war bonnet," Falcon Hawk said, suddenly at Maggie's side, his gaze following hers. "In my time, I have not seen much war, except for small skirmishes with various enemy tribes. Yet I show off my father's emblems of achievements as though they are my own."

He motioned with a slow swing of a hand

toward other things of which he was proud. "As you also see," he said proudly, "there are my own trophies, medicine bundles, and sacred pipe bag. These prove that this chief is from a family of wealth and power. No one is allowed to have such things except through expensive ceremonies or extraordinary experiences."

Falcon Hawk turned to Maggie and framed her face between his hands. "*H-isei,* these I wish to share with you," he said thickly. "Can you say that enough time has passed for you to forget this husband who has passed on to another world? What is the allotted time for white women to mourn? Did you love him much, so that your mourning will last longer than usual? Do you feel free now to confess your feelings to this Arapaho chief?"

Maggie was melting beneath his searching dark eyes. His hands on her flesh caused her head to swim. All she wanted was to be kissed by this handsome man and to be held within his arms. The passion she was feeling was deliciously sweet. How could she find the strength to tell him the truth about herself?

Instead of kissing her, as Maggie had guessed he might, he suddenly placed his hands to the fastenings of her poncho and just as quickly removed it over her head.

As Falcon Hawk dropped the poncho to the floor, his eyes were drawn suddenly downward. His mouth opened in a mortified gasp when he discovered exactly why she had determinedly left the filthy garment on during their entire time together. She had been hiding beneath it the secret that she was with child, and so pregnant it did seem that she might deliver at any moment!

"You . . . are with child?" he gasped, his eyes shifting upward, staring into Maggie's. "You kept this from me? Knowing how Falcon Hawk felt about you, you did not tell the truth about being heavy with child? Did you not trust me enough to tell? What did you think this Indian might do?"

"At first, no, I was not sure if I could trust you," Maggie admitted, nervously wringing her hands. "Then, as I began realizing how you were attracted to me, as I was to you, I was afraid that you would look at me with disgust should you know that I was large with child. I—I could not stand that, Falcon Hawk. As now, you are looking at me as though you hate me. Please tell me that you don't. Please don't hate me."

Unable to help his feelings of anger at the thought of this woman carrying another man's child, he turned and fled from the tepee, his fists clenched tightly at his sides.

Devastated by Falcon Hawk's reaction, Maggie stared at the entrance flap for a long moment, then crumpled to the floor in tears. She had been wrong. She had been so wrong in not telling him the truth. Now what was she to do? What was to become of her? Would he banish her from his village and never give another thought to her? It was much too far to the trading post to travel there before having her child.

She hung her head in her hands and cried until she felt a presence in the tepee besides herself. Lifting her face quickly, she found herself being scrutinized by a beautiful Arapaho maiden whose eyes were wide, angry, and filled with what was obviously a keen jealousy.

"Who . . . are . . . you . . . ?" Maggie murmured, wiping tears from her cheeks.

"I am called Soft Voice," the maiden said in a tone that was more hateful than kind, yet her voice was indeed as soft as the wind on a beautiful spring morning.

"What do you want with me?" Maggie said, slowly rising to her feet, then taking cautious steps away from Soft Voice.

"Falcon Hawk sent me," Soft Voice said, lifting her chin boldly.

"Why?" Maggie asked, her voice strained.

Soft Voice's two long braids bounced as she took angry steps toward Maggie, causing Maggie's heart to thunder wildly. She eyed the knife sheathed at Soft Voice's side. She could not help but think that perhaps Falcon Hawk had sent this woman to make her pay for having lied.

Chapter Eight

"Remove your clothes and give them to Soft Voice," The Arapaho woman said, her voice cool and impersonal.

Maggie shrank farther away from Soft Voice. "No," she said, folding her arms protectively across her chest. "I refuse."

"You must remove clothes to have bath," Soft Voice demanded. "Give dirty clothes to me. They will be discarded."

"Do you mean thrown away?" Maggie asked, her eyes widening. "Why?"

"Everything should be done as Falcon Hawk instructs," Soft Voice said, turning and nodding toward two other Arapaho women as they came into the tepee. One was carrying a basin of water, the other a lovely buckskin smock, lying in soft folds across her arms. Soft moccasins lay in the palms of this woman's hands.

"Falcon Hawk?" Maggie said softly. "He is

responsible for all of this?"

This gave her hope. If he hated her, he would not care about how she looked. She had expected him to return and tell her that she must leave. Perhaps he had softened in his anger toward her. Yet it was surely only because he pitied her and this child that would soon be born to her. The hope that he still loved her had faded away into nothingness.

"Yes, Falcon Hawk gave the orders," Soft Voice said. Her eyes narrowed angrily as she gazed down at Maggie's swollen stomach. "Soft Voice obeys because he is chief, and his word is supreme in this village of Arapaho."

Soft Voice took a step closer to Maggie. She extended a hand, palm side up, toward her. "Now give me your garments so that I may be on about my own personal business," she said icily.

Her face hot with a blush, Maggie glanced from one woman to the other, not wanting to get undressed in front of them. She stood quite still for a moment longer, then was relieved when the woman who had brought the dress and moccasins laid them aside and brought a blanket to hold up in front of Maggie to give her the privacy she needed to undress.

Nodding a silent, relieved thank-you to the woman, and knowing that Soft Voice would not leave until she had the clothes, Maggie began undressing. Item by item she pitched them over the blanket, and when she was completely nude, she took the blanket from the kind Arapaho woman and wrapped it around her.

"I hope that I can bathe in private," Maggie

then said, lifting her chin haughtily toward Soft Voice. She realized that this beautiful Arapaho woman would never be her friend. It was in the depths of Soft Voice's doe-brown eyes and in her voice that she was Maggie's enemy.

Maggie was not sure if it was because Soft Voice hated all white people, or if Maggie was singled out because she was not only white, but very pregnant and taken in by the handsome Arapaho chief. Whatever the reason, it was obvious that Soft Voice could scarcely tolerate standing there, doing as Falcon Hawk had ordered.

"Your privacy is granted," Soft Voice said, waving the other women from the tepee. Soft Voice took one last, lingering look at how the blanket swelled out away from Maggie in the middle, gave a disgusted groan, then swung around and left, carrying Maggie's soiled clothes.

Breathing a sigh of relief to at least have that confrontation behind her, Maggie sat down beside the fire pit, close to the basin of water. She stared into the flames of the fire, tears near, grateful for the hope that Falcon Hawk might forgive her for not being altogether truthful with him. Did his forgiveness extend as far as still loving her? She could never stop loving him. She would do anything to recapture his total love! She wanted to stay with him—not only until her child was born, but forever.

Thinking that was an impossible dream now, she dispiritedly placed her hands into the basin of water and began splashing it on her face and then the rest of her body, drying herself with the blanket.

As she lifted the buckskin smock and slipped it over her head, she found it to be angel soft. She then placed her feet inside the moccasins, finding them comforting to her swollen, tired, and aching feet.

Combing her fingers through her hair to get the tangles out, Maggie sat down on a blanket and eyed the pot from which still wafted delicious aromas, yet she did not venture to eat. She wasn't sure if the food would stay down. She felt totally isolated and alone.

At least she was safe, she thought with a sigh. Her child would not be born with only its mother to bring it into the world.

"Secrets," she whispered disconsolately to herself. Since her father's death, she had been forced more than once to keep secrets. First she had kept the knowledge of the hidden money from Melvin. . . .

Her insides grew cold at the thought of the satchel of money. She must get it hidden before some of the Indians searched her belongings. She was almost certain that she was going to be in Falcon Hawk's tepee until she was well enough to travel after the birth of her child. She must get the satchel from her wagon and hide it, perhaps beneath Falcon Hawk's many belongings.

Pushing herself up from the blanket, Maggie crept to the entrance flap and nudged it aside to take a cautious look outside. When she saw no one close by, she moved stealthily to the wagon and climbed inside. Although it was now dark outside, she knew where to look without the aid of any light.

Her fingers soon found the satchel. Hugging it to her bosom, she left the wagon and hurried back inside the tepee. Her heart pounded as she searched desperately with her eyes for the perfect place to hide the money, then settled on the far back side of the tepee, beneath the bed, where rolled-up blankets and other paraphernalia were stored.

She knelt down there and, moving everything aside, breathlessly dug into the dirt with her fingers until the hole was deep enough to hide the money.

After everything was back in place, she turned to return to the fire, but something else drew her attention.

The sound of voices singing took Maggie back to the entrance way. She lifted the flap and gazed toward the center of the village. Gathered around a great outdoor fire, many of the Arapaho men, women, and children were singing, stopping long enough to tell tales, then singing again. It seemed to Maggie that a grand time was being had by all, but to her it was all steeped in mystery.

She was reminded of the treaties between the white people and the Arapaho that had confined these gentle people to the Wind River Reservation. An Indian agency had been established along the Little Wind River to serve the needs of the Indians.

She peered more intensely through the darkness, searching for Falcon Hawk in the crowd around the fire. When she did not see him, she went back inside his tepee.

She settled down by the fire. It was sinking

into a pile of smoking coals, the night creeping more closely about her. She shivered, feeling the aloneness, realizing that she must find the strength that she had remaining to focus on having her child. But it was hard.

As she waited for Falcon Hawk, she looked over his various weapons, her gaze stopping at one in particular. It was a lance. It had a head of flint, cunningly shaped, and was about three inches long. It was lashed to a slender stick of brown wood with sinew, and near the head were attached several brightly colored feathers. It was a beautiful weapon, one of grace.

Sighing, she looked toward the entrance way again, then pushed herself up and again went to the flap and lifted it. She looked skyward. The stars were bright in the clear, dark sky, promising a calm night.

But, dear Lord, she silently pleaded—where was *Falcon Hawk?*

Falcon Hawk was on bended knee on a high butte overlooking his village, offering a prayer to the Great Unseen Power.

"Oh, Great Mystery, the Great Unseen Power, my heart is open," he said, gazing into the star-speckled heaven. "I give my soul into thy keeping. No thought is within me save of thee. Lead this Arapaho chief into decisions that will best suit his future. Lead me to accept that this woman my heart hungers for is large with another man's child. This husband has died, leaving the woman and child alone in the world. Give me the strength and knowledge to make wrongs right for her.

Allow me to get over my anger at her for keeping this from me."

Falcon Hawk rose to his full height and stretched his arms and hands heavenward. "Oh, Great Unseen Power, my heart is open. Lead me into ways that I may know myself and my destiny. Always I ask for peace and harmony in all things. Tonight I ask for guidance, for I love a woman of a different skin coloring. Give me the strength to accept this child she carries as though it were my very own. I cannot live without Panther Eyes now that I love her."

Falcon Hawk lowered his arms and his eyes. He stood there for a moment with his head bowed, feeling the sort of peace known to him only when he was alone with the Great Unseen Power.

A slow smile flickered on his lips, and he nodded to the silent bidding of the Great Mystery.

"*Haih-nyah-weh*—thank you, Great Mystery. I shall heed your advice. I shall go to my grandfather," he whispered, as though in response to words having been spoken to him. "He is everything wise in this world."

He descended the high ground and hurried back to his village. He felt especially close to his people tonight as their voices lifted to the sky in song. He wanted to join them, but he needed the company of the wise one tonight.

Taking long strides, he soon came to his grandfather's colorfully painted tepee. Lifting the flap, he went inside. He moved softly across the mats spread over the floor of his grandfather's dwelling, then sat down opposite the fire from him.

Falcon Hawk gazed across the fire at Long Hair.

He was sitting cross-legged in his loose buckskin robe, the light of the fire flickering over his face and in his eyes. He wore a necklace of arrowheads which symbolized long life. As always, his long hair was drawn in a bunch over his forehead, all sticky and matted.

When Long Hair looked across the fire and discovered Falcon Hawk there, he grinned, bringing even more wrinkles into his leathery face.

"What brings you to visit this old man?" Long Hair said, lifting his fan made of an eagle's wing to shade his eyes as he squinted them in an effort to get a better look at his grandson. "Does it have to do with this woman you have brought into our village? I have heard that she is heavy with child. Where is the man who is this child's *neisa-na?*"

"This man, this child's father, is dead," Falcon Hawk said, crossing his legs and resting his hands on his knees. "I found this woman alone. She was lost in her travels. I brought her here. Only after she was here did I realize she was with child. But that was too late for your grandson's feelings. Falcon Hawk's heart was already filled with love for the woman. This chief, your grandson, wishes to keep her and the child. This chief, your grandson, wishes to marry the white woman. But your blessing is needed. Oh, wise one, tell me that you give such a blessing—that this grandson is wise in allowing such a love to enter his life."

Long Hair lowered his fan and began patting it against one of his knees. "This woman is white. She will bring you trouble," he said, his voice strained. "All white people are trouble."

"This woman is different from most whites I

have ever known," Falcon Hawk murmured, in Maggie's defense. He was trying to blot out from his consciousness the fact that she had kept truths from him, trying his best to understand why she had. "If I bring her to you, you will see. Shall I, *Naba-ciba?* Will you meet her?"

"That is not required," Long Hair said, laying his fan aside. He folded his arms across his chest. "Soon, but not tonight." He paused, then said. "When is the child due?"

"I would think any day now," Falcon Hawk said, nodding.

"And you would have feelings also for this child born not of you?" Long Hair said, his voice low and measured. "You would raise this child as your own?"

"Loving the child's mother as I do, it would not be a hard thing to love the child as well," Falcon Hawk said, nodding.

Long Hair gazed for a long time at Falcon Hawk, then gave him a wave of a hand in a silent gesture of dismissal. "Go," he said. "You are the grandson of a wise old man. So are you then as wise. If your heart belongs to this woman, who am I to say that you should deny such feelings? Go. You have my blessings. But be wary, my grandson, of what I have warned. Trouble. All white people are trouble."

Falcon Hawk's eyes danced as he rose to his full height. He went around the fire and leaned down and gave his grandfather a hug, then left the tepee, feeling exhilarated.

With bold steps, he went to his tepee. When he entered, he found Maggie lying on a blanket, sleeping. He knelt beside her and softly touched her face, awakening her.

Maggie looked up with a start at Falcon Hawk. Her heart pounded as he took her hands and urged her to her feet. She scarcely breathed when he lifted the smock and revealed her bare, swollen stomach. She allowed it because he was so gentle, and because she could see in his eyes that he had forgiven her and was ready to accept her as she was.

When he placed a hand on her stomach, she grew warm through and through at his gesture of acceptance. She closed her eyes in ecstasy when he smoothed his fingers upward and cradled her firm, milk-filled breasts with his hands.

When he moved his hands away, allowing the smock to drop back in place, and then lifted her chin so that he could kiss her, Maggie's head began spinning with desire. Her knees weakened from the beautiful feelings soaring through her when their lips met. She twined her arms around his neck and returned the kiss with ardor, but was interrupted when Soft Voice suddenly appeared in the tepee.

Maggie and Falcon Hawk moved apart quickly. Falcon Hawk went to Soft Voice and angrily took the tray of food she had brought. He knew that she had come with this offering of food only to spy on him. He did not scold her this time. He just gave her a look that made her take only one last angry glance at Maggie; then she turned and ran from the dwelling.

"She meant well," Falcon Hawk said, placing the tray of food beside the fire. "Come. We will eat and talk. There is much to say. There is much for you to explain, is there not?"

Maggie shyly nodded, then went and sat down beside him as he handed her a bowl made from the knot of a cottonwood tree, cut in half and then hollowed out.

He lifted another vessel and dipped it into the kettle that hung from a tripod over the fire. He filled her bowl with elk stew, then took an assortment of dried meat from the platter of food that Soft Voice had brought to them and placed this on a tin plate that he also offered to Maggie.

She ate ravenously as he watched her. Within his eyes she could see an eagerness and delight. She smiled at him, relieved when he began eating also, which kept him too busy to start asking her questions that she might find hard to answer.

The time soon came, though, when their plates were shoved aside. Falcon Hawk wiped his mouth with the back of his hand, then moved closer to Maggie's side. "While you wore the large poncho, it seemed you were well fleshed-out," he said softly. "But now I know it is only your stomach that is large."

He ran a finger slowly up the column of her neck, making a sensual shiver soar through her. "Here stands a flawless white throat," he said admiringly. "Your arms are dainty, and your legs are long and tapered beautifully. Once the child is gone from inside you, you will be small again. When we make love, I will be holding someone delicate."

"When we . . . make love?" Maggie stammered.

"It is certain that we will make love after you

have your child," Falcon Hawk said matter-of-factly. "You will stay. You will be my *h-isei*. The child will be reared as mine."

"It will?" Maggie gulped. Then she placed a hand on his arm. "How can you be so generous after I kept the truth from you?"

"There were good reasons, were there not?" Falcon Hawk said, taking her hand and holding it to his lips, kissing her fingertips.

"I feared telling you for many reasons, but mainly because I did not want to lose your love," Maggie murmured. "I do love you so, Falcon Hawk. I have from almost the moment I first saw you."

Falcon Hawk nodded. "I believe that is so," he murmured. "Yet it puzzles me how you could fall in love with one man while another is lying fresh in death. Was your love for this man frivolous? Will yours for me be the same?"

"Falcon Hawk, I never loved my husband as one does who feels passion for a man," Maggie tried to explain. "My feelings for him were gratitude for taking me in when I had no one else. I felt much for my husband, but never passion. When we made love, I felt nothing. I shared his bed only to make sure his manly needs were fulfilled. I owed him that much."

Falcon Hawk drew her next to him and held her at his side. "It is good to know," he said, sighing heavily. Then he turned to her, his finger leading her face around, so that their eyes could meet. "Why were you alone? Why did you need this man to fill a void in your life?"

"My mother died long ago," Maggie said

somberly. "My father died only a few months ago. My father's partner in business robbed me of my inheritance. I fled the horrible man and my past. Melvin, the man who became my husband, took pity on me. We made a home together and then, only a few days ago, I found him dead, obviously from a heart attack. Being heavy with child, I had to leave right away, to find someone who might help me deliver my child."

"I, too, have lost a father and mother," Falcon Hawk said, staring into the flames of the fire. "My father, who was called Dreaming Wolf, was chief before me. He chose to give up his life on purpose, during a skirmish between a small band of Ute and the braves of our village. He always said it was better to die in battle than to wither as he had watched my grandfather wither. My mother's name was Pure Heart. She wandered off while mourning the death of my father, and no one has since seen her."

"How horrible," Maggie gasped.

"Many winters ago, my grandfather stepped down from his role of chief and the people elected my father in his place, just as they elected me chief in the place of my father," Falcon Hawk said, his voice drawn. "It is a title I proudly bear, but I would gladly give it back to my father if given the chance—even to my grandfather, who is idling his life away in memories."

Falcon Hawk placed his hands on Maggie's waist and turned her to face him. He delicately touched her stomach, running his fingers around the solid, round ball of it. "No more talk of parents. You and the child are now safe," he said, then clutched her shoulders and drew her close and kissed her.

"You are so beautiful," he whispered as he drew his lips slowly away from hers.

Maggie blushed and lowered her eyes. "How can you say that?" she murmured, her heart sweet and melting under this special attention from the man she loved. "I am so big. I am so clumsy."

"This soon will pass," Falcon Hawk said as he stepped around her, moving toward his bed. "Come. You will sleep on my bed tonight. I will sleep on robes by the fire."

Maggie went to the bed. He took her elbow and helped her down onto the robes and blankets. He gently placed a blanket over her, then gave her another soft kiss.

"No more secrets between us?" he whispered against her lips, then went and stretched out beside the fire, his back to her.

Maggie snuggled herself into the blanket, breathless over how things had turned out between them.

He had forgiven her. He was even planning for her to stay. She was going to marry this marvelous, handsome Arapaho chief. And he had promised to do right by her child. He was an extraordinarily good-hearted man, for he was even going to raise the child as though it were his!

She turned on her side, suddenly afraid. Everything seemed too suddenly perfect. Surely something would make this dream turn into a nightmare.

A feeling of guilt went through her when she remembered that she had kept still more secrets from him—the rape and the fact that she had hidden a satchel of money beneath this very bed on which she was to sleep. One day he would surely know the full truth about even these things. Would he feel betrayed again? Would he forgive her a second time?

She closed her eyes, trying to force sleep upon herself and to place these fears behind her.

Chapter Nine

A sharp, stabbing pain in her abdomen wrenched Maggie awake. She grabbed at her stomach, gasping as the first pain subsided into another. "I'm in labor," she whispered, her eyes wide. The pains were coming frequently. She had not thought that it would happen this quickly.

Easing up on her elbow, Maggie looked at the blankets and robes upon which Falcon Hawk had slept. He was no longer there.

"Oh, no. Where *is* he?" she whispered to herself.

She looked desperately around the tepee. The fire in the fire pit cast long dancing shadows along the walls, and she could not tell if it was night or day.

Then she gazed up at the smoke hole, discovering a sky that was just turning blue as night crept away.

"He's surely gone for his morning bath in the

river, or for more firewood," Maggie whispered, trying to convince herself that he would return soon and realize that she was going to give birth today.

She did not want to think of going through the ordeal without him at least being near.

She wanted his comfort. She wanted his love. She wanted his acceptance the very moment her child took its first breath!

If he could accept this child, as he had accepted her and her shortcomings, then it would make it so much easier for her to cast the thought of the child's father finally from her mind, forever.

So much depended on Falcon Hawk. Her *life* depended on him. Her total happiness depended on him.

Another stabbing pain grabbed Maggie's consciousness. Sweat poured from her brow, and she gritted her teeth as she forced herself to tolerate the pain that came with giving birth. She threw her blanket aside and spread her legs. Clutching her stomach with her hands, she lay back and closed her eyes, her mind swimming with dizziness as the pain worsened and came in even shorter intervals.

Fear gripping her heart, wondering what was keeping Falcon Hawk, Maggie slowly tried to leave the bed. But as soon as her feet made contact with the mat-covered floor, another pain grabbed at her stomach, the contraction tight and long this time. The pressure was almost too much to bear as the baby pushed inside the birth canal.

She waited until this pain eased away, then

again tried to set her feet on the mats. She had to reach the entrance way. If Falcon Hawk was within earshot, she would get his attention.

Yet, she feared the worst—that he would not be there for the birthing. What if no one came to help her? Finally she set her feet level on the mats and pushed herself from the bed.

Gripping her stomach as though steadying it, she moved her feet an inch at a time across the soft mats. When another pain shot through her, she had to bear it right where she was standing. The pain was so intense that her head swam, and she felt as though she might faint if it did not subside soon.

When it did, she huffed and puffed and sweated until she finally reached the entrance way. With a trembling hand, she brushed the flap aside and leaned her head out. Her hopes of finding Falcon Hawk anywhere near were dashed. She saw no sign of him, nor did she see his horse among those in a corral a short distance from his tepee.

Then she realized something else. Her wagon was gone, as were her chickens, rooster and cow.

But that seemed a trivial thing to be worrying about when another pain shot through her. This one was so intense that she screamed and crumpled to the floor, her arm and hand partially extended through the entrance way.

Her eyes closed, and softly crying, she was scarcely aware of the shuffling of feet as someone came and stood over her.

"And so it is time," Soft Voice said sarcastically, drawing Maggie's eyes open.

"You!" Maggie said in a strained whisper. "Oh,

Lord, no. Please send for Falcon Hawk. Please send for someone else to help me. I don't want *your* help. You . . . act as though you hate me. I don't . . . trust you."

"White woman be quiet with words," Soft Voice said, bending down to place her hands at Maggie's waist, slowly helping her up from the floor. "Soft Voice help with delivering of child. If you do not like, you can run away."

Maggie had no choice but to lean against Soft Voice as she began helping her back toward the bed.

"As though I am in any condition to walk, much less run, anywhere right now," Maggie said, laughing sarcastically. She looked somberly at Soft Voice. "Where is Falcon Hawk?"

"He was called away before sunup," Soft Voice said matter-of-factly.

"Oh, no," Maggie cried as she slowly stretched herself out on the bed. "Where did he go? Why?"

"Word came that perhaps his mother has been sighted," Soft Voice explained, slowly lifting Maggie's buckskin smock over her head. "But rest assured, white woman. He left word that all women of the village should be alerted that you could deliver today. He has left orders. We women know what must be done."

Knowing that Falcon Hawk cared enough to make sure that she was to be attended to should have made Maggie feel better about things, yet she didn't. She could hardly bear to be in the same tepee as Soft Voice, much less have to listen to her spiteful tongue all day and be at the mercy of whatever she did during the childbirth.

"You say that besides yourself, others will help?" Maggie asked, glad when Soft Voice drew a blanket up over her nudity.

"I am sure that they heard your scream as I did," Soft Voice said, her jaw tight and her dark eyes angry as she peered down at Maggie. "They will come soon."

"Perhaps they did not hear my scream. Go now and tell them that I am soon ready to have my baby," Maggie said, lifting a hand towards Soft Voice. "Please?"

Another sharp pain stole her fears away. She closed her eyes and gnawed on her lower lip, knowing nothing at this moment but how her whole body was reacting to the pain. She was not even aware of Soft Voice's hands on her stomach, kneading it.

Only when the pain slowly subsided again was she aware of Soft Voice's hands. For a moment, time seemed frozen. Then, realizing how gently Soft Voice was kneading her stomach, Maggie smiled up at her.

When Soft Voice did not return the smile, Maggie's faded. "Why don't you like me?" she asked, wiping perspiration from her brow with the back of a hand. "From the very first moment we met, I could tell that you hated me. Does it have to do with Falcon Hawk? Are you . . . in love with him?"

"Soft Voice does not have to tell white woman anything about her feelings," Soft Voice said. "It is not for Soft Voice to say who Falcon Hawk decides to give his heart to. He *has* given you his heart, has he not?"

"I am not free to speak for Falcon Hawk," Maggie said, feeling it best not to reveal anything of Falcon Hawk's promises to her to Soft Voice. She was even more in Soft Voice's power now than before.

"It is the color of your skin, hair, and eyes that intrigues him," Soft Voice mumbled, lifting her chin haughtily. "While you are with child, I think he could have no interest in you! Yet I must wonder if the child will be born with white or copper skin? Have you known Falcon Hawk longer than he has professed to us?"

Maggie paled, realizing that she was accusing Falcon Hawk of not only fathering her child, but also lying about how he had come across her on the trail!

"You call your chief a liar?" she dared to say, knowing that she might enrage this woman even more against her. Yet perhaps Soft Voice had set her own trap by showing that she did not trust Falcon Hawk's words. This might give Maggie some leverage with the beautiful, spiteful woman.

"How would he react if he knew that you thought he was someone who could not be trusted, or believed?" Maggie said guardedly.

Soft Voice's lips parted and her eyes widened, but she had no chance to reply. Four women came hastily into the tepee, some carrying basins of hot water, others soft cloths and assortments of things that Maggie did not recognize.

The women moved to the bed, two on each side, with Soft Voice standing at the foot.

"Move on to your knees and elbows," Soft Voice flatly ordered.

"What?" Maggie gasped out. "Why should I?"

"Do as you are told," Soft Voice said, jerking the blanket away from Maggie. "Now."

Maggie scarcely breathed as the women on each side of the bed pounded stakes into the ground at each corner of the bed. "What are those for?" she finally asked, her voice shallow and trembling with fear.

"You will grasp the stakes as the child comes," one of the women said, her voice soft and comforting. "Now do as Soft Voice instructed. Move to your knees and elbows. Then grasp the stakes. As your pains come, hold tightly to the stakes. It will give you leverage."

Maggie rolled her head back and forth. "No, I won't do it," she cried. "This is not the custom practiced by my people. I will lie on my back to have my child. That is the natural way!"

Soft Voice leaned over the bed and glowered down at Maggie. "You are not among whites now," she said in a hiss. "You chose to have your child among us. *Nyuh!* Then you will have the child in the tradition of the Arapaho!"

Several hands came to her and began turning her over onto her stomach. She slapped at the hands until she discovered that she was much too weak to protest further. No matter how much she hated the idea, she had no choice but to have her child on her elbows and knees!

Her hands were led to the stakes as she moved to her knees, her stomach heavy beneath her. She gripped hard as another pain shot through her. Strange how it came to her that it did seem easier this way. The pains were not as severe.

And it was wonderful to have something to hold on to as she fought to withstand the worsening pain.

Once again she was without contractions. She hung her head, sweat pouring from her brow. She closed her eyes and panted as several soft hands kneaded and comforted her body.

Then she heard a sudden commotion behind her. She turned her head sideways and opened her eyes, shocked to find a man among those who were in the tepee with her. She tried to scramble for a blanket, but the hands that had only moments ago been comforting her were keeping her from covering herself from the eyes of the man.

"Please leave," she cried, begging the elderly man in strange garb with her eyes. "Leave me with some dignity, please."

Soon she discovered exactly who this was—a healer! A medicine man. He started singing and dancing around the bed, shaking a rattle made of a scaly fish back mounted on stuffed buckskin with feathers tied to one end. He fanned and brushed her with these feathers as he continued chanting in a singsong fashion.

"Please don't do that," Maggie cried, shivering with distaste. "Leave me alone!"

When he stopped, Maggie inhaled a deep sigh of relief. Then she tensed when she saw that he was not leaving, but only continuing his healing ritual. He lighted incense of sweet grass, then went to her and began rubbing her stomach with a chewed root, then with a horned toad.

Maggie almost fainted from the sight of the

toad. "Stop!" she screamed again. "Get out! Leave me alone! Do you hear? Stop!"

The medicine man took the toad away from her and dropped it into a buckskin bag, then began brushing her all over with feathers again, chanting all the while.

Maggie hung her head and sobbed, realizing that all her protests were in vain. She cried out when the sharpest pain yet shuddered through her abdomen. She clung to the sticks and bore down, grunting. She could feel hands on her abdomen, kneading and encouraging the birth. Then she felt hands move up inside her birth canal and the child soon following the trail of the hands outside her. Its cries attested to its passage into the world with a set of healthy lungs.

"It is a girl child," Soft Voice said. "Her skin is very white. Her eyes very blue."

Proud and relieved, Maggie allowed the women to help move her around, so that she could lie on her back again. Breathing hard from her exertions, she gazed down at the child being held within Soft Voice's arms.

"My child," she said softly, holding her arms out for her baby. "Give me . . . my child."

Soft Voice gave Maggie a strange smile, then turned and left the tepee with the wailing baby.

Maggie was stunned. She was speechless as she stared at the entrance way, thinking that surely Soft Voice was playing some sort of terrible trick on her and would return soon to relinquish the child to her rightful mother.

But when Soft Voice did not come back and

Maggie realized that her child was being purposely kept from her, she began screaming and tried to get up from the bed, but too many hands were there, holding her in place.

"Why?" Maggie cried, searching the women's faces for answers. She found no one willing to give her a reason for her child's having been taken from her, yet she was relieved that she saw gentleness and caring in those who still held her in place.

"Please," Maggie begged, looking from woman to woman. "Tell me why Soft Voice took my baby away."

When again no one offered a response, Maggie resumed trying to fight her way from the bed, but too soon fell back, exhausted from the effort, feeling empty and drained of spirit and hope. She closed her eyes and turned her face from those who proceeded to bathe her, soon placing on her a clean, soft buckskin robe. She sobbed until she felt there were no more tears to shed, then turned her eyes quickly around when she heard Soft Voice's voice among the women talking at the foot of the bed.

"Your tears are dried?" Soft Voice said as she gazed steadily into Maggie's eyes.

"Where did you take my baby?" Maggie asked, her throat aching and sore from screaming and crying. She struggled to lean up on one elbow, but her weakness caused her to fall again onto her back. "Why did you take my child away? Why?"

"The infant has been taken to Many Children Wife to feed from her breasts instead of yours," Soft Voice said, smiling down at Maggie. "Why?

Because this is what Falcon Hawk commanded should your child be born before he returned to our village."

Maggie's heart leapt, then seemed to stand still as she gave Soft Voice an incredulous look. "My child is feeding from another woman's breasts?" she gasped. "And you say that is because Falcon Hawk said that is the way it should be?"

She managed then to push herself up on her elbow and stay there. "You are lying!" she shouted, tears again splashing from her eyes. "Falcon Hawk wouldn't do that. Go and get my child immediately!"

Again gentle hands held her on the bed as she struggled to get up.

Again she fell back, exhausted.

Then waves of anger swept through her as she looked up at Soft Voice. "This is all your doing and you know it," she said from between clenched teeth. "When Falcon Hawk returns and discovers what you have done, you will regret it."

An older woman placed a gentle hand on Soft Voice's arm and ushered her outside, then came back in and stood at the foot of the bed. "You have no true quarrel with Soft Voice," the woman said softly. "We all are here at Falcon Hawk's command. The child was taken to Many Children Wife also at his command. Now rest. When Falcon Hawk returns, you can get the answers that we are not free to tell you."

Maggie squeezed her eyes together tightly, trying not to envision her child at someone's else's breasts. If she allowed herself such thoughts, she felt as though she might sink into insanity.

One of the women came to Maggie's bedside with a bowl of soup. "You have lost much strength and blood in having the child," she said, drawing Maggie's eyes open. "You must eat to regain this strength."

Maggie turned her eyes away, disbelieving all that was happening to her. Suddenly she had been thrust into a world completely different from her own. And although Falcon Hawk had treated her kindly and had even professed to love her, she now doubted everything he had ever said or done. She felt more like a captive than one who was loved!

Knowing that she must regain her strength in order to get back her rights as a woman and mother, Maggie scooted up into a sitting position and took the bowl of rabbit soup. She looked guardedly from woman to woman as she ravenously ate until the bowl was empty, then asked for a refill.

Later, when she was alone, she fought sleep. She wanted to be awake the very instant Falcon Hawk came into the tepee. She wanted to lash out at him with questions and accusations.

But she soon succumbed to her weakness and began drifting off, softly sobbing, praying that the hurt in her heart would go away.

Nestled in comfortable blankets beside a campfire, Frank Harper awakened with a start. He sat up and looked guardedly around him, then up at the sky as the sun began rising in a brilliant red splash along the horizon. He shoved his blankets aside and rose to his full height and stretched, then stared down at the dying embers of his campfire.

"What a damn dream," he said, bending on one knee before the fire to place fresh wood on it. "Margaret June had a baby? Damn, the baby even had my eyes."

He shuddered and stretched out again by the fire. He laughed, wondering what on earth would bring on such a dream as that, which was in truth a nightmare to him.

With every fiber of his being he hated children.

He would never have a squealing brat around, not even one fathered by him.

Chapter Ten

The next morning Maggie was awakened by a new sort of pain. Groaning, her hands slipped beneath her blanket and up the soft gown to her breasts. They were aching and throbbing. When she cupped them within her hands, she found them hard and heavy.

Instinct told her that only a child suckling from them could alleviate such pain. The milk needed to be released.

"I want my baby," she sobbed, softly kneading her breasts, yet finding that made them ache even more.

She turned on her side with her back toward the entrance way and drew the blanket over her. She wanted to escape into the dark void of sleep again, to forget the pain . . . to forget Falcon Hawk. . . .

A sudden presence behind her made Maggie turn slowly. Blood rushed to her face with excitement and relief when she found Falcon Hawk standing there, a child cradled in the safety of his arms.

Although she could not see the child's face or body because of the blanket wrapped snugly around her, Maggie knew that the small infant was hers and that she had been wrong to hate Falcon Hawk. It was obvious now that those who had taken her child from her had been wrong to do so. They had surely misinterpreted Falcon Hawk's instructions.

Stronger today, and momentarily forgetting her throbbing breasts, Maggie scooted into a sitting position. Beaming, her eyes filled with happy tears, she held her arms out for her baby.

"Oh, thank you, thank you," she murmured. "You've brought my baby to me. Falcon Hawk, please give her to me. How badly I want to hold her. Because of Soft Voice, I have yet to even see my daughter up close."

Falcon Hawk gently lay the child within Maggie's beckoning arms. He knelt down beside the bed and lovingly stroked Maggie's brow as he watched the blanket being unfolded to reveal the tiny thing to his woman's tear-filled eyes.

He too looked, long and searching, as the blanket came away from the child. He had seen many newborn babes, but those had displayed soft copper skin and dark eyes.

This child had the fairest of skin, with a pinkish tint, and golden-red curls tight across her head. The child being asleep, he could not see her eyes, but he knew them to be blue.

This had not puzzled him. Although he would have preferred a child that he was going to raise as his own to have dark eyes, or the panther-green eyes of her mother, he had already accepted the blue eyes which were surely the eyes of the child's father. To himself, he had already named the child.

Sky Eyes.

Haa, she would be raised with the Arapaho name Sky Eyes.

Maggie marveled over her daughter, unable to stop smiling as she touched her all over, from her head to her tiny toes. She sighed as her daughter's fingers circled one of her own and clung to it.

Maggie thought that the only thing wrong with this scenario was that her daughter was contentedly asleep, not crying to be fed. Even the pressure of the tiny thing against her breasts was almost unbearable.

Yet her daughter continued to sleep soundly.

At least Maggie did not yet have to look into her daughter's eyes, seeing Frank's. Soft Voice had said that her daughter's eyes were blue—a dreaded blue!

"Is she not beautiful?" Maggie murmured, smiling lovingly up at Falcon Hawk. "And she is so soft. Touch her, Falcon Hawk. See just how soft and sweet she is."

Falcon Hawk reached a hand to the child and slowly ran his fingers over the softness of one arm and then the other, and then across its tiny stomach, which seemed well filled with Many Children Wife's milk.

"Soft Voice has been so hateful to me, Falcon Hawk," Maggie suddenly blurted out. "And when she took the child away, even before I got to hold her in my arms and see her, that was the worst of her hatefulness. Yet, the other women did not correct her and tell her to give the child back to me. Why is that, Falcon Hawk? How could they have all been mistaken about what you told them to do?"

Falcon Hawk began folding the blanket back over the baby, Maggie hardly aware yet that he was doing this. She was awaiting his response. Until this morning, he had been silent, almost painfully so.

"How could they have taken my child to another woman's breasts?" Maggie demanded. "Why would they have, unless . . ."

Her heart pounding, wide-eyed and breathless, Maggie realized what Falcon Hawk was doing. She watched each corner of the blanket slowly hiding the sight of her child from her wondering eyes.

She was puzzled as to why he was doing this. The tepee was warm from the lodge fire. She was going to soon waken her daughter to place her lips to her aching breasts!

"Why?" Falcon Hawk said, avoiding her eyes. "It is because most of my direct orders were followed." He gently picked the child up into his arms and began rocking her back and forth as he continued his explanation. "It was my command to take the child to Many Children Wife, to feed from this woman's breasts. But it was not my intention that it should be done without you first seeing and holding her."

His confession made Maggie grow suddenly weak all over. Her pulse raced so hard that she felt faint. "No," she gasped. "Why would you do that to me? The child is mine. Only I should offer it breasts for suckling!" She doubled her fists on her lap as she watched her child in his arms. "How could you do this to me? Why would you? And if you had meant for someone else to raise the child as theirs, why did you bring her to me today? To make me suffer? To make the pain even worse when you take her from me again?"

She gasped and wanted to scream when one of the women she remembered from yesterday came into the tepee and took the child from Falcon Hawk's arms and carried her from the dwelling.

"What is going on here?" Maggie said, her voice a faint whisper. Then her voice grew stronger. "Give me back my baby!" She tried to get up from the bed, but fell back down as her knees buckled beneath her. She had not yet gained the strength she needed to take command of her own life.

When Falcon Hawk sat down on the bed and started to draw her into his embrace, she pummeled his bare chest with her fists.

"I hate you!" she cried. "How could I have ever allowed myself to love such a man? How was I so stupid not to see that nothing between us could ever work out. You are a most deceitful man!"

Falcon Hawk allowed her to beat at his chest until she fell limply back down onto the bed, sobbing and breathing hard.

Then he leaned over her and drew her up into his arms and cradled her close as he caressed her back, softly beginning his explanations. "Nothing I have done has been intended to upset you," he said gently. "Although I can understand why it has, please believe me when I say that it pains me to do anything that hurts you."

Too weak to fight him anymore, Maggie leaned limply against him and sobbed. "Then why are you doing it?" she said, her tears wetting his sleek, copper chest. "Taking my child away is cruel. If you loved me, you would not even consider doing such a thing."

"My love for you is as deep as the rivers and as high as the stars in the heavens," Falcon Hawk whispered, holding her shoulders so that their eyes could meet and hold. "What I do with the child is because of my love for both you and the child. Look at me. Listen. Try and understand."

Maggie winced as pains began shooting through her breasts again, followed then by a dull, steady throbbing.

"Go ahead. Tell me. But I doubt that I shall believe you," she said tightly. "You who said there should be no more secrets between us, and you do this with my child? All along you knew that you would. That was a terrible secret to keep from me."

"It was not meant to be a secret," Falcon Hawk said, puzzled at how she would wince now and then and close her eyes, as though in some terrible, gripping pain. "I realize now that you should have been told. But I did not get the chance. I was called away. Word came that my mother had been sighted in another village. I had to follow the lead, although I found that it was a false one. By going for her, I neglected you. For that I am sorry."

"There can be no good reason for you to take

my child away from me," Maggie said, finding the strength to jerk herself away from Falcon Hawk. She eased down onto the bed and turned her back to him. "Leave me alone now. I need my rest." She turned glaring eyes up at him. "But be assured that once I regain my strength, I shall go for my child. No one will ever take her away from me again."

"Before long you shall have her to yourself, anyhow," Falcon Hawk said. He took her hand and refused to let it go when she tried to yank it away from him. "Give this a few days. Try and understand. Allowing the child to be with Many Children Wife for a while will make your life and the child's life with my people more comfortable."

"I don't intend to stay here with you and your people," Maggie stormed, then mellowed when he took her hand and kissed her fingertips, as though he adored her. Her eyes wavered into his. "You do behave as though your love for me is true, yet if it were, you would not deny me my child."

"Listen to Falcon Hawk," he said gently. "Open your heart to what I have to say."

"You can talk and I shall listen, but my heart is closed to you forever," Maggie said, finally able to release her hand from his. She reached it beneath the blanket in an effort to keep him from claiming it again.

"You voiced aloud the love you have for this Arapaho chief," Falcon Hawk said, his midnight-dark eyes imploring her. "And Falcon Hawk has voiced his love for you. Along with this love come the teachings of the Arapaho so that you can live among us as one of us. So does this apply to the child."

"My child is mine, alone," Maggie said icily. "No decisions should be made for her except by me."

"You say that now in your anger," Falcon Hawk said, reaching to smooth a fallen lock of hair back from her brow. "But if you would allow yourself to listen to reason, and to see beyond your anger, you would understand this that I have chosen to do for the sake of the child—and you, who will soon become my wife."

"I won't marry you," Maggie said, stubbornly lifting her chin. "I plan to return to Kansas City as soon as I am able."

"You left that city to escape your past," Falcon Hawk said in a growl. "You choose that past over what I offer you now and in the future?"

"Yes," Maggie said, although the thought of coming face to face with Frank ever again sent cold chills through her. But she would face him. Also, she would see that he got arrested for his evil deeds. Through her recent trials and tribulations, Maggie had learned how to cope with many things. Including having to face that evil man.

Falcon Hawk took Maggie's wrists and drew her closer to him. "You listen to Falcon Hawk, *now,*" he growled. "Then if you wish to leave, it will be arranged. Tomorrow you will be in your wagon, going away from this man who loves you."

Maggie's lips parted as she gazed into eyes that always threatened to steal her senses away, even now, while she was so angry and hurt by what

Falcon Hawk had done. She breathed hard, trying to hide the pain in her breasts.

"It was important to Falcon Hawk that your child suckle from the breast of a woman of my village," he said. "The child is partially Indian now, its body nourished with Indian milk. Soon, when I feel that the nourishment from Many Children Wife is enough, your daughter will be brought back to you. Never will she be taken from you again. She will suckle from your breasts alone. You are my woman. The child will not be only yours, but also mine!"

Maggie was stunned by his explanation, and by how innocent his reasoning was. To him it seemed logical enough. To her it was wonderful to finally know why he had done this, and to discover that it had not been done maliciously, but because he loved not only her, but also the child!

There was a moment of silence as they gazed intensely into one another's eyes. Then Maggie flung herself into his arms, sobbing.

"I'm sorry for having doubted you," she cried. "But it seemed so cruel to take my baby from me in such a way. Even now I hunger to have her in my arms."

Pressing herself against Falcon Hawk in such a way caused her breasts to pound. She winced and eased away from him, gently cupping her breasts through her gown, sobbing as she lowered her eyes in pain.

"What is the matter?" Falcon Hawk asked, softly gripping her shoulders. "I can tell that you are in pain. Where is this pain?"

"My breasts," Maggie sobbed, gazing slowly up

at him. "They are hard and throbbing. Although I understand that you think it is important for my child to nurse from one of your women's breasts, I need my child's lips at my own. The milk is hardening. That is why I am hurting so. Please help me with the pain, Falcon Hawk. I don't think I can bear it much longer."

"*Haa,*" Falcon Hawk said, kneading his chin. "I have heard of such pain and what causes it."

"Then you will get my child so that I won't have to suffer any longer?" Maggie asked hopefully.

"There are other ways to stifle such pain," Falcon Hawk said, his eyes locking with hers, as though deep within them lay the question of her approval.

"Show me," Maggie cried, tears rolling down her cheeks. "Do whatever you must. I can hardly stand the pain much longer."

His heart pounding, for he had for so long wanted her in ways that had been denied him until she healed from the childbirth, Falcon Hawk placed his fingers at the hem of the buckskin gown and began slowly brushing it up, over her.

"Trust that what I do is done with much love," he said, as he lay her gown aside. His eyes devoured her silken nudity, roaming over her, seeing just how beautiful she was.

Wide-eyed and scarcely breathing, Maggie watched Falcon Hawk move his trembling fingers to her breasts, cradling them.

He flinched when he heard her groan. When he looked up and saw that she closed her eyes, he knew that it was not passion causing such a reaction, but pain.

"What I am going to do will not be as good as if your child were suckling from your breasts," Falcon Hawk explained, drawing Maggie's wondering eyes open. "But at least it should somewhat alleviate the pain."

She gasped with surprise when he leaned over her and began sucking milk from first one breast, then the other, spitting the milk from them into the fire each time he emptied his mouth.

When she first realized what he was doing, Maggie expected to be repelled. But strangely, it did not affect her in such a way. Instead her head began to spin with pleasure. His lips on her nipples and his hands on her breasts were starting raging, savage embers within her that she had never experienced before.

When he was finished and drew his mouth and hands away, Maggie sat there quietly and numbly staring up at him. It was at this moment that she realized just how much a woman could want a man.

She could forgive him anything!

And she would try with every fiber of her being to understand why her child was being denied her. This would soon pass and then what lay ahead had the promise of sheer bliss. She would awaken every morning with this dear man. She would share the wonders of lovemaking each night with him.

Yes, she was ready to make the small sacrifice he was asking of her to ensure that in the end, she would have him.

Almost swallowed whole by his own passionate feelings, Falcon Hawk placed his hands on Maggie's shoulders and drew her against him. "Is the pain less now?" he whispered, brushing his tongue lightly and seductively across her lower lip.

"The pain in my breasts?" she whispered back. "Or elsewhere? Falcon Hawk, it hurts me so to be near you, yet unable to give myself wholly to you. I must heal first. Then . . . then . . ."

"Then I shall take you to paradise," he whispered huskily, yanking her closer to him. His mouth bore down upon her lips, now knowing the extent of her love for him.

His feelings for her poured from deep within his soul as he ground his mouth over her lips, his tongue searching for hers, trembling through and through when she touched hers, tip to tip, with his. They groaned and clung, unaware of someone entering the tepee, watching. . . .

Soft Voice stood with her hands clutched into tight fists at her sides, her face somber and bitter as she glared with defiance at Falcon Hawk, then at Maggie.

Unable to stand watching the man she loved kissing someone else so passionately, Soft Voice fled from the tepee. She swore to herself that she would find many ways to make this white woman's life miserable. Soft Voice now understood why Falcon Hawk had taken the white child to Many Children Wife to be nursed. It was because that would make him as close to the child as to the white woman.

"Why did I not realize this earlier?" Soft Voice

was fuming to herself. "I even helped. I took the child from the white woman and gave it immediately to the breasts of a woman of my village!"

Soft Voice stamped over to Many Children Wife's dwelling and watched the white child nursing contentedly from one of Many Children Wife's milk-filled copper breasts, while Many Children Wife's own child suckled from her other breast. She glowered as she watched the white child's fingers contentedly kneading the breast from which she was getting nourishment. Soft Voice now wished that she had taken the child to the forest, where no one could have ever found it, instead of taking it to a woman who even now nourished it with healthy milk!

"You came to see the white child?" Many Children Wife said, directing her dark eyes up at Soft Voice. "Why do you frown so? She is a pretty child. White woman who bore the child is pretty, also. Soon she will marry our chief."

Many Children Wife paused. "Ah, that is why you frown, is it not?" she said. "You saw our chief as one day *your* conquest."

Soft Voice spun around and stamped away, not wanting everyone to see inside her heart, especially if her plan to stop this marriage between the man she loved and the white intruder was to succeed. She walked away, her head spinning with various ploys to part them.

Frank drew his reins tight, stopping his horse. He stared blankly at the burned-out trading post. "Damn," he spat out. He would now have to travel onward, to the trading post on the reservation land of the Shoshone and the Arapaho Indians.

He didn't look forward to entering Indian territory. Everyone knew that the treaties signed to settle the Indians there had been signed with blood—Indian blood. He feared that too many might be eager to spill white man's blood if given even the slightest excuse.

He would have to make sure he did not give them cause to spill his, Frank thought, slapping his horse's reins and riding onward.

Chapter Eleven

Two Days Later

The hours and the days dragged by for Maggie as she awaited the day when she would finally be given her child to keep and to feed from her own breasts. Although Falcon Hawk had brought her child to her each day to hold and to pamper between her daughter's feedings, it had been hard to relinquish her into the arms of another.

Today Maggie ate her afternoon meal ravenously and eagerly. Falcon Hawk offered her another bowl of corn chowder, smiling at her, reveling in her loveliness and the way she beamed like the sunshine. Never had he seen such a sunny smile, nor such radiance on a face. And in her eyes there was not only anxiousness, but a peace that came from deep inside her.

He knew the cause and could not help but feel somewhat guilty for forcing Maggie to wait for her child. But it had been the only way to mold their future together, as though Falcon Hawk, Maggie, the child, and the Arapaho, were one person, one breath, and one heartbeat.

Maggie's eyes were dancing as she giggled and nodded to indicate that she was still hungry. Soon she would be with her daughter forever. Although Falcon Hawk called the child Sky Eyes, Maggie had named her Mary Elizabeth. She did not speak this name aloud much, for Falcon Hawk had been adamant that while the child was being raised as Arapaho, she would be known by an Arapaho name!

She had not argued this, for to her the child would always be Mary Elizabeth.

"You are this happy to become a full-time mother today?" Falcon Hawk said, ladling chowder into her bowl.

"Yes, and why shouldn't I be?" Maggie asked, smoothing the beautiful doeskin dress with bead designs more snugly around her legs. "Two long days, Falcon Hawk. You should admire my patience. I am not much practiced in patience. My father spoiled me rotten."

"As will this man who will soon be your husband," Falcon Hawk said, handing her the bowl.

"Before we go for the child, there is something you must know," Falcon Hawk said, his voice guarded.

The sudden seriousness in Falcon Hawk's tone of voice caused Maggie to look suddenly over at him, a warning flashing off and on again inside her wary consciousness.

"What is it?" she asked, her voice drawn. She

set her bowl aside, even though it was still half-filled with the chowder. "What do you have to tell me?"

She turned to Falcon Hawk, beseeching him with her wide green eyes. "Is it about the child?" she asked warily. "She was all right yesterday, Falcon Hawk. Has something happened that I haven't been told since I last saw her?"

"Sky Eyes is fat and healthy and beautiful," Falcon Hawk said, taking her hands and holding them to his bare chest. "Sky Eyes must go through a ritual before she can be returned to you. It will be done this morning with an audience of many. You and I will be among this audience."

"What . . . sort of ritual?" Maggie gasped, paling. She tried to draw her hands free, but Falcon Hawk held them tightly to him, his dark eyes searching hers for some sort of understanding.

"It is a custom of my people, one that you may fight against, yet must accept to prove that you willingly hand your child over to live her life as Arapaho, not white," Falcon Hawk said softly. "I can see that you are frightened. Just listen with an open heart as I explain. Then perhaps you can accept what is to be done today with your daughter."

"Go ahead," Maggie said, fear gripping her at the very pit of her stomach. "Tell me."

"Today your daughter's ears are to be pierced," Falcon Hawk said guardedly, watching her reaction, expecting it.

"Her ears are to be . . . pierced?" Maggie stammered, paling even more. "No. I won't allow it."

"All Arapaho children's ears are pierced," he said, releasing one of her wrists, to point to the small hole in his right ear, and then his left. "This was done when I was but a few weeks old. So must it be done to your child."

"No," Maggie said, her voice smaller and pleading. "Please don't let this happen. It will be painful."

"Ear piercing while children are infants makes them grow up well and become men and women," Falcon Hawk said, drawing her next to his chest. "*Haa,* there will be some pain felt by the child. But that is good. It is said that the more the child cries during the operation, the better it is thought to be. The crying signifies that hardship and pain have already been endured, and therefore the child will grow up into strong adulthood."

"That is the custom of the Arapaho, not mine," Maggie softly argued.

"Your child is becoming Arapaho, so she shall practice all customs of Falcon Hawk's people," he said flatly.

He lowered his mouth toward her. "Trust this man who loves you with all his being," he whispered against her lips.

When he kissed her hard and demandingly, Maggie felt all her protests melting away, as savage embers began claiming her once again. She moaned against his lips and twined her arms around his neck, wanting him so much and wanting to understand these things that seemed so foreign to her.

In the long run, she knew that her child would

be better off if she were completely accepted by the Arapaho. She trusted Falcon Hawk to give this child a wonderful, loving future.

She knew that he would do nothing to harm her.

When Falcon Hawk released her and placed a blanket around her shoulders, she rose to her feet beside him. Without further argument, she left the tepee with him, noticing the crowd assembled around Many Children Wife's tepee. As she came closer, she saw that the bottom of the dwelling had been curled up, enabling the people to see inside, to witness the ear-piercing.

Cold sweat pearled along Maggie's brow when she wondered how the piercing might be done, closing her eyes momentarily as she envisioned her child already screaming with pain.

Someone playing a steady, rhythmic beat on a drum caused Maggie's eyes to open. She stared at an elderly man who was just outside the entrance of Many Children Wife's lodge, standing before a drum, facing it yet no longer playing it. He was instead telling war stories in a low voice, gesturing with his hands as he spoke. At the mention of each valorous deed, he struck the drum sharply two or four times, the women of the crowd crying "*Niii!*"

Falcon Hawk took Maggie's elbow and ushered her to step close to the man with the drum. "The elderly warrior you see at the drum is called the piercer, the one who will pierce your daughter's ears today," Falcon Hawk said in a low voice, as he bent closer to Maggie. "This warrior received Falcon Hawk's best horse for the deed."

Maggie looked quickly up at him, her lips parting with a gasp.

"You gave up Pronto to this man?" she finally said.

Falcon Hawk nodded. "This I did proudly," he said, smiling. "For *you* I gave up my stallion. For you and your child—a child who will soon be mine also."

Maggie was awed by this generous gesture of Falcon Hawk's, stunned that he would give up his horse for anyone or anything. There had seemed to be something mystical in their relationship. And now the horse would belong to an elderly warrior who did not seem able any longer even to get into a saddle, much less ride the animal.

"What can I say?" Maggie murmured, touching his cheek gently.

"Say nothing," Falcon Hawk murmured, taking her hand and lowering it to her side, not yet wanting such public admiration from the woman he loved to be seen by his people. "Just accept and trust. That is all Falcon Hawk asks of you today and all tomorrows."

Maggie leaned closer to him so that their hips brushed. "I do trust you," she whispered. "And oh, how I love you."

Falcon Hawk's eyes danced as he heard the words that made music in his heart.

Then when the elderly warrior ceased his tales and went inside the tepee, Maggie's insides tightened as she followed Falcon Hawk into the interior, which was brightly lit by a roaring fire in the fireplace.

Her eager eyes searched for her child, and she

grew warm and mellow inside when she found her baby lying comfortably in a moss-packed buckskin bag laced to a cradleboard. Her arms felt empty as she stared at her child, so badly wanting to go to her and rescue her from what was about to happen.

She comforted herself by knowing that after this was over, the child would be in her own comforting arms. If need be, if her child cried with pain for longer than the ritual lasted, she would rock her child the whole night through.

Before she realized what was happening, Falcon Hawk had left Maggie's side. She noticed his absence when she saw him bend over her child and take her baby from the cradleboard. When the elderly warrior stepped up to the child with a heated sewing awl, it took all of Maggie's willpower not to snatch the baby away from Falcon Hawk and run away with her.

But remembering Falcon Hawk's assurance that she could trust him, and knowing that this was necessary if she was going to make a life for herself and her child with him, Maggie clasped her hands behind her and watched as the awl was held over her baby as the elderly warrior began to talk.

"The awl symbolizes a spear," he said somberly. "The pierced hole is the wound, the dripping blood represents ear ornaments."

Without further hesitation he pierced the first ear, sending the child into a loud wailing.

Maggie forced herself to recall Falcon Hawk's words—that the more the child cried during the operation, the better it was thought to be, for the crying signified that hardship and pain had already been endured, and therefore her child would grow up well into adulthood.

The second ear was pierced, accompanied by more wails, and then greased twigs were inserted in the holes to keep the wounds open so that the piercing process would not have to be done again.

Maggie was surprised when Falcon Hawk came quickly to her and laid her sobbing infant in her arms.

"She is now yours for all time," Falcon Hawk said, watching how Maggie cuddled and spoke softly to her daughter, which seemed to quickly stifle the child's urge to cry. The child was in her rightful place, in the arms she belonged.

Maggie gazed lovingly up at Falcon Hawk, trying hard to remember how to say thank-you in Arapaho. As she spoke, it came to her, as though by magic.

"*Hahou,*" she murmured. "Oh, thank you, thank you."

Falcon Hawk nodded, then ushered Maggie from the tepee and through the crowd.

Soft Voice watched, angry and hurting inside, knowing that the piercing of the child's ears had drawn the child closer to Falcon Hawk. This filled her with rage and jealousy, yet she was not able to act on her feelings.

But she would, and *soon!*

Chapter Twelve

Maggie felt as though she were walking on clouds, so happy was she to finally have her child to herself. She went into Falcon Hawk's tepee, unable to take her eyes off her beautiful daughter. Mary Elizabeth was no longer crying; the pain of the ear-piercing seemed to have been washed away by the tears that she had shed during the ritual.

"Come and sit with Sky Eyes beside the fire," Falcon Hawk said, guiding Maggie by her elbow onto a soft cushion of furs and blankets.

"Do you insist we call her Sky Eyes?" Maggie asked, her eyes wavering when they met his. She did not want to tell Falcon Hawk that the name Sky Eyes would always remind her of the color of her daughter's eyes, which would forever remind her of her daughter's father!

"It is best, just as it was best that Sky Eyes fed from the breast of an Arapaho woman," Falcon Hawk said. "The child would have never been accepted if she had not been fed with Indian milk. She will be even more easily accepted if her name is Arapaho."

He helped her down onto the cushion of blankets and furs, then sat down beside her. "Falcon Hawk makes these decisions because he loves you," he said gently. "Not to spite you."

Maggie smiled sweetly up at Falcon Hawk. "I think I know that," she murmured, then settled herself into the comforting cushion beneath her. "And I shall not question my daughter's Arapaho name ever again."

She stretched her legs out before her and laid her child on them. As she unfolded the blanket in which her child was snuggled, she slowly rocked her legs back and forth. She proudly studied Sky Eyes as she was revealed to her, as though it were that first time. Her daughter seemed just as inquisitive now, for her blue eyes were on Maggie, wide and studious.

"Such tiny lips and look at the small, upturned nose," Maggie murmured, folding the last corner of the blanket away. Her hands went gently over her daughter's soft arms and legs. Gently she lifted one of her feet and marveled at its smallness. When Sky Eyes made a soft cooing, contended sound and her lips twitched into a tiny smile, Maggie's heart was stolen away.

As was Falcon Hawk's.

"Do you hear how she makes noises of happiness?" Falcon Hawk said, in an effort to prove to Maggie that the length of time she had been forced not to be with her daughter had not harmed her in any way.

accepted if she had not been fed with Indian milk. She will be even more easily accepted if her name is Arapaho."

He helped her down onto the cushion of blankets and furs, then sat down beside her. "Falcon Hawk makes these decisions because he loves you," he said gently. "Not to spite you."

Maggie smiled sweetly up at Falcon Hawk. "I think I know that," she murmured, then settled herself into the comforting cushion beneath her. "And I shall not question my daughter's Arapaho name ever again."

She stretched her legs out before her and laid her child on them. As she unfolded the blanket in which her child was snuggled, she slowly rocked her legs back and forth. She proudly studied Sky Eyes as she was revealed to her, as though it were that first time. Her daughter seemed just as inquisitive now, for her blue eyes were on Maggie, wide and studious.

"Such tiny lips and look at the small, upturned nose," Maggie murmured, folding the last corner of the blanket away. Her hands went gently over her daughter's soft arms and legs. Gently she lifted one of her feet and marveled at its smallness. When Sky Eyes made a soft cooing, contended sound and her lips twitched into a tiny smile, Maggie's heart was stolen away.

As was Falcon Hawk's.

"Do you hear how she makes noises of happiness?" Falcon Hawk said, in an effort to prove to Maggie that the length of time she had been forced not to be with her daughter had not harmed her in any way.

Chapter Twelve

Maggie felt as though she were walking on clouds, so happy was she to finally have her child to herself. She went into Falcon Hawk's tepee, unable to take her eyes off her beautiful daughter. Mary Elizabeth was no longer crying; the pain of the ear-piercing seemed to have been washed away by the tears that she had shed during the ritual.

"Come and sit with Sky Eyes beside the fire," Falcon Hawk said, guiding Maggie by her elbow onto a soft cushion of furs and blankets.

"Do you insist we call her Sky Eyes?" Maggie asked, her eyes wavering when they met his. She did not want to tell Falcon Hawk that the name Sky Eyes would always remind her of the color of her daughter's eyes, which would forever remind her of her daughter's father!

"It is best, just as it was best that Sky Eyes fed from the breast of an Arapaho woman," Falcon Hawk said. "The child would have never been

Maggie these past days, yet brushing these regrets aside as quickly as they came. What he had done had been for the good of the child and for the good of his woman. And now it was all behind them. Soon he would marry his Panther Eyes and everything would be as it should be!

Many Children Wife came into the lodge just then. The space at the door was hardly large enough to fit her healthily plump body.

She smiled at Maggie when she discovered the child eagerly nursing, then at Falcon Hawk. She turned to reach outside, then brought a cradle into the tepee. She waddled to the far side of the tepee and placed the cradle at the foot of Falcon Hawk's bed. Then, without saying anything, only continuing to smile, she left the dwelling.

"How nice," Maggie said, marveling at the kindness of Many Children Wife in giving up one of her many cradles so Maggie could have one for her own. "And it's so beautiful."

Her gaze swept over the cradle. It was made of buckskin embroidered with porcupine quills and beads and was suspended on ropes from four legs made of oak.

"Many Children Wife made the cradle for Panther Eyes," Falcon Hawk said, giving the cradle a slight shove to make it slowly swing back and forth. "The colors and symbols express a wish that the child may reach the age of womanhood and inhabit her own lodge."

Falcon Hawk placed a hand to Maggie's chin and lifted her eyes to meet his. "The cradle is a symbol of your acceptance by Many Children Wife," he said softly.

"Truly?" Maggie murmured.

"*Haa,*" Falcon Hawk said. "Soon all of my people will share this acceptance of my woman."

As he lowered his hand, Maggie looked at the cradle again. She wondered what the small buckskin pouch was that hung from the peak of the cradle. The pouch was diamond-shaped and was covered on both sides with beads.

"What is inside the pouch?" she asked, turning wondering eyes to Falcon Hawk. "Surely she left it there by accident."

"No. No accident," Falcon Hawk said, rising to his feet. He got the pouch and showed it to Maggie. He sat down beside her again and opened the drawstrings of the small bag.

When he reached inside and withdrew something tiny, dried, and curled, Maggie's eyes widened. "Why, it . . . it looks like a navel string," she said.

"Your daughter's navel string," Falcon Hawk said, giving her a closer look. "The navel strings of girls are preserved. Soon you, the child's mother, will stuff the pouch with grass and then sew the navel string into it. Sky Eyes will keep this amulet with her for safekeeping until it is worn out."

Maggie smiled weakly at him. This was one more custom she had to accept, even if she did not understand. It was all a part of her new world. She hoped that soon it would no longer seem so alien to her.

Aware that her child was no longer nursing, Maggie looked down at her and discovered that Sky Eyes was peacefully asleep. It was hard to move her daughter, reveling in the touch of her tiny body against her own flesh. She sat there for a moment longer, her eyes absorbing the sight of her daughter and her body taking in the warmth of her daughter's, as though it were sunshine casting its wondrous beams down upon her.

When her arm began to feel cramped from holding Sky Eyes in one position so long, Maggie was forced to move her back to her lap. She held Sky Eyes up just enough to give Falcon Hawk the space he needed to wrap the child again in the warm doeskin blanket.

"Tonight she sleeps where I can hear her breathing," Maggie whispered, smiling at Falcon Hawk. "I shall cherish the sound, Falcon Hawk. Absolutely cherish it."

He helped her to her feet. As she walked toward the cradle, she hummed lullabies that she remembered her mother humming to her even when she was too old for such fussing. Falcon Hawk walked ahead of her and hung the amulet on the cradle, then watched Maggie gently place the child on a soft bed of furs.

"Sleep well, my darling daughter," Maggie whispered, giving the cradle a slight shove that sent it rocking softly from side to side. "The angels are smiling down at you. My mother is among those angels. She is so proud of her granddaughter."

Tears came into her eyes at the mention of her mother, then those thoughts of her long-ago past were washed away when Falcon Hawk came up behind her and circled his arms around her, his hands on her breasts, softly kneading them.

"Tonight your daughter was *your* gift," Falcon Hawk whispered as he brushed his lips against

Maggie's. "Soon you will be *Falcon Hawk's.*"

She trembled with ecstasy at the thought of how it might be. She wished that it could be now. But her body was not as ready as her heart. She hoped that the healing time would pass swiftly.

Six Weeks Later

Finally the day that Maggie had been waiting for arrived. Her body was strong again, eager for the touch of the man she loved.

Maggie's heart began to pound and her insides grew warm at the thought that she was now well enough to know the wonders of this man's love-making. Tonight, as they listened to her sleeping child's breathing in their tepee, they would make love. She knew that to be so, and knew that it would be nothing like being with Melvin in those dreadful moments in the dark each night. In Falcon Hawk's arms, she felt alive with hungers she had never experienced with Melvin. She knew these feelings would be doubled while making love with her handsome Arapaho chief.

Ah, but what a night it was to be! At last she was going to be awakened to ways of truly loving a man. She had already nursed Sky Eyes to sleep for the night. Soon she would offer her breast to Falcon Hawk, but not to suckle milk from.

"Your thoughts," Falcon Hawk said as he entered the lodge and seated himself beside her. "Where did they just take you? I saw something there that caused my loins to awaken."

"And so they should," she murmured, looking almost bashfully up at him. "Darling Falcon

Hawk, I was thinking of making love with you. I am well enough now to do more than sleep next to you in your bed."

Having never before been as brazen, Maggie's pulse raced and her face flushed. The thudding of her heart was so intense, she felt as though her whole body was throbbing from it.

Maggie was almost being swallowed whole by the passion that was overwhelming her. For a moment she closed her eyes and felt his arms come around her. Her knees became weak as he turned her to face him and he pushed her dress down away from her. For a moment time seemed to stand still, and Maggie felt as though she were scarcely breathing as Falcon Hawk's eyes moved slowly over her in a sensual caress.

When he lifted his eyes and smiled a slow, seductive smile, Maggie could not hold herself back any longer. She flung herself into his arms, and he kissed her, his mouth grinding into hers, his hand setting small fires along her flesh as his fingers moved downward.

When his hand reached the juncture of her thighs and he began caressing the center of her desire, she was awakened to feelings she had never experienced before. Melvin had never touched her in such a way. He had never taken the time to show her that it could feel good for a woman, also. He had laid her down and mounted her, the fulfilment of his desires the only goal of their lovemaking.

Now Maggie was realizing what she had missed. Frank had made her acquaint sex with pain. Melvin had made her acquaint sex with nothingness.

Ah, but how different it was with Falcon Hawk. His hands and his lips were arousing her to heights that almost frightened her. Her whole body seemed to be one large heartbeat.

She was dizzy.

She was thrilling!

And all she wanted was more and more and more.

When Falcon Hawk stepped away from her, Maggie reached out for him, not wanting to let him go.

"I must undress," Falcon Hawk said, chuckling, pleased that she was being so free with her feelings with him. Some women did not know how to accept the sensual side of love. This woman seemed capable of giving as much as receiving. And that was good. He had chosen wisely when he had sorted through all of the women in his life and had chosen her as his soul-mate. Their life together would never be mundane or boring. Their nights would always be filled with fire—with savage embers!

After his last garment was tossed aside and he had slipped his moccasins off, Falcon Hawk took Maggie's hand and led her to the bed.

Slipping his hands down to her tiny waist, he leaned her back onto the bed, then lay down beside her. He turned her to face him and gazed with a rapid heartbeat at her luscious, soft mouth and her thin, yet lovely shoulders, where her hair lay in soft waves.

First he caressed her ivory-pale breasts until

she moaned with ecstasy. Then she twined her fingers through his thick black hair and brought his lips to her breasts. He eagerly tongued the nipples into tight peaks, then nibbled them with his teeth.

Again his eyes shifted downward. He took in a great gulp of air as anticipation built within him to fully possess her where the hair between her legs lay like a shadow.

He smoothed a hand down over her body, past her flat belly and to the muff of hair beneath which lay the mysteries of her femininity. He could hear her breath coming faster as his fingers parted the fronds of hair and touched the softness of the lips.

Maggie was so consumed with this wondrous, sweet passion raging through her, she could hardly bear lying still as Falcon Hawk explored her where her heart seemed to be centered. When his fingers touched the swollen nub of her womanhood, then began slowly caressing it, she closed her eyes, alive with a slow fire that licked its way through her body. Falcon Hawk was glad when he saw that she was hot with desire and lifted her hips to meet the wondrous caress of his fingers. His fingers worked more earnestly over her swollen nub. He caressed. He softly pinched. He tickled.

But knowing that was not enough for him, or her, his lips lowered to her mouth. He gave her a hungry kiss, their tongues meeting in a sensual dance as he found her opening herself more to him where his fingers played and searched.

When he thrust a finger into her, she moaned,

startled by the intensity of the pleasure this gave her. It was as though she had burst into undying flames as he moved his finger rhythmically in and out of her. Each time he thrust it inside her, he seemed to be seeking to touch her deepest depths, playing her now as though she were an instrument.

She clung to him and threw a leg over him, her eyes opening widely when this brought his swollen shaft against her to rest patiently and hot against the flesh of her thigh.

His free hand sought one of hers. When he found her hand, he circled his fingers around it and urged it to his manhood. When he placed her hand on him, and she felt the satiny texture, the very heat of it, Maggie felt as though she might swoon with the strange sensations this caused deep within her. She had never touched her husband in such a way. He had never asked it of her. His interests had always centered on himself, and she had thought that was natural.

Now she was learning from a masterful teacher how it *should* be, and she was going to be a most astute student!

Falcon Hawk inched his mouth only a fraction from her lips. "Move your hand on me," he whispered against her cheek. "Clasp it hard." He circled his hands over hers, teaching her how to make him feel an even more intense pleasure than that he already felt.

"Move your hand in this fashion," Falcon Hawk whispered, gazing with passion-heavy eyes into hers as he swept her hand in an up-and-down motion over his throbbing hardness.

"*H-isei, h-isei,* my woman, my woman," he groaned as he closed his eyes. He threw his head back, his teeth clenched with the pleasure. He moved his hand away and let her take over, and he lay there for as long as he thought it safe, before he reached that time when he might explode into her hand instead of her womb.

He continued caressing her and thrusting his finger into her, in time with the movements of her hand, and then he moved away from her and knelt at her side.

Maggie expected him to mount her and take his pleasure quickly now, but instead he was still postponing it. Her eyes grew wide and questioning when he started worshipping her flesh with his tongue, starting with the long column of her throat, working his way down to lick her breasts, and then across her flat tummy, which rippled with pleasure in the path of his tongue.

Then when he moved again and held her legs apart, giving him room to kneel between them, Maggie's face turned crimson with a blush, his tongue now on her most sensitive spot, sending her heart and mind into a sensual spin.

Placing her hands at his head and parting her legs further, she encouraged his mouth closer. Never had she thought that such rapture was possible. His caresses were causing her to melt. There was only the world of feeling, touching, burning and throbbing. Her breath came faster as the passion came near to exploding.

But Falcon Hawk knew when to stop and to concentrate on bringing them both to the peak of passion at the same time. He rose over her. As he kissed her passionately and long he thrust his throbbing hardness within her. Their heartbeats and moans mingled as the pleasure mounted and mounted and he moved more quickly within her.

Maggie closed her eyes and lifted her hips closer. She wrapped her legs around his waist and locked them together at her ankles. She clung to Falcon Hawk as he ground his mouth into her lips, his pulse racing, the heat within his loins raging.

Then they found the ultimate release. They cried out as their bodies trembled with pleasure. Maggie received Falcon Hawk's intense thrusts eagerly, her own climax continuing, as though her mind was filled with millions of sunbeams and rainbows.

And then Falcon Hawk rolled away from Maggie. He stretched out on his back, panting.

Maggie closed her eyes, hardly able to believe that this had just happened to her. She had felt totally alive! Falcon Hawk had loved her enough to want her to feel the same depths of passion as he.

And she had!

More than she had ever thought was possible.

She turned to Falcon Hawk and draped an arm over him, gazing lovingly at him as his eyes opened and he returned the look. "I love you," she said, giving him a soft kiss. "I adore you. Thank you for making me so happy, for taking me to paradise, as you promised. I never thought that paradise could be found on this dreary earth. But tonight I discovered just how wrong I was."

"You did not know this with your husband," Falcon Hawk said, placing his hands at her arms and drawing her above him. "The passion seemed too new to you. Is that true?"

"*Aa,* that is so," Maggie said, blushing. One word at a time, she was learning their language, just as she was gradually learning other things.

"You seemed practiced at first, but then I could tell by your reaction to the different ways of my loving you that it was new to you," he said, placing a gentle hand on her cheek.

"I only appeared to know about loving at first, because it was you who were loving me and causing everything that I did to come so naturally to me," Maggie said, tossing her long hair back from her shoulders. "Did I please you as much as you pleased me?"

"Panther Eyes, does this Arapaho chief act disappointed?" Falcon Hawk said, chuckling as he searched with his manhood for entrance inside her, the blood already filling his member again with wanting her.

"No," Maggie said. "You do not act the least bit disappointed."

She sucked in a wild gasp of pleasure and closed her eyes when she felt him fill her so magnificently again. She leaned down and placed her hands on his chest and began moving with him, then stopped and lifted her hands away from him, seeing the scars on his chest that she had not yet asked him about.

But now did not seem the appropriate time.

She closed her eyes and enjoyed the renewed splashes of pleasure rising within her, but never forgetting her child that was only a heartbeat away.

Maggie felt as though she could never be as content as now, and still a lifetime of contentment lay ahead of her!

She threw her head back and allowed the bliss to overwhelm her again as Falcon Hawk lifted her rhythmically with his powerful thrusts.

Grumbling to himself, Frank opened his saddlebag and pulled out his shaving gear. He had found the other trading post yesterday and had finally found some answers about Margaret June. After describing her to those in charge of the trading post, they had nodded, saying that they knew her but she was now going by the name Maggie.

But the man who had married Margaret June, or Maggie, Frank did not know from Adam!

"He's probably the one that gave Margaret June the nickname. He probably married her for her money," Frank ground out between clenched teeth. "My money, damn it."

He carried the shaving gear to the bubbling stream and placed it on the ground, then leaned over and splashed water onto his face.

Then he opened his leather bag and pulled out his mug of soap and shaving brush. He dunked the brush into the water, then circled it over the soap.

"There had better be a good portion of that money left, or by God they'll both have hell to pay," he said, lathering his whiskers with the suds.

His plan was to find that settlement where Margaret June was called Maggie and where Margaret June played at being a wife and where Margaret June had the money . . . !

Chapter Thirteen

The fire pit was glowing with dying embers as Maggie sat close beside it on a cushion of furs, her child nestled in her left arm as Sky Eyes nursed hungrily. The air was filled with a morning chill, and Maggie had left the soft doeskin blanket wrapped snugly around Sky Eyes, preventing her mother from being able to marvel anew over the tiny toes and fingers.

But Maggie enjoyed watching the tiny lips receiving nourishment from her nipple and hearing the contented sounds as the warm milk filled her daughter's small tummy. At this moment it did not seem that she had ever been denied this special pleasure, even for a short time. The wonder of her child within her arms erased all ugliness from her mind. The remembrances of her unhappy past were fading more and more every day, as though someone were pulling a shade down, hiding the rape behind it.

Hearing Falcon Hawk make a movement on the bed, she turned her eyes to him. She could feel her heartbeat quicken to see him sleeping so peacefully without a stitch of clothes on. Her eyes moved slowly over him, admiring his sleek copper skin and his muscled shoulders, arms, and legs.

A hot flush came to her cheeks as she gazed upon that part of his anatomy that was now small and unresponsive, recalling so very vividly to what lengths it could grow, and how thick and velvety it felt to her fingers when she touched it. She recalled with an arousing passion how he had so magnificently filled her, making her ache even now to have his rhythmic thrusts within her again.

Deep within her came a spreading of warmth as she recalled how he had awakened her to feelings she had never known possible. Her skin tingled at the thought of being with him again in such a way. She closed her eyes and remembered how his lips, tongue, and hands had set her afire. If she thought hard enough, she could feel them even now. She sighed as desire spread through her.

Realizing that her child's lips had become still on her breast, Maggie opened her eyes and gazed lovingly down at her. "You slept all night and you are asleep again already?" she whispered, lifting Sky Eyes away from her breast.

A small droplet of milk still clung to the corner of her daughter's mouth. Maggie lovingly smoothed it away with the flesh of her thumb.

So that her breasts would not be exposed to the chill of the morning any longer than needed,

Maggie soon had her gown back in place. Then she rose slowly to her feet and carried Sky Eyes to her cradle.

Humming a soft song, Maggie rocked her daughter slowly back and forth in her arms for a moment. Then, although reluctantly, she laid Sky Eyes on the thick cushion of furs and blankets in the cradle.

"I adore you," Maggie whispered.

Her eyes widened with surprise when she felt a hard body slide in behind her, and felt hands slipping up inside her gown.

"My woman's skin is cold," Falcon Hawk said, his fingers warm against her flesh as he crept them higher on her leg, stopping at the soft muff of hair at the juncture of her thighs. "Come to bed, Panther Eyes. Let your Arapaho brave warm you all over."

Maggie gasped with delight when he cupped the mound between her legs within his powerful hand, cradling it as though it were something sweet and delicate.

"If you don't stop that, my legs will be too weak to carry me to the bed," Maggie whispered huskily, not wanting to move, enjoying what he was doing too much.

"Then Falcon Hawk will carry you," he teased.

His fingers moved to her shoulders. He eased her around to face him, then whisked her up into his arms.

Her heart pounding, Maggie clung to his neck. Her lips quavered as his mouth came to hers in an explosive kiss. One hand cupped a breast through her gown, while the fingers of his other hand caressed her where her center of desire was throbbing.

When he laid her on the bed, she lifted her arms willingly as he pulled the gown up and over her head, glad when he had tossed it aside. She was not in the least aware that the room was cold and that the fire needed tending. All that she could feel was the heat rising within her.

Maggie inhaled a breath of pleasure when Falcon Hawk knelt over her and cupped one of her breasts with his hand, sending the nipple into a ripened hard peak as his tongue swept over it and then as his teeth began nipping at it.

Only moments ago, Maggie's child had fed from that breast, giving her one kind of pleasure. Now Falcon Hawk was giving her another sort, which made her head spin with rapture.

Falcon Hawk's masterful hands began moving all over Maggie's silken body, eliciting moans from deep within her when he touched or fondled her pleasure points. Smiling, she closed her eyes and enjoyed this way of beginning a new day. She tossed her head from side to side when his tongue then began to make a heated path across her body, stopping where she was still softly tender from their lovemaking of the previous night.

When he spread her legs and gave her his special pleasuring, her breath quickened. She chewed on her lower lip, not wanting to cry out with the pleasure, afraid that she might awaken the whole village and then never be able to face them again from the shame of it!

* * *

Soft Voice had been awakened earlier than usual by something she could not identify. Restless, she had dressed and was taking an early walk through the village. Something had taken her close to Falcon Hawk's tepee. That something was the knowledge that the white woman was still there with him. Soft Voice understood that the white woman should be well enough to enjoy sensual pleasure. She had no doubt that Falcon Hawk and the white woman would soon make love, if they had not already.

Gathering her blanket more snugly around her shoulders, Soft Voice peered with squinted eyes through the early hours of the morning at Falcon Hawk's dwelling. She saw no shadows of fire on the inside walls, so surmised that the fire had all but gone out. That had to mean that Falcon Hawk was still asleep, for placing wood on the embers in the fire pit was the first duty of a brave each morning.

Sighing, Soft Voice started to walk onward, then stopped with a start when she heard a noise coming from Falcon Hawk's tepee. She grew cold inside with anger when she realized that what she was hearing were moans of pleasure! And it was not a man's voice emitting such sounds! It was a woman's!

"He is making love to her!" she whispered harshly to herself. She circled her hands into tight fists, her fingernails breaking the skin of her palms as she squeezed her fingers even more tightly together. "He does plan to make her his wife. But did I not already know this? He treats the woman's child as though she is his! Why not the woman!"

Soft Voice knew that she should go on past, to get the sound of the lovemaking behind her, but she could not move. She grew angrier the more she heard, knowing that she had lost this man whom she had dreamed of conquering since she had been old enough to know that he would one day be a great leader of their people.

Even after she had married another handsome brave, her eyes never left Falcon Hawk when she was near him. When he had become chief, and after her husband had been killed by a crazed pack of wolves, she had become even more determined to have Falcon Hawk.

He had never returned her smiles and had shunned her advances. But she had continued trying everything to get him interested in her.

She had kept his lodge clean. She had kept food in his cooking pot. She had sewn for him. And he allowed all of these things, only to use her as one might use a slave, and *she* had allowed it, hoping to spark something within him that might make him want her.

"Never has he let me warm his blankets for him," she thought painfully. She had seen other women sneak in and out of his tepee when no one else was watching. She had died a slow death inside each time.

"Now it is never, ever to be," she said, wiping tears from her eyes.

Something compelled her gaze to shift upward, where the proud, lovely eagle was sleeping, its head tucked gracefully beneath one of its mighty wings.

Knowing how Falcon Hawk cherished this bird, having tamed it to be his since the bird was a few weeks old, Soft Voice realized what losing it might do to him.

It could break his heart as Soft Voice's heart was broken!

She had only to untie the one leg and it would be free. . . .

Her jaw tight, her eyes squinting angrily in the morning light, Soft Voice tiptoed to the perch and was careful not to alarm the bird into making a racket.

Very quietly, she untied the knot. Very gently she gave the eagle a nudge. When it jumped with alarm and flapped its wings with fright, it soon discovered that this time when it did this, the action took it from the perch. Instinct drove him upward into the sky.

Smiling mischievously, Soft Voice watched the bird until it was lost to her sight against the dark heavens.

Shifting her gaze downward, she glared at Falcon Hawk's tepee. "Take your pleasure *now,* for when you step outside and discover your pet gone, you will hurt as I hurt," she whispered, then stamped away toward the river.

Although the water was icy cold this morning, she would take a swim. The sting of the water might help erase the sting in her heart.

Yet she doubted that would ever go away.

Not unless she could make the white woman

vanish, as she had the bird!

She smiled at the thought.

Falcon Hawk shifted his position and lay over Maggie, one knee nudging her legs farther apart. He entwined his fingers with hers and held her hands above her head as he lowered his mouth to her lips. He took her mouth by storm and probed at her softly with his throbbing hardness, then entered her and began his rhythmic thrusts, driving in swiftly and surely. Her hips arched and moved with him, helping to draw him even more deeply within her. Their bodies strained together hungrily, the sensations within Maggie searing.

Falcon Hawk released her hands and moved his palms over her, then surrounded her with his hard, strong arms and pressed her body up into his.

His lips moved to her neck, down to the hollow of her throat, then to a breast. He lapped his tongue over one and then the other, making her shiver sensually.

Again his mouth went to her lips and they clung and kissed, her slim, white thighs opening even more widely to him as she reached her legs around his body, locking them at her ankles. Feeling the excitement rising, she gripped him tightly and abandoned herself to the torrent of feelings that washed over her.

Falcon Hawk's head was spinning with the pleasure. He fought to go slowly, yet the sensations were working through him in hot, sharp pains.

He slowed his thrusts, then quickened them.

He lay with her now, cheek to cheek, his breath hot on her flesh, hers on his.

The curl of pleasure was spreading and then there was no holding back. He stiffened, sucked in a long breath, then sank deeply into her again and felt the release as his hardness trembled and sent the seeds of his desire deeply inside her womb.

Just as she could feel Falcon Hawk receiving the deepest of pleasure, Maggie felt a great surge of warmth flooding her body. Tremors cascaded down her back as the air became heavy with pleasure, and her throbbing center sent delicious waves of ecstasy through her, filling her, drenching her with a delicious warmth.

"I will talk to my grandfather soon about a ceremony that will make you my wife," Falcon Hawk whispered against Maggie's cheek, his hands trembling as they cupped her breasts. "This will make you happy?"

"I never want to leave you," Maggie whispered, caressing his sweat-pearled back.

"You are accepting the customs of my people well," Falcon Hawk said, rolling away from her. He left the bed and gathered up his clothes, slipping into his fringed breeches.

Maggie once again stared at the scars on his chest. For many reasons, she had put off asking him what had caused them. But mainly, she knew that she did not enjoy talking about things of the past that pained *her* heart. She believed Falcon Hawk felt the same. Surely whatever had caused the scars on his chest had not been a pleasant experience, not one that he would enjoy discussing.

But now, since they were so comfortable

together, she felt that she could ask him. "Falcon Hawk, I've never asked, but what caused the scars on your chest?" she ventured, reaching for a doeskin dress among the several that Falcon Hawk had brought to her one day. She went to him where he now stood beside the fire. "Or is it too painful to talk about?"

She knew that she had her own painful secrets. She glanced at the bundles beneath the bed. There lay one of her secrets. She had not yet found an ideal time to tell Falcon Hawk about the money, now doubting she ever would. He would wonder if she had kept other secrets—in particular, the one that she wished never, ever to tell!

Falcon Hawk slipped a fringed buckskin shirt over his head, then knelt down beside the fire pit and began laying twigs across the glowing embers. "It is not painful at all to talk about," he said, giving Maggie a look over his shoulder. "These were received while participating in the Sun Dance of my people. It is an honor to show such scars."

"An honor?" Maggie gasped, slipping her feet into soft moccasins. "And this is one of the customs I will be a witness to?"

"In time," Falcon Hawk said, nodding. He added larger pieces of wood in the fire pit as the small twigs took hold and spread their fire upward and about.

"Should we ever have a son, I would not want him to participate in anything that obviously causes such pain . . . such scarring," Maggie said, shuddering at the thought.

"Any son born Arapaho takes pride in participating in the Sun Dance," he said, turning to face Maggie. "As do the parents as they watch the performance."

He sat down on the soft cushion of pelts and reached a hand out for Maggie. "Come. Sit by the fire with me," he said. "Let us talk as the dwelling warms."

"Shouldn't I begin preparations for breakfast?" Maggie said, sitting down beside him.

"As you know by now, the Arapaho have no regular time for meals," Falcon Hawk reminded her. "Women cook when men are hungry, except for supper time which is a fixed affair, especially in winter. Food gives strength. When the cold winds blow, much strength is needed."

"I dread the arrival of winter," Maggie said. "Although I lived in a cabin last winter, it did not keep the winds from creeping in through the cracks and through the drafty door and windows."

"You will find that the Arapaho tepee locks in the warmth of the fire and keeps out the winds of the winter," Falcon Hawk said, taking her hand and squeezing it affectionately.

"Tell me about your people," Maggie said, leaning into his embrace as he slipped an arm around her waist. "I have so much to learn."

"We lead a simple life and there is happiness among our people," Falcon Hawk said, gazing dreamily into the fire. "But long ago, before the white man came, our people were much happier, their hearts singing each morning when they arose, for the country was rich. The country was *theirs.* There was plenty of grass for their horses and for all the wild game to make them fat. There was everything to make the heart of the Arapaho glad."

He paused, and she could see a sadness enter his eyes before he began speaking again, this time in a monotone.

"And then, long ago, when the white men came, everything began changing for all Indians," he said. "These men were treated kindly, yet they were asked to go away. But they would not go. They stayed. More came. They killed the buffalo. They burned the grass. They cut down the trees and dug up the ground. Then we tried to fight them. That was no good. There were too many white men. Too many guns. The Indians would kill only one white man while the white man turned on them and killed many of our people."

Falcon Hawk held up his hands. He made the sign for putting his thumb on a piece of paper. "It was a sad day when our people, the Arapaho, were forced to surrender all their rights to their home, their country, and independence, and agreed to fight the white man no more."

He turned his dark eyes to Maggie. "Where once my people roamed at will, we are now confined and kept under military surveillance," he said, his teeth clenched. "Is it not a form of prison? Can you not understand why the Indians cannot help but hate most whites? Or that my ancestors were rebellious?"

Shame filled Maggie's heart at the thought of what her ancestors had forced on not only the Arapaho, but all Indians. She crept into Falcon

Hawk's arms. "How could you love me?" she cried. "I am white. My child is white. My ancestors may have even been among those who forced you into this life that you are made to tolerate."

Falcon Hawk drew away from her. He framed her face between his hands. "My woman, you are white, but this is something that you did not ask for," he said softly. "It is my true belief that should you have been given a choice while in your mother's womb, you would have chosen to be born Arapaho! If not, you would not be so accepting of Falcon Hawk and his beliefs! Is this not so, my woman?"

"Yes," she murmured. She smiled softly up at him. "Perhaps sometime way back in history, someone of my family *was* Arapaho. Would it not be grand to discover that perhaps my great-great-grandmother or grandfather fell in love with an Indian, the same as I?"

Falcon Hawk smiled down at her, then drew her gently into his embrace. "*Haa,* that is a good thought, but something we could never prove," he said. "So we will just be content with how you are, no matter what has formed your heart and soul into the person you are."

Falcon Hawk lifted her chin with a finger. He kissed her softly, knowing that she was right for him in every way.

But he still had his grandfather to convince! Although old grandfather had told Falcon Hawk to follow his heart, still Falcon Hawk knew that his grandfather was not happy that this path had led to a white woman. It was important to Falcon Hawk that his grandfather truly accept this woman who would soon be his wife. His grandfather's feelings were important to Falcon Hawk.

But Falcon Hawk had seen in his grandfather's eyes as he gazed at Maggie that he did not approve of her, and his grandfather's eyes sometimes said more than words ever could.

Frank slid easily out of his saddle, looking guardedly around him at what seemed a deserted settlement. It was midday, when someone should be stirring outside, if not in the garden, then elsewhere.

Surely his informant was wrong about Margaret June living here. With all the money that she had stolen from the safe in Kansas City, she would have been able to live in a grand style.

Slipping his pistol from its holster, Frank walked stealthily toward the front door of the cabin, then crept inside.

The stench of rotted flesh splashed into his face instantly, burning his eyes, nose, and throat. Through the stillness he could hear the buzzing of flies—swarms of them.

When his eyes became conditioned to the dimmer light inside the cabin, what he saw made him jump with alarm. He placed a hand at his throat, realizing that beneath that thin, fly-covered blanket was a body.

"Oh, God. Margaret June?" he said, quickly flipping his pistol back inside its holster.

Although he had hated her this entire trip, he did not want to discover her beneath the blanket. He would never forget how sweet and pretty she was.

Now, when he thought that she might be dead, it was easier to remember her innocence, than it was to remember how angry he had been at that moment when he discovered that she had stolen all of the money from the safe.

Deep down inside himself he would never forget how it had felt to hold her, to make love to her. Even though she fought him, he had realized much passion at her expense.

His loins ached even now at the thought of that moment of sexual release, knowing that even if this wasn't Margaret June lying dead beneath this blanket, he had no hope of ever feeling her warm body against his again. She would kill him first—that is, if he did not get that first shot at her.

Bending to one knee, Frank shooed the flies away, then placed his trembling fingers at one corner of the blanket and slowly rolled it away until at least the face was revealed to him.

Relief flooded his senses when he discovered that it was a man, not Margaret June.

This must be Melvin, he thought. Her husband. But why had she left him unburied?

Thinking that foul play might be responsible, and wanting to check the body to see what might have caused the man's death, Frank jerked the blanket away from Melvin.

He was puzzled when he saw no gunshot wounds, no points of entry caused by any weapons. He had thought that Melvin might have been killed by an Indian's arrow.

"Seems it was a natural death," Frank concluded, covering the body again.

Slowly he went around the cabin, inspecting

everything. Margaret June seemed to have left in a hurry. Where the hell to, though?

He rushed back outside to get away from the stench.

Checking everything out before venturing onward, he found that the chicken house was empty. In fact, all the animals were gone.

As he started to leave the chicken house, he clumsily tripped over some upturned dirt. He stared down at the hole in the ground, then shrugged and went back outside.

Margaret June was gone all right. He swung himself into his saddle. But she for sure hadn't gone to the damn trading post for assistance. And he'd checked everything beyond that. In between were only Indian villages. Could she have . . . ?

Relentless in his pursuit of Margaret June, Frank wheeled his horse around, determined to look for her in every Indian village on and off the reservation. If she couldn't be found there, then she had to have succeeded at eluding him forever!

He narrowed his eyes angrily at the thought that she might have outsmarted him.

Chapter Fourteen

Maggie giggled as her stomach growled from hunger. She leaned into Falcon Hawk's embrace, gazing lovingly up at him. "I was raised to eat breakfast every morning," she said softly. She placed a hand on his cheek. "Darling, I'm going to go and gather eggs for my breakfast. Won't you please eat some scrambled eggs with me this morning?"

"Scrambled eggs do not tempt me to eat," Falcon Hawk said, chuckling low. "It is not a food that I care to introduce into the diet of the Arapaho."

He swung her playfully away from him, giving her a gentle swat on her behind. "Go," he said. "Gather your eggs. Scramble them and enjoy eating them. I will go and feed my eagle, then go and meet with old grandfather. I will share with him whatever he eats this morning. He gets lonesome for this grandson since the white woman has entered his grandson's life."

"When will I meet him?" Maggie asked, picking up her egg basket.

"When the time is right," Falcon Hawk said, his teasing smile fading. "He has many harsh feelings against the *nih-a-ca*. You are white. I am afraid that will be as far as he will see once you are taken to have council with him."

"Then must I?" Maggie said, fearing rejection by this elderly man who meant so much to Falcon Hawk.

"In time, yes," Falcon Hawk said, gathering her within his arms. He brushed her lips with a soft kiss. "But now, before Sky Eyes awakens, why not go and gather your eggs and have your breakfast?"

"You were so kind to build a chicken house for me so that my rooster can strut midst the chickens and so that the chickens could be comfortable enough to lay eggs for my meals," Maggie said, gazing into his eyes, loving the dark mystery of them. "When Sky Eyes is old enough to eat solid foods, the yolk of an egg will be one of the first nourishing foods I shall introduce her to."

"And when will she drink milk from the cow instead of your breasts?" Falcon Hawk said, slipping his hands up and cupping her breasts through the soft doeskin of her dress.

"She was denied my breasts for too long," Maggie said, her smile waning. "Now that I can hold her to my breasts for her to feed from them, I shall delay as long as possible taking her from them."

"And share them with this man you love," Falcon Hawk said huskily. He yanked her closer and gave her a deep, passionate kiss.

When he released her and stepped away from her, he laughed softly when he saw that she seemed as dizzied by the kiss as he.

"Night comes too slowly for this Arapaho chief," he said, giving her a laughing smile over his shoulder as he walked away from her.

Shaken by the kiss and her suddenly aroused need for him, Maggie's weakened knees would not carry her immediately behind Falcon Hawk as he left the dwelling. She placed a hand over her heart, feeling its fierce pounding. "Who says we have to wait until it becomes night?" she whispered, laughing softly to herself.

Her smile was wiped away by a fierce cry just outside the tepee. She paled and almost dropped the basket at the sound that was so piercing and filled with despair.

"Falcon Hawk!" she cried, fearing that someone had attacked him.

She dropped her basket and ran outside, then stopped quickly when she found Falcon Hawk standing by the eagle's perch. She gasped when she saw that it was empty. The rope that had held the eagle to the perch was dangling, untied, gently swaying back and forth in the breeze.

As many people came running to see what had caused Falcon Hawk's cry of despair, he turned and gazed down at Maggie. "My friend, the eagle, is gone," he said throatily. "I must go after him! I must find him!"

Before Maggie could say anything, Falcon

Hawk was running toward the corral. Wide-eyed, she watched him saddle a horse from the many he had chosen to take the place of Pronto. It was a rust-colored gelding, very muscled and spirited.

Maggie watched Falcon Hawk as he rode away in a slow lope, his eyes ever searching the trees overhead for his beloved pet. She knew that he would not give up the bird easily. Perhaps he might even search the canyons and trees the whole day through, leaving Maggie to fend for herself until his return. Somehow this did not set right with her. She had grown to depend on Falcon Hawk's closeness. She had not yet been totally accepted by his people. This made her uneasy to be there, alone, at their mercy.

She must busy herself to make this day go faster. Maggie turned slowly around, feeling many eyes on her. She smiled weakly at her audience, then rushed back inside Falcon Hawk's tepee.

She stood before the fire, finding it hard to catch her breath, then decided that she must go on with her regular chores of the morning, even if it was with an audience.

Determinedly she picked up the egg basket and marched outside, breathing a sigh of relief when she found everyone gone, except for one woman.

"Soft Voice," she said, stiffening, not yet trusting the woman. Maggie had grown to tolerate Soft Voice's sudden appearances. She always began a conversation with her, although hesitantly. The way Soft Voice looked at her most times sent chills up and down Maggie's spine.

"Good morning," Maggie then said, when Soft Voice offered no conversation this time. She then whirled away from the Arapaho woman and went on to the chicken house that Falcon Hawk had constructed for her only a short distance from his tepee. She knew that she was not alone. She could hear Soft Voice's moccasin-padded footsteps behind her.

Ignoring Soft Voice, Maggie went inside the hen house and began gathering eggs from beneath the hens, some of which flew from their nests, squawking angrily.

Not wanting to leave her child alone for too long, Maggie hastily gathered the rest of the eggs. When she was finished, she turned to return to the tepee, but was made to stop so quickly that several eggs tumbled from the basket when she found Soft Voice blocking her way.

"Please step aside," Maggie said stiffly, giving Soft Voice a haughty stare.

Surprisingly, Soft Voice did as she asked, then fell into step with her as Maggie attempted to walk away from her.

"The chickens are strange-looking birds," Soft Voice finally said. "But they seem profitable enough to have. The eggs that they lay are quite healthy."

"Healthy?" Maggie said, arching an eyebrow as she looked over at Soft Voice. "Yes, I guess they are quite large, aren't they? They make a delicious breakfast food."

"Breakfast?" Soft Voice said.

"The morning meal," Maggie explained. "Breakfast is the morning meal, a custom practiced by white people."

"Ah, I see," Soft Voice said, forcing herself to

be friendly in an effort to succeed later with her plan to see this white woman look foolish in the eyes of Falcon Hawk, so that he would no longer be under her spell.

As usual, Maggie could not help seeing how beautiful Soft Voice was. It amazed her that Falcon Hawk could look past such beauty and choose someone who did not compare with Soft Voice's appearance. Maggie had never thought herself beautiful, but she knew that Falcon Hawk had seen something else in her, perhaps something which Soft Voice could not offer him. Maggie had been around Soft Voice long enough to know that she was a spiteful witch.

Maggie sent her eyes slowly up and down the beautiful maiden. Today she wore the basic dress of the Arapaho—two deerskins sewn together and adorned with pendants of beads, the cap sleeves and yoke covered with quill work. The dress did not reach her ankles. She wore moccasins to which leggings were attached that extended to the knee.

Soft Voice's hair was worn in two braids from behind her ears, parted from her forehead to her nape. The part was painted a brilliant red. Maggie had not yet asked why, but today seemed to be the perfect opportunity, since Soft Voice was still there, even determinedly following her into the tepee.

"Why do you paint the part of your hair?" Maggie asked as she set her basket of eggs on the floor. She started to reach up to touch the part, then dropped her hands back to her sides when Soft Voice took a quick step away from her. "And what is it that is used to give it the pretty color?"

"The paint along the part of the hair is called The Path Of The Sun," Soft Voice said. "Ochre, sometimes vermillion, is used to get the particular color."

Maggie started to ask Soft Voice something else, but to her surprise and puzzlement, Soft Voice suddenly turned and left. Maggie shrugged and went to check on Sky Eyes, finding her sleeping soundly, her lips moving as though sucking on Maggie's nipple.

"Still having dreams of angels?" Maggie said, smoothing the quilt adorned with designs of animals more snugly beneath her daughter's chin.

Maggie ran her hand softly over the quilt, admiring it. She had sewn it together lovingly those long hours beside the fire in her cabin while Melvin had either been working in the garden until dark or had his own pleasure in reading a book by the soft light of the fireplace and a lone kerosene lamp.

The memories of those nights with Melvin were hardly painful any longer. They were good, pleasant memories, the sort that would last forever. His kindness had blessed her. That could never be forgotten.

Only a few days after she had given birth to her daughter, Falcon Hawk had brought Maggie's belongings in from her wagon. She had cherished having with her the small cedar chest that Melvin had made with his own hands, which contained the baby clothes and quilts that she had made for her child.

She had made use of the jams after finding

ways to make bread over the fire in the tepee. She had shown Falcon Hawk how she churned butter.

He had acquired a taste for all of these things now. So in part, he was accepting her customs, as she was his.

At first, the early crowing of her rooster had annoyed him. Then it had become a part of the sounds that he had grown accustomed to since childhood—the sound of the wind, the barking of the dogs, and the neighing of the corraled horses.

"I have brought ochre with me to paint your hair," Soft Voice said suddenly from behind Maggie.

Startled, Maggie turned around, her eyes wide. "You have brought your paints to paint my hair?" she gasped, surprised at Soft Voice's generous, sweet nature today—and not trusting it.

"Come. Sit by the fire," Soft Voice said, gesturing with her free hand; her other hand held a small container of paint. A hairbrush stuck from one of her front pockets, and a tiny hand mirror shone from the other.

Maggie felt the gnawing in her stomach as her hunger mounted, yet she did not want to miss this opportunity to find at least a measure of friendship with this woman who had shown in many ways that she hated her.

"All right," Maggie said, settling down beside the fire.

"What I do pleases you?" Soft Voice asked, as she began drawing the brush through Maggie's long and lustrous hair.

"*Aa*, it pleases me," Maggie said, casting a questioning smile over her shoulder at Soft Voice.

"You will tell Falcon Hawk that you are pleased with what I am doing for you?" Soft Voice said, momentarily pausing from brushing Maggie's hair.

Maggie was beginning to suspect why Soft Voice was doing this now. In a sense, Soft Voice was using Maggie for her own selfish purposes. Yet she had gone this far; she could not stop what had begun.

"*Aa,* I will tell him," Maggie confirmed.

Soft Voice smiled widely and proceeded to brush and then braid Maggie's hair. "Falcon Hawk lost his bird today," she said, a sharp edge in her words. "That is sad, is it not?"

"Very," Maggie murmured. "He idolized that bird. He had raised the bird from a chick. They were friends, as people become friends."

Maggie paused, giving Soft Voice time to reply, but when she didn't, she continued talking as Soft Voice continued working on her hair.

"At first I did not understand why Falcon Hawk would keep an eagle as a pet," Maggie murmured. "But when I saw his devotion to the bird, I saw no harm in having it as a pet. He said that it is quite natural for the Arapaho hunter to bring back animals and birds to rear in captivity."

"Did you have pets in your white community?" Soft Voice asked, now daubing the paint along Maggie's part.

"*Aa,* I had a cat for ten years and I would have had her longer except that she was run over by a horse and carriage," Maggie said sadly. She would never forget Scratch, her black-and-white cat. She could even now vividly recall the scent and feel of her cat's soft fur. She fondly recalled holding Scratch close to hear her purr. Strange, though, that when she had buried her cat in the garden, she had come to know a new awareness of her own breath and being.

"One of my friends had a canary," Maggie also said. "It was quite beautiful. Its song was lovely." She recalled the white-painted, wooden bird cage, with its baroque flourishes, lovely to the eyes and to the touch.

Maggie sighed, then said, "It's unfortunate that Falcon Hawk's eagle's rope became untied," she said. "I wonder if he will find him?"

"No," Soft Voice said, a touch of sarcasm in her words. "Once the eagle's wings are spread in freedom, its wild instincts soon take over. Even if Falcon Hawk found the eagle, the eagle would no longer recognize him as a friend."

"I wonder how the eagle got loose?" Maggie said, giving Soft Voice a sidewise glance over her shoulder. She stiffened when she saw a strange gleam in the woman's eyes and a slow smile on her lips.

Maggie's heart skipped a beat, and she turned her eyes away from Soft Voice and the truth that she did not quite want to know that was hidden behind the devious smile and squinted eyes.

Soft Voice reached her small hand mirror around and thrust it into Maggie's hand. "See?" she said, quickly changing the subject. "Do you not look beautiful?"

Maggie was too uneasy about what she had discovered to truly see anything beautiful. Yet as she peered into the mirror she could not help but see that what Soft Voice had done had improved her looks. With the braids, and wearing the doeskin dress with its fancy beadwork, she did take on the look of an Indian.

She gazed at herself a moment longer, then gave the mirror back to Soft Voice.

Soft Voice's eyes widened. Maggie was an intelligent sort. Had she gathered from Soft Voice's behavior that she was behind the disappearance of Falcon Hawk's eagle?

Soft Voice's insides turned cold at the thought that Maggie might tell Falcon Hawk her suspicions! She had to do something to distract her from doing this!

"I have done something for you today," Soft Voice said quickly. She moved around and knelt down before Maggie and took her hands. "You will now do something for Soft Voice?"

Maggie was expecting Soft Voice to beg for her silence about what she suspected, so she was surprised by Soft Voice's request.

"Can Soft Voice share a breakfast of scrambled eggs with you?" Soft Voice pleaded, giving Maggie her sweetest smile. "You learn my customs. I learn yours?"

Maggie stared questioningly into Soft Voice's dark eyes, not wanting to share anything at all with this devious woman. And even though she suspected that Soft Voice was using this request as a ploy, Maggie felt drawn into doing as she asked. It would be wonderful to have a true friend to share these moments with. If only Soft Voice could be someone sincere, someone to trust. . . .

"*Aa,*" Maggie said, easing her hands from Soft

Voice's. "I will prepare us a breakfast of scrambled eggs."

"*Hahou,*" Soft Voice said, seemingly pleased enough as she went and got the basket of eggs and handed them to Maggie.

Just as Maggie reached for her frying pan, Falcon Hawk entered the tepee in an angry fury. Maggie and Soft Voice exchanged quick, questioning glances.

Chapter Fifteen

Falcon Hawk ignored Soft Voice as though she weren't there. His eyes were centered on Maggie as he stepped up to her and clasped her shoulders with his fingers. "You will go with me to get another eagle," he said. "The one I called my friend, the one with the long, golden feathers, is long gone from me."

Maggie was too stunned at first to respond to him.

She gave Soft Voice a lingering stare and noted how it made her uneasy. Then she shifted her eyes back to Falcon Hawk. Although she truly believed that Soft Voice was responsible for the disappearance of the eagle, it was not Maggie's place to tell Falcon Hawk her suspicions. That could make Soft Voice hate her even more, and perhaps cause the Arapaho people as a whole to dislike her. She could be labeled a troublemaker among their people!

"I'm sorry you didn't find your eagle," Maggie finally said, reaching a gentle hand to Falcon Hawk's cheek. "But this that you are asking of me—I don't know, Falcon Hawk. Do you truly want me to go with you? Won't I just be in the way?"

She shifted a troubled glance at the cradle, then looked Falcon Hawk in the eyes again. "And darling," she murmured, hearing a low gasp of anger behind her. Soft Voice could hardly stand to hear this white woman calling this Arapaho chief "darling."

"Falcon Hawk," Maggie said, correcting herself, so as not to give Soft Voice reason to hate her. "What of Sky Eyes? I don't want to leave her for any amount of time, much less as long as it would take for you to find an eagle's nest."

"We will not be gone much past the sun's setting," Falcon Hawk said, dropping his hands from her shoulders. He went to the cradle and knelt beside it. He peered at the sleeping child, pride swelling within him. Each day brought him closer in feelings toward her. She was from the womb of the woman he loved. That made the child almost as special as her mother.

"But even then, Falcon Hawk," Maggie said, kneeling down beside him, touched to the very core of herself when she saw the look of pride in his eyes as he gazed down at her daughter. "That would be so long. What of Sky Eyes?"

"Many Children Wife would care for her," Falcon Hawk said matter-of-factly.

"I would be glad to care for her in your absence," Soft Voice said, as she came and stood over them. "I would take her to Many Children Wife for her feedings, then bring her back to her cradle. I shall even sing Arapaho songs to her."

Maggie paled at the thought of Soft Voice caring for her baby. She moved swiftly to her feet and placed her hands in tight fists at her sides, waiting for Falcon Hawk to speak. Maggie had learned that when it came to decisions about the Arapaho, it was not Maggie's place to speak up. Not even when it concerned her very own child. She said a soft prayer that Falcon Hawk would make the right decision.

Falcon Hawk pushed himself up to his full height. He gave Soft Voice a quiet, questioning stare, then suddenly took her by an elbow and ushered her toward the entrance way. "Go and tell Many Children Wife that the child will soon be brought to her for the day," he said smoothly.

Maggie scarcely breathed when Soft Voice cast her an angry, spiteful look over her shoulder, then stepped outside with Falcon Hawk.

"Thank the Lord," Maggie then breathed aloud, sighing heavily, as though someone had just lifted a weight off her shoulders. She knew that if Soft Voice could go as far as releasing the lovely eagle from its perch, she could most definitely not be trusted with a child. And this baby was white, the child of a woman Soft Voice despised.

Maggie turned and gazed down at her daughter. "How peacefully you sleep," she whispered, clasping her hands nervously behind her. "You are so trusting now, my sweet. But when you grow as old as I, you will be wary of betrayal."

Hands slipping around and cupping her breasts

through her dress caused Maggie's thoughts to melt into something sweet and wonderful. As Falcon Hawk turned her around into his embrace, she stood on tiptoe and welcomed not only his arms, but a kiss that gave her a thrill that she knew she should not allow. This was not a time for going to the blankets with her beloved. There was much more on his mind, as well as on hers.

His thoughts were centered on finding another bird.

Hers were on the welfare of her child while they were gone.

She did know, though, that as long as Sky Eyes was with Many Children Wife, no harm would come to her.

Yet did Many Children Wife know not to allow Soft Voice near the child?

Was Soft Voice trusted too much among her people?

Falcon Hawk stepped away from Maggie and began gathering the paraphernalia that he was going to be using to capture another eagle. "Wrap Sky Eyes snugly," he said over his shoulder. "Take her to Many Children Wife, then return to me. I have already saddled a horse for you."

He turned to give her a questioning look. "You do ride horses, do you not?" he asked.

"*Aa,*" Maggie said, laughing softly. "I learned long ago, as a child. My father taught me everything. Swimming. Riding. How to shoot guns. Although I was called a tomboy at that time, I realize now why he required this of me. He was preparing me for the uncertain future."

"And he was a wise man," Falcon Hawk said.

"Yes, very," Maggie said, a tinge of sadness in her voice.

Lifting Sky Eyes into her arms, Maggie stood momentarily snuggling her against her bosom, then left the tepee. As she walked toward Many Children Wife's lodge, she could feel eyes on her and she did not have to turn to see whose. She knew.

She stiffened her spine and went onward even though Soft Voice's eyes seemed to be boring through her skin.

The sun made a warm haze on the floor of the valley, yet every feature of the landscape was distinct in shape, color and loveliness. The top of the mountains was lined in blue, only a little darker than the sky.

The horses rode onward at a soft lope, a winding river at their side. Maggie sat stiffly in the saddle, unable to get Soft Voice off her mind.

"Did I fail to tell you how beautiful you look with your hair braided and painted in the Arapaho fashion?" Falcon Hawk said, suddenly breaking the silence.

Maggie turned wavering eyes to Falcon Hawk, knowing to whom must be given the credit for the cause of Falcon Hawk's admiration. If only she could become acquainted with another young Arapaho woman whom she could call a friend. As it was, she was dealing with an enemy, and the relationship became unnerving as each day passed.

"Thank you," she said, offering Falcon Hawk no more explanation about how or why she wore her hair this way today, nor telling him who had done it for her. From this time forth, it would be her own fingers that braided her hair. She would ask Falcon Hawk to get her the paint that was required for the special coloring effect. Never would she allow Soft Voice to get that near her again!

Fortunately, the subject of her hair was quickly forgotten, when suddenly above them were eagles, too many to count, dipping and gliding and soaring. The sight drew Maggie's breath away.

Mesmerized, she watched as the birds took turns swooping down to snatch a tasty morsel from the river.

"Are they not something mystical?" Falcon Hawk said, drawing a tight rein, stopping his horse.

"So very beautiful," Maggie sighed. "But, Falcon Hawk, something puzzles me. They aren't as thickly feathered as your pet eagle was. And they are gray rather than black and white."

"What you are seeing are immature birds," Falcon Hawk explained, as he took her horse's reins while she slipped down from her saddle. "It takes anywhere from two to five years before youngsters reach the glory of their famous white head and tail feathers. Mature birds have a wingspan of six to eight feet."

"Are you going to catch one of those birds?" Maggie asked, amazed that anyone could have the skill to catch such a bird. "They may be immature, but they look as though they might be too large to catch."

"*Nah,* I will not take any of those birds from

the sky," Falcon Hawk said, circling the reins of both horses around one of his hands. He began leading the horses and walking beside Maggie, his eyes never leaving the soaring birds overhead. "It would be a cruel thing to take freedom from those that have already tasted of it. This I know. When the Arapaho were forced on a reservation, their freedom was taken from them."

Falcon Hawk paused. Maggie saw a haunted expression in his eyes as he spoke of reservation life and freedom. Guilt spread through her, understanding why he felt this way, and knowing that it was her own kind that had caused such hurt and despair and humiliation not only to the Arapaho, but to all Indians.

She was glad when Falcon Hawk began talking again, helping her guilt fade away into something like awe as she listened to him speak so knowledgeably and lovingly of the eagles.

"I am taking you where I discovered a nest of many young chicks," he said. "There I will take my next bird friend. I will also be leaving many behind for the parents to teach the meaning of being an eagle—of being wild, free and majestic."

When they brushed past a tree, Maggie spied a long, snug, stout nest resting in the fork of a limb. "Is that an eagle's nest?" she asked, stopping to point at the one she had discovered.

Falcon Hawk laughed softly as he gazed at the nest. "*Nah.* That is not an eagle's nest," he said. "This belongs to a Baltimore oriole. For as long as spring comes to the reservation, the Baltimore orioles make their safe nests for their eggs. The

Wyoming winds gently rock their babies. That is when you know that the Great Unseen Power is still here, watching over *all* of his creatures."

"You are so wise about animals and birds," Maggie said, falling into step beside him as he walked onward.

"Old grandfather taught me everything of birds and animals," Falcon Hawk said, smiling down at Maggie. "The stories he told me made my life more peaceful, just as his love and his compassionate understanding have helped others in time of trouble through all the long years past."

He paused, then continued, "Old grandfather has a gift that makes everyone feel better about themselves. He has a way of putting a person at ease."

Falcon Hawk continued walking, leading Maggie away from the river for a short distance, toward a cluster of trees. "Old grandfather taught me that the most mysterious and most majestic of all winged creatures is the eagle," he said, his gaze on the trees now, the birds behind them, still soaring over the river.

"No other bird so stirs the imagination of the Indian," Falcon Hawk said. "We have watched it soar into the heights of the great blue. We have seen it communing with the clouds. It fears nothing. It even braves the face of the sun with open eyes. The eagle is *wakon*. It is mighty medicine. It is a bird of power, sought by all tribes."

"I witnessed many an eagle's flight myself as a child," Maggie murmured. "Father was a bird-watcher. Many a time I stood beside the mighty Mississippi River looking through my father's binoculars as the eagles soared overhead. I found them so fascinating. Never did I realize their importance to Indians."

"You are learning my ways quickly," Falcon Hawk said, giving her a sidewise glance.

"And why should I not?" Maggie said, returning his glance. "I have a masterful teacher."

Falcon Hawk chuckled. Then his eyes were drawn quickly around and he became tense, his gaze directed upward, discovering an eagle bringing fish to its nestlings only a few yards away. Without saying anything else to Maggie, he quickly tethered the horses to a low tree limb, then took Maggie's hand and led her behind the tree.

"Soon another parent bird will come with food, and when both are gone again we must get into the shelter that I made beneath the nest before I returned to the village to get you," Falcon Hawk said in a guarded whisper.

"Shelter?" Maggie whispered back. Her eyes scanned around her, looking for anything that might resemble this shelter that he was talking about. "Where is it? Why will it be used?"

"Look beneath the nest in the tree," Falcon Hawk said, leaning down closer to her, hoping to keep his voice from traveling to the keen ears of the eagle. "After I discovered the eagle's nest, I waited for the parent eagles to be gone long enough and then dug a deep pit and covered it with boughs. As soon as we are given the opportunity, we will hide in this pit. We will then wait patiently for the time to capture one of the nestlings."

"How can you do that if you are in a hole in

the ground?" Maggie whispered back.

"After the nestlings are fed, they will try to fly," Falcon Hawk said. "They do not learn to fly without mishap. When one falls onto the boughs of our hiding place, I shall grab it. It will then take the place of the one that flew from my tender care."

"What if this eagle escapes?" Maggie asked guardedly.

"It was my misfortune to lose one eagle," Falcon Hawk said stiffly. "It will not be my misfortune again."

Maggie looked away from him and tried to blot out the twisted smile on Soft Voice's face when they had spoken of the missing bird. Maggie could not—would not—put herself in the position of causing everyone to see her as a busybody or a meddler by voicing her suspicions about Soft Voice.

It took everything within her at this moment not to spill out those suspicions to Falcon Hawk!

She focused on the eagle's nest. "It must've taken the eagles weeks to build such a large nest as that," she whispered as she leaned up closer to Falcon Hawk's ear.

"The eagles build a nest each breeding season," he said.

Maggie jumped with alarm when Falcon Hawk suddenly grabbed her hand. "Come," he said tightly. "It is time to enter the hiding place. The parent birds have gone, but they will not leave the nest untended for long."

Maggie followed quickly alongside Falcon Hawk, then waited until he pushed aside the boughs that he had placed over the large hole in the ground. When this was done, she followed him into the deep, dark dungeon-like pit; the earth was damp and cold around her as she huddled next to Falcon Hawk while he quickly covered the pit again with the boughs.

Unable to stop herself, Maggie began to tremble from the chill of the air and the cold dirt on all sides of her. She was glad when Falcon Hawk sensed her discomfort and surrounded her with his warm, muscular arms.

"How long do you think we will have to wait?" Maggie whispered, peering upward through the break in the boughs.

"Until we have a bird," Falcon Hawk said.

Maggie's eyes widened, her thoughts catapulted back to her daughter. She did not want to spend a full night away from Sky Eyes. Earlier Falcon Hawk had said they would be home soon after the sun set. Now his determination to get a bird made her doubt that!

"You must understand the importance of taking another eagle," Falcon Hawk whispered, his cheek warm against Maggie's. "I am of the Eagle clan. We of this clan sing our songs to the eagle. There are eagle dances and eagle ceremonies. The eagle's paintings are used in the heraldry of our clan. If the eagle is dreamed about in an initiation ceremony, many privileges are given the dreamer. Among these are the right to paint the eagle crest upon a medicine shield. It is painted upon my father's shield, which is now mine."

As they waited, Falcon Hawk continued talking in a whisper to Maggie. "Eagle feathers are a symbol of power," he said. "The most prized feathers are the tail plume of the war eagle—the long, finely formed feathers with black tips. One perfect tail is worth one pony."

He paused and held her closer. "But this Arapaho chief does not keep birds to kill for feathers," he said. "Falcon Hawk takes feathers only as they are shed when the bird enters its moulting season."

"I'm so glad," Maggie sighed. "They are too beautiful to kill just to possess feathers."

"They are not only beautiful, but sacred as well," Falcon Hawk said. "Some believe that the great sky eagle is both bird and human and might on occasion lay aside its feathered form and come among men."

Maggie started to respond, but her words were cut short when she caught sight of a quick spread of wings overhead as one of the eagles returned to the nest. She was in awe as she watched the eagle. Riding a wingspan of six feet or more, and with a sublime air, it swept over its youngsters and presented its talons as if grasping for food.

Maggie sucked in a wild breath of air as she got her first look at the nestlings as, one by one, they began climbing onto the edge of the nest. Soon they were perched side by side, visibly wobbly as they tried to balance themselves.

"Falcon Hawk, they are so cute," Maggie whispered.

He drew away from her and turned his eyes upward, a smile fluttering across his lips. "Cute?" he said, his voice soft with admiration. "Maybe now. But soon majestic."

They both watched the pair of eagles sail about the tree nest, showing their young how to fly.

"The two grown eagles seem so devoted, not only to the nestlings but also to each other," Maggie said, her eyes never leaving the soaring birds.

"Eagles mate for life," Falcon Hawk said, momentarily turning his gaze to Maggie. "The same as you and I, my woman. We have mated. It is for life."

Hearing the sincerity in his words, and realizing that at this very moment Falcon Hawk was renewing his commitment to her, made a sweet warmth spread through Maggie. She wanted nothing more at this moment but to be taken into his arms and kissed.

But too soon his thoughts were back on the birds. Maggie hoped that he would be successful today, for she wanted him all to herself tonight!

"Look," Maggie said, pointing to the baby birds as they began testing their wings, hopping between limbs and flying from tree to tree. Many flights ended in a tumble to the ground.

And then it happened. One of the birds fell onto the boughs overhead. Maggie gasped when she saw the speed with which Falcon Hawk thrust his arm through the boughs and grabbed the bird by the tail, then by its legs as he drew it down into the pit with him and Maggie.

Maggie could not tell what was happening then. The evening shadows had already begun to lie long and black on the ground, making the pit even darker.

"What are you doing with the bird?" she asked softly.

"I have brought with me hidden beneath my shirt a doeskin bag," Falcon Hawk said. "I am placing the bird there for safekeeping."

"Won't it suffocate?" Maggie asked anxiously.

"There are holes cut into the fabric," Falcon Hawk said, then everything grew quiet. "We must wait until total darkness shields our movements. Then we will leave and return to my lodge and see what I have caught. A male or female."

"And how will you know?" Maggie asked, anxious to get a good look at the bird.

"I will measure its feet to determine its sex," Falcon Hawk whispered. "Females grow larger than males and are several pounds heavier."

"Then the females are the dominant of the two," Maggie said, laughing softly.

"Birds, yes," Falcon Hawk said, chuckling. "Humans, no." He paused, then added, "Does that bother you?"

Maggie slipped an arm through his. "My love, I wouldn't have it any other way," she said softly.

"Not since I met you, that is," she added quickly. In her mind's eye, she was reliving the way Frank had forced himself on her, hurting her, humiliating her. At that moment, she had discovered the meaning of dominance and how strength could be misused.

With Falcon Hawk and with Melvin she had discovered that a man's domination did not have to mean anything ugly or intolerable!

The world was growing darker outside, and the night sounds were beginning to erupt around them when Falcon Hawk began shoving the boughs aside.

Maggie was glad to finally be able to leave the pit. As the moon's glow poured from the heavens, she rode proudly beside her Arapaho chief, anxious to return to his lodge for many reasons. Not only to be with her daughter, but to be with Falcon Hawk through the long hours of night. She felt as though she belonged. And that feeling was deliciously sweet.

Chapter Sixteen

Maggie was hardly aware that night had dropped its dark cloak from the heavens. She was sitting on a thick bear pelt beside the fire. Life was unhurried in the glow of the warm lodge fire.

Contentedly sucking from the taut nipple, Sky Eyes's fingers kneaded Maggie's breast. Smiling, Maggie watched Falcon Hawk examining the small eagle. It was scruffy now, but would soon have an imposing look. Falcon Hawk had told her that the look of the eagle would change entirely during its first four to six years.

Now all that she could see was its mottled feathers, large, trusting eyes, and a yellow beak and legs.

Maggie's smile faded. She couldn't help thinking about its parents, knowing herself the pain of having to relinquish her child to another.

Yet she consoled herself at the remembrance of seeing many nestlings circled around the huge nest, balancing themselves before taking turns learning to fly. With so many, perhaps this one had not been missed. She would concentrate on the pleasure having the bird gave her beloved Arapaho chief.

"My new friend is a female," Falcon Hawk suddenly said, after measuring the feet of the bird. "Although I will hate to do so, I will have to give her up later. She must be allowed to find a mate and give birth to many more eagles. It would be selfish of me not to allow it."

"When will you do that?" Maggie said, surprised to know that he would set the bird free, especially after having grown to love it.

"I will know by her plumage," Falcon Hawk said, balancing the bird on one of his forefingers. The bird seemed to enjoy its new home—its new master. "The appearance of adult plumage with its snowy white head and tail indicates sexual maturity. That is what aids in attracting a male."

He paused and turned gleaming, warm eyes to Maggie. "It will one day find its soul mate," he said huskily. "As I have found mine."

Maggie's face grew hot with a blush. She felt the first stirring of warmth flooding her insides, in anticipation of what was soon to follow. Realizing that her need for him was so strong, she could not help but feel wanton.

Turning her eyes from this man that she adored, she gazed down at Sky Eyes, finding her in a deep slumber, her lips still on Maggie's breast.

"Dreaming of angels again," Maggie whispered, gathering the blanket snugly around Sky Eyes as she drew her away from her milk-heavy breast.

"Darling daughter, I have dreams, also, but at this moment they are not of angels. They are of a man. A wonderful, gentle man, who is so kind, he has not only claimed me for his wife, but you also, as his daughter. Mary Elizabeth, how could we both be this lucky?"

Moving slowly to her feet, Maggie took Sky Eyes to her crib and laid her on the cushion of blankets on her tummy, making sure that her face was not covered. Maggie touched her daughter's cheek almost meditatively, then bent and kissed her brow while she covered her with the patchwork quilt that Maggie had made solely for the child.

"You linger long over Sky Eyes?" Falcon Hawk said as he came up behind Maggie and snaked his arms around her, cupping her breasts which she had not yet returned to the confines of her dress.

Maggie closed her eyes with ecstasy and leaned back against him. His fingers on her breasts were warm and delicious as he fondled them, her nipples cresting against his thumbs as he circled them.

"She is . . . so beautiful," Maggie said, groaning as Falcon Hawk's hands slipped farther down, taking her dress with them, so that it soon dropped to the floor. She melted against him when his hands cupped her muff of hair where, beneath it, the center of her desire was already throbbing with anticipation.

She sighed and bent her head back, so that she was cheek to cheek with Falcon Hawk when he thrust an eager finger within her and began slowly moving it, as though it were his manhood, giving her pleasure that she would always savor.

Leaning harder against him, Maggie edged her backside into the bulge that was pressing hungrily into her, yet still confined within his buckskin breeches.

Suddenly Falcon Hawk's hands went to Maggie's waist and turned her to face him. She melted into his arms and their lips met in an explosion of kisses, her hands on the waist of his breeches. Her fingers trembled as she hastily shoved this garment over his hips, relieved when it fell away from him, giving her full access to that part of him that sprang free, hard and long and ready.

Maggie's heart raced as she circled his hardness with a hand and began moving her fingers over him in a slow motion. She could hear him groan against her lips and could feel him stiffen when her fingers began moving faster, sometimes in a circle, or sometimes in an up and down pumping motion.

Falcon Hawk could feel the heat rising, splashing through him in volcanic torrents. His eyes were shut tight in exhilaration. It was happening too quickly. He wanted her. He wanted to feel the warmth of her body around his throbbing member, not only her fingers. He recalled her tightness, and a trembling of sexual anticipation flowed through his body.

He gently shoved her hand away, then kneeled before her, again teaching her what true paradise was as he began running his warm-flowing breath over her, and then his tongue.

Her knees growing wobbly with the ecstasy of the caresses, Maggie closed her eyes and held her head back so that her hair hung long and lustrous down her back. She clung to his shoulders and bit her lower lip, not wanting to cry out with the pleasure that she was feeling.

Falcon Hawk, dizzied with his building need, rose to his full height and swept her fully into his arms and carried her to his bed. Gently, as though she were a delicate porcelain doll, he laid her on the bed.

Joining her on the bed, he knelt over her. He brushed kisses on her cheek and neck, and then across her breasts. He stroked her hair, licked her eyes closed, and sent nibbling kisses along the long, slim column of her neck, then kissed her breasts and belly.

Maggie lay in a dreamlike ecstasy when she felt his hardness exploring and searching for entrance where she lay open to him. Slowly, slowly, sliding deep and deeper, he went into her until she sighed and trembled with the rapture of feeling him totally filling her.

She wrapped her legs about him and urged his thrusts to begin. She placed her hands at his cheeks and drew his mouth to hers, kissing him with a passion she had never known existed until he held her within his powerful arms.

She could feel the moist heat that joined their bodies. Both of them paused in exquisite anticipation, their eyes meeting and holding, exchanging silent passion, and then they were kissing again, his lips grinding into hers until she felt as though she were one with him.

His hands on her breasts, her nipples rising up tight and hard against his palms, they reached that rush of delight together.

Their bodies shook and quaked and rocked.

Their tongues danced together.

They groaned out their pleasure against each other's lips.

Their hands sought each other's, clasping.

Soft Voice had seen Maggie and Falcon Hawk's return. She had crept from her tepee and had gone to hide behind another lodge, close to Falcon Hawk's, watching the shadows being cast from within. When she had seen Falcon Hawk's and Maggie's shadows embrace and had even been able to tell that he had lifted her up on his bed, she had crept closer behind his tepee and had listened to the silence, and then the sounds of bodies seeking pleasure from each other.

She had wanted to run away and fling herself over a high butte, to plummet to the ground, dead, for this was the only way to rid herself of her intense feelings for this chief whom she had always dreamed of possessing.

But something had held her there, immobile, as she had listened to the sounds that bodies made when they came together while making love.

She had heard the sound of kissing.

She had heard the final insult, the groaning that meant that the peak of passion had been found inside the chief's lodge.

Turning her back to Falcon Hawk's tepee, stung to the core by what she had heard, Soft Voice lowered her face into her hands. She forced back tears that wanted to come from her eyes. She forced back feelings that made her want to rush inside and plunge knives into the sweat-soaked bodies.

Her head rose in a jerk, her eyes narrow, her lips pursed venomously. Softly she left her place of hiding and wandered past the tepees where she could hear laughter and storytelling, and others where she could hear the same sounds that had just been exchanged in Falcon Hawk's lodge.

Her gaze was locked on one tepee in particular.

Falcon Hawk's grandfather's!

She had to encourage Long Hair to deny his grandson the right to marry this white woman. This was her only remaining chance to win Falcon Hawk's love for herself.

She could be as warm and as attentive within his arms. She could make love as fulfilling as the white woman. She could be everything to Falcon Hawk. Everything!

Yes, Long Hair was her only chance. He thought she was beautiful. If he were a young man, he would take her as his bride and she would show Falcon Hawk a thing or two!

But as it was, Long Hair was an old man with an old body. She wanted a young man with a young body to answer to hers.

Falcon Hawk. He was the only one she wanted. Only Falcon Hawk!

Her steps even more determined, Soft Voice soon reached Long Hair's lodge. From the outside shadows she could see that his fire was still warm and inviting and that he sat beside the fire, perhaps contemplating his death, or perhaps the life that lay behind him. She had noticed, of late, that he was living more in the past than the present. It was a sad thing to witness a person reverting to childhood when once this person was so vital and handsome.

And she could recall, when she was just old enough to notice differences in men, that even when Long Hair had been in his sixtieth winter, he had been someone to enjoy gazing upon.

"Long Hair," Soft Voice said as she brought her lips close to the entrance flap. "Long Hair, it is I, Soft Voice. Would you have my presence for a while beside your fire? Soft Voice is lonesome. Are you as lonesome tonight?"

Long Hair fluttered his fan of feathers against his bare chest as he peered toward the entrance flap. His heart did a quiet leap within his chest at the thought of the beautiful Soft Voice needing his presence to fill the void that she was feeling tonight.

He understood the void. She had not been able to win Falcon Hawk over as her own. There was not much to say, yet just having her there with him might make this old fool feel young again, if only for a moment.

"Enter," Long Hair said, gesturing with a wave of his fan toward the entrance way. "Share the fire with an old man, if you desire."

Her heart pounding, knowing that she must be clever with words while with Long Hair, Soft Voice went inside. When he patted the thick cushion of pelts and blankets at his side, she did not hesitate to sit close to him. If she looked hard enough, she could still see some of the features that had made him a most sought-after brave by the women of the surrounding villages all those many years ago.

Settling down beside him, Soft Voice smiled weakly. "You are very kind to take pity on this lonesome young woman tonight," she said, fluttering her eyes at him. "*Hahou,* old grandfather."

"The nights seem to grow colder and longer for this old man," Long Hair said, tapping his feather nervously on his bare knee, where the blanket that he had draped around his middle had fallen aside. "It is good to have someone who not only looks good, but smells good, sit at his side."

Soft Voice pretended a sudden shyness as she lowered her eyes, then she looked slowly up at him again. "Old grandfather, I too feel the longer and colder nights. Does it seem fair to you that your grandson is keeping a white woman warm tonight instead of a woman of his own people? Would I not warm his blankets as well, old grandfather?"

Long Hair gazed intensely at her for a moment, feeling stirrings that were familiar to him, yet long past, then looked quickly away from her. "If this grandfather could dictate to his grandson, you would be his choice for a wife," he said, staring now into the fire, yet enjoying the embers that were awakened again inside his loins. It made him feel as though he were a virile young man again, at least for this moment. He knew that the feeling would soon be gone and he would feel empty again.

"If you feel this way, old grandfather, then why do you not command your grandson to cast off the white woman?" Soft Voice begged, having tossed aside any thoughts of being clever. "Deny your grandson this thing that is not right for him when he comes to speak to you of marrying the white woman. Encourage your grandson to marry a woman of his own kind—to marry Soft Voice!"

Long Hair turned his eyes quickly to Soft Voice. "Do you forget that my grandson is now chief, and his word is final in everything?" he said, his voice thin.

"You are his elder and he listens to you and would do what you requested over what he wants for himself," Soft Voice said, moving to her knees. She boldly took one of Long Hair's hands, clasping it to her breast. "Please, old grandfather? Please? For Soft Voice will you do this thing that you know is right—not only for Falcon Hawk, but for all our people."

Long Hair slipped his hand from hers and placed his gnarled, bony fingers to her cheek. He ran his fingers over the smoothness of her flesh, recalling so many times in his past when he had done this. His insides ached to remember so much that he had enjoyed with women, particularly with his beloved wife.

Soft Voice leaned into his hand, pretending that she felt something for him by his gesture. "If you were but a young man, I would not have eyes for Falcon Hawk," she said, closing her eyes. "It would be you that I would desire. Only . . . you . . ."

His heart thumped like many drums beating inside his chest, and he realized that he was not as dead inside as he had thought. He drew his hand away as though touching her was the same as touching a live, hot coal.

Soft Voice opened her eyes and gazed at him. She scarcely breathed, for fear that she had overstepped the bounds of what was right with this old man who had been at one time a great chief of his people. She was relieved when he did not show anger at her, or humiliation, but the friendliness that had always been shared between them.

"You have come to speak of my grandson," Long Hair said, laying his fan aside. He drew his blanket up and around his thin, narrow shoulders, suddenly conscious of being withered and old. "But there is nothing this grandfather can say or do. My grandson has his own desires. It is not my place to take them from him."

"Then you will not talk to him?" Soft Voice said, her voice breaking. "You will not encourage him to see that women of his own kind are lovelier than this white woman?"

"This grandfather has already given his grandson a blessing," Long Hair said solemnly.

"You have?" Soft Voice said, her voice a raspy gasp.

"He is yet to come, though, to speak of the ceremony," Long Hair said, giving Soft Voice a smile. "Then I will again voice my thoughts to him."

Soft Voice lowered her eyes and sighed. "I see," she murmured. "I cannot ask for more than that."

Long Hair placed a finger to her chin and slowly lifted it. "You are beautiful," he said, nodding. "Look to other men. Find one that will satisfy you soon. You will then be fulfilled as you never will be should you continue seeking that which can never be yours."

Soft Voice's eyes filled with tears. As they spilled over onto her cheeks, she rose quickly to her feet and rushed from the tepee.

Long Hair shook his head slowly back and forth, then a slow smile curled his narrow lips. He was glad for her visit; she had made him realize that he was not all that old after all!

He lifted a pipe and lit it, then leaned closer to the fire, his eyes filled with dreams and laughter again.

As Maggie watched the small eagle sleeping in a box filled with straw, she dared to run a hand over its soft, downy feathers, then covered the box again with a soft buckskin that had holes cut into it for air.

Maggie rose to her feet and went to peer down at her daughter. Even seeing her did not take her wariness away, for Falcon Hawk had left to talk to his grandfather again about the ceremony to make Maggie his wife. She could still feel the old man's eyes on her whenever she moved about the village among the other people, or as she walked toward the river for a bath or to get water in a jug. The old grandfather would be more pleased if she packed up and left, she was sure.

Settling down beside the fire, Maggie began embroidering a gown that she had sewn by hand for her child. She sank the needle into the cloth and brought it back out again without truly seeing the soft leaf design that she had just formed. She was filled with too much dread to see anything. If only she could be a little mouse tucked into the corner of old grandfather's tepee so that she could hear what was being exchanged between the two men.

Falcon Hawk inhaled smoke from Long Hair's pipe for a few solemn moments. Then Long Hair laid the pipe aside. Tonight was a night for callers. Long Hair felt suddenly important.

"What has brought you to your grandfather's lodge this night?" he asked, seeing the uneasiness with which Falcon Hawk sat, seemingly unable to find the right place to rest his hands, finally settling on clasping them to his knees.

"You have already given your blessing to my union with Panther Eyes," Falcon Hawk said, his voice drawn. "I have come tonight to get a second blessing and to talk of plans for a celebration. At this celebration my woman will be accepted into the tribe, and she will become my *nata-cea*."

Long Hair allowed his blanket to fall away from his shoulders so that it rested around his narrow hips. He crossed his arms over his chest and smiled over at Falcon Hawk. "It is a good grandson who asks for this old grandfather's blessing twice," he said, obviously pleased.

"You have waited patiently for this time in your life, the practice of marriage coming late to the Arapaho," Long Hair said, nodding. "You who are thirty winters of age speak of marriage now when you have much honor and property. That is good."

Falcon Hawk's eyes brightened, thinking that

his grandfather would accept his bride. Then his eyes wavered as his grandfather continued speaking.

"You should not need to be told this, but grandson, it seems necessary for me to say it, since you show such determination to marry the white woman," Long Hair said, his voice solemn and somewhat cold. "But never would this grandfather want his grandson's wife to be non-Indian—to be white."

"But old grandfather, have you not seen that she is a true-blood Indian in her heart, where it counts?" Falcon Hawk said in Maggie's defense.

"Nothing can change the color of her skin, hair, and eyes," Long Hair mumbled. He lifted his eagle wing fan and began nervously tapping it on one of his bare knees.

"Has she not accepted the changes brought into her life since she has been a part of our lives?" Falcon Hawk said more determinedly.

Long Hair ignored this. Instead, he said, "Do you wish to have white sons and daughters?"

"Have you not seen that I have already accepted the child that came from the womb of my white woman as though she were my own daughter?" Falcon Hawk said, feeling it was wrong to continue in this argument with a man that he had idolized since he was a child. But for Maggie, he must cast everything aside except claiming her as his wife.

"And you see that as wise?" Long Hair said, quirking an eyebrow.

"It is something acceptable in my eyes, *haa,*"

Falcon Hawk said. "And as for children born of my union with the white woman, do you doubt the virility of your grandson? Surely my son will resemble me."

"And if you are wrong and your son should be white?" Long Hair said testily.

"Should that be so, my son will be a son in all ways that matter, no matter the color of his skin," Falcon Hawk said firmly.

"My grandson, it is our sacred trust to keep the bloodline pure to preserve our people," Long Hair said in his last argument to Falcon Hawk.

"*Naba-ciba,* do you not remember the changes in our lives already?" Falcon Hawk said, resting a hand on his grandfather's shoulder. "You must accept this one more change. My heart has already been given to Panther Eyes. She is my breath, my every heartbeat. Not to have her would mean I would feel half a man."

Long Hair's eyes faltered. He laid his fan aside and reached out for Falcon Hawk, drawing him into his tight embrace. "Then go to her," he said softly. "No more will be said against this that you want to do, ever. Again, my grandson, our people's chief, you have this old grandfather's blessing. But do one last thing for your grandfather. Go and fast and think this through carefully and pray for guidance."

"*Haa,* this I will do," Falcon Hawk said, embracing his grandfather at length.

Then he rushed from Long Hair's tepee and went to Maggie. She looked up from the fire, silently questioning him.

Falcon Hawk fell to his knees beside her and

whisked her into his arms. "It is done," he whispered. "There is much to celebrate, my beautiful Panther Eyes."

Their lips met in a crushing kiss. Maggie clung to him, her heart filled with joy.

But when he drew away from her, his eyes pleading into hers, she knew that he had not yet told her everything.

"What is it?" she said, her voice drawn. "Why do you look at me in such a way?"

Falcon Hawk took her hands in his. "There is something I must do, not only for my grandfather but for myself," he said solemnly, his eyes searching hers for acceptance of what he was saying. "I must leave you for four days."

"Four days?" Maggie gasped, paling. "But why?"

"I will be fasting and praying for guidance in all things," Falcon Hawk said, drawing her into his arms. "The days will go quickly for you. You have your daughter. You also have the eagle. Before I leave for my fast, I will stay one more day and teach you how to begin the eagle's training. It will be something of enjoyment for you. You will see."

"Four days?" Maggie said, a shudder swimming through her at the thought of being at the mercy of Soft Voice for so long.

Frank Harper was deeply into Indian territory, riding bold and unafraid as he watched for his first sighting of a village. He would take his time observing it from afar to see if there were any signs of a white woman there. Then he would move on to the next village if he came to the conclusion that Margaret June wasn't there.

He rested his hand on his holstered pistol, no less determined to find her now than yesterday and all the yesterdays since he had discovered the empty safe.

"She's going to pay," he whispered to himself as the cold breeze of night stung his cheeks. "In the worst way, she's going to pay."

He chuckled and sank his spurs into the flanks of the horse, sending it into a harder gallop across the moon-drenched land.

Chapter Seventeen

The day was warm and breezy. Maggie carried Sky Eyes out into the sunshine of the meadow, where Falcon Hawk was training and exercising his new eagle friend. A blanket had been spread on the soft grass for her. Not taking her eyes off the eagle as it was being urged to take flight from Falcon Hawk's arm, a string attached to one of the bird's claws, Maggie eased down onto the blanket.

She could see that it would take great skill and patience to train the eagle. But she could tell that this challenge was to Falcon Hawk's liking. His patience showed each time the bird was coaxed into the air and it fluttered clumsily to the ground; Falcon Hawk picked it up and started the process all over again.

Feeling that it was warm enough for her daughter to soak up some of the sun that felt so good to Maggie, she nudged the blanket aside. She watched her daughter's eyelashes flutter against the brightness of the day. Soon the baby relaxed enough to begin taking in her surroundings.

"I offer a beautiful day to a beautiful daughter," Maggie said, allowing one of Sky Eyes's fingers to clasp one of her own.

Falcon Hawk's deep, contented laughter drew Maggie's eyes back to him.

"Did you see?" Falcon Hawk shouted. "She took flight, if only for a moment."

The bird was back on Falcon Hawk's wrist, eating a healthy portion of meat that was being offered to her.

"Urge her to do it again for me," Maggie said, smiling at Falcon Hawk. She shadowed her eyes from the sun with her free hand and watched as once again Falcon Hawk dropped his arm, making the small eagle flutter away from it, then back again as Falcon Hawk lifted his arm and gave a slight jerk on the string that was attached to the eagle.

Again Falcon Hawk rewarded the bird with a morsel of meat.

"The idea is to teach the bird to rise from my arm at command, and return," Falcon Hawk said. "When the bird does as commanded, it is fed warm flesh of other freshly killed fowl. If the flesh is warm from the killing, so much the better. But otherwise it must be heated over a fire, if not by the sun."

"Am I expected to exercise the bird and train her in such a way all the while you are gone?" Maggie asked, rocking Sky Eyes as the child began softly whimpering. "I'm afraid I'm not as practiced as you, Falcon Hawk. The bird might get away from me."

"If you choose not to do this, then just take time with it in the lodge," Falcon Hawk said, reeling the eagle in after another successful short flight. "It might be the last chance to allow it to be free without securing it by its leg outside on the perch. She is not all that anxious to fly, as you can see. She will enjoy just walking around inside the lodge. But watch out for the fire. She would not enjoy having her wings singed."

"I will make sure nothing happens to her while you are gone," Maggie said, firming her jaw as her thoughts drifted back to Soft Voice. "She will be waiting for your return, as will I."

The sun began to slant in the sky, and shadows fell in straggling patterns beneath the trees in the distance. Maggie wrapped Sky Eyes in the blanket and rose to her feet, the child fussing now.

"I will retire to your lodge and feed Sky Eyes," Maggie said as she began walking away. "You will be coming soon, darling?"

"*Haa,* soon," Falcon Hawk said, petting the soft, downy feathers of the eagle. "Just a little more exercise for my friend here and then you and I will warm the blankets, will we not?"

"I may not let you leave once we are there," Maggie tossed over her shoulder, laughing softly, yet deep inside wishing that she could make what she said possible. She dreaded his departure for four long days.

Yet she knew that she had no choice but to accept and make the best of the time while he was gone by learning more about the Arapaho

way of life, to surprise him when he returned.

Again as she entered the village, she felt Soft Voice watching her, making her grow stiff and cold inside. Surely Soft Voice now knew of their impending marriage ceremony and also that Falcon Hawk was going to be leaving for several days.

Maggie knew to expect Soft Voice to take advantage of Falcon Hawk's absence in some way. She feared whatever tactic Soft Voice might use to rid the village of the white woman and her child.

Glad to finally be in the safe confines of Falcon Hawk's lodge, Maggie sat down beside the glowing embers of the fire and offered her breast to her child. She rocked Sky Eyes slowly back and forth as the baby took her fill from the proffered breast. Maggie closed her eyes, blocking everything from her mind except for Falcon Hawk and how he would soon transport her to paradise again with his skills in lovemaking. He did things to her she had never imagined.

She grew warm in the pit of her stomach even now, remembering the wonders of his lips, tongue, and hands. She sucked in a wild breath as she recalled the very touch of his manhood and how it so magnificently filled her and sent rapture through her, taking her to the moon.

"And is she filled yet with your sweet, warm milk?" Falcon Hawk said as he came like a sunburst into the tepee, the eagle trustingly clutching his arm with its claws.

Her thoughts having only moments ago strayed to that most sensuous of moments between them, so that she had scarcely heard what he was saying, Maggie blushed as she glanced up at Falcon Hawk. "What did you say?"

Falcon Hawk looked at her knowingly, understanding her blushes well, and what usually prompted them. He laughed softly as he knelt and placed the small eagle into its protective box lined with straw, then went to Maggie and looked down at the child.

"Did you not know that she was asleep?" he said, bending low to take the child from Maggie's breast. "Your mind was not on the nursing child. It was on your man."

"Yes, on my man," Maggie said, pushing herself up from the cushion of furs. She slipped her dress over her shoulders and past her hips, then allowed it to fall to her ankles, where she gently kicked it away.

She followed Falcon Hawk to the cradle and stood behind him as he placed Sky Eyes on her blankets. When she knew that Sky Eyes was safely asleep in the cradle, Maggie crept her arms around him and drew his backside against her. She pressed her breasts into his back teasingly, while one of her hands slipped down past the waist of his breeches and cuddled his manhood within her eager fingers.

She heard his groan of pleasure and could feel his manhood growing within her fingers, pulsing as though it had a life of its own against the palm of her hand.

When it reached its full thickness and length, she began to move her fingers over him. Falcon Hawk closed his eyes and stiffened, her fingers feeding pleasure into his system as a child takes nourishment from its mother's breast. He took all that he could, then reached for her hand and loosened its grip around his stiffened rod.

Freeing her hand from his breeches, he took her by a wrist and turned to face her, pulling her against him. He kissed her hard as his other hand went to her buttocks. He circled one round, soft globe, his fingers sinking into the tender flesh to draw her even more tightly against him. Once she was so close that not even a breath of air could squeeze between them, he began grinding his hips into her so that she could feel his hardness.

Maggie's insides heated up as the friction he was causing against her flesh made her wild with need of him. She lifted a leg and wrapped it around him, drawing his hardness against the core of her femininity, where it throbbed hungrily with the need to be touched, to be fondled, to be licked. . . .

Brazenly she rubbed herself against the bulge in his breeches. Yet that wasn't enough. She wanted to feel the heated flesh of his manhood. She wanted to open her legs to it so that once again he would thrust himself into her. She was weak with desire, the passion floating through her like waves warming sand on a beach.

Stepping away from Falcon Hawk, Maggie smiled seductively up at him and reached her hands to the waist of his breeches. In a flash he was standing nude before her, his copper skin gleaming beneath the soft glow of the embers in the fire pit.

Her gaze raked over him, admiring anew the muscles, his skin's sleekness, the midnight dark mystery of his eyes, and his lips that seemed made for kissing.

Her pulse racing, Maggie went to the bed and stretched across it, beckoning him with outstretched arms and hands.

He went to her, and without any more preliminaries, entered her quickly and deeply, his thrusts demanding and hard.

Maggie locked her ankles around him and rode him, his hands cupping her breasts, the nipples hardening against his palms.

His mouth came to hers with a kiss that matched no other kiss shared between them. They kissed long and hungrily, their tongues flicking, their breaths hot and sweetly mingling.

Then to Maggie's surprise, Falcon Hawk rose away from her. He turned her over and placed his hands to her waist, urging her to her knees. The blood pulsing through his veins, almost dizzying him, Falcon Hawk moved behind her and gripped her buttocks with trembling fingers as he sought entrance within her in this way, from behind.

Maggie's surprise was soon lost in the ecstasy that rose anew within her. She thrust her behind higher in the air to make herself more accessible to him.

As he thrust more deeply and more quickly, she closed her eyes and felt herself lethargically floating away. He filled her soft, warm place for a while longer in this way, then turned her onto her back again.

Maggie began to squirm and sigh as he kissed

and licked her body hungrily, starting at her breasts, then moving lower, past her stomach. When he found her throbbing center of desire he paid homage to it until he feared her groans of pleasure meant that she was too ready not to mount her again.

He moved over her and thrust himself deeply within her and began his rhythmic strokes, kissing her, his arms engulfing her. Together they found the wonders of pleasure again. They shook and trembled, then lay quietly side by side, breathing hard.

"I truly must be on my way," Falcon Hawk said, breaking the silence.

Maggie's body was still awake to passion. She closed her eyes, not wanting to hear that he must go.

"Did you hear me, my woman?" Falcon Hawk said, turning to her and framing her face between his hands. He brushed a kiss across her lips, then her breasts. "I truly must leave you now."

"So soon?" Maggie finally said, sighing heavily. She closed her eyes and trembled when his lips nibbled at her breasts once again. "You will leave me like this, when I still hunger for you?"

"You will hunger even more for this man who loves you after you have been forced to be away from him for four days and nights," Falcon Hawk said, chuckling low.

When he rose from the bed, Maggie's eyes opened wide. She turned on her side and looked poutingly up at him. "Make love just one more time before you leave?" she said in a begging fashion. "Please? Just one more time?"

Falcon Hawk had his breeches only halfway up his legs, then jerked them off again.

Laughing he jumped back on the bed with Maggie. "One more time, then perhaps two?" he said, giving her navel a teasing kiss.

"Would it be horrible if I asked for a third time today with you?" Maggie asked, stroking his thick hair with her hands. She then twined her fingers through his hair and drew his mouth to hers. "I love you so. I could make love with you without stopping forever, my darling."

"Do not say what I might test you on later," Falcon Hawk said, chuckling. He knelt over her and began probing his thickened shaft into her love cocoon. "Just one more time and then you must accept that you must say good-bye for a while."

Maggie coiled her arms around his neck. "Love me then, my darling," she whispered. "Whatever on earth are you waiting for?"

He made a final thrust and was inside her. She clung to him. She rocked with him. She closed her eyes to everything but now and the wondrous mysteries of their entwined bodies.

Chapter Eighteen

Four Days Later

Sky Eyes was propped up on a cradle board beside Maggie in front of a cozy fire, where elk stew simmered in a pot over the flames. Maggie's fingers ached as she tried to learn the art of the needlework of the Arapaho, wanting to surprise Falcon Hawk upon his return.

Maggie glanced at Soft Voice. She had not wanted to accept her offer to teach her how to perform this beautiful needlework, but Soft Voice had insisted in front of other Arapaho outside Falcon Hawk's dwelling, giving Maggie no choice but to agree.

Maggie looked at the pot hanging over the fire pit, from which delicious, tantalizing aromas wafted. This was the fourth day of Falcon Hawk's fast. She had made sure that she had food waiting for him to fill the emptiness in his stomach which surely by now was intensely painful.

Glancing upward at the smoke hole at the apex of the tepee, she noticed that the sky was still quite blue. There were many hours left in the day. Hopefully, by the time the sun set behind the mountains he would be with her again and would have won the battle over all that troubled him. Her main dread was that while communing with his Great Unseen Power, he might change his mind about taking her as his wife.

"You are working hard," Soft Voice said, forcing herself to sound friendly, while deep within her lay a resentment that was simmering into something she could hardly tolerate.

She smiled mischievously at Maggie, whose fingers were clumsily working with the awl of bone and thread of dried sinew. She laughed to herself, purposely leading Maggie astray in her teachings. This white woman would be humiliated when she gave her completed blanket to Falcon Hawk. He would see that this white woman was stupid and useless. He would no longer want her for his wife!

Maggie cocked an eyebrow, pausing to gaze at what she had done. The points of the quills were sticking out and the embroidery was coming loose from the blanket.

"I feel that I have lots to learn and much practicing to do before I can make anything that comes anywhere close to the beauty of your blanket," Maggie said, hating to have to tell Soft Voice that anything she did was acceptable.

Maggie was beginning to resent everything about Soft Voice, and she trusted her even less than before. Something was amiss even today about Soft Voice being there, yet Maggie knew that she had no choice but to wait and see just what.

"Soft Voice has made many blankets," Soft Voice bragged. "White woman has made only one."

Maggie quickly corrected Soft Voice. "I have made more than one blanket in my lifetime," she said, gazing at the beautiful patchwork quilt wrapped loosely around her daughter. "But what I had to work with while making it was different from that which I am being taught to use to make an Arapaho blanket."

Soft Voice followed the line of Maggie's eyes and looked at the baby's quilt, truly admiring its handiwork.

But she would not comment favorably. She wanted to tear this woman's pride and self-esteem down inch by inch, not build it up.

Soft Voice reached over and stretched one end of Maggie's Arapaho blanket out. She shook her head back and forth. "The work you do today is not pretty at all," she said, forcing a heavy sigh. "Perhaps you would do better with paints than with porcupine quills. Or perhaps you would do better with small glass beads of many different colors."

Feeling her cheeks heating up with a blush, Maggie yanked the blanket away from Soft Voice. "Give me time," she said with determination. "I will learn."

"Today is the fourth day of Falcon Hawk's fast," Soft Voice said, resuming her needlework as she sewed the colored and flattened porcupine quills firmly on the surface of the blanket that she was decorating. Before using the quills, Soft Voice had softened them in her mouth and flattened them with a bone.

"*Aa,* it is his fourth day," Maggie said, once again clumsily working with her blanket. She paused and gave Soft Voice a wary stare. "And it should not matter to you at all when he is to arrive. Today. Tonight. Or perhaps even tomorrow."

Soft Voice's fingers stopped and her eyes looked sharply into Maggie's. "You use the Arapaho word 'yes' so naturally," she said icily. Then she smiled slowly. "But that is the only word I have heard you say. You are slow at learning. You will make a lazy wife."

Maggie gasped and her cheeks flamed with anger. She started to order Soft Voice from the lodge, but again realized that any action she took against Soft Voice might in turn be used against herself.

Soft Voice was Arapaho.

Maggie was white.

"And you would make a better wife?" Maggie said, her eyes flashing.

"*Aa,* that is so," Soft Voice said, surprised that Maggie was not ordering her from the lodge.

Maggie ceased sewing, placing her needlework aside on the floor. She leaned closer to Soft Voice. "Then why aren't you married?" she asked, smiling slowly. "You had one husband, why not another?"

"There have been those who have wanted Soft Voice," Soft Voice said impudently.

"Then why aren't you married?" Maggie insisted. "In truth, you lie when you say there have been men who wanted you. Do not all braves see beneath that soft smile and know that you are not as you seem? I see right through you, Soft Voice—and you call me stupid."

Soft Voice tossed her needlework aside and rose quickly to her feet. She doubled her hands into tight fists at her sides and glared down at Maggie. "You do not speak to an Arapaho woman in such a way," she hissed. "When Falcon Hawk hears what I tell him about your spiteful ways, he will banish you from his lodge and his village."

"As he will you when I tell him the suffering you have caused," Maggie said, slowly rising to her feet. She took a step closer to Soft Voice and spoke directly into her face. "Shall I tell him about the eagle? About who set it free?"

Soft Voice's lips parted in a soft gasp, and her eyes wavered. "What do you truly know about it?" she said, her teeth clenched. "What do you know about *anything?*"

"You can call me stupid as many times as you wish, or try to make me believe that I am ignorant, but it won't work, Soft Voice," Maggie said, placing her hands on her hips. "Now get out of here and don't come back. But hear my threat well. If you cause me any more trouble, I'll tell Falcon Hawk about the eagle."

Maggie paused and placed a finger to her chin, as though contemplating something, then said slyly, "Perhaps I will tell him anyway. Then we shall see who gets banished from where."

Soft Voice raised a hand and was ready to slap Maggie when the entrance flap was lifted and an elderly woman whom Maggie had not yet met came into the tepee.

The woman's sudden arrival stopped the altercation between Maggie and Soft Voice. Soft Voice dropped her hand immediately to her side and stepped back so that the elderly woman could come farther into the lodge.

Maggie took a step back and swallowed hard, hoping that her face was not flushed too much. She didn't want anyone of this village to know that she had gotten so angry with someone of their own kind. She gazed in wonder at this woman. She was short, plump, and short-winded. Her gray hair hung in long, waist-length braids. Her eyes were narrow, and she was dressed in a loose, flowing deerskin dress that was resplendent with beads in patterns of flowers. She wore a spot of red paint on each cheekbone and on her forehead. She knew that the color red symbolized old age, but Maggie had also been told by Falcon Hawk that paint on the face in general signified happiness or a wish for happiness.

"Thread Woman, it is nice to see you," Soft Voice said, taking the elderly woman by an elbow and easing her down on the soft pelts before the fire. Soft Voice glanced uneasily at the blanket that she had shown Maggie how to sew, hoping that Thread Woman would not see the mistakes. She would soon realize that no one could make such mistakes unless led into them purposely.

Thread Woman nodded, then looked at Maggie as Maggie settled down opposite the fire from her, beside her child. "I have come to make acquaintance with white woman," Thread Woman said in a gravelly voice. "This old woman would have come sooner, but ailments kept me between my blankets by the fire."

Maggie rose to her feet and went around the fire, extending a hand toward the elderly woman, hoping that she would find her friendly, instead of hostile. It was hard to tell by her expression how she felt. Her eyes and expression were lost somewhere in the craters of her wrinkles.

"It is good to make your acquaintance," Maggie murmured, glad when Thread Woman took her hand. "*Hahou,* for coming. I am very pleased to meet you."

Thread Woman nodded, held Maggie's hand for a moment longer, then released it. "Falcon Hawk still fasts?" she said, glancing around the tepee.

"*Aa,* he still fasts," Maggie said, returning to her cushion of blankets and furs beside Sky Eyes.

"And what is your purpose for being here, Soft Voice?" Thread Woman asked, looking up at Soft Voice, who had yet to sit down or leave.

A visible uneasiness crept over Soft Voice. She gave Maggie's blanket another glance, then smiled crookedly down at Thread Woman. "Soft Voice is here to fill the void left by Falcon Hawk," she said softly. "White woman needs a friend. Soft Voice offers such friendship."

Wise in years, Thread Woman stared up at Soft Voice for a moment longer, then turned a questioning gaze to Maggie, and to the blanket spread out awkwardly at her side. "And so Soft Voice is teaching you needlework to help pass the days?" she said, arching a thick gray eyebrow. "Show it to me, Panther Eyes. Let me see the skills she has taught you."

Soft Voice moved as quickly as a panther leaps to grab the blanket. She placed it behind her and began inching away from Thread Woman. "You do not wish to see it just yet," she said, her voice drawn.

Maggie saw how Soft Voice was behaving, and suddenly understood that Soft Voice was not keeping the elderly woman from seeing the blanket for Maggie's sake.

It was her own hide she was trying to protect!

It was *she* who had shown Maggie how to make these stitches with the crude instruments and strange quills.

It was obvious now to Maggie that Soft Voice had purposely taught her wrong, to make her look stupid in the eyes of the Arapaho, especially Falcon Hawk.

She moved to her feet and went determinedly to Soft Voice. She took the blanket from her. "Soft Voice, you need not hide my imperfections," she said tauntingly. "Thread Woman's name must have been given to her because of her skills in sewing. Let her see your skills in *teaching*."

Soft Voice inhaled a gasping breath, and her eyes widened as Maggie spread the flawed blanket out on the floor for Thread Woman to see. It took only a moment for Thread Woman to see what had happened, and why. She cast Soft Voice an angry look.

"You have showed her how to do everything wrong," Thread Woman said, her voice cold. "Leave. Be shamed for what you have done.

This woman belongs to our chief. Never forget that again, Soft Voice!"

Distraught, Soft Voice stared in disbelief down at Thread Woman, then fled the lodge in a rush.

There was a moment of strained silence between Maggie and Thread Woman as the two women gazed at each other.

"Come. Sit beside me. Bring your needlework," Thread Woman then said, patting the cushions at her side. "I am everyone's friend. I will be yours. Let me help you correct your mistakes before Falcon Hawk returns."

Stunned that the elderly Arapaho woman would chastise Soft Voice in such a way, and then take Maggie into such a sudden friendship, Maggie was at a loss for words. She wanted to say thank you over and over again. But there was something about Thread Woman's demeanor that made her think that thank-yous were not necessary. Thread Woman had seen the wrong in Soft Voice's actions. She could see that Soft Voice had planned to make a fool of this woman who would soon marry their chief!

Gathering all of her needlework equipment and the blanket into her arms, Maggie went smilingly to Thread Woman and sat down beside her.

"The child sleeps well," Thread Woman said, gesturing with her bony hand toward Sky Eyes, who was in a deep, peaceful slumber. She laughed softly as she gazed at the child's fat cheeks. "She also eats well."

"*Aa,* she does both well," Maggie said, her eyes dancing, feeling as though she had finally found a friend. She would have preferred having a friend of her same age, but right now, when friendships were few, it was enough for her to have Thread Woman there.

"I have come to you today not only to make your acquaintance, but to also tell you that Falcon Hawk's grandfather is ailing somewhat," Thread Woman said. She eyed the kettle of stew simmering over the fire. "Perhaps later we could go together to offer him warm food?"

Maggie's smile faded and her heart skipped a nervous beat. She dreaded having to go to Falcon Hawk's grandfather's lodge. He had not yet approached her in any way to speak to her. And always when he looked at her, he seemed to look through her, as though she wasn't there or as though he despised her.

She was hurt by this, knowing that he must hate her to treat her so coldly. Yet she had no choice but to show kindness toward him. Today it would be without Falcon Hawk at her side.

She gazed at Thread Woman, thinking that perhaps this elderly woman might make things less difficult for her when she went to offer Long Hair a bowl of her steaming elk stew.

"*Aa,* I will go with you with food to Long Hair's lodge," Maggie murmured. "I am sorry to hear that he is ailing."

"His health changes from day to day," Thread Woman said, taking Maggie's blanket from her arms. "One day he seems well, the next it seems he will die before sunset." She paused and gazed into the fire. "Strange how four sleeps ago he seemed to come to life, as a man would of fewer years. In his eyes there was something akin to being in love."

Thread Woman shrugged and gazed back down at the poorly worked blanket. "Although I had often wished in the past to be chosen as Long Hair's special woman, this old woman knows she is too old to think of romance," she said, cackling. "So is Long Hair too old for such thoughts and desires. I am certain that what I saw was an old man reverting to his past for pleasant thoughts."

Thread Woman paused, then began rattling on about sewing, making Maggie feel much more at ease. She did not feel at all comfortable listening to talk of Falcon Hawk's grandfather's behavior.

"We must tear out all that you have done and start again," Thread Woman said, her gnarled yet deft fingers already removing the needlework from Maggie's blanket. "You will not have the blanket finished before Falcon Hawk arrives home, but you will show him a good start. He will be pleased. Shame, shame on Soft Voice. Falcon Hawk must be told, and this old woman will be the one to do it. What else might the child do because she wants Falcon Hawk for herself? She must be stopped now before she goes so far that Falcon Hawk will send her from the village."

"Do you mean forever?" Maggie dared to ask.

"Once banished, always banished," Thread Woman said. "Now let us begin." She pulled her quill-flattening bone from a pocket, revealing thirty notches cut into it. "This old woman has made thirty robes in her lifetime. And that is not the last. There will be many more before this old woman takes her last breath."

Maggie became attentive while she listened and watched Thread Woman, admiring her skill both with needlework and in telling stories.

"Whenever this old woman makes and gives away a robe, she receives a horse for it," Thread Woman said, cackling. "Horses then are traded for valuable threads, cloths, and beads. It is quite a bargain this old woman makes."

Maggie listened and nodded when she felt the need, learning that a robe with white quill work symbolized old age and that fifty small dew-claws of buffalo were hung as pendants, or rattles, along the lower edge of what was called a twenty-lined robe.

She would remember well that a buffalo robe usually had twenty lines of quill-embroidery across it and was called *Niisa-uxti*. There were seventeen lines and then three more close together, along the bottom of the robe. These lines were ordinarily yellow.

Maggie and Thread Woman worked until the blanket was at least one fourth done and then Thread Woman pushed herself up suddenly from the floor. "It is time to take food to Long Hair," she said, already dipping some elk stew into a wooden bowl. She glanced over at the child, then at Maggie. "Let us go quickly so that your child will not be alone for more than a few moments."

Maggie laid her needlework aside and followed Thread Woman from the lodge. Just as they stepped up to Long Hair's tepee, Thread Woman thrust the bowl of stew into Maggie's hand.

"You take. You give the offering of food," Thread Woman softly encouraged her. "It is important that Long Hair sees the kind side of you. He has never been fond of whites."

Maggie swallowed hard, smiling a silent thank-you at Thread Woman for her thoughtfulness.

Then, as Thread Woman lifted the entrance flap aside, Maggie went inside. Her footsteps faltered when she found Long Hair sitting beside his fire, looking no less weak now than at any other time. She wondered if he played with people's feelings sometimes to draw sympathy from them.

"Long Hair, I have brought you some nourishment," Maggie said, holding the bowl toward the old man. "Elk stew. I hope you will find it to your taste."

Long Hair fluttered his fan of feathers against his bare chest, his eyes squinting up at Maggie.

She grew cold inside as she waited for some response from him, then wondered if he could ever find it in his heart to like her!

Again she moved the bowl toward him. "Please take it," she murmured.

Long Hair's gaze shifted to the bowl of stew, then to Thread Woman, and then back to Maggie. He nodded and held a hand out for the bowl.

Smiling with relief, Maggie gave it to him. But her smile waned when he still did not say anything to her, only giving her that look that made her want to die! He had yet to say one word to her! She was hurt deeply by this, knowing that he must hate her to treat her so coldly.

Maggie turned and fled from the lodge alone, leaving Thread Woman behind with Long Hair. Sobbing, Maggie ran back to Falcon Hawk's lodge and threw herself down on his bed. She was hurt to the core by Long Hair's rejection of her, fearing that he could cause her to lose Falcon Hawk's love. Long Hair was known as a man of influence, having himself at one time been the chief of this band of Arapaho. Surely he could find ways to stop his grandson from marrying a white woman.

"Blessing, indeed," Maggie cried. "He did not mean it when he gave Falcon Hawk his blessing!"

Soft Voice stood behind Falcon Hawk's lodge. She had stood there all the while Maggie and Thread Woman were sewing. She had stayed there until Maggie's return from Long Hair's lodge. Knowing Thread Woman's plan to reveal Soft Voice's deceit to Falcon Hawk, Soft Voice had dreaded Falcon Hawk's return.

When she heard how distraught the white woman was over not being accepted by Long Hair, Soft Voice felt that she did have an ally in him after all! She would have to find a way to reward him!

She crept around Falcon Hawk's lodge and watched Long Hair's tepee, waiting for Thread Woman to leave. When she did, Soft Voice went there herself. When she stepped inside, she stood silently just inside the doorway and watched Long Hair eagerly eat the stew. Something came over her that she found hard to understand. She had come with the intention of playing a game with the old man, but as she watched him her heart softened. He was loved by all. He had all of Falcon Hawk's better qualities.

She was not sure why, or what might be possessing her, but today she was even able to look past Long Hair's wrinkles and see him as the handsome man he once had been.

Her pulse racing, she stepped out of the shadows.

When he tilted his old eyes up at her, she smiled a genuine smile, then went and sat down beside him.

"Why have you come to this old man's lodge?" Long Hair asked, setting aside his empty bowl. "It has been four sleeps since you filled my tepee with your sweetness. Why did you stay away?"

"My age and yours," Soft Voice said, lowering her eyes.

When his hand came to her chin and lifted it, so that their eyes could meet, she felt a strange dizziness overwhelm her.

"While with you, this old man is young again," Long Hair said thickly.

"I see you as young," Soft Voice said.

The thudding of her heart told her that her words were true. Suddenly it seemed that Falcon Hawk's image was vague within her mind. She now realized at last that she could never have him. But this old man wanted her. She could see it in his eyes. She could feel it in his touch!

"You see past your feelings for Falcon Hawk and have found feelings for this old man?" Long Hair said, feeling a slow heat rising in his loins.

Soft Voice did not respond. Instead she stood over him and began slowly undressing. With her clothes tossed aside, she stepped closer to Long Hair. She closed her eyes and trembled as his hands began moving over her. Since her husband's death, she had hungered for a man's touch. And not just any man. She wanted a man with much property, one who belonged to a noble family of chiefs. Long Hair was such a man.

Long Hair reached for Soft Voice's hands. He drew her down on the soft furs spread out on the floor beside him. Tossing his blankets away, he lay down over Soft Voice and became a virile man again.

He relished the feel of her soft body against his. He quavered at her touch, at her youthful kiss. He wrapped her in his arms and brought her even more tightly against him, their bodies soon quaking as the peak of their passion was reached.

Afterwards, Soft Voice lay beside Long Hair, her eyes closed. She was surprised at his virility. She was surprised at how she had enjoyed being with him in such a way!

She tried to blot out all thoughts of Falcon Hawk. She wanted to love Long Hair. She even hoped that his seed would become fertile within her womb, and she would have a child born of their union. Then there would be no question as to who she should love!

"You are more beautiful than all the stars in the skies," Long Hair said, stroking Soft Voice's breasts. "Had I met you when I was a youth, ah, but there would not be a night when I would not make love to you. As it is, this old man may not often be as virile as he was tonight. Would it be fair to you to ask you to stay and be my woman? Could you look past those nights when I could not take you in my arms and love you?"

"Whether you make love or not, being in your arms is all that would matter," Soft Voice whispered, snuggling against him. "I have needed someone for so long. You have also been plagued with needs."

"You will not care what the people say about an old man and young woman finding love and happiness together?" Long Hair said, brushing a kiss across her lips.

"I care not what anyone says," Soft Voice said venomously.

Long Hair arched an eyebrow at her tone of voice, but forgot it when she rose above him and straddled him, and he found that he was able to find entrance inside her again with his manhood. He breathed hard as he thrust up into her as she held her head back, sighing.

He closed his eyes, reveling in his ability to once again have the *naii-tate-ihi*—the fulfillment of desire.

Upon a high peak, Falcon Hawk gazed across the glorious land that lay below him. White clouds sailed across the valley, their shadows rippling over the treetops, wandering farther until they nestled against the distant mountains. The ceaseless wind swept the grass in the meadow below him into a continuous, undulating surface, silver-crested.

Up this high, everything was quiet. Falcon Hawk heard not the birds in the trees nor the rippling of the stream that snaked across the land below him. There was just himself and the Great Unseen Power—and the prayers he had been uttering to the heavens for the past four days, when he had not been gathering the necessary ingredients for the medicine bag that he had fashioned from a badger skin.

His medicine bag now contained a root to be used when necessary by him and his wife against cough. He had also gathered a root frequently used in the tribal ceremonies of the Arapaho. He had also placed within his bag a pebble-like formation found in the side of the body of a dead buffalo, called *hanatca,* "buffalo bull." This stone would be used on sores to cure them.

Falcon Hawk had built a monument of stones on the hill where he had fasted, as was the common practice. He had found a buffalo skull and had used it as a pillow when he slept.

Weak and emaciated, yet feeling warm within his heart that the Great Unseen Power had blessed him and his future with Maggie, Falcon Hawk gathered up his medicine bag and began walking slowly down the side of the steep hill. His footsteps were slow, his knees wobbly, his heart pounding with weakness.

When he reached his horse, he barely had the strength to get into the saddle. Then he wheeled the steed around and headed it toward home.

"Haih-nyah-weh, thank you, Great Unseen Power," he uttered as his head bobbed and he felt waves of dizziness sweeping through him. *"Hahou* for making me see the right for having chosen the white woman for my wife. *Hahou* for giving me visions that make me know that my people are ready to accept this woman into their hearts."

He lifted his head heavenward. "I am not yet so sure about my grandfather," he whispered. "His blessing was weak and not filled with true goodwill."

He hung his head and continued riding onward, in his mind's eye seeing Maggie as though she were there touching the very core of himself with her sweetness and devotion. Although he had found answers and peace about many things these past four days, most of all, this time spent away from his woman had confirmed his love for her.

Only for her.

Chapter Nineteen

Maggie took Sky Eyes from her breast and slipped the corner of her dress back into place. Gently, she folded the blanket around her daughter, then laid her in her cradle. She rocked the cradle for a while, humming softly, then sat down by the fire again, continuing her long wait for Falcon Hawk. She slipped another piece of wood onto the fire. She rose to her knees and gave the stew another stirring, knowing that it was overcooked by now, though it would still be nourishing. That was all that mattered.

She reached for a small bundle that she had placed close to the ashes of the fire and uncovered one corner, smiling when she found that the bread she had made to pass the evening hours was still warm. She hadn't eaten any of it yet. It was for Falcon Hawk, so that he would have something special to eat with the elk stew.

A small portion of scrambled eggs lay on a

platter beside the fire, where she had left it after Sky Eyes had begun crying to be fed. Having had stew for each of her meals this day, she had craved the eggs in this later hour to fill the hunger that waiting had caused.

She was no longer hungry, yet she hated to discard the eggs into the fire.

A stirring in the eagle's box drew Maggie's eyes to it. When large, friendly eyes peeked at her over the top of the box, where the eagle had managed to push the cloth aside, an idea popped into Maggie's mind. Ever since Falcon Hawk had gone, Maggie had fed the eagle the fresh meat left in the bag outside the door by the village hunters. But perhaps the eagle would like a different snack tonight.

Maggie reached for the platter of eggs and took it to the eagle. Kneeling, she took a pinch and offered it to the bird, whose beak opened and plucked it away from her.

"Why, you *do* like it, don't you?" Maggie said, feeding the bird as quickly as she herself had consumed the eggs. Maggie laughed softly. "When Falcon Hawk comes home, I can tell him that I'm not the only one in this lodge who likes scrambled eggs."

"Did I hear someone speak my name?" Falcon Hawk said as he entered the lodge. He tried to appear strong, even though his knees were threatening to give way. His stomach reacted to the aroma of the food cooking over the fire by growling. His mouth watered at the recognizable fragrance of Maggie's special way of making bread.

But he refrained from rushing to the food and eating it like someone who had lost his senses. Instead he went to Maggie and drew her up into his arms and gave her a long, lingering kiss, reveling in the feel of her body against his and how she clung to him, proving that she had missed him as much as he had missed her.

Maggie kissed him with passion as he ground his mouth into hers. She sobbed against his lips, happy that the long ordeal of waiting for him was finally over.

The growling of his stomach and his gaunt look when he had entered the lodge made her realize that his homecoming should be spent in feeding him. The rest would come later, after he had his strength back to carry her to their bed to make rapturous love.

"Darling, darling," Maggie said, stepping away from him, giving him a wavering stare. "You look as though your fasting has taken its toll on you."

She took his hand and half dragged him down with her beside the fire. She ladled out a big bowl of stew, which she quickly gave him, his spoon ready. She uncovered her bread and broke off a large chunk and gave it to him.

She then sat down beside him and watched him eat ravenously. "You were gone too long," she said solemnly. "Just look at you. Your cheeks are sunken. Your eyes are dark and hollow." Her eyes roamed over him, and he was glad that he had on a shirt so that she would not see how much weight he had lost during those four days and nights of refusing to take nourishment.

Maggie took her coffeepot from the hot coals at the edge of the fire and poured coffee in a mug for Falcon Hawk and handed it to him. Although it was scorching hot, he swallowed it in fast gulps, then handed the empty cup back to her.

"More of everything," he said, wiping his mouth clean with the back of his hand. He chuckled. "This Arapaho chief almost forgot how good food tastes."

Maggie poured another cup of coffee and gave it to Falcon Hawk, then began ladling more stew into the bowl. "Did you achieve what you wanted while fasting?" she asked, giving him a sidewise glance. "Am I to . . . still be your wife?"

"Was there ever any doubt that you would be?" Falcon Hawk said, setting aside the coffee and taking the steaming bowl into his hands.

"You fasted because of me," Maggie said, settling down in front of him on her knees and clasping her hands in her lap. "Is that not so, Falcon Hawk?"

"The fast was meant to give my grandfather comfort more than it was for Falcon Hawk's own peace of mind," he said. "But it is good that I took time for fasting. I have returned home feeling cleansed of doubts, of feeling sometimes as though two persons are battling feelings deep within my soul."

"What do you mean?" Maggie asked, waiting for his response after he ate several more spoonfuls of the stew. She placed another chunk of bread at his side, which he grabbed up and ate as quickly.

"The loss of my mother has troubled me

deeply," Falcon Hawk then said, his eyes looking into the flames of the fire. "Always I need the closeness with the Great Unseen Power to accept that she has been taken from my life in such a cruel way. It is hard to think that perhaps she died while wandering all alone, away from her people. So you see, the fasting was good, after all. *Haa,* it was good that my grandfather suggested it. It was good that I took the four days for fasting and communing with the Great Unseen Power."

"It is so sad about your mother," Maggie said, her heart flooded with sadness at the memory of all her own loved ones who had gone on to their final resting places before her. "Perhaps one day you will find out that she is alive. Wouldn't that be wonderful?"

"That hope always stays alive within my heart," Falcon Hawk said, setting his empty bowl aside. When Maggie started to take it to refill it, he covered it with his hand. "No more. My stomach is comfortable now."

He glanced over at the cradle. "Sky Eyes has grown much these past four days?" he asked, turning his eyes back to Maggie.

"*Aa,* very much," Maggie said, moving onto his lap and straddling him. "And also your eagle." She placed her hands to his cheeks, where a stubble of whiskers was rough to her palms, and brushed a kiss across his lips. "Darling, the sweet bird was fed each day with meat brought by your warriors." She leaned away from him, her eyes dancing into his. "Also tonight I discovered her love for something else. I fed her my leftover scrambled eggs. Falcon Hawk, that bird gobbled those up like they were cherry pie."

"Cherry pie?" Falcon Hawk said, arching an eyebrow.

Maggie laughed softly. "I forget that you don't have knowledge of such food eaten by white people," she said. "One day, if we can obtain enough cherries, I shall make you a cherry pie."

She ran her hands up and down the stubble of his face. "Never have I seen you with whiskers," she murmured. "Although my husband sometimes wore a beard, it seems strange to see even such a feathering of whiskers on your face."

"Time was not taken to pluck whiskers from my face, nor to take a bath," Falcon Hawk said, lifting her from his lap. "That chore will be tended to after I meet with old grandfather." He took her wrist and pulled her down again, his lips teasing hers with feather kisses. "Then, my beautiful white woman, I will make wrongs right for you. You have been neglected four nights. This fifth we will make love until the sun rises over the mountains in the morning."

"I dreamed of you every night that you were gone," Maggie said, cuddling up into his arms. "Please hurry with your bath. But should you bother your grandfather this late?"

"Most are still awake in the village," he said. "The fires within cast many shadows on the inside walls of the lodges. So was my grandfather's shadow cast on his."

"Thread Woman and I became acquainted while you were gone," Maggie said as she moved from Falcon Hawk's lap. "She is such a sweet and generous woman."

"She brought her awls and needle and sewed while you became acquainted?" Falcon Hawk said, rising to his feet. He combed his lean fingers through his long, flowing hair. "Scarcely does she go anywhere lest she is sewing while talking."

"*Aa,* she brought her sewing tools," Maggie said, fighting back the urge to tell him about Soft Voice's added deceits and insults. It was so hard not to.

But it was no longer necessary for her to worry about revealing truths about Soft Voice. Thread Woman had said that she would tell Falcon Hawk about Soft Voice's scheming ways. "Thread Woman also brought me news of your grandfather. She said that he was not well. She and I took stew to your grandfather. Yet he did not seem all that ill to me."

"Sometimes he pretends," Falcon Hawk said. He swept Maggie into his arms and gave her a soft kiss, then swung away from her toward the entrance way. "Ready the blankets for us. This time my absence will be brief."

"Please do hurry, my love," Maggie whispered to herself as Falcon Hawk stepped from the lodge.

Feeling giddy with excitement now that Falcon Hawk was home again, Maggie began readying things for the night, so that when he returned from the chores he had to do before retiring, she would be all that he would need to see to.

Singing to herself, Maggie gathered the dirty dishes and stew pot and set them outside for washing the next day. She readied the coffeepot for brewing early the next morning.

Then she went to the eagle to pet her one last time. When she found her fast asleep, Maggie instead drew the soft cloth over the box, then turned and eyed the bed.

Her heart raced with anticipation of the long night that lay ahead of her.

Falcon Hawk's attention on his grandfather's lodge was so intense that he jumped when someone stepped out of the shadows and began walking beside him. When he looked down and saw that it was Thread Woman, he raised a quizzical eyebrow.

"Thread Woman, you are wandering outside your lodge at this hour of night?" he asked softly.

Thread Woman tilted her head and squinted up at Falcon Hawk. "There are things that you should know that the white woman will not say to you for fear of angering our people," she said in her gravelly voice.

Falcon Hawk stopped. His heart skipping a beat, he feared what this elderly Arapaho had to say about his woman. He knew that it would be the truth. No one could be as honorable and truthful as this old lady. She had been his grandmother's best friend.

"What is this that you have to say about my woman?" he said guardedly, his eyes searching for the truth in the squint of Thread Woman's.

"It is not about your woman that I come to you beneath the moon and stars," Thread Woman said. "It is about Soft Voice and what she is doing *to* your white woman."

Falcon Hawk's jaw tightened and his eyes blazed angrily. "What is it that she is doing?" he asked, his teeth clenched. He should have expected Soft Voice to cause problems in his absence. If he had his way, he would rename her! The name Soft Voice did not fit one who was spiteful and scheming!

Thread Woman explained at length about how Soft Voice had purposely taught Maggie to do needlework wrong. Then she said something that stunned Falcon Hawk even more, so much so that he felt numb from the knowing.

"She is . . . moving her things in with old grandfather?" Falcon Hawk gasped, disgusted at the very thought of what this had to mean.

Thread Woman had to say no more. Soft Voice was suddenly there, her arms filled with some of her belongings, shaken to find Falcon Hawk with Thread Woman and knowing why their heads were together in such a serious conversation. When Falcon Hawk turned and glared at her, she lowered her eyes. Stiffening, she readied herself for a verbal lashing by her chief.

Thread Woman went on her way, leaving Falcon Hawk and Soft Voice alone beneath the dark veil of night.

"How could you do these things?" Falcon Hawk said, finding it hard not to grab her and shake her. "First you torment my woman—and now my grandfather? Do you not know that he is a man of integrity, wisdom, and good standing? This grandson will not allow you to corrupt him!"

When Soft Voice still did not look up at him, Falcon Hawk placed a rough hand at her chin and forced her eyes up to meet the anger in his. "You take your belongings back to your lodge now," he flatly ordered.

When Soft Voice stubbornly stood her ground, Falcon Hawk pointed toward her lodge. "Falcon Hawk has spoken!" he said, his voice raising in pitch. "How could your parents allow you to make a fool of my grandfather? How?"

"They have always wanted the best for their daughter," Soft Voice finally said, giving him a defiant stare. "If not you, then your grandfather."

"You are wicked to the core," Falcon Hawk hissed. "Go. Take your face from my sight!"

"We have already made love," Soft Voice blurted out. "Do you not see the meaning in that? It has proven to him that he is still a virile man. Do you not see the importance in that? I have given him back something that he thought he had lost."

Her eyes softened. "And Falcon Hawk, I discovered love in his arms," she murmured. "Although he is old, there is much about him that I still see as young."

"You only use him for your scheming purposes," Falcon Hawk said, refusing to believe her. "Take yourself home and pray to the Unseen Great Power to forgive you for taking advantage of an old man who was content in his life as an old man."

"You are wrong in ordering me from him!" Soft Voice said, then turned and stamped away.

Thinking that the sound he heard might

actually be her sobbing, which could mean that she was sincere about his grandfather, Falcon Hawk raked his fingers nervously through his hair. He closed his eyes and said a soft prayer to his Great Spirit, then went on to his grandfather's lodge. He took a deep breath before stepping inside.

Chapter Twenty

As Falcon Hawk stood in the shadows of his grandfather's tepee, unnoticed as yet by this beloved old man, Falcon Hawk silently studied him. When he had discovered what Soft Voice had done, he had felt as though someone were stabbing him in his heart.

Yet the changes he saw in his grandfather made Falcon Hawk take a second thought about this old man who had taken a young woman to his bed. His gray hair no longer lay twisted atop his head, matted and sticky-looking. It now lay across his shoulders, clean and shining. The robe he wore was clean and fresh and resplendent with colorful designs made from porcupine quills.

But Falcon Hawk was keenly aware that those were not the most important changes in his grandfather's appearance. He wore a contended look; his eyes gleamed proudly as he smiled to himself while gazing into the dancing flames of his lodge fire.

There was no doubt in Falcon Hawk's mind what had caused these changes in his grandfather, and it hurt him to the core that it had to be Soft Voice instead of any number of the other women who would have willingly offered themselves to Long Hair to be his wife. Why couldn't it have been Thread Woman? Falcon Hawk knew that her feelings for his grandfather were sincere. His grandfather deserved someone like Thread Woman.

Long Hair was revered. He was loved. He was admired by everyone!

He had once been a powerful chief until he had handed this title to his son many winters ago after his wife had left him to travel the long road of the hereafter with her ancestors.

Now Falcon Hawk was chief, and tonight he might not have made a wise decision in sending Soft Voice back to her dwelling. He recalled the many times his old grandfather had urged his grandson to take Soft Voice as his woman.

Now Falcon Hawk understood why. His grandfather had even then truly been enamored with the young woman, yet had not allowed himself to think that she might have eyes for him. Everyone knew that Soft Eyes wanted Falcon Hawk.

But except for his grandfather, it seemed, everyone knew that Falcon Hawk most definitely did not want her. And that was surely because his grandfather did not see how any man could not want her!

This was the first time his grandfather had

looked at another woman in the same way he had looked at his dearly departed wife. As far as Falcon Hawk knew, this was the first woman his old grandfather had taken between his blankets with him since the death of his wife!

Shaking his head slowly back and forth, confused as to what to do now or how to treat this delicate matter, Falcon Hawk paused only a moment longer, then stepped out into the bright light of the fire, drawing Long Hair quickly out of his reverie.

"*Naba-ciba,* this grandson has returned from his fasting," Falcon Hawk said. He went to his grandfather and bent low to give him a lingering hug.

Then he sat down beside the fire much more stiffly than usual. He even felt it awkward to look into his grandfather's eyes which were surely filled with question since this was not Falcon Hawk's usual demeanor in the presence of his beloved old grandfather.

There was a strained silence, then Falcon Hawk's jaw tightened. He realized that he must either accept what had happened between his grandfather and Soft Voice or quickly voice his unhappiness about it. If he delayed, he never could feel later that it was right to speak of this to him.

Yet Falcon Hawk remembered the pride in his grandfather's eyes and the changes in his appearance. That had to count for a lot and help sway Falcon Hawk's decision!

"Look my way, grandson," Long Hair said, reaching a bony hand to Falcon Hawk's shoulder. "You know, do you not, about the woman who has shared my bed? This is why you hesitate to look into your *niba-ciba's* old eyes."

When Falcon Hawk turned his head to meet his grandfather's gaze, something beyond, in the farther recesses of the tepee, half drew his breath away. Soft Voice had already brought some of her bundles into the lodge. Among these he could see her hairbrush and hand mirror. A pair of her moccasins were sitting beside his grandfather's bed as though they belonged there.

His heart pounding, he looked quickly away and found his grandfather still staring at him, patiently awaiting a response.

"*Haa,* this grandson knows," Falcon Hawk said thickly.

"And it is in your behavior that you do not approve," Long Hair said, easing his hand from Falcon Hawk's shoulder to fold it with his other hand on his lap.

"It is not for this grandson to approve or disapprove," Falcon Hawk said, wanting to take away the words almost the moment he had said them.

But he could not humiliate his grandfather by telling him his heartfelt feelings about what had happened. In fact, Falcon Hawk knew that he must get to Soft Voice and tell her that she could continue taking her belongings to old grandfather's lodge after all, before she came to Long Hair and spoke viciously of what Falcon Hawk had done. He would cut this council short.

"Then it will not be further spoken about," Long Hair said, nodding. He reached for his fan of feathers and began tapping it on one of his knees. "Your fast. Tell this old grandfather about it. Do you feel at peace now with your decision to marry this white woman?"

"I never felt anything less than at peace with the decision before I agreed to fast," Falcon Hawk said, sliding a piece of wood into the lodge fire. "The fast was out of respect for you, *Naba-ciba.* But it was good that I did this. I return to our village feeling renewed and cleansed of all bad feelings brought on by my mother's absence. Perhaps I can now accept that she is gone."

"Dreams have told me that she will return," Long Hair said solemnly. "But it is best that you accept that she is gone should my dreams be wrong. It is better on your heart. It will beat without stings of sadness."

"*Naba-ciba,* it is time to go on with the sweet side of my life," Falcon Hawk said, envisioning Maggie waiting for him back at his lodge, anxious to enfold her within his arms. "You will participate in the celebration which welcomes my woman into our village of Arapaho? You will also join the celebration of our marriage?"

"*Haa,* this old grandfather will be there," Long Hair said, lifting a hand to Falcon Hawk's shoulder. He drew his grandson into a fond embrace. "Be happy, my grandson. My feelings are peaceful toward this decision that you have made. It is well."

Falcon Hawk felt a gush of love swell within his heart for his grandfather. He hugged him tightly, then slipped from his arms and rose quickly to his feet. There was more reason for a hasty exit other than wanting to get to the woman he loved. He *must* go to Soft Voice quickly and tell her the reversal of his decision, much as he hated to humble himself in such a way.

But it was for his grandfather that he would do this dreaded thing. Only for his *naba-ciba.* Most definitely not for Soft Voice.

He bade his grandfather a farewell, then left the lodge and stepped out into the quiet hour of night. As he moved his eyes around him, he no longer saw shadows being cast against the inside walls of the dwellings. All that he could see was the dancing light of the lodge fires as they flickered in the night.

There was one exception. When he looked toward Soft Voice's lodge, he saw her sitting outside the entrance flap, her head bowed into her hands. His ears caught the sound of soft sobs, and again he had cause to believe that she might have sincere feelings for his grandfather. One did not cry over a loss that was not important.

She cared.

In a dignified manner, Falcon Hawk walked past the silent lodges until he came to Soft Voice. Standing over her, he waited for her to lift her eyes to him. When she did not, he knelt down beside her and placed a hand on her arm.

"Your tears prove to me that which I find hard to believe," Falcon Hawk said as she slowly looked up at him. "Be warned that if they are false tears and you hurt my grandfather, or if you humiliate him in any way, you will regret having ever lifted your eyes into his."

"Why do you say this now, when you have already banished me from Long Hair's lodge?" Soft Hair said, wiping tears from her face with the back of her hand.

"I have seen my grandfather and the happiness

that you have put into his eyes and heart," Falcon Hawk said, unintentionally gripping her arm harder, only realizing it when she winced in pain. He dropped his hand away from her. "Because of this, I have reversed my decision about your sharing his blankets and lodge with him."

"You . . . have changed your mind?" Soft Voice said, her eyes widening in utter disbelief.

"*Haa,* and perhaps foolishly so," Falcon Hawk grumbled. "But hear this, Soft Voice. I still see past your outward beauty. I still see your inner, spiteful self! If this is a game you are playing, it will be your last in this village of Arapaho!"

This sort of warning did not set well with Soft Voice. She tightened her jaw and glared into Falcon Hawk's eyes. Her love for him had turned to loathing. She truly hated him. Oh, for so many reasons did she hate him! And she would not stop trying to find ways to avenge his having turned her away from his heart.

"You need not worry about your grandfather's feelings any longer," Soft Voice said, forcing herself to sound sweet and soft. "This woman truly cares for Long Hair. You will see the proof of this by things that I do for this man who has offered me his heart."

Falcon Hawk gave her a lingering stare, then turned on a moccasined heel and forced himself to place his worries aside. He had to take a bath in the river. He had to remove the stubble from his face. All of this he must do before he slipped between the blankets with his woman.

The moon was reflecting off the river in great splashes of white. Falcon Hawk stripped off his clothes, then dove headfirst into the water, shivering at his first contact. He bobbed back to the surface and swam with long strokes down the narrow aisle of the river. Then suddenly he realized that someone else was swimming alongside him. When he turned his head, he was stunned almost speechless to find Maggie there, splendidly nude.

"I waited long enough," Maggie said, swimming up close to him, glad when he wrapped his arms around her as they both placed their feet on the pebbled bottom of the river. "Sky Eyes was asleep. I thought it safe enough to join you in the river."

"Do you not feel the cold bite of the water?" Falcon Hawk asked, pushing wet strands of hair back from her brow.

"*Aa,* I feel the coldness," Maggie said, brushing a kiss across his lips. "But I knew that you would soon warm me."

"I have yet to remove the whiskers from my face," Falcon Hawk said huskily, his manhood growing hard against her stomach as she pressed herself even more tightly against him. "They will scratch you while we make love."

"I don't care about whiskers," Maggie whispered, sucking in a wild breath of ecstasy as he began moving himself against her flesh. Even though the water was cold, she could feel the heat of his manhood. "I only care about being together. The four days were so long. Darling, never leave for such a long time again. Please?"

"The duties of a chief sometimes take him away from his people—and his wife," Falcon

Hawk whispered against her cheek, his breath coming quickly now as passion rose within him. "Sometimes it can be for days. Sometimes it can be for only one night. But think of this while I am gone—waiting always enhances the pleasure."

"Your grandfather?" Maggie said as Falcon Hawk swept her fully into his arms and began carrying her toward the shore. "Did you find him well? Did you and he once again agree about everything that had to do with me? Will he stand in the way of our happiness?"

Falcon Hawk chuckled. "You are filled with many questions," he said. "Let me answer them all by saying that my council with my grandfather went well enough so that you need no longer think of anything but your future with this man who loves you."

Maggie still could not let it rest about his grandfather. He had been anything but cordial to her when she had taken the stew to him. The way he looked at her! She wasn't sure if she could trust his word to allow Falcon Hawk to marry her!

"He said nothing negative about me?" she persisted as Falcon Hawk carried her to dry ground.

"Nothing," he said, placing her on a blanket that she had purposely spread for them before she had entered the water. Her clothes lay in a neat stack beside the blanket. She had gathered his and had placed them beside hers.

He knelt over her, thinking how beautiful she looked beneath the light of the moon. He meditatively ran a hand over her breasts, lower then to her stomach, feeling her flesh twitch sensitively at his touch. He cupped the mound of her desire and slowly thrust a finger up inside her. He smiled down at her when he heard her gasp of pleasure, then his smile faded and he momentarily withdrew his finger.

"My grandfather is very well indeed," he said dryly. "He has a young lover now to warm his bed at night."

Maggie's eyes widened and she leaned up on an elbow. "Oh?" she murmured. "And shouldn't you be glad? You sound as though you resent this woman."

"This grandson has just cause to," Falcon Hawk said, his jaw tightening. "The woman is Soft Voice."

"Soft Voice?" Maggie said, paling.

"*Haa,* Soft Voice," Falcon Hawk uttered flatly. "And I trust her very little. Especially where the feelings for my grandfather are concerned. I feel that she is taking advantage of him."

"Is there something that you can do to stop her?" Maggie asked.

"*Nah,* nothing," Falcon Hawk said solemnly. "But I gave her a warning. Now we must wait and see if she heeds it."

He placed a hand at the nape of Maggie's neck and drew her lips to his. "No more talk of other people's romance," he whispered huskily. "The true romance is here, lying within my arms."

"Yes, yes," Maggie whispered against his lips as they moved gently against hers.

"Are you cold?" Falcon Hawk asked, his lips

whispering against hers. He breathed in the sweet scent of her. "We can go to my lodge."

"No, I'm not cold," Maggie whispered back, twining her arms around his neck, his warm breath mingling with hers. She was growing languorous at his touch. "Not while you are here to set fires along my flesh. Take me, my darling. Take me now. Let us make maddening love."

Molding her closer to the contours of his lean body, he entered her in one burning thrust. She shuddered with desire and placed her legs around him. He moved rhythmically within her. Her hips moved, answering his heat and excitement.

Delicious shivers of pleasure coursed through her as he cupped her swelling breasts, feeling magic in his caress. His mouth seared into hers with intensity. Her breasts pulsed warmly beneath his fingers.

Falcon Hawk could feel the nerves in his body tensing as the passion rose hot in his loins. His mouth slipped down to the creamy flesh of Maggie's breast and he flicked his tongue over her taut nipple. Each thrust within her brought him closer to that moment of magic. He came to her thrusting even more deeply, his arms around her, holding her now as though in a vise. He kissed her hungrily, his breath quickening as he trembled with readiness.

Groans of pleasure filled the air as their world melted away, total bliss claiming them as their bodies quaked and rocked together with a fiery climax.

A rush of air whistling through the trees and over their sweat-soaked flesh made Falcon Hawk roll quickly away from Maggie. He took the corners of the blanket and drew it over them both, then once again he knelt over her.

Maggie's hands reached up and rediscovered the contours of Falcon Hawk's face as one of his hands molded her breast. His mouth sought hers, on fire with renewed passion.

She came alive with his touch, shivering with pleasure as his manhood grew once again hard and velvety against her flesh. He leaned over her with burning eyes. As he thrust deeply within her and began his even strokes that lifted her clear to the heavens, his mouth covered hers with a reckless passion.

With a moan of ecstasy, she gave him back his kiss. She clung to him and the wild, sensuous pleasure captured her again in its web. This frantic passion that she was feeling devoured her, spreading . . . spreading . . . spreading. . . .

Again they reached that plateau of pleasure they were seeking. Laughing afterwards, they shivered as they dressed and ran hand-in-hand to his lodge.

Once inside, he drew her around and gave her a hard, pressing kiss, causing her head to reel. She trembled as she became alive again beneath his caresses. They almost tore the clothes from each other as they raced into another torrid lovemaking.

"All night," Maggie whispered as he carried her satiny nude body to his bed. "Make love to me all night, my darling Arapaho chief."

Falcon Hawk gazed down at her with passion-heavy eyes. "*Haa,* all night," he said thickly and laid her across the bed as he took in the sight of her again, seeing her as vibrant and glowing and flawless.

His hand ran down the length of her body, making her skin quiver. She drifted toward him and sought his lips with her own. The tenderness grew slowly into a surge of passion. Their bodies strained together hungrily, their hot moans filling the cold night air.

Having made camp in a canyon, where the smoke of his fire might not be detected, Frank placed his saddle on the ground, then laid his head on it as he stretched out on a blanket. His eyes watched the flames eating away the wood in the fire pit that he had circled with round, smooth rocks. He was close to a Shoshone camp. Tomorrow he would begin observing it. Tomorrow he might even go into the camp and boldly ask about any sighting of a white woman in a covered wagon. He could not waste much more time in mere observation. Although risky, it was much quicker to come out and openly ask the Indians questions.

After taking another deep puff from his cigar, he flicked the stub into the fire. He took a last sip of coffee, then tossed the tin cup aside and lay down on his rolled-out blankets, covering himself with another one.

"Tomorrow," he whispered as lazy, midnight sleep crept over him.

Chapter Twenty-One

The next morning, the day of the celebration of acceptance, except for a few drifting clouds, the sky was unspeakably fresh and blue. The puffy white clouds were darker-edged toward the far horizon. A gray wolf stood near a hillock observing a band of antelope sweeping ghostlike across a distant ridge. The eagle was majestic on its perch outside Falcon Hawk's lodge, some of its baby feathers lying on the ground beneath it.

As Maggie stepped from Falcon Hawk's tepee in a beautiful white doeskin dress with intricate beadwork designs, her heart hammered. It seemed to be keeping time with the great medicine drum that sat in the heart of the village. It had just begun to vibrate its steady beats into the air when the Arapaho warriors began singing their brave heart-songs.

Maggie rested the cradle board in the crook of her left arm and held her chin proudly, knowing that she looked as close as possible to how the Arapaho women looked today because Thread Woman had come and fussed over her for hours, beginning at sunrise.

As Thread Woman painted the part in Maggie's hair after having braided it, she had taken the time to explain more about the red paint than Soft Voice had. Thread Woman's paints were contained in hollowed-out bear tusks ornamented with a large pearl. Her favorite paint was red made of red iron oxide.

Thread Woman had explained that these red pigments were ground in small mortars and mixed with certain greases so they would smear easily. She had stopped to point at her face, proud of the round dots, lines, and large red spots on her cheeks and forehead.

After Thread Woman had finished with Maggie's hair, she had brought out a neat little case in which she carried her face powder, telling Maggie that face powder was regarded very highly among the Arapaho. As Thread Woman had placed the fluffy powder on her face, Maggie felt its softness and enjoyed its pleasant smell.

Thread Woman had explained that the powder was used not only on the face, but also on the bodies of adults and children much as talcum powder. It was prepared from the red dry-rot of the heart wood of the pine. This material came in chunks and was easily crumbled and reduced to a powder.

"The idea of a beautiful complexion is to have it red," Thread Woman had said as she put the final touches to Maggie's face. "It is the color which the sun gives to those whose bodies are lifted to the healing rays of the light that shines from the sky world."

Maggie was proud to carry with her today so many visible signs of proof to Falcon Hawk's people of her eagerness to become one with them. There were only two nagging doubts that entered her mind now and then, especially now when she could feel not only one set of eyes on her, but two.

Glancing quickly toward Long Hair's lodge, she found him and Soft Voice just leaving his tepee, their eyes having quickly discovered her as she walked toward the center of the village where everyone was congregating in one large circle around the skyward-reaching flames of an outdoor fire. Maggie could see mixed emotions in the old grandfather's eyes and a mixture of hate and envy in Soft Voice's.

When Soft Voice took Long Hair's hand, it did not seem to Maggie that it was because she was proud to have been chosen by this admirable man. She did it to show that she had not failed at her attempts to get a man in high standing to fall in love with her.

Disgusted at the thought that Soft Voice might make a fool of Long Hair, Maggie turned her eyes quickly away and was glad to find Falcon Hawk walking toward her with eager steps. A smile fluttered on her lips when she again saw just how handsome he was—so tall and wide-shouldered and sinewy of muscle, his expression quietly alert and showing strength and confidence.

Her gaze raked slowly over him, seeing that

his hair was perfectly groomed, black, and very straight over his shoulders. His attire for this special occasion was a shirt of deerskin, resplendent with porcupine quillwork and reaching to his knees, with added cape-like sleeves fringed along the forearm and wrists. His skin-tight leggings bore horizontal painted stripes and panels of quill along the seam, with fringes of horsehair wrapped at the base with quillwork.

Falcon Hawk met Maggie and gently took the cradle board from her, his eyes never leaving her.

"You are a vision," he finally said, his eyes gleaming into hers. "Thread Woman makes you Arapaho in color. You are even more beautiful than I have ever before seen you."

Maggie's cheeks heated with a blush. "I want you to be proud of me," she murmured. "I never want to make you feel awkward over me with your people."

"Red, white, yellow," Falcon Hawk said, chuckling low. "I would love you if even you were the color of the sky!"

Maggie laughed softly. Then, feeling as though she were walking on clouds, she fell into step beside Falcon Hawk and became frighteningly aware of being closely scrutinized when the crowd fell back and made room for them. She tried to focus her eyes on the platform that sat on the one side of the fire, while the drummer beat out his steady rhythm on the other. She could feel the circle of people close around her and Falcon Hawk.

She said a silent prayer that her Lord would

get her through this day without disappointing Falcon Hawk.

So much depended on today.

If his people found any cause not to accept her, then what would Falcon Hawk do?

He was their leader. His woman must be as loved as he, so that his leadership would not waver in its strength.

Maggie sat down on the platform, which was covered with thick, rich pelts. She smiled at Falcon Hawk as he propped up the cradleboard beside her, then moved to the other side of her and sat down. Her heart pounded and her throat went dry, wondering what would happen next.

To focus on something else for the moment, to give her heart time to settle into a more normal beat, she looked past the people and gazed at the small eagle outside on its perch. It seemed content enough, as though it belonged. Before the sun had crept high over the mountains, she had fed the eagle a handful of scrambled eggs. Falcon Hawk had followed that with a fresh catch of meat, warm from the kill.

"Spoiled," she had said, giggling as she watched the eagle devour all of its offerings. "Cute, but spoiled."

She was glad to know that this was one eagle that would not be killed just for its show of feathers! Those eagles that were free were at the mercy of everyone and everything.

Falcon Hawk leaned closer to Maggie. "Let me explain things to you as they happen," he said in a whisper. "The drum is an essential part of every meeting of the Arapaho. It represents the heartbeat of Mother Earth. Its beats send messages to the Great Unseen Power. The drum player determines the types of dances by his song and drumbeat. The one who plays for us today is called Crying Wind."

Maggie's breath was stolen away when several male dancers appeared, their attire eye-catching and beautiful. They wore skin-tight leggings and breastplates consisting of long, white bone beads called *hairpipe.* The number of bones indicated the wealth of the owner.

They also wore headdresses made from porcupine hair, trimmed to stand erect and made to fit the top and back of the head. Two eagle feathers were attached to the top of each. They each wore only brief breechclouts and carried spinners, sticks that were generously decorated with brightly colored feathers attached loosely to the end, which began spinning and twirling when the dancers began their demonstration.

"They do a traditional dance," Falcon Hawk explained.

Maggie nodded and continued watching. The dancers moved in a steady circle around the fire on the grass, their steps varying from a shuffle or a trot to a violent lifting of the knees and stamping of the feet upon the ground. Not only did the feet perform in this dance, but also bodies and arms.

Some were dancing so vigorously that they had to pause every two or three minutes, during which time the drum tapped briskly until the dancers began performing again.

Their feet came down with a resounding whack and then gave a softer hop or shove ahead, accompanied by gestures of the arms and twisting of the body. The *dum, doom, dum, doom* of the drum gave the rhythm.

These dancers left and others appeared.

"You will now observe the hoop dance," Falcon Hawk said, smiling at Maggie when these dancers began their performance, followed quickly by others.

During the hoop dance, the women dancers used a number of wooden hoops, holding and spinning them around their arms, legs, and waist in order to form intricate designs.

These were followed by the women's fancy shawl dance. This was the counterpart of the men's fancy dance. These dancer's outfits were made of shiny, colorful, satin-like materials. This dance style involved high cross steps and pirouettes.

Then followed the rabbit dance, where couples followed a lead couple around in a zigzagging line. The couples had to maneuver to keep up while keeping their two-step in time with the drumbeat.

Maggie found herself caught up in the merriment of the long day—drummers pounding in resounding rhythm, the Arapaho people's voices reaching high to sing their ancient songs.

It was all an event of sight as well, colors brilliant and sharp on the garments of slow-moving, proud Arapaho women.

To Maggie it became a spiritual thing—so moving, entrancing, and alive! She nodded her head as the songs became longer and more powerful, the dancers' feet pounding, pounding, in powerful performances.

And then everything became quiet and solemn. The silence was like a soft, steamy vapor lifting from a foggy river on a humid summer morning.

Falcon Hawk took Maggie's hand and urged her to her feet. Her knees almost buckled with fear as she was led to several elderly warriors who sat together, as though in council. Among them was old grandfather, Long Hair.

As Maggie and Falcon Hawk stopped before the gathering of elders, Falcon Hawk placed a hand to Maggie's elbow to steady her. She cast him a nervous smile, then gazed attentively back down at the old men, her eyes moving to Long Hair's fan of feathers as he held it over his eyes, shielding them from the sun as it crept lower along the western horizon.

"I, the chief of this band of Arapaho, bring this woman for acceptance into our village," Falcon Hawk said, pride thick in his voice. "Elders, it is my wish that you give her your welcome and blessing. She will then be as one with our people."

There was a strained silence, then one of the elders—the "introducer"—spoke. "Let the rites begin," he said, rising to his feet. His long and flowing gown dragged the ground as he moved to Maggie and took her hand.

The silence in the village was vast and haunting to Maggie as she followed the elderly man to a stone that had been placed amidst the people. He urged her to stand upon it. New moccasins were brought to Maggie. She humbly accepted them.

"The stone and moccasins and the white woman having accepted them are proof of her stability and strength," the introducer said.

He stepped aside and a priest stepped forth, also dressed in a long and flowing gown, his waist-length hair whipping around him as the breeze grew in intensity as evening began to fall. He raised his hands toward the heavens and began singing in a monotone.

"Ho! All ye of the Heavens, all ye of the Air, all ye of Earth, I bid you all to hear me! Into your midst has come a new life. Consent ye, consent ye all, I implore. Make her path smooth, then it shall travel beyond the four hills!"

Falcon Hawk's chest filled with pride, knowing that the deed was now done, and thinking on the last verse of the song and its meaning. The four hills were the hills of infancy, youth, manhood, and old age, and the appeal to the powers of the earth and the air was a recognition of man's dependence upon their created things.

In these things, his woman was now a total part, and she was now Arapaho in the eyes of not only himself, but his people.

As the elderly men rose and began mingling with their kin, Falcon Hawk went to Maggie and led her from the rock. He smiled down at her as she clutched the moccasins to her chest. "It is done," he said, taking her by the elbow and leading her through the throng of people.

She looked up at him, glad that it was over. Although fascinating, it had been a long day.

When they hadn't been watching performers and listening to the singers, they had been feasting, the honey-buttered fry bread and the Indian tacos tantalizing to her taste buds.

Now she could relax and get on with her life, a true part of Falcon Hawk's people.

"I'm exhausted," she said, leaning against him as they approached Falcon Hawk's tepee. "I hope that Sky Eyes is still asleep. I'm grateful to Many Children Wife for taking Sky Eyes home earlier in the day and seeing to her welfare."

"She will always be there for us and Sky Eyes," Falcon Hawk said, smiling down at her. "And when your breasts fill with milk for a second child, even then will she be there for us."

"A second child?" Maggie said, gazing up at him. "How I would love having your child."

"*Nyuh,* then it will be so," Falcon Hawk said matter-of-factly.

Maggie sighed contentedly. The night stretched out before her like some vast spell of blue enchantment. She had never been happier. When she went inside with Falcon Hawk and they unclothed for bed, she moved into his arms and got lost in his touch and kisses, her face burning in the darkness as his lips began teasing her sensitive places.

But for only a moment.

She was so tired, her eyes drifted closed and soon she was fast asleep.

Falcon Hawk leaned up on an elbow, gazing disbelievingly down at her, then laughed softly and stretched out beside her, himself welcoming the lethargic wonder of sleep, knowing that tomorrow would be theirs—and not only tomorrow. Forever!

He cuddled close to Maggie and went to sleep with a smile on his face.

Chapter Twenty-Two

Taking one of her robes that she had brought from her former life, Maggie slipped it around her shoulders and sat down beside the fire pit. She stared into the glowing embers that remained of the fire and began stirring them with a stick. She watched the sparks spitting here and there, reminding her of the fireworks she had seen in Kansas City on the Fourth of July.

Her thoughts turned to the celebration for her acceptance into the Arapaho community. She could still remember the sounds, could still feel the vibrations soaring through her body as the drums had beat and the feet had thudded. She could still taste and smell the delicious food that she had eaten.

Now she faced the other celebration with much anticipation—when she would become Falcon Hawk's wife in the tradition of the Arapaho. She thrilled at the thought of being able to call this noble man her husband.

"Husband," she whispered to herself.

Yes, she liked the way that sounded as it flowed softly across her lips.

Maggie grew suddenly tense and looked guardedly at the entrance flap. She leaned an ear toward it. There it was again. The sound of the shuffling of feet. Whoever it was came closer. Fear splashed through her. It was past midnight. Who was wandering around outside?

Maggie recalled the hate in Soft Voice's eyes whenever Soft Voice looked at her. It was no less now that she had moved in with Long Hair. It had been born of jealousy and seemed to still be eating away at Soft Voice.

Thread Woman's voice broke through the silence, shaking Maggie out of her dread.

"Falcon Hawk?" Thread Woman said, scratching on the outside of the flap. "Panther Eyes? Please awaken."

Maggie glanced over at Falcon Hawk. When she discovered that he was still soundly asleep, she rose quickly to her feet and stepped outside with Thread Woman. They gave each other a hasty embrace, then Maggie stepped away from the kind woman, questioning her with her eyes.

"Why are you here?" Maggie whispered. "It's so late."

"Soft Voice came to me and awakened me," Thread Woman said, casting a nervous glance toward Long Hair's lodge.

Maggie's gaze followed Thread Woman's. She grew cold inside when she noticed that his fire had not burned away to dying embers as most did at this time of night. She could see the light of the fire brightening up the inside walls of the tepee. She could make out the shadow of Soft Voice as she knelt over something.

Maggie's eyes widened and she grabbed one of Thread Woman's hands. "Soft Voice came to you," she said warily. "Why? Is something wrong with Long Hair?"

"That is so," Thread Woman said, her eyes dark and sad. "I have come for Falcon Hawk. Since he is the only living relative of Long Hair, it is he who must give permission for the sacred wheel ceremony to be performed over his grandfather."

"I don't understand," Maggie said. "What is the sacred wheel ceremony?"

"There is no time now for explanations," Thread Woman said, patting Maggie on the back of her hand. "It is important that we awaken Falcon Hawk now. You and I will talk later."

Maggie was filled with questions. She still didn't even know what was wrong with Long Hair! She wasn't sure how ill he was! And what part did Soft Voice have in this sudden failing health?

This time it did not appear that Long Hair was only pretending to be ill to get the notice of those around him. Thread Woman was taking this quite seriously!

So then should I, Maggie thought.

"I'll get Falcon Hawk," she said in a rush of words.

"I will return to Long Hair's bedside," Thread Woman said, already walking away toward Long Hair's tepee.

Maggie hurried back inside Falcon Hawk's

dwelling. She knelt over the bed and placed a gentle hand on his smooth copper cheek. "Darling?" she whispered, trying not to alarm him by the sudden awakening.

Falcon Hawk's eyes fluttered open. He flashed Maggie a knowing smile and grabbed her wrists and started pulling her onto the bed with him.

"So you have awakened me because you want loving?" he said. He released one of her wrists and slipped a hand inside her robe, cupping a breast within his palm.

He forked an eyebrow when he did not get the response that he had expected from her, then drew his hands away from her and sat quickly up on the bed.

"What is it?" he asked, searching her face with his eyes. "You are solemn, as though you have brought me bad news."

He looked past her at the closed entrance flap, then back into her eyes. "Has someone come for me?" he said guardedly. "Do they wait outside for me?"

"Thread Woman was here, but she is now with Long Hair," Maggie said. Falcon Hawk was already off the bed and stepping into his fringed breeches.

Falcon Hawk looked at Maggie, his dark eyes flashing angrily. "If anything has happened to my grandfather because of Soft Voice, she will pay," he said between gritted teeth. "He must truly be ill or Thread Woman would not awaken me from a sound sleep in the middle of the night."

"Those were my thoughts exactly," Maggie said, nodding.

Falcon Hawk slipped into his moccasins, then went to Maggie and clasped his fingers onto her shoulders. "Come with me," he pleaded.

Maggie's insides tightened. Her eyes wavered as she gazed up at him. "Your grandfather doesn't like me," she murmured. "I'd best stay behind." She nodded toward Sky Eyes's crib. "And I'd best stay with the baby."

"She sleeps all night and will not miss you," Falcon Hawk said. "And my grandfather has accepted you."

"But he has yet to say one word to me," Maggie said, her voice breaking. "I . . . will only be in the way. I might make him uncomfortable if I am there."

"There are reasons why he does not speak to you, but now is not the time for me to say why," Falcon Hawk insisted. "I will tell you later. At this moment, time is my enemy, too quickly passing while I am not at my grandfather's bedside."

Seeing that she was causing this delay and wanting to do everything to please Falcon Hawk, Maggie nodded. "All right," she said, already walking toward the entrance flap. "I shall go with you. Let's go now before any more time passes."

Together they went to Long Hair's lodge. When they stepped inside and found Soft Voice kneeling beside Long Hair's bed, sobbing as she determinedly clutched one of his hands, there was a strained silence. Not only because Long Hair lay gasping for each and every breath, but because Soft Voice appeared to genuinely care that he was ill.

Falcon Hawk rushed to the other side of Long Hair's bed. He ignored Soft Voice and placed a gentle hand to his grandfather's brow.

"*Naba-ciba,*" Falcon Hawk said softly. "Can you open your eyes and see this grandson who has come to give permission for the Sacred Wheel Ceremony? Can you speak enough to tell me what ails you?"

Long Hair slowly opened his eyes and looked at Falcon Hawk. He laughed softly. "This old grandfather discovered tonight that he is truly old, after all," he said, raising a hand to pat Falcon Hawk's shoulder. He closed his eyes and groaned as pain engulfed him anew. He clutched at his chest. "The heart is also old . . . too old for your grandfather to behave like a young man with a beautiful woman whose desires are unquenchable."

Falcon Hawk cast Soft Voice an accusing stare, causing her to blush and hang her head. "You were making love when this happened to my grandfather?" he hissed over at Soft Voice.

She said nothing. Only nodded.

"Leave my grandfather's lodge," Falcon Hawk growled.

Maggie went to Soft Voice and knelt down beside her and took her by an elbow, urging her to her feet. "It would be best if you leave," she repeated, jumping with alarm when Soft Voice jerked away from her and glowered at her. "It is best for everyone if you leave."

Soft Voice lifted her chin stubbornly and shook her head slowly back and forth.

"Soft Voice, if you truly care for Long Hair, you will do what is best for him," Maggie said, once again taking Soft Voice by the elbow, ushering her toward the entranceway.

Soft Voice burst into a torrent of tears as she cast a worried glance over her shoulder at Long Hair. "I do love him," she wailed. "I did not want this to happen! I . . . only wished to make him happy. Is it wrong to want to make someone happy?"

"If it was done without selfish motives," Maggie said, taking Soft Voice outside into the dark veil of night. "And you know that nothing you do is without motivation, with yourself as your only main interest."

"What do you know about the wants and needs of Arapaho women?" Soft Voice said, leaning into Maggie's face, her eyes filled with venom. "You are white," Soft Voice hissed. "Through and through you are the dreaded color of white."

Maggie gasped and stepped quickly aside when Soft Voice stamped on past her. Having never met such a complex, confusing person before as Soft Voice, she sighed heavily.

Then she went back inside Long Hair's tepee and sat down on the far side, in the shadows, as Falcon Hawk still stood over his grandfather, talking softly while Thread Woman stood close by, listening.

Maggie feared intensely for this old grandfather's life. It was obvious that he had suffered a heart attack. The reason for it made Maggie uncomfortable for the lovely old man. She was afraid that if the news spread through the Arapaho village it might make Long Hair feel ashamed in the eyes of his peers. He had thought himself a young, virile man again. It had turned out that he was perhaps older even than his years.

She watched Thread Woman leave.

Falcon Hawk left his grandfather's bedside and came to Maggie. He knelt down beside her. "The permission has been given for the Sacred Wheel Performance," he said, reaching a gentle hand to Maggie's cheek. "My grandfather's heart is weak. Perhaps the Keeper Of The Wheel can bring strength back into his heart so that he can live at least long enough to see his first great-grandchild."

Their eyes were drawn around when Thread Woman and the Keeper of the Wheel entered the dwelling. Maggie's eyes quickly went to what the elderly gentleman was carrying. It was a bundle, yet she could see that what was inside it was shaped like a wheel, perhaps a foot and a half across.

Falcon Hawk sat down beside Maggie, and as the Keeper covered the floor in the tent with sage and cedar to be used as incense, Falcon Hawk began softly telling what was happening, and why.

She listened attentively and watched anxiously when the Keeper sat down in the middle of the back of the tent and brought the wheel out of the bundle.

"The hoop of the wheel represents a snake," Falcon Hawk said in a whisper. "It is kept enclosed in the bundle until it is time for it to be ceremonially wrapped and sacrificed for the good of the one who is ill."

He paused and took a look at his grandfather,

whose eyes were closed, his hands folded together over his chest. Then he continued with his explanation. "The Sacred Wheel is always in the keeping of a special individual, whose approval must of course be secured before the ceremony can be made. Silence must be observed now. There will only be words spoken if the Keeper wishes to utter a prayer."

Maggie scooted closer to Falcon Hawk. The Keeper had taken a cloth from his bundle and was praying in a monotone. Then he became quiet and began wrapping the cloth around the wheel. When the wheel was fully covered, the Keeper stood over Long Hair with it, then took up his bundle and left the lodge.

"That's all there is to it?" Maggie whispered, her eyes wide.

"Sometimes there is more, sometimes not," Falcon Hawk said, rising to his feet.

Maggie followed him to his grandfather's bedside, then turned and stiffened when she discovered Soft Voice standing behind her.

Maggie turned her eyes up at Falcon Hawk just as he realized that Soft Voice had returned.

Falcon Hawk started to scold Soft Voice, but his grandfather's voice behind him caused him to hesitate to tell Soft Voice that she had gone too far this time. She had not listened to the bidding of her chief!

"Come to me, lovely woman," Long Hair said, beckoning for Soft Voice with a trembling hand. "Come and sit at my side and listen to these words of wisdom."

Soft Voice's eyes grew soft as she smiled down

at Long Hair, now ignoring everyone else in the lodge except for the old grandfather.

She knelt at Long Hair's side. She took one of his hands and held it affectionately, resting his hand on the bed beside him. "I am sorry for having caused your affliction," she said, her voice soft, sincerity in her tone. "It was never Soft Voice's intention to harm you, only to make you feel like a man again—in every sense." A sob escaped from the depths of her throat and she lowered her eyes. "This woman is not so clever, it seems."

She then lifted her eyes to Long Hair again. "Do you wish that I remove my belongings and not return?" she asked weakly, another sob lodging in her throat.

"*Nah,* do not leave me to live alone again," Long Hair said, his old eyes pleading into hers.

"But I am not good for you," Soft Voice said, reaching a hand to his brow, softly caressing it.

"You are good for me in many ways, except for one," Long Hair said, his lips quavering into a light laugh. "Stay. Be my companion. Warm my body at night with yours. But do not expect me ever again to perform like a young man. That time of my life is long past. Only briefly did I have the pleasure that I felt as a young man. Now it is time for me to behave as a man of my age must." He paused. "Or the heart will betray this old man who loves a younger woman."

"No matter that you do not love me in that particular way again, I want to stay," Soft Voice said, placing her cheek against his. "I have grown so fond of you."

It was taking all the strength that Falcon Hawk could muster not to yank Soft Voice away from his old grandfather. But something held him back. Although deep down inside himself he feared that she was using his grandfather, there was much in her voice and behavior that spoke to him of her genuine love for Long Hair.

Maggie clutched Falcon Hawk's hand, understanding these feelings that were surely battling inside him. She jumped with alarm when he suddenly broke free of her grasp and went to stand over Soft Voice and Long Hair. She scarcely breathed as he gave Soft Voice a look of utter contempt and warned her again as she gazed sheepishly up at him.

"My grandfather is the earth, the moon, the stars to me," he warned. "If you stay with him, it will be until he takes his last breath. I will not stand by and watch you hurt him."

Long Hair reached for Falcon Hawk's hand and drew him down close beside him. "It is good to have such strength in a grandson's love and devotion to his grandfather," he said. "And do not think that this old man cannot fend for himself. Grandson, Soft Voice's feelings for me are true. I have felt it in the way she has embraced me. A wise old fool like myself cannot be wrong about such things."

Maggie saw the contempt in Soft Voice's eyes as she gazed up at Falcon Hawk. Maggie knew that although Soft Voice might truly love Long Hair, she still had strong feelings for Falcon Hawk, even if they had changed to hate. Maggie did not trust her, yet she kept her opinion to herself. Falcon

Hawk would know how to handle Soft Voice if ever she needed tending to.

Long Hair turned his gaze to Maggie. He lifted a hand toward her, beckoning for her to come to him.

Maggie swallowed hard, wondering if he was finally going to speak to her, and if so, what would he have to say?

She was frightened of what his first words to her might be, yet she moved to Falcon Hawk's side and knelt down so that she could be close enough to Long Hair to hear his words distinctly. Sometimes he used the Arapaho language while speaking with his grandson. Hopefully he would speak in English while talking to her.

"White woman who has stolen my grandson's heart, this old grandfather wishes to say that he welcomes you now, with open arms," Long Hair said, taking her hand and squeezing it. "I have not spoken to you to tell you my feelings, because in the Arapaho tradition, no grandfather and daughter-in-law speak."

Maggie's eyes widened and she sent Falcon Hawk a quick glance. Only moments ago she had asked him why his grandfather never talked to her and had been told that Falcon Hawk would explain later. Now she knew! The knowing warmed her through and through. How wonderful to know the true reason. And once he started talking to her, he went on and on. Oh, how she loved it! She loved him! She cherished him!

"It is our custom that no grandfather and daughter-in-law speak," Long Hair said again, stopping to take a deep, quavering breath. He then began again. "Of course, you are not in truth my daughter-in-law, yet in a sense you are. You have promised yourself to Falcon Hawk, making you as close to this old grandfather in relationship as a daughter-in-law might be. But your presence here today, to be with this old grandfather during the Sacred Wheel Ceremony proves that you care. It is now that you know that this old grandfather returns the devotion of his grandson to you."

He stopped and motioned for her to hug him. She knelt over him and reveled in the embrace. "*Ha-hou,*" Maggie whispered. "Thank you for your blessing and for not hating me for interfering in your life."

"You are no interference," Long Hair said, fondly patting her back. When he smiled, his old, faded eyes twinkled, giving way to the warmth inside. "You are my grandson's intended."

Maggie eased from his arms. "How are you feeling?" she asked, smoothing a comforting hand up and down one of his frail arms. "Did the ceremony make you feel stronger? Will you be well?"

"How can this old grandfather not be well when he has two young women to love him?" he said, chuckling low. His eyes drifted closed. "But this old man is tired. Leave now, but come often. There is much to say now that I have chosen this once to forget Arapaho tradition which keeps silence long and cold between grandfather and grandson's woman."

Maggie moved to her feet alongside Falcon Hawk. They both gave Soft Voice a look of warning, then left Soft Voice and Thread Woman alone with Long Hair.

The sun was just creeping up from behind the distant mountains as Maggie and Falcon Hawk walked toward their dwelling. "He's made me so happy," Maggie said, beaming. "He has made my world with you complete and filled with peace. I am so grateful to your grandfather for this."

"He is a man of good heart," Falcon Hawk said, drawing the entrance flap aside so that Maggie could go inside his dwelling. He followed her and knelt beside the fire pit and began laying wood on the glowing embers. "And perhaps Soft Voice's heart is not as scarred as I thought. She does seem sincere about my grandfather. For that, for *him,* I am glad."

Maggie felt a rush of coldness moving through her veins as she remembered again Soft Voice's eyes and what seemed to lie in their depths. Total contempt for Falcon Hawk!

A shudder embraced her at the thought. But soft whimpers coming from the cradle soon stole all thoughts from her except for those of her child.

She stood over the cradle, watching Sky Eyes slowly awakening. The baby stretched, yawned, kicked, and licked her lips. She was a picture of innocence.

But what of *her* future? Maggie despaired to herself. Soft Voice had been as innocent and sweet at one time, also!

"They are two lonely people who are finding refuge in one another's company," Falcon Hawk said, still contemplating this relationship between his grandfather and Soft Voice. "Although I wish it could have been Thread Woman instead of Soft Voice."

Maggie turned and gave him a lingering look, seeing also an innocence in this man who would soon be her husband. She silently vowed that she would never allow Soft Voice to touch his life again.

Chapter Twenty-Three

The days had passed quickly since the last ceremony. But this day, during the long ceremony that preceded her becoming Falcon Hawk's wife, time had seemed to drag by. It was now evening. Scores of fires outside each tepee were lifting lazy blue wreaths of smoke against the velvet black of night. The Indian drums thudded through the dark, and a great wolf in the distance lifted its hoarse, raucous voice in a howl.

Maggie sat on a fur-shrouded platform for the second time in three days, Falcon Hawk beside her. Sky Eyes had been given into Many Children Wife's care at daybreak, just prior to the first drumbeat that announced the beginning of the day's events that would continue until late in the evening, when all would look to their chief and the woman of his choice.

Dressed beautifully in a brand-new doeskin dress made by the skillful fingers of Thread

Woman, with every exquisite design drawn from nature, Maggie tried to forget the slow ache that was beginning in her back after sitting for so long in one place. She had welcomed the rabbit-fur coat that Thread Woman had been so kind to bring to place around her shoulders when the cooler breezes of the evening picked up into an uncomfortable wind.

And still the dancers continued to perform, going into one routine after another, each more colorful than the last.

Maggie looked slowly around her at the various tribes that attended this celebration. Not only were there many Arapaho, but several Cheyenne and Shoshone were also present.

Falcon Hawk had explained to Maggie how invitations had been sent out to these guests, each of whom had brought not only gifts, but food. Falcon Hawk had shown her his bundle of invitation sticks before he had sent them out.

Falcon Hawk had kept the fifteenth stick of the set. It had the same ornamentation as the other sticks, and would serve to check the authenticity of each guest's invitation when he or she arrived.

As the guests arrived, they had laid their sticks across the vessel of food they brought. Many gifts had also been brought, mainly horses. When Maggie saw them, she had been amazed at their appearance. Most were painted yellow with spots on their shoulders and stripes down their backs and sometimes across their hindquarters. There were also circles around the eyes, and their manes and tails were yellowed. A few horses of dark color were painted green.

His heart kind toward those who had come to share this special day with him, Falcon Hawk had himself parted with special gifts. A Cheyenne woman who had provided more food than any others, received several blankets. Some visiting Cheyenne had received gifts of money to enable them to return home.

All in all, forty of Falcon Hawk's horses had been given away.

"There will be the crow dance, and then the dancing will cease until after vows have been exchanged between us," Falcon Hawk whispered, leaning close to Maggie's ear. "It has been a long day, yet only because there are so many who care and who give their blessings on our union. My heart is filled with much warmth and gratitude for these people who celebrate with us. So it is the same, I am sure, for you, my beautiful Panther Eyes."

Maggie cast him a warm smile, in her eyes a gentle loving for him. "My heart is filled with much I could never be able to describe," she whispered back, placing a hand on his smooth copper cheek. "I love you, my handsome Arapaho chief. I would sit through a full week of ceremonies if it meant that you would, in the end, be my husband."

"When I first saw you, and even when you wore that ugly poncho, I knew that you would be mine. When I looked at you, I saw nothing beyond that beautiful face and entrancing eyes and hair," Falcon Hawk whispered, his eyes shining into hers.

"Ah, but what a surprise when I discovered that I had chosen a lovely, shapely maiden."

A brief wave of nausea swept through Maggie, causing her smile to waver. She slipped a hand over her abdomen, wondering if she could be pregnant again so soon. Surely she could! Many weeks had passed since she gave birth. And she just realized that she had not had a normal monthly flow since the Sky Eyes was born. She had attributed that to breast-feeding. Had she been wrong?

Maggie forced a smile so that Falcon Hawk would not suspect that she was feeling ill—and perhaps the reason for it. She wanted to keep the news of her possible pregnancy from him until they were alone, to savor it together.

She prayed that she *was* pregnant with his child. That would make her world complete as her metamorphosis into being an Arapaho continued.

"There was something in your eyes a moment ago," Falcon Hawk whispered, forking an eyebrow. "It was not a look of contentment. It was a mixture of pain and confusion. Tell me why, Panther Eyes."

"I feel nothing but radiant," Maggie whispered back, telling no falsehood, for she did. In so many ways, she did.

Falcon Hawk searched her eyes for a moment longer, then turned his gaze back to those who were performing before the platform, in the wide circle where the people sat. Falcon Hawk shifted his gaze and was amazed to see a look of bliss on Soft Voice's face as she sat beside Long Hair.

He watched her for a short while, then became absorbed in the dancing and the throb of the drums, nodding and tapping his fingers on his knees as he folded his legs before him. He could feel Maggie's eyes on him still. He had dressed in his most elaborate garments today, the designs brilliant in color and definition.

He had Thread Woman to thank for this. Indeed, he had Thread Woman to thank for many things. She had made Maggie feel more comfortable in her lessons about Arapaho life than anyone else could, even himself. The old woman had ways about her that most every other woman who knew her envied.

His thoughts shifted to his old grandfather and again to how he would have liked to see him take Thread Woman into his tepee and blankets, for she was alone, widowed many winters ago during the wars between Ute and Arapaho.

But Long Hair looked upon this gentle old lady only as a friend.

Falcon Hawk felt that his grandfather needed a friend during his last years on this earth more than a young woman who entranced him.

Not wanting to think further on Soft Voice in any respect, and as eager to get through these performances as his Panther Eyes, Falcon Hawk focused his full attention on the dancers. He had performed the crow dance many times in his youth and now he was proud to be a spectator. He was proud of the cause for such performances today. Finally he would seal all of his tomorrows with the woman he loved.

The drum was on the eastern side of the huge,

outdoor fire. Four sticks were used to suspend it, the painted ends sticking in the ground, the drum hanging from the forks at the top. The underside of the drum was called *haatetc,* the ocean; the upper side was red, representing the sun.

Singing, eight men sat crowded closely together around the drum, all beating it in unison with sticks, the ends of which were wrapped with cloth. Each man moved his entire body as he beat the drum. Their singing was in the throat, but very constrained, without any attempt to produce a clear sound. The drummers looked either at the drum or straight in front of them, without watching the dancers.

The dancers were dressed in many different fashions. Some wore crow tails, others wore feather ornaments, and some were entirely naked except for a breechcloth. Knee bands with rattles or bells were worn by many. Most carried ceremonial objects. One man was painted red over his entire body, others yellow, and some black. More than one man was painted black on one side and yellow on the other.

As the dance progressed, some performers danced rather violently, others slowly, quiet and subdued.

Maggie's eyes widened as many women entered the dance, among them Thread Woman. All women but Thread Woman danced much more slowly and heavily than the men. Thread Woman raised her feet and skipped along with a little swing, her face radiant as the fire shone into the deep craters of her wrinkles.

Maggie and Falcon Hawk exchanged smiles,

then returned their eyes back to the fire. Earlier in the day, there had been many other special dances—one for food, another with bows and arrows, and a third with spoons. There had been several breaks, when everyone had stopped and had eaten the feast set before them, soon resuming the many different clever kinds of dances.

Maggie was enjoying this dance the best—for it was the last!

The drumbeats stopped. The dancers left the circle and became as one with the others who had been their audience. Maggie's throat went dry when Long Hair rose shakily from his blankets and walked to the center of the congregation, his back to the fire as he began talking, motioning to everyone with a slow swing of the hand, in order not to miss anyone as he spoke.

Falcon Hawk reached over to take one of Maggie's hands and held it lovingly as Long Hair began his speech in a low monotone.

"My friends, this old grandfather is deeply grateful that you have come here on account of my grandson, who is to marry," Long Hair said, his voice filled with deep emotion. "It is the wish of men that when their grandsons marry, they choose wisely."

Long Hair turned his old, wizened eyes to Maggie and smiled, yet still spoke to everyone. "My grandson has made his choice, and this grandfather says with much feeling and pride that my grandson has chosen well. Even though the distance is great in their skin coloring and traditions, this woman who trusts her heart to my grandson has shown her ability and willingness to learn the ways of our people."

Tears swept from Maggie's eyes, so deeply touched was she by this old man's words and his total acceptance of her. She smiled at him and mouthed the word thank-you in Arapaho to Long Hair.

When he slowly nodded her way, she knew that he understood what she had said, and was glad to receive this word deeply into his heart, to carry with him until he closed his eyes and began his long walk on the road of the hereafter.

Maggie wiped the tears from her cheeks and glanced at Falcon Hawk, for Long Hair's undivided attention was now focused on him. Again, as she listened to Long Hair's words, she was moved to tears. She absorbed each of his words—words that she would never forget.

"My grandson, it pleases me that you are marrying," Long Hair said, smiling into Falcon Hawk's eyes. "Do good for your woman. Always treat her well. Those who try to be good are treated well. And now look to your future of many children. It has been a long time since this old grandfather has held a child in his arms. Give this grandfather a grandchild before the heavens open for me to join our ancestors in the sky."

Maggie placed a hand over her abdomen, now wanting more than ever to be pregnant. If not now, she would make it happen soon. Not only for herself and Falcon Hawk, but for this wonderful old grandfather.

Falcon Hawk nodded a silent thank-you to his grandfather. Maggie watched Long Hair resume his place beside Soft Voice, then shifted her gaze to the young woman, growing cold inside when she saw the hatred in the depths of her brown eyes as she stared openly at Falcon Hawk. Maggie knew that such a hate could be like an open wound festering inside one's soul. It could make Soft Voice do anything for vengeance. Anything!

Maggie's thoughts were interrupted when Falcon Hawk moved from the platform and stood before her, holding his hands out for her.

Weak in the knees, and with a thudding heart, Maggie rose to her feet and went to him, their hands clasped, their hearts intertwined.

She melted inside when he began speaking his vows to her, having never heard anything as beautiful during the marriage ceremonies that she had attended in Kansas City. These words that he spoke were not something written down in a book that could be used over and over by other people. These were from his heart, the very depths of his being.

"With reverence I take you, Panther Eyes, as my wife. Never will I give you up. I wish to live in happiness with you while the sun travels the sky and the stars light the dark heavens with their magical light. Our lodge will be a good and safe haven for our children. I promise you, my woman, that from this time we will live long together. The way we travel on earth will be clear and smooth before our footsteps. Our life will be good. Sickness will be far away. During both day and night we will be together, hands and hearts linked, as one body, heartbeat, and soul."

When he stopped, awaiting her vows to him, Maggie's eyes misted with happy tears and she willingly spoke her thoughts aloud to him and all others to hear.

"With reverence I take you, Falcon Hawk, as my husband," Maggie began, her chin lifted proudly, her gaze locked with his. "I will never give you up. And I promise to stay pure for you. I wish to live in happiness with you, always, and promise you a lodge of happiness and good heart. I promise you that my womb will be warm with child many times so that our family can multiply, to share this love that we have for one another. During the day and the night, I will be there to fulfill your every need. I lift my voice into the sky and say these things loudly so that the sky, the stars, the good wind, and the good earth will hear me, for these things are a part of us, as are your people. Listen well to what I say, Falcon Hawk, when I proclaim that I proudly become your wife today, for in you I have found peace, love, and happiness. I have found that which I never knew before you became known to me. Let there be long life for us, Falcon Hawk. I am blessed to have found you."

Falcon Hawk was so moved by her words that he felt that surely everyone observing this ceremony thought that the drummers had returned to their drums, when in truth it was his heart pounding inside his chest. He gazed down at Maggie, taken anew by her loveliness and her gentle, caring ways. If anyone was blessed this night, it was he!

Without further thought, Falcon Hawk drew Maggie into his embrace. "You are now my wife," he whispered into her ear. "In all ways you are mine."

"You are my husband," Maggie whispered, tears splashing from her eyes again, awed by the reality of this moment, and that it was actually happening. "Oh, how happy you have made me."

A great outpour of chanting began, and the drums threw their thump-thumping sounds into the air when Falcon Hawk lifted Maggie up into his arms and began carrying her away from the circle of people toward his lodge.

Maggie clung to his neck and gave him a soft smile and a mischievous look. "Wouldn't you rather join the feast again with everyone?"

Falcon Hawk smiled into her eyes. That was all the answer that she needed.

"I thought not," she said, laughing softly.

Falcon Hawk carried Maggie into the lodge and to the bed, where he gently laid her down. He leaned over her, and his fingers slowly disrobed her. When her breasts were bared to him, he bent and kissed first one and then the other, drawing a sensual sigh from between Maggie's lips. She closed her eyes and reveled in the fire that was being lit inside her.

Frank Harper had gone from village to village, watching from afar. When the Cheyenne left in large numbers from their village, his curiosity had been aroused enough to follow them, especially since his observances had proved to him that there was no white woman living among them. He had stayed far enough behind for them not to notice him, and when he found that their destination was an Arapaho village, he had taken a position on a butte close enough to the village to observe whatever celebration was taking place.

When Maggie had stepped into view, dressed in Indian garb, Frank had almost fainted from surprise. He had watched curiously throughout the whole, long day and into the hours of night, and had not taken his eyes off Maggie until now, when he was forced to watch her being carried away in the arms of an Arapaho warrior.

"I'll be damned," he said, scratching his brow. "I think she just married the Injun."

His thoughts went to the money, wondering where it was and how it might be used if he didn't get his hands on it.

Although he felt he should move swiftly, he must be careful, he thought. If he were caught sneaking around in the village and Maggie explained that he was her worst enemy, he wouldn't live long enough to spend the damn money.

He stretched out beneath his blankets, shivering. So close to the Indian village he had not been able to build a fire. And he knew that he might have several days ahead of him without a fire or fresh game to eat. He had to find means to get the money without actually going into the village himself. He would wait until he found one of the squaws wandering through the forest gathering herbs or whatever else the damn squaws might be after. He would force the squaw to work in his behalf, or die.

Chuckling, he drew another blanket over him and hugged himself with his arms. "At least I've finally found the bitch," he whispered. "Enjoy your little love nest, Maggie. This marriage of yours will be short-lived."

Chapter Twenty-Four

Falcon Hawk cradled Maggie in his arms for a moment, taking time to savor the quiet times of their love sharing. Then he moved to his knees over her, bending and pressing his lips softly against hers as his hand swept slowly down her body, her flesh like silk against his fingers. His tongue brushed her lips lightly, then he slid his mouth down to one breast and covered its taut tip with his lips. Ecstatic waves washed over Maggie, and she was experiencing a deliciously sweet euphoria.

Maggie felt Falcon Hawk's hunger when his lips came to her again, hard and seeking, his body now against hers, the throbbing hardness of his shaft probing where she quickly opened herself to him. As he pressed into her softly yielding folds, his fingers caressed the swollen center of her desire, sometimes softly pinching, sometimes moving only in gentle circles with his fingertips.

One hard thrust and Falcon Hawk was deeply within her tight cocoon of love, magnificently filling her. His fingers played. His lips kissed. His body moved rhythmically into hers.

And she clung to him, receiving all he offered her with her own, practiced movements. Her hands moved over his body, marveling anew at the sleekness of his copper skin and at the muscles that molded to her hands as she stroked his shoulders, his back, and his arms with the tips of her fingers. She met his thrusts with uplifted hips; then she placed her legs around him and drew him even more deeply within her.

Falcon Hawk buried his face between her breasts, his hands now at her buttocks, holding her in place as the slow thrusting of his pelvis took him to a higher plane. He had the lethargic feeling of floating, as though he were being carried somewhere high among the clouds, soaring with the mighty eagle.

His stomach churning wildly, Falcon Hawk increased his speed, going deeper, deeper. His mouth moved back to her lips and closed hard upon hers. He kissed her in a frenzied fashion, the pulsing crest of his passion drawing near. He was already feeling that first burning center of his passion scalding his insides. He moaned against Maggie's lips, reveling in how her warm breath mingled with his, wondering how he had ever lived without her. She was now as much a part of him as he was himself. She was everything to him!

Their bodies tangled as the lovemaking grew more heated and their hands searched and caressed each other's pleasure points. Maggie was feeling a drugged passion overwhelming her; she had never before felt this free and alive even while making love with Falcon Hawk.

But it would make sense that she wouldn't have. She was only now his wife. Belonging to him totally made everything right and beautiful.

Before it had only been a dream, one which circumstances might snatch away in a heartbeat.

Now she was his. And he was hers! Today their love and commitment to each other had become complete.

Nothing would ever come between them.

Nothing.

Falcon Hawk could feel the storm building within. He held Maggie in a torrid embrace as her hands clung to his sinewed shoulders. He paused, kissed her softly, then gave one last shove within her that caused him to go over the edge into total ecstasy. He shuddered his seed into her. Her body trembled violently, answering the call of his. Their sighs and groans filled the night air.

Once they were down from their flight to paradise, Falcon Hawk gave Maggie a lingering kiss, then rolled away from her. He lay on his side, tracing her body with his fingertips.

"My *nata-cea,*" he murmured. "You have made that word have meaning to me. It is a word most magical."

Maggie smiled at him, reaching a hand to draw a thick lock of hair back across his muscled shoulder. "My *na-ac,*" she murmured. "Until I met you, I never thought much about that word, or the importance of it. But now it is everything to me." She leaned closer and gave him a feathering of a kiss. "*You* are everything to me."

Falcon Hawk leaned up on an elbow. "Listen," he said, cocking an ear toward the entrance flap. "The drums no longer play. The people no longer sing or talk. The celebration is over and the guests have left. The village is as quiet as the night."

"*Aa*, my love. All is perfectly content in quietness. Perhaps I should go and get Sky Eyes," Maggie said, moving to a sitting position. "Many Children Wife needs her rest. Poor thing. Because of her own children and then ours, she did not have the opportunity to be a part of the celebration."

"Her celebration of life is in the many children she brings into this world," Falcon Hawk said, grabbing Maggie by her wrist and drawing her down over him. "And perhaps that is not a bad thought. Just how many children do we wish to have sit around our lodge fire with *us?* We already have a daughter. Shall we expect a son to be next?"

Maggie giggled. She placed a gentle hand to his cheek. "I would hope so," she said softly. "And perhaps we shall know if it's a son in less than nine months."

Falcon Hawk leaned up on one elbow, his lips parted. His eyes locked with hers as a smile blossomed on his face. Then his gaze shifted. He splayed his fingers across her abdomen, as though meditating, and stared down at the flatness of it, but recalling how round and perfect it had been before Sky Eyes was born.

"A child grows within your womb now?" he said, marveling at the thought of it being his.

"Yes, a child," Maggie said, tears of joy flowing from her eyes. "*Your* child."

"You are certain?" Falcon Hawk said, lifting his gaze to hers. "It can happen so soon?"

"I am almost certain," Maggie said, laughing softly as he drew her into his quick embrace. She clung to him. "My darling, I hope so. Would not that make our happiness complete? To have a son in your image? How I would adore him."

"Another daughter in your image would be just fine with this Arapaho chief," Falcon Hawk said, leaning away from her so that their eyes could hold again. "There is plenty of time for sons."

Maggie melted into his arms. She clung to him and kissed him as he leaned her back down onto the bed.

"We can join Sky Eyes a little later," Falcon Hawk whispered against her lips. "I want you to myself for a little while longer. Just a little while."

Maggie curled into his embrace, already floating again on clouds of euphoria.

Soft Voice lay cuddled against Long Hair, scarcely breathing herself as she had listened for Long Hair's breathing to become smooth and deep, indicating that he was finally sound asleep.

She tightened her jaw, and her eyes flared angrily when she thought back to how long Thread Woman had stayed beside the lodge fire with them after the celebration. It had seemed to Soft Voice that Thread Woman would never leave, the two elderly people talking on and on about the day and the wedding.

Soft Voice had pretended an interest and had listened intently, yet all the while fuming inside, not so much now because she was jealous of the woman who had married Falcon Hawk. It was because Soft Voice hated Falcon Hawk with a passion.

And even though he was her chief, that meant nothing to her anymore. He had made her look foolish more than once. She would never rest until she made him pay—and pay and pay!

A rumbling sound beside her made Soft Voice lean over Long Hair, smiling when she discovered that not only was he asleep, he was snoring. Finally she was free to leave. He would never even realize that she was gone. What she had to do would take only a few minutes.

Stepping lightly on the padded floor of the tepee, Soft Voice paused again before pushing herself completely up from the bed. Her insides tightened, aware that Long Hair was no longer snoring.

And then again it began. He let off sounds that reminded Soft Voice of the very first rumblings of thunder that she had so often heard wafting from behind the distant hills before a storm.

Having confidence again to leave the bed, Soft Voice moved to her feet and ever so quietly walked barefoot to the one side of the tepee, where she knelt down beside several bundles of Long Hair's personal belongings.

Her fingers trembled as she sorted through the

buckskin pouches and bags, then smiled devilishly when she recognized the one that she was searching for.

Before taking the buckskin pouch from the others, she cast a nervous glance over her shoulder at Long Hair. Warily, she watched him for a moment.

When he did not so much as stir, she turned her attention back to the pouch. Releasing its drawstring, she reached inside and circled her fingers around several "buttons," or the aboveground parts of the peyote cactus. She knew that these were used in the peyote ceremony. Peyote offered solace, but if too much was taken, it could cause a terrible illness, and sometimes death.

Its effect on animals could be deadly!

She knew exactly which animal she would feed it to tonight. Falcon Hawk's horse! Tomorrow Falcon Hawk would find his steed ill, even dead. She wanted that to be a warning to Falcon Hawk that not everyone was his friend—that he did have enemies!

As far as Soft Voice was concerned, *she* was his worst enemy, her hate for him worse than even that of the Ute tribe with whom the Arapaho still did not find a meaningful peace.

With the peyote in her possession, Soft Voice tiptoed toward the entrance flap. Before leaving the lodge, where the fire was now only glowing red embers, she turned and took one last look at Long Hair. She smiled and nodded, knowing that he would never know that she was responsible for anything tonight except warming his body with hers. When the true colder hours of the night were upon the village, yes, she would be there for him. He was also there for her. She did enjoy this new sort of friendship that she had found with old grandfather, a friendship that lay much deeper than they had found while making love. Being with him, feeling as though she belonged, was now enough.

She only hoped that he would never discover that she was the one who was doing these evil things against his grandson. She would be banished not only from Long Hair's life as quickly as the command could come from his heart, but also the Arapahos'. She would be forced to wander alone, never recognized again as a part of her people.

But she was willing to take this chance. She had to get even with Falcon Hawk. She would not rest until she did!

The outdoor fire had burned away into glowing ashes. As she moved stealthily past it, she recalled the celebration that had lasted long into the day. She cringed and bit her lower lip when she remembered the vows that Falcon Hawk had spoken to Maggie, and those she had spoken to him. In her many dreams, it had been Soft Voice standing with Falcon Hawk, looking endearingly into his eyes! In her dreams she had been swept away in his arms and carried to his lodge for a full night of lovemaking.

Instead, that had all been denied her.

And so would she deny Falcon Hawk many things!

She moved past the lodges and toward the corral, her eyes quickly singling out Falcon Hawk's horse. Careful not to cause a stir among the animals, she moved on tiptoe across the dew-dampened grass, then crawled beneath the fence where Falcon Hawk's horse stood away from the others.

Moving slowly, scarcely breathing, Soft Voice held out her hand to the horse and allowed it to sniff at what she held. She was afraid that because of the peyote's bitter taste, the horse might refuse it. Then her plans would be ruined.

Her heart leapt and she smiled when the beautiful horse's teeth grabbed the peyote buttons between them. She stepped back away and watched the last of the peyote disappear into the animal's mouth. She edged her back up against the fence and tightened inside when the horse emitted a soft whinny and began frantically shaking its head back and forth.

Minutes later she caught sight of a white froth boiling from the corner of the horse's mouth, and she knew that she had succeeded in her mission. If the horse didn't die, at least it would be ill when Falcon Hawk found it.

Knowing that she must return to Long Hair's lodge as quickly as possible, Soft Voice crawled beneath the fence again and began running away from the corral. When she heard a loud thud behind her, she stopped and turned and found that the horse had fallen to the ground on its side.

"Die, die," she whispered, her voice a hiss.

She turned on a heel and ran briskly toward the village and then through it, panting hard when she was finally safe inside Long Hair's lodge. She stayed deeply in the shadows until she caught her breath, then strolled nonchalantly to the bed and crept onto it.

Smiling, she cuddled up beside Long Hair, but she found it hard to sleep. She was anxious for Falcon Hawk to make his discovery.

She would revel in his sadness.

Chapter Twenty-Five

The first morning of their marriage seemed magical to Maggie. Before Sky Eyes awakened, hungry, Maggie and Falcon Hawk had made love again, this time more slowly, savoring every minute.

Falcon Hawk had built a warm lodge fire, and Maggie and he had sat beside the fire pit, their eyes on Sky Eyes as she had gotten her fill of warm milk.

Sky Eyes was back in the cradle again, fast asleep. Maggie had eaten her fill of scrambled eggs and Falcon Hawk was outside the lodge, feeding his eagle meat that he had first warmed over the fire before offering it to his pet.

Maggie was brushing her long hair, feeling a gentle peace within her, something akin to how a cat must feel when it lies by a hearth or on the lap of its owner, purring.

"If only I could purr," Maggie whispered, laughing to herself. "Then Falcon Hawk could *hear* my contentment at being his wife."

She shrugged and laid her hairbrush aside, knowing that he needed no more proof than she had shown him last night in ways that mattered the most. Their bodies had been perfectly tuned, a symphony of two.

Falcon Hawk's voice rising in pitch outside his lodge as he spoke to someone made Maggie's eyes move to the entrance flap. Falcon Hawk was obviously distraught over something.

Flipping her hair over her shoulders, she ran to the entranceway and rushed outside, puzzled when she didn't find Falcon Hawk, or anyone else for that matter, except those who were just emerging from their own lodges to begin their chores for another day.

Where did he go? It wasn't like him to leave without telling her.

"Chief Falcon Hawk is at the corral," a young brave said, as he came and stopped breathlessly at Maggie's side. "He sent me to tell you. He has given me permission to enter your lodge to get his medicine bag that contains his horse medicine. He told me where it could be found."

"Medicine for his horse?" Maggie asked. "Why does he need it?"

"Each morning it is my duty to check on the horses in the corral to make sure no one has stolen any from us," the young brave said. "Today I found Chief Falcon Hawk's horse lying on the ground. He is very ill."

Maggie noticed that the young brave was nervously shuffling his feet as he glanced from Maggie to the entrance flap, apparently anxious to do as his chief had commanded as quickly as possible.

She nodded to him. "Go and do as you've been told," she said, following behind him as he entered this lodge that she no longer solely referred to as Falcon Hawk's. Now it was also hers.

A sudden fear entered her heart as she watched the young warrior go directly to Falcon Hawk's buckskin bags. Although the satchel of money was buried in the ground, she could not help but be afraid that this young man might uncover it. Her heart pounded as the young brave continued searching. She breathed much more easily when he finally chose one particular bag over the others.

"*Ha-hou,*" the boy said, then left at a run.

Maggie went limply to the bed and sat down for a moment. She had practically forgotten the money. Now she realized just how things might change if the satchel was ever found.

Yet she was afraid to dig it up and take it elsewhere, for fear of being caught doing it. For now, she must leave it and pray that Falcon Hawk would never find it. He would know then that she still held dark secrets locked within her heart.

She wanted to go to Falcon Hawk, but her eyes moved to Sky Eyes's cradle. Something inside told her not to leave the child unattended, not even for a few minutes. Things were happening that made her wary of her child's safety. First Falcon Hawk's prized eagle was set free, and now Falcon Hawk's horse was ill.

Her thoughts crept back to Soft Voice and the suspicions about this young maiden that she could not shake off. Could she have given

Falcon Hawk's horse something to make it ill?

She shook her head, trying not to linger on such thoughts. It did not seem logical that Soft Voice would have any more reason to hurt Falcon Hawk. She had found a man who loved her more than she deserved.

Or was she the sort who always wanted more?

"Will she wreak havoc in our lives forever and ever?" she whispered to herself, hearing the despair in her voice.

"You wish to go to Falcon Hawk?"

Thread Woman's voice behind Maggie drew her around to face her.

"I spoke your name outside the lodge, but you did not hear," Thread Woman said, moving farther into the tepee, toward Maggie. "You are troubled, I am sure, about Falcon Hawk's horse. Go. Be with Falcon Hawk as he tends to his animal. I shall care for Sky Eyes."

"Oh, Thread Woman, would you?" Maggie said, meeting Thread Woman's slow approach. She grabbed Thread Woman's hands and squeezed them affectionately. "You are so kind always to me. How can I ever repay you?"

Thread Woman laughed softly. "The reward is in being with you and the child," she said, her old crinkled eyes dancing into Maggie's. "Maggie, don't you know that you make this old woman feel young again?"

"That's so nice of you to say," Maggie said, dropping her hands and embracing Thread Woman instead.

Then she stepped away from her and looked toward the cradle. "Sky Eyes ate and just went to sleep a short while ago," she said, nodding toward the cradle. "If she should awaken, she shouldn't be hungry."

"That is good, for this old woman's milk dried up many, many winters ago," Thread Woman said, cackling low. "Holding her will be enough for this old woman."

"And also for Sky Eyes," Maggie said. "She is growing used to your arms, as well as my own. She also is learning your face. She studies faces so intently, have you noticed?"

"She will be an intelligent, beautiful woman," Thread Woman said, nodding. She eased slowly down beside the fire, then motioned toward the entrance flap. "Go. Go to Falcon Hawk."

Maggie grabbed a shawl that she kept just inside the door on one of the lodge poles since the mornings were beginning to reveal the nip in the air that autumn brought to this vast, beautiful land.

Outside, she broke into a run and soon was kneeling beside Falcon Hawk, her heart suddenly heavy with sadness as she gazed down at the steed that had once been so powerful. It was not dead, but was severely ill and lay breathing hard, its dark, trusting eyes gazing up into Falcon Hawk's.

"What's wrong with him?" Maggie asked. She shuddered when trickles of foam rolled from the corners of the horse's mouth and it whinnied softly and tried to lift its head from the ground.

"It is my estimation that the horse ate something foreign," Falcon Hawk said, laying his drawstring bag aside after taking something from it. He looked around him at the different sorts of weeds that peeked through the grass, and into the distance, where just outside the fence stood many more varieties of weeds, hedges, and even some sprouts of herbs.

"Is your horse going to die?" Maggie asked, watching the heaving of the animal's sides, as though it were struggling for every breath.

"Falcon Hawk will not allow it to happen," he said flatly.

Maggie looked at what Falcon Hawk had taken from his bag. "What is that?" she asked, seeing several spotted beans and strange sorts of roots lying in the palm of his hand.

"These are bean amulets, which consist of horse-fetlock, and the root of a plant called *hiwaxu-haxhiwaxu*—horse root," Falcon Hawk softly explained as he forced these things into his horse's mouth. "These are fed to a sick horse or rubbed on the nose of a tired horse to refresh it. Today I do both. Feed and rub."

Maggie scarcely breathed as Falcon Hawk tended to his horse, watching for the horse's reaction and hoping that it would be quick. She silently prayed that Falcon Hawk was not too late—not only for the horse's sake, but for Falcon Hawk's. He loved his animals. They were a part of him. Not long ago he had lost his eagle. He had parted with Pronto, and now he might even lose this second horse.

It appeared as though it was Maggie's fault, for all of this had happened since she had become a part of Falcon Hawk's life. She only hoped that he did not begin thinking along those same lines.

He could grow to resent her.

Maggie jumped when the horse raised its head and flung it against Falcon Hawk, rubbing its soft muzzle up and down Falcon Hawk's arm.

Falcon Hawk ran his free hand along the horse's withers, then down its flanks. "You must get up now," he said softly to the horse. "It is now or never, my beautiful animal."

Maggie moved to her feet and stepped back when Falcon Hawk rose above the horse. The young brave who had been standing by, silently watching, gave Falcon Hawk a rope. Falcon Hawk draped it around his horse's neck and began slowly tugging on it.

Maggie clasped her hands behind her, watching her husband fighting for the animal's life. The horse's legs wobbled as it finally moved to its feet.

Falcon Hawk spoke into one of the horse's ears. "You must not only stand, but also walk," he said, again running his hands along his horse's withers. He gave Maggie a nod over his shoulder. "Come. We will walk together. We will give my horse the necessary exercise to get its strength back."

Maggie paled and placed her hands to her cheeks. "Are you certain that is best for the horse?" she asked, then realized that she was questioning her husband's judgment when he gave her a sour glance.

She didn't expect a further response. She tied a knot in her shawl beneath her chin and waited until the horse was bridled. Then she went to Falcon Hawk's side and took his hand.

She caught her breath when Falcon Hawk

tugged on the reins and the horse took a tentative step forward, his legs no less wobbly now than moments ago.

"The horse is going to fall back to the ground!" she cried, giving Falcon Hawk a nervous glance.

"There will be no fall," Falcon Hawk said, softly clucking to the horse. "This is a horse of spirit. My steed will fight for its life!"

Maggie walked ahead, then waited while Falcon Hawk coaxed the horse to follow him. Her eyes were wide and her heart thudded when the horse began moving slowly through the grass and through the open gate as the young brave opened it at Falcon Hawk's command.

The longer the horse was on its feet, the stronger it became. Soon Maggie and Falcon Hawk were walking briskly, the sunshine a gift today from the heavens as it warded off the chilly breeze that blew against Maggie's face and lifted her hair from her shoulders.

"You see?" Falcon Hawk said, pride in his voice. "The horse grows stronger with each breath it takes. The horse medicine has again saved a proud steed of the Arapaho!"

Maggie leaned against Falcon Hawk and put her arm around his waist, now able to forget her worries about the horse. Instead, she was enjoying the freedom that she felt taking this morning walk outside the village. She laughed as a covey of partridges were stirred from the knee-high grass, causing them to flutter aimlessly into the sky. She watched rabbits scatter in all directions. She enjoyed the beautiful bounce of the deer as they fled from the sound of the horse's hooves.

Maggie closed her eyes and enjoyed the splash of the air on her face, now warmed by the sun. She reveled in this special moment with Falcon Hawk, the time when he had saved his beloved horse. The wrong to the horse had been righted, yet Maggie could not totally cast aside her doubts about Soft Voice.

Her eyes were drawn open and her insides tightened at the sound of approaching horses. She shaded her eyes with a hand, peering intensely at those who were coming hard on their horses, soon discovering that they were Cheyenne. The closer they came, the more faces she recognized from the wedding celebration. She could not understand why they were returning, when in truth they should by now have been at their own village.

Falcon Hawk soon recognized the horsemen also, and it troubled him that they had felt the need to return. It was certain that they were headed for his village with a strange sort of determination!

Mentally he counted those among these Cheyenne who had come for the celebration. This particular band had not brought women. Because of the distance of their camp, there had been only a few braves who had accepted his invitation.

Realizing that they were all there, in the same number they had come for the celebration, heightened Falcon Hawk's curiosity. They had surely not come across trouble on their journey. They looked as well and as elaborately dressed as when they had sat in the circle of his friends.

Then why . . . ? He brought his horse to a stop

as the Cheyenne braves halted their mounts on each side of him.

"Why have you turned back toward my village of Arapaho?" Falcon Hawk asked, questioning each of them with a slow, sweeping gaze. "Do you return for a second celebration and sharing of food? Do you wish to linger again over a smoke from the sacred pipe?"

One of the braves nudged his horse closer to Falcon Hawk. In friendship he clasped one of his hands on Falcon Hawk's shoulder. "My friend, this Cheyenne brave brings you news that should fill your heart with joy," Brown Antelope said, smiling into Falcon Hawk's eyes.

"News?" Falcon Hawk said, forking an eyebrow. "About what?"

"About *who* should be your question," Brown Antelope said, a pleased smile on his face. "My friend, this band of Cheyenne stopped at a Ute camp for food and rest and a smoke. While there, someone familiar to me served me food. When I looked into her eyes, I saw *yours.* Falcon Hawk, your mother is alive and well. She lives with the Ute, as though one of them!"

Falcon Hawk gasped, feeling as though what he had heard was surely not true, yet hoping that it was.

His mother was alive!

Then his eyes wavered, knowing to which Indian camp she had wandered. The Ute. The longtime enemy of the Arapaho.

Suddenly it came to him that perhaps she had not wandered away at all, but instead had been captured.

"Tell me where this camp is, and how many Ute are there," Falcon Hawk said, his voice a hiss.

Maggie's insides rippled cold, fearing that her husband might soon become a warring chief and that she might lose him in the process! Her life could change all that quickly! And she could not fathom a future without this man who had blessed her with his heart!

She turned wavering eyes to him, afraid.

Chapter Twenty-Six

"I see anger in your eyes and hear it in your voice," Brown Antelope said, lowering his hand from Falcon Hawk's shoulder. "There is much I do not understand about how your mother came to be in the Ute camp. Tell me about it."

"When my father died some moons ago, my mother disappeared," Falcon Hawk said, taking all of his willpower not to ride off at once to get his mother back from those who had never been friendly with the Arapaho. But he knew that first he must reward his Cheyenne friends for bringing him this information. They would smoke the sacred pipe with him and share a meal.

Then he would go for his mother!

"So she wandered off?" Brown Antelope said, wonderingly. "This is why she is at the Ute camp?"

"I at first thought that she did," Falcon Hawk said, now feeling foolish for not having suspected something worse. "Now I feel that she may have been taken captive by the Ute."

"She did not behave as a captive or slave," Brown Antelope said, shrugging. "She mingled with the Ute as though she were one of them. When she was not serving guests food, as the other women did, she was sitting among the women her age, happily sewing and chatting."

"She is . . . happy?" Falcon Hawk said, his voice low and measured. He was puzzled over why his mother could live with the Ute as though a friend, even as one with them, when throughout her lifetime, warring was an ugly thing between the Arapaho and Ute!

"She did seem to be," Brown Antelope said, his eyes squinting into Falcon Hawk's. "Yet she is Arapaho. Why is that, Falcon Hawk?"

Not having answers, Falcon Hawk turned his eyes quickly away from Brown Antelope. He had never been as confused about anything and was finding it hard to accept it as true that his mother was happy with the Ute.

Yet the one thing that stayed foremost in his mind was that she was alive!

She was alive!

And he would go for her—soon.

He turned his eyes back to Brown Antelope. "Come. Come with me and my wife to my village," he said, trying to keep the battle he was feeling deeply hidden inside his heart, although he wished to emit a loud scream into the heavens about these tumultuous feelings that seemed to be drowning him!

He stiffened his arm around Maggie's waist,

having almost forgotten that she was standing beside him. She had not offered any conversation since the arrival of the Cheyenne.

And he understood. She was as confused as he. And surely as happy for him, to know that his mother was alive and would soon be there for them to become acquainted as mothers and daughters-in-law should.

"A rest and smoke will be good before we return to our homeward journey," Brown Antelope said, nodding. "And if you wish, Falcon Hawk, these Cheyenne warriors will join you as you go to council with the Ute over your mother's return to your care. The Ute are not our enemy, as they once were, and perhaps are still the Arapahos'. Our dialogue comes soft and friendly, not tight and warily and filled with suspicion."

Falcon Hawk thought for a moment, contemplating the offer which had been spoken from the heart. "It is with much humility that this chief accepts your offer," he then said, reaching over to clasp a hand with Brown Antelope.

Their hands parted. Falcon Hawk led the way as Brown Antelope rode beside him on his great white steed, the other Cheyenne dutifully following.

Maggie was feeling much better about things. She could breathe more easily about this task that lay before her husband. It was apparent that it could be done without war. With the Cheyenne riding into the Ute camp with Falcon Hawk, there would be a guaranteed peaceful council, instead of one that held threat within each of the words that might be spoken there.

Maggie turned quick eyes to Falcon Hawk. "Can I go with you?" she found herself saying before she had thought about the logic of her accompanying Falcon Hawk on such a mission. It was just something that she suddenly wanted to do. She felt that he needed her at this time when he was confused about his mother's actions.

And if Maggie were to become Arapaho in all thoughts and deeds, going with her husband into the camp of another Indian faction could be a valuable lesson to her. She no longer feared leaving Sky Eyes. She had two wonderful women who cared for the child, Thread Woman and Many Children Wife. In Maggie's absence, the child would never be without someone's love and attention.

Falcon Hawk was taken aback by Maggie's sudden request. He gazed into her eyes, touched to the very core of himself that she would leave Sky Eyes long enough to travel with him on this mission of the heart. He knew that leaving Sky Eyes was a great sacrifice to her for any amount of time. Now she was willing to be parted from her child for her husband's welfare.

"*Haa,*" he said thickly. "It is good that my wife will accompany this husband. My mother will need a woman's company on her return to her true people. Your sweetness will be good for my mother."

"Then I can go?" Maggie said, her eyes anxiously wide.

"*Haa,* you can go," Falcon Hawk said, smiling down at her. "But what of Sky Eyes?"

"So many spoil her, she will not even be aware

that her mother is gone," Maggie said, laughing softly.

She turned her eyes ahead, feeling the warm spreading of contentment within her. She did not see how she could be this lucky to have such a man as Falcon Hawk. He was a strong, noble man, a great leader of his people. There was great strength in his kind ways.

When she left Kansas City, bitter and hurt from having been raped by a vile man, it had been impossible for her to see a future that could be so different, so unique as this world that she had found among the Arapaho.

She wondered how on earth it was possible for Falcon Hawk's mother to want anything but the life that she had surely known among her true people, the Arapaho. Maggie was most anxious to see why she had gone into the camp of Falcon Hawk's enemy.

Everyone left their lodges in the Arapaho village when they realized that the Cheyenne had returned. Falcon Hawk put his horse in the corral and turned to face his people as Brown Antelope came to stand beside him on one side, while Maggie stood on his other.

Falcon Hawk began explaining about how Brown Antelope and his Cheyenne comrades had found his mother in the Ute camp. Maggie's heart ached when she heard Falcon Hawk's voice break when he said his mother's name, as though doing so, and knowing where she was, was tearing at his very soul.

She was glad when the explanations were over and the gathering became more lighthearted. A large fire was lit in the center of the village. Blankets were brought and spread, as well as food and drink.

Maggie went with Falcon Hawk into their lodge. As he lifted a leather pouch from his belongings, she gave Thread Woman a quick hug, then checked on Sky Eyes, who was awake in her cradle, kicking and cooing contentedly.

"Your mother has been found," Thread Woman said, as she went to Falcon Hawk and gazed up at him. "You will go for her soon?"

"First council with the Cheyenne who have brought the good news, a smoke, and then we leave for my mother," Falcon Hawk said. He held his leather pouch in his hand, then placed his free arm around Thread Woman's frail shoulders and drew her into his gentle embrace. "Soon your friend will sew and talk with you again."

Thread Woman emitted a throaty sob, then stepped away from Falcon Hawk and resumed her place beside the lodge fire. In her eyes there was much happiness. Her fingers worked more eagerly than usual with her needlework.

Again Maggie was made to feel breathless and afraid that the satchel of money might be found while Falcon Hawk went to the back of the lodge and began sorting through his belongings. She sighed with relief when he seemed to find what he was after. Once again she had been saved from his anger and hurt. This made her know that one day soon she should tell him her last unhappy secrets and get it over with. But now there were other things that needed tending to.

She turned to Thread Woman. "I'm going with

Falcon Hawk to the Ute camp," she said, kneeling down beside the elderly woman. "Can you stay longer? Can you stay with Sky Eyes until I return?"

Thread Woman idled her fingers for a moment as she looked up at Maggie, then reached a hand to Maggie's cheek. "You need never ask," she murmured. "Thread Woman is here always for you."

Maggie gave Thread Woman a long hug, then turned to Falcon Hawk again, marveling over what he had taken from the buckskin bag in which he had stored his warring gear. She watched as he took each item from his bag.

Although Falcon Hawk did not expect a fight with the Ute, he felt the need to dress with cautious readiness. The amulets that he chose today consisted of an armlet of badger skin, painted green and yellow inside, to which was attached a gopher skin, an owl-claw, several feathers, bells, some of the red seeds called southern berries, and a few skin fringes painted yellow with green ends.

The badger-skin wristband was always used to increase the speed of the horse that the warrior rode. The claw helped the wearer to seize the enemy. The motion of the feathers drove away the enemy, and the bells represented the noise of the fight. In case of need, one of the red seeds was broken off and chewed.

When Falcon Hawk came to Maggie, she left with her husband and joined the others outside. She sat down with him among the circle of Cheyenne and Arapaho. She watched Falcon

Hawk produce a pipe and stem from the leather pouch that he had brought from his tepee. She admired the pipe as he fitted it together. He had spoken of it to her, telling her that the pipe of the Arapaho was called *saeitca.*

The pipe was about two feet long and two inches in diameter. The stem was as thick as the bowl and was white and made of wood. The bowl was black and made of soapstone.

Falcon Hawk had taught her that the pipe was a sacred instrument in which was smoked the consecrated incense so pleasing to the Great Unseen Power. The stem was a wand through which the breath of the petitioner was drawn, in order that he might receive power within him from on high.

Because of this, the wand was decorated with objects that were believed helpful in attracting power. Symbolic paint was applied to the wood that it might resemble the sky and thereby please the Great Mystery.

As Falcon Hawk filled the pipe with tobacco, he treated it with much respect, reverence, and awe. After he lighted it, the pipe started its journey around the circle, the smoke drawn into their mouths through the consecrated stem used to make one think clearly. Today each participant took a draft of the smoke and blew it out slowly.

When the pipe had made the full circle and was handed to Maggie, she gave Falcon Hawk an uneasy glance. When he nodded, indicating that he wanted her also to partake in the smoke, she paled.

She motioned toward herself and mouthed the

word 'me?' to Falcon Hawk, so that only he would see her discomfort at the thought of smoking from a pipe, not only this pipe but any that might be offered her. In her culture no women dared smoke unless they were harlots.

Yet the more she hesitated and looked into Falcon Hawk's eyes, the more she knew what was most certainly expected of her.

She looked away from him and realized that she was the only woman among those who were sitting in the circle. Only now had she even become aware of this. If other women had been sitting in council, would they have been expected to smoke from the instrument? Or was it because she was the wife of their chief?

The Cheyenne who were sitting at her left side suddenly reached around her and gave the pipe to Falcon Hawk, but all the while Falcon Hawk's eyes did not leave Maggie.

She swallowed hard and watched as he held the pipe out before her, in a quiet insistence that she was most definitely expected to smoke from it.

She searched his eyes, glad to now see a quiet amusement enter their depths. She could even tell that he was finding it hard not to break into a smile!

She now realized that it was not imperative that she participate in the smoke, but that he was only testing to see if she would.

Quite determinedly, yet with her eyes dancing, Maggie took the pipe and thrust the stem between her lips. She gave Falcon Hawk a teasing smile as she took her first puff from the pipe. As the smoke entered her mouth, the smile was wiped almost as quickly from her face. Never had she tasted anything as vile! And as the smoke rolled back into her eyes and up her nose, she felt that she had never smelled anything so horrible!

She quickly withdrew the pipe, fighting back the urge to cough, for she was nearly choking on the rank smoke.

Falcon Hawk smiled at her as he eased the pipe from between her fingers. Maggie could feel her face reddening with the further need to cough, but held it back. She would not give Falcon Hawk the satisfaction of seeing how uncomfortable she was.

And for some time afterward, while the warriors began talking and eating, she sat with the inside of her throat burning and smarting, refusing even the tempting food that was set before her.

By the time the council was through, the bar of sunlight on the distant mountains had eaten far into the valley, and above it loomed a line of dark and threatening clouds.

Falcon Hawk rose to his feet and gazed at the sky. He kneaded his chin, then turned to Brown Antelope. "We will not let storms or darkness stop us," he said, clasping a hand on his Cheyenne friend's shoulder. "Do you ride with us still to the Ute camp?"

"No threatening cloud stops the Cheyenne from deeds that need to be done," Brown Antelope said, his jaw set.

Brown Antelope turned his gaze to Maggie. "She goes?" he said, forking an eyebrow.

"This woman is not only my wife, but my

best friend and companion," Falcon Hawk said, snaking an arm around Maggie's waist and drawing her next to him.

"It is good to have such faith in a woman," Brown Antelope said, nodding.

"She has given me every reason never to falter in my faith toward her," Falcon Hawk said.

He then grew somber. "We must delay leaving for a while longer," he said solemnly. "My thoughts go to my father. I must take time to take them to him, to pray at his waiting place."

Maggie turned and watched him go, understanding his need to be with his father, just as she felt so often the need to be with hers.

Her eyes sad and lonely for those times of so long ago when she had laughed and shared so much with her father, she watched Falcon Hawk leave at a brisk run, then walked away and waited for him at the corral.

Falcon Hawk ran swiftly from the village to a hill that overlooked the serenity of the river. There he slowed his pace and walked stolidly toward a scaffold that had been built high, beyond the reach of coyotes. A sadness engulfed him as he gazed upon the pelt-wrapped figure that lay upon this scaffolding.

His father had not been buried yet, awaiting the return of his wife to give his spirit rest. Yet the funeral rites had been performed, and quickly, for the souls of the dead were known to seek company for their long and final journey.

Falcon Hawk stopped beside the scaffold and reached his hands and eyes toward it. "My father, hear me," he cried. "This son soon brings your wife to say final good-byes. So than shall you rest, *neisa-na.* So then shall you be placed in the ground of our ancestors."

Falcon Hawk bowed his head and clasped a fist over his heart. "This son misses you, *neisa-na,*" he said throatily. "If you could but still be with me to see and know the love I have found in a woman. She is as pure and sweet as your woman, *neisa-na.*"

With that said and done, he ran from his father's waiting place and soon met the others at the corral. He sorted through the animals and chose a gentle mare for his woman.

Several young braves came and attentively saddled the horse for Maggie. Another brought a long buckskin cape.

"To wear if it storms," one of the others explained as the cape was laid over Maggie's arm.

Maggie gazed heavenward, her insides cold as she watched the zigzag of lightning forking over the heavens, remembering another storm and the fire that had followed. Never would she ever forget those savage embers!

"Let us go now," Falcon Hawk said, lifting her into her saddle.

Maggie reached down and touched his face. "When we return, it will be with your mother," she murmured. "I'm so happy for you, my darling. So happy."

He stepped over to his horse and swung himself into his saddle. When he lifted his reins and nudged the flanks of his horse with his moccasined heels, she followed his lead and was soon riding beside him into the face of the storm as the clouds rumbled toward them.

Frank Harper lay flat on the ground, his face barely exposed over the edge of the cliff. He watched the Cheyenne leave with Falcon Hawk, Margaret June, and many Arapaho warriors.

Earlier, he had seen the Cheyenne return to the village. He had watched the passing of the pipe. His eyebrows had gone up in surprise when he saw Margaret June place the pipe to her lips and partake in the smoke.

Now he was just as puzzled when he saw her riding away with the Cheyenne and Arapaho.

"Where the hell are they going now?" he grumbled, then cast his eyes heavenward when lightning zigzagged across the darkening sky.

He looked over his shoulder at the cave he had found behind a cover of bushes and decided that it was best to take shelter before the storm hit in its fury.

A fire. He needed a fire to ward of the chill. He could build a fire in the cave. The smoke would spread into the rain and become invisible. He had only a few supplies left that could be eaten without being cooked. Soon he would have to depend on catching game and therein lay the chance of being caught by the Arapaho.

"I can't delay gettin' answers from that bitch for much longer," he whispered to himself as he quickly gathered wood for a fire. "When she returns. Yes, when she returns."

As he saw it he was running out of tomorrows.

Chapter Twenty-Seven

Several of Falcon Hawk's warriors, accompanied by Brown Antelope, broke away from the others and rode on ahead to the Ute Camp with gifts of peace. The worst of the storm was hanging longer over the mountains than had been expected, but the rain was beginning to fall in blinding sheets where the entourage of Arapaho and Cheyenne traveled.

Falcon Hawk wheeled his horse to a stop and grabbed Maggie's reins. "You must return home," he shouted above the whine of the wind, securing his hooded buckskin cape as he tied its thongs at his throat. "There is no need to endanger your health. Return to our daughter. Sit by the fire and be warm."

Maggie huddled beneath her own buckskin cape, her face and hands the only parts of her body that were exposed to the cold rain. "But I wanted to go with you," she shouted back. "I won't become ill. Don't you remember? I withstood the ravages of that other terrible storm on our way to your village."

"*Then* you were not my wife, and I knew not that you were with child," Falcon Hawk said, already motioning toward two of his warriors in a silent command to come to him. "Nor did either of us have a choice. There was no place to take shelter. This time, you are only a short ride back to the village. There you can have shelter and warmth. Go now. My warriors will see you safely home."

Maggie's thoughts went to Sky Eyes and the importance of being able to nurse from her mother's breasts, realizing that should Maggie become ill, the child would once again be kept from her, to feed solely from Many Children Wife's breasts.

"Yes," she said somberly, wiping sprays of rain from her face. "You are right. I will do as you say. I'll return to the warmth of our lodge."

"It is good that you see the wisdom in that decision," Falcon Hawk said, leaning over to brush her lips with a kiss. "I shall return home soon. The Ute camp is not that far and we should be back soon after daybreak tomorrow."

"I shall wait anxiously for your return," Maggie said, wheeling her horse around in the direction of the village. She nudged her moccasined heels into the flanks of her horse and rode away from Falcon Hawk, accompanied on each side by an Arapaho warrior.

She looked from one to the other. "It isn't necessary that you come with me," she shouted into the wind. "Go. Ride with Falcon Hawk. This mission he is on is important. He must be sure to have enough backing should the Ute decide not to allow him to take his mother from their camp."

"What you say is true, but we do as our chief says," one of the warriors said, the other affirming this with a determined nod.

Maggie gazed at them a moment longer, then ducked her head low over the horse, trying to fend off as much rain as she could as it began rolling from the heavens in a torrent. When she caught first sight of the tepees ahead, she sighed with relief.

She urged her horse into a hard gallop, imagining the warmth of the fire and the sweet feel of her child snuggled against her breast.

Frank was drawn from the shelter of the cave when he heard the approach of horses below. Grabbing a leather poncho and slipping it over his head, he left the cave. Leaning into the rain and squinting as it stung his flesh, he watched the three horsemen arriving at the village. He continued watching, his heart skipping an anxious beat when he realized that one of those riders was Margaret June! The two Arapaho warriors with her rode with her to her tepee, then took her horse and went to the corral as she fled inside her lodge.

"Well, I'll be damned," Frank said, kneading his chin. "She's come back. She'll be without his protection."

His eyes narrowed angrily when he caught sight of the Arapaho warriors running into the village, soon disappearing into their own lodges. Although they were lost from sight, that did not mean they would not hear someone coming into the village.

No, he concluded. He still had to use the same plan that he had thought up earlier. He had watched the women coming and going from the village, going either to the river for water or to the scattering of trees nearby to gather herbs or firewood. If not for the storm, now would be a perfect time to watch for a woman and abduct her. With Falcon Hawk gone, his plan would work without fail!

"What a hell of a time to rain!" he said aloud, turning on a booted heel and stamping back inside the cave.

Tossing the wet poncho aside, he sat down on a blanket beside the fire, rubbing his hands over the flames. "It can't rain forever," he whispered, chuckling.

Shivering, Maggie tossed off her wet cape. Thread Woman rose to her feet, took Maggie's hands, and began rubbing them briskly, sending the warmth from her body into Maggie's.

"You have returned home?" Thread Woman said, looking with question into Maggie's eyes. "The storm forced you to return?"

"Yes, the storm," Maggie said, frowning. "I so badly wanted to go with Falcon Hawk. He needs me. Yet, worrying about the danger of my becoming too chilled in the rain, he told me to return home."

Thread Woman placed a hand to Maggie's elbow and led her to the fire. "Warm yourself, my child," she murmured, now smoothing some wet locks of Maggie's hair back from her brow. She nodded toward a pot of soup that she had just had time to make before Maggie returned. "The soup is simmering. Eat. It will warm your insides."

Maggie knelt before the fire, rubbing her hands over the flames. "You are always so kind," she said as Thread Woman ladled some soup into a wooden bowl. "It will be so wonderful to watch my daughter grow to love you as I do. She will be blessed with your presence. She already is."

Maggie took the soup, reveling in the warmth of the bowl against the flesh of her fingers. When Thread Woman gave her a spoon, Maggie eagerly sipped the soup between her lips, feeling the warmth travel downward to warm her throughout.

"Sky Eyes still sleeps," Thread Woman said. "And you will need to rest yourself." She cackled as she lifted her needlework from the floor. "This old woman will go to her own lodge and rest."

Maggie cast a worried glance up at Thread Woman. "You will catch a chill if you leave now," she said, hating the thought of this lovely woman coming down with a cold that could go easily into pneumonia with someone of her age. It had happened to Maggie's grandmother many years ago. She had watched her grandmother struggle for her very last breaths before dying from sheer exhaustion from the ailment.

"Lean your ears toward the lodge covering," Thread Woman said, smiling down at Maggie. "Do you not hear it? Silence. The rain does not mark its tattoos on the lodge any longer. It is either too fine a mist, or it has stopped. Either way, it is not enough to keep this old lady from going to her own dwelling."

Loving Thread Woman's independence, Maggie laughed softly. "No, I doubt that it would," she said.

"You are now safely home and warmed," Thread Woman said, leaning a kiss to Maggie's brow. "Falcon Hawk will return as safe and as well, and very happy. His mother will be with him. This is something that makes Thread Woman very happy also."

Thread Woman then went away from Maggie and left the lodge. Maggie set her empty bowl aside and stared aimlessly into the fire. "Yes, *I'm* safe, but what of Falcon Hawk?" she whispered, shivering at the thought of the Ute being unfriendly toward her chief and his warriors. "I wish you were here, darling, just as safe as I, in our lodge."

Frank stepped from the cave and stretched his arms over his head, a broad smile etched across his face. "It's stopped," he said to himself. "The damn rain's stopped."

He went to the very edge of the butte and stared down at the Arapaho village, singling Maggie's lodge out from the rest, then looked slowly toward the river and the cluster of trees that sat back from the village.

Now all he had to wait for was a dumb squaw wandering away from the village to set his plan into motion. He hoped he would see one before

Falcon Hawk returned. That was the only way he could make his plan work.

He sauntered back inside the cave and squatted beside the fire. He doubted any squaw would go wandering from her lodge this late in the afternoon, or in the dampness. Tomorrow, when the sun rose and everyone had to resume their chores—*then* he would capture him a squaw!

Falcon Hawk yanked his wet cape off and spread it across the saddle in front of him to dry as the sun began squinting from behind the white clouds that had replaced the dark, bulbous clouds of only moments ago. Steam rose from the ground on all sides of him. Small animals came out of hiding and scattered as the horses thundered across the straight stretch of land. Birds soared with open wing overhead, the sun drying them after they had been soaked during the storm.

Falcon Hawk's hair lifted and fluttered in the breeze as he sent his horse into a harder gallop. The day was almost gone, night only a few heartbeats away. But he would reach the Ute village soon. He had not slowed his speed of travel even during the heaviest part of the storm.

His heart was hammering at the thought of soon seeing his mother. Yet the wonder of why she was there with the Ute muted his happiness.

But soon he would have the answer.

He would be reunited with his mother! He would return her to her true people! Ah, but then would not his life be complete?

This one last blessing from the Great Unseen

Power seemed a miracle, one that Falcon Hawk would give thanks for until his last breath whispered across his lips.

When several horsemen came into sight, riding hard toward Falcon Hawk, he recognized Brown Antelope and Falcon Hawk's own Arapaho warriors. His gut twisted, fearing what news they might be bringing to him.

He hurried onward and met their approach, bringing his steed to a halt as he reached them.

"What news do you have of my mother?" Falcon Hawk said, gazing from man to man.

Blazing Arrow nudged his horse closer to Falcon Hawk's, in his eyes a deep concern. "She is well," he said. "But, Falcon Hawk, when I approached her, she did not come to me. She did not know me!"

So taken aback by this was he that Falcon Hawk gasped and he teetered on his horse. "You say she did not know you?" he asked incredulously. "How can that be? You and I have been friends since we were young braves. You were in my mother's lodge almost as much as I. She knew you well, Blazing Arrow. She must know you *now*."

Brown Antelope edged his horse to the other side of Falcon Hawk's. "She knows no one," he said, clasping a hand to Falcon Hawk's shoulder. "And I questioned Chief Scar Hand. He explained that your mother was found by one of his braves, wandering along a riverbed. He questioned her then. She was blank of mind. Chief Scar Hand's brave took your mother to his village. There they welcomed her and cared for her."

Falcon Hawk shook his head slowly back and

forth. "It is true that Chief Scar Hand would not know my mother," he said. "He was never invited as a guest into our village. This is why he allowed her to stay instead of bringing her to her true people. He knew not to whom she belonged!"

"That is so," Brown Antelope said, nodding.

Falcon Hawk looked quickly up at Brown Antelope. "Did Chief Scar Hand receive the gifts with an open heart?" he asked, his voice breaking. "It is with an open heart that we will be received into his village? Is he willing to give my mother up to Falcon Hawk, her son?"

"Without question," Brown Antelope said, again nodding. "His warriors are not thirsty for war. They will not wave their bows and rifles as you approach their camp. They will be lowered to their sides in a gesture of welcome."

"Is this to say that peace might be finally achieved between Arapaho and Ute?" Falcon Hawk said, finding it hard to think this might actually happen, much less speak it aloud.

"Because of your mother, yes, I see that this has happened," Brown Antelope said, easing his hand from Falcon Hawk's shoulder. "They await our arrival. Your mother will be ready to depart with you."

"There will be no need to sit in council and smoke?" Falcon Hawk said.

"Not unless it is your desire to do so," Brown Antelope said, taking his reins and nudging his horse's flanks as Falcon Hawk rode in a slow lope onward.

"My deepest desire is to get my mother back to her people, perhaps then smoke later with the

Ute," Falcon Hawk said, yet thinking that to pass by the opportunity to smoke the peace pipe now with the Ute might be to cause the hatred to build again between them and Falcon Hawk's people.

"Chief Scar Hand will understand," Brown Antelope said, nodding. "He also has a mother."

Falcon Hawk urged his horse into a hard gallop across the land, then drew a tight rein when he came to the outskirts of the Ute camp, where their lodges looked like dark, hovering shadows against the backdrop of the mountains as the evening passed into night.

Falcon Hawk dismounted and led his horse into the village by foot. The farther he went, the more people came out of their lodges, silently watching.

Then he caught his first sight of his mother as she stood outlined against the bright, roaring outdoor fire. His heart thudding like a hammer inside his chest, he dropped the horse's reins and broke into a mad run.

Forgetting that she had lost her memory, he went ahead and swept her into his arms, reveling in the familiar smell and feel of her, glad to know that during her strange sickness she had not lost any weight. She was still as soft and fleshy in his arms as before. She was still as clinging, as before.

Clinging? Falcon Hawk realized with a sudden knowledge that she *was* clinging to him as though she knew him! And she *was* saying his name over and over again! She did know him!

Falcon Hawk eased away from her and held her at arm's length. *"Ne-ina?"* he said, his voice breaking. "It is I, Falcon Hawk. You do remember this son who loves you so much?"

Tears rolled down Pure Heart's cheeks. She reached a hand to Falcon Hawk's cheek and caressed it. "*Ne-ina,* how would I not know my son?" she murmured, then again clung to him. "Until I saw you, my mind was blank of the past. But oh, Falcon Hawk, one look at you and everything snapped into place. Falcon Hawk, take me home. Please take me home. I have yet to visit my husband's grave."

Tears rolled from Falcon Hawk's eyes. He did not care that anyone who saw him might think he had become as timid as a mourning dove. His happiness was too complete not to cry!

"*Haa, ne-ina,* this son will take you home," he whispered into her ear. "This son will take you to your husband's grave. And this son will take you to meet your daughter-in-law."

Pure Heart eased from his embrace. "You say that this mother now has a daughter-in-law?" she said, looking up at him with wide, dark eyes.

"*Haa,* that is so," Falcon Hawk said, smiling down at her. "And you will love her as much as I."

"You have spoken vows with Soft Voice?" Pure Heart said, hope in her eyes.

"No. Not Soft Voice. Another woman has filled my life with joy," Falcon Hawk said softly.

"Who is this woman?" Pure Heart said somberly, disappointed by his decision.

"You shall soon see, Mother," Falcon Hawk said, squaring his shoulders proudly. "You shall soon see."

"I have missed so much," Pure Heart said, casting her eyes downward. "Oh, so very much."

"Not anything that can't be made up to you," Falcon Hawk said, taking her hands in his. He could hardly wait to return home so that the two special women in his life could become acquainted. He had never thought it would happen.

Smiling, he turned and welcomed Chief Scar Hand with a hug, finding it hard to believe that he was doing such a thing with one who had been an enemy as long as he was old—thirty winters.

"Hahou," Falcon Hawk said thickly as he stepped back from Chief Scar Hand. "Thank you for taking care of my mother during her time of lapse of memory. It is with a humble heart that I extend to you an invitation to come to my village and enter as a friend, not as an enemy. We will smoke the pipe of peace there? It is my desire to take my mother home now, and smoke later. Would a council of peace and harmony later meet with your approval?"

"It is the same as done, my friend," Chief Scar Hand said, over his heart making the sign of friendship with his fingers.

Falcon Hawk nodded, then sighed happily as he swept his arm around his mother's waist and led her toward his horse. Everything in his life seemed now well. He could not think of anything that might cause his world to turn ugly and questionable again!

Chapter Twenty-Eight

A sense of nausea had awakened Soft Voice with a start. As she leaned up on one elbow, the feeling worsened. She could even feel a bitter bile rising up into her throat.

Not wanting to awaken Long Hair, especially not to the sound of her retching, Soft Voice eased quietly from the bed and slipped her loose buckskin smock over her head, then went barefoot into the early dawning of a new day. As the nauseous feeling swept over her again, Soft Voice covered her mouth with her hand and began running through the village toward the shine of the river. She knew that she could not hold it back much longer. She was dizzy now, her throat burning as the bitterness rose and fell and rose again.

When she finally reached the river, she fell to her knees and allowed the bile to splash from her mouth into the water. She clung to her abdomen as she retched, over and over again, until finally no more was there to spill from inside her.

Feeling weak and lightheaded, Soft Voice moved away from the soiled water to find comfort in that which was clear and refreshing as she splashed it onto her face. She even took a swallow of the water from her cupped hands, then took more into her mouth and splashed it into all of its corners, finally removing any debris that may have been left there to attest to this strange bout of sickness this morning.

Settling down on her haunches on a cushion of moss beside the river, Soft Voice held her face in her hands and slowly rocked back and forth. Still too lightheaded to return to Long Hair's lodge and too weak to take her morning bath in the river, she squatted there for a while longer. She must get this past her. Today Falcon Hawk would be returning with his mother! Soft Voice wanted to see Pure Heart so that she herself could witness that the woman who would have been her mother-in-law was truly all right.

Although Soft Voice now knew that she could never be anything special to Pure Heart, she did not admire Falcon Hawk's mother any less. This woman had been most kind to Soft Voice. She had even favored Soft Voice over the other women in the village to be the wife of her son.

"Nothing is as she or I wanted," Soft Voice whispered to herself, tears falling from her eyes. "I did love him so, Pure Heart. Your son was everything to me. Now I have Long Hair. He is a dear, sweet man, but he is not Falcon Hawk. How I still wish that your son were mine!"

Lost so deeply in hurtful thoughts, Soft Voice had not heard the muffled footsteps behind her. And when a hand moved quickly around and fingers locked over her mouth, stifling any scream that she tried to release from the terrified depths of herself, she almost fainted from the fright.

Her eyes widened over this hand that was imprisoning her mouth when she felt the very identifiable tip of a knife being thrust against her back, making her too afraid to try to fight back.

"Don't try anything, squaw," Frank said in a snarl. "Cooperate with me, or you're dead."

Frank saw her weak nod, showing that she understood the danger that he posed to her. "If you so much as make a sound, you won't last long enough to realize it was the knife that took your life from you," he warned.

When he thought that she was in full understanding of what he said, Frank slowly eased his hand from her mouth, then took her by a wrist and turned her to face him.

Soft Voice's fear showed on her face as she found herself gazing into blue eyes that seemed so cold—so passionless. She scarcely breathed as the stranger began slowly moving the flat side of the knife along the smooth, beautiful plane of her face.

"Now ain't you a pretty one?" Frank said, chuckling. "Even prettier than Margaret June. If I didn't have business on my mind, I'd have a time wrestling you to the ground." His free hand slipped quickly up her dress, soon cupping the muff of her hair at the juncture of her thighs, making her groan with disgust.

"Warm and soft," Frank said, running his fingers over her furry mound, purposely seeking the cleft that he found when he parted the fronds of hair.

Soft Voice flinched and her eyes grew narrowly angry when he began rubbing his thumb over the cleft that normally gave her much pleasure when touched. But this man's fingers there made her feel ill all over again.

No matter if the knife was still threateningly close, Soft Voice moved quickly away from Frank, drew her dress tightly down, and held it in place.

"A hellion, are you?" Frank said, laughing. "I disgust you, do I? Well, squaw, that don't matter none to me. And don't worry about me raping you. I've got more important things on my mind this morning."

Soft Voice sighed with relief. "If you did not come to rape me, then why are you here, interrupting Soft Voice's morning?" she asked warily. She fought back another wave of nausea, not wanting to humiliate herself in front of this stranger, evil, vile man that he was. It was humiliation enough to even be in his presence, held captive.

She was beginning to wonder about her nausea, realizing that it could be the first sign of pregnancy. The thought of having a child out of her few times of lovemaking with Long Hair gave her more cause to be careful not to antagonize this stranger. She must do as he said or she would never be given the chance to bear this child to rival Falcon Hawk's children.

That is, if she was truly pregnant, she quickly thought to herself, hoping that she was. For so many reasons she needed such a child born from the peace that she had found with Long Hair. Not only would the child seal their bond, but also prove his virility to his people!

Yes, she did see the importance in that, wanting this man who allowed her to warm his blankets each night to be envied by others who were not as fortunate to have a child in their later years of life.

"It's not so much that I chose you deliberately to set my plan in motion," Frank said, holding the knife to his side. "But you are the first squaw to happen along this morning. So you are selected to be the one to help me."

"What is it that you wish for Soft Voice to do?" Soft Voice said, subconsciously laying a hand protectively over her abdomen, silently praying to the Great Unseen Power that a child was growing within, in her womb.

"Squaw, it's not what I wish," Frank said, taking a threatening step closer. "It's what you are going to do."

"Is it against my people that you wish me to do this thing?" Soft Voice said, her voice guarded.

"No, not against your people," Frank said, seeing confusion enter her eyes. "It's the white woman in the village who interests me," he quickly added. "Only the white woman."

Soft Voice's eyes widened and her heartbeat quickened. "Maggie?" she said softly. "The one who is now called Panther Eyes by my people?"

"Panther Eyes?" Frank said, arching an eyebrow, then he laughed throatily. "Yes. Panther Eyes."

"What about her?" Soft Voice said, her heart racing, perhaps seeing an ally in this white man. "What am I to do?"

"You've got to find a way to bring her to me," Frank said, lifting her chin with a forefinger. "Do you understand? Go and get her and make sure no one sees you do it. And you can't take long. Soon everyone in your village will be wandering around, doing their chores. I don't want them to see me. Do you understand?"

"*Aa*—yes," Soft Voice said, nodding her head anxiously. "But why do you want her?"

"Don't ask questions," Frank said, bodily turning her and heading her in the direction of the village. "Go now. Bring her here. Find a way to get her to do it without making her aware that I'm here. And hurry. Falcon Hawk could return anytime."

Soft Voice nodded and began walking briskly away, then stopped and turned to face him with questioning eyes. "And the baby?" she asked. "Do you also want the baby?"

Frank kneaded his chin. "Hers?" he said.

"*Aa,*" Soft Voice said, her heart pounding in her eagerness to rid herself not only of Maggie, but also of the white child Falcon Hawk had taken in as his own.

"Is the child the Injun's?" Frank said, thrusting his knife back inside its sheath.

Soft Voice's jaw tightened at his reference to "Injuns." But casting her aversions aside for the sake of her own needs, she gave him a pensive stare. "In some ways yes," she murmured. "In some ways, no."

"What the hell is that supposed to mean?" Frank said, nervously raking his fingers through his hair.

"You shall see," Soft Voice said, then turned and broke into a run toward the village. Her mind was active, searching for ways to get Maggie from the lodge, as well as the child. Maggie was probably still asleep, unless she had been drawn awake to give the child its early feeding.

"How can I get her to leave with me without drawing suspicion from her?" Soft Voice whispered to herself as she came into the outer fringes of the village. To her relief, there was still no one moving about outside. The sun had not yet come from behind the mountains to send its glow down the smoke holes of the tepees.

"Peyote," Soft Voice said, stopping suddenly as the thought sprang to her. "I shall prepare a drink with peyote in it for Maggie. If she is asleep, I shall force it down her throat before she has a chance to realize what is happening. If she is awake, I shall offer her a drink from a cup."

Going to the place where she had hidden the rest of the peyote in a leather pouch beneath a rock after having fed Falcon Hawk's horse enough to cause him to become ill, Soft Voice shook several hard buttons of peyote into her hand and returned the pouch back to its hiding place.

Spreading the skirt of her smock across the ground, she lay the peyote buttons there and began crushing them with a rock until all that remained was some fine, loose powder. Scraping this powder into the palm of her left hand, she rose to her feet and went to Maggie's tepee.

Outside the entrance flap, Soft Voice leaned an ear close and listened for any sounds inside the lodge. When she heard none, she crept on inside. Smiling wickedly, she stood over Maggie's bed, finding her in a deep sleep on her back.

Soft Voice went to the leather pouch that hung just inside the lodge, where the drinking water was stored, and poured a half cup full. Then she sprinkled the powdered peyote into the cup and turned and moved stealthily back to Maggie's bed.

Easing herself onto the bed beside Maggie, Soft Voice was careful not to jar it, which might awaken Maggie and reveal Soft Voice ready to perform mischief on her.

After she was securely on the bed, she leaned over Maggie's face and began pouring the liquid into Maggie's mouth.

When Maggie's eyes popped open and she began choking and trying to get up, Soft Voice sat down upon her, pinched Maggie's nose closed with one hand, and finished pouring the rest of the drugged liquid into Maggie's unwilling mouth.

Maggie coughed and sputtered. She pushed at Soft Voice, her eyes wild as she felt her head beginning a strange sort of spinning. Close to unconsciousness, she closed her eyes and went limp.

Soft Voice would not allow Maggie to drift completely off. It was necessary for Maggie to walk, for Soft Voice to be able to get her to the white man. And Soft Voice's one arm needed to be empty so that she could carry Sky Eyes. It did not seem possible that she was going to be rid of both

Maggie and Sky Eyes at the same time! Her heart pounded at the prospect of being the one to tell Falcon Hawk, upon his return, that his wife and child were gone—surely abducted in their sleep, she would say.

Leaving Maggie lying somewhere between sleep and consciousness, Soft Voice went to Sky Eyes and wrapped her securely in a blanket, then lifted her up into her arms. After securing her safely in the crook of her left arm, she went back to Maggie and gave her a slight shake.

Maggie's eyes opened and she smiled drunkenly up at Soft Voice. "Good morning," she said, her voice slurred. Her eyes revealed a blankness.

"Come with me," Soft Voice said, taking one of Maggie's hands, urging her to her feet. "Take a walk with me. It is a pretty day, Panther Eyes."

"Pretty . . . day . . . ?" Maggie stammered, rising shakily to her feet. She nodded, her head bobbing. "*Aa*, pretty. Everything is pretty."

Soft Voice smiled wickedly at Maggie. "Very," she said, laughing beneath her breath. "Just you wait and see just how pretty it is."

Maggie trailed along beside Soft Voice, not even aware that Soft Voice had Sky Eyes, nor that Sky Eyes was just beginning to whimper from hunger. In a daze, her eyes glassy, she circled behind her lodge and went toward the river.

When they got to the cluster of trees where Frank was waiting, Maggie did not even see him, much less recognize him. She could not hold her eyes open any longer. She crumpled to the ground at his feet, slipping into a black void of unconsciousness.

Frank nudged her with the toe of his boot. He laughed throatily, then gave Soft Voice a crooked smile. "Damn if you didn't come through for me quicker than I thought you could," he said. He stepped over Maggie and took the child from Soft Voice's arms. "Let me take a look at this one."

Sky Eyes began wailing hungrily as Frank unfolded the blanket from around her face. He forked an eyebrow, surprised to find that the child had all white features. "Why, she ain't Injun at all," he said, giving Soft Voice a questioning look.

"In appearance she is white," Soft Voice explained. "But otherwise she is being taught to be everything Arapaho."

Frank shifted his gaze to Maggie. "Even she's dressed like a squaw," he said. He shrugged aimlessly. "But if she's married to an Injun, I guess she has to act like one."

"Soft Voice can return to her lodge now?" she dared to ask.

"Not so fast," Frank said, giving her a dark stare.

Soft Voice's heart skipped a beat. "After I helped you, you are still going to harm me?" she said, backing away from him.

"Naw, nothing like that," Frank reassured. "I just need you for one more chore."

"What is that?" Soft Voice said, tensing.

"You've got to help me get Maggie and the child to my hideout," he said. "Then you can go. You know that if you tell anyone about me, I'll find a way to stick you with the knife so that you don't tell anyone anything anymore."

"Soft Voice glad to be rid of white woman and

child," she said, lifting her chin proudly. "Never will Soft Voice tell where they went, or with whom. Soft Voice glad she is gone. She has brought nothing but trouble into my life."

"That'a girl," Frank said. He went to Soft Voice and gave her the child. "You carry the child. I'll carry Maggie. And then you can return to your lodge like nothin' ever happened."

Soft Voice rocked Sky Eyes slowly back and forth, fearing her wails might awaken someone. She looked nervously over her shoulder, glad to see that there still were no stirrings in the village.

Then she followed Frank, even as he climbed the high butte that was far back from the village.

After Maggie and Sky Eyes were laid on blankets beside a small fire inside the cave, Frank placed a hand on Soft Voice's waist and yanked her against him.

"I ought to show you how a white man makes love, but time don't allow it," he said, but still crushed his mouth to her lips, giving her a fiery kiss.

Soft Voice squirmed free and glared up at him, wiping her mouth clean with the back of her hand.

Then she turned and ran from the cave, not stopping until she was back inside the safety of Long Hair's lodge, where he still slept as soundly as a baby.

Breathing hard, yet trying not to awaken him, she stripped herself of her clothes and climbed into bed, cuddling up against him. Finding so many reasons to be happy this morning, she closed her eyes and snuggled even more closely into the shape of Long Hair's back. She had rid her life of Maggie and the white child and just perhaps she was bringing a life into the world!

If the child was a son, how it would be revered by all Arapaho, for it would be the son of a man who was once chief, a leader still, noble and grand in every way!

"A son," she whispered, slipping a hand down to her abdomen. "A son . . ."

Chapter Twenty-Nine

Frank laid the child aside, its wails now reaching nerve-racking levels. He kept glancing toward the entrance of the cave, afraid that someone might happen by and hear the crying. There were two ways of silencing the baby. He could smother her or he could see that she was fed. He shuddered at the thought of taking the life of a child, so knew that he must find a way to feed her.

"Margaret June," he whispered, gazing down at the woman whose body still inflamed his insides at the memory of their brief encounter. He had hoped that she would participate and enjoy his lovemaking. Instead, it had turned out to be something that she could not even tolerate.

Enraged, he had taken her anyway, brusquely, angrily. . . .

His eyes flashing, his jaw set, Frank reached down for his canteen of water. Smiling crookedly, he screwed the lid off the canteen, stood over Maggie, and slowly poured the water onto her face. Anything to get her awake, to silence the child.

And *then?*

He would find out about the money.

Maggie was jerked quickly awake by the coldness of the water. Sputtering, she wiped at her face. The water stung as it rolled up her nose and choked her as it splashed into her mouth.

Frank tossed the canteen aside. He knelt over Maggie and jerked her head up from the ground. He met her eye to eye as she wiped the last of the water from her eyes and came slowly out of her lethargic state.

"Margaret June, Margaret June," Frank droned mockingly. "Look at you. Just look at you. If you had stayed with me in Kansas City, you'd be dressed in the finest silk and satin gowns and living in grand style. But here you are, living among savages—a savage yourself, it seems."

Maggie gazed with disbelief up at him as her senses began to return, numb from what had happened and from seeing herself at the mercy of the same man who had taken advantage of her innocence those many months ago.

"Frank," she gasped, paling. "Lord, Frank. You found me."

She tried to rise from the ground, but her knees were still too weak. In flashes, her memory was returning to her. She recalled Soft Voice standing over her in her lodge, forcing her to drink some vile liquid. She could recall trying to fight Soft Voice off, but the lethargy had taken hold of her too quickly.

Sky Eyes had stopped crying for a moment or two, but now again burst into loud, hungry wails, sending Maggie's heart into a tailspin of fear and despair. Her daughter had also been abducted.

Knowing that her daughter's life was in danger gave Maggie the strength to jerk herself away from Frank. Shakily she rose to her feet. Her eyes did not have to search far for her child. Sky Eyes's cries led her right to her.

"Feed that damn brat and shut her up," Frank said, helping Maggie over to Sky Eyes. "Then you and I have some business to discuss."

"I have nothing to discuss with you," Maggie said, giving him a venomous glance. "I fled you once. I shall again. And heaven help Soft Voice when I tell Falcon Hawk what she did to me, and—and to Sky Eyes."

"I don't care one ounce what happens to that pretty Injun that brought you and the child to me," Frank said, shrugging. "All's I want is the money you stole from me. And, pretty lady, I intend to *have* it."

Maggie bent down and swept Sky Eyes into her arms, then sat down beside the fire. She reached for a blanket and covered her breast area before uncovering her breast, not wanting Frank to see any part of her anatomy that might arouse his hunger for her again.

Yet rape was not his prime need now. Greed had led him from Kansas City. He had traveled many miles, perhaps even going through hardships, to find her and the money. And it would suit her just fine to give him the money if it meant that she would never have to think about him again. He would have the money. She would have peace of mind.

Placing Sky Eyes's lips to her breast, Maggie stared at Frank where he knelt on the other side of the fire from her, his eyes watching the child feeding.

"Throw aside the damn blanket so's I can see better," Frank said, glowering over at Maggie. "Let me see your breast, Margaret June, and how the child feeds from it."

"You've seen my breasts once, but never again," Maggie said in a low hiss. "And if you want to see a child feed so badly, why don't you settle down and marry and have a child of your own?"

Her words came back to haunt her the minute she said them, and she wished that she could take them back. She could tell by the way he studied the child that he might be counting the months since their sexual encounter and realizing that he need not marry to have a child. He would know that he had already fathered one!

She was relieved when he shrugged his shoulders, then gave her a glowering stare. "Where's the damn money, Margaret June?" he said, his voice a low, threatening hiss.

She hated with all of her heart to give in to this man's demands. She had taken what was rightfully hers in Kansas City. She had felt that having the money was her only way to overcome what Frank had done not only to her, but to her father as well.

But she had no choice now but to give it back to him. She could not allow Frank Harper to ruin her daughter's life.

For that reason, it was not going to be all that hard to hand the satchel of money over to Frank, and truthfully, she would be glad to be rid of it. Its threat lay over her like a dark cloud, for never did she want to tell Falcon Hawk about having kept this secret from him.

"I've buried the money," she said, giving Frank a stubborn stare.

"Where?" Frank said. "Tell me where it is. I'll go get it."

"You can have it only if I'm allowed to go for it," Maggie said warily. "But I must first get my daughter to safety."

"She'll stay with me," Frank snarled, his eyes narrowing. "She's my guarantee that you'll return with the money instead of a pack of Injuns."

"I won't agree to those terms," Maggie said stiffly.

"You don't have any choice, as I see it," Frank said, kneading his chin. "Where is it, Margaret June? Where's the money?"

"In . . . my lodge," she gulped out. "Buried in my lodge."

"Well, what are you waiting for?" Frank said, gesturing with a hand. "Time's a wastin'. And don't allow anyone to see you go to your lodge to get the money." He turned his cold, blue eyes to her. "I don't want no interferences. Do you understand? This savage you are living with. I know he's gone. Should he return while you are getting the money, lie. Tell him anything that will get you back here with my money."

Frank rose to his full height and went to kneel down beside Maggie. In a flash he had yanked

Sky Eyes from her breast and was holding her at arm's length away from her.

"My child!" Maggie said, her voice only a bare whisper. "Give my child back to me."

"You want her?" Frank said, chuckling. "Go and get the money and I'll give her back to you, unharmed. Tell anyone I'm here and she's dead."

Knowing that he was capable of most anything, Maggie nodded. She secured the dress over her breast, her eyes never leaving Sky Eyes, who was content and making sweet, gurgling sounds, waving her arms and kicking her legs. "I'll do as you say," she murmured. "But first you *must* give me my child. I can't leave her with you. I just can't."

"Do you think I've come all this way to allow a woman to fool me into believing she can be trusted?" Frank said, slowly wrapping the blanket around Sky Eyes, except for her face. "Nope. Don't think so. Now do as I say. Go and get the money if you want to get your daughter back."

"But even then, will you allow us to go free?" Maggie said, rising shakily to her feet, the effects of the peyote still not having worn completely off.

"If you value your child's life," Frank said, gazing down at Sky Eyes. "And *yours*. You have to promise to allow me to leave unharmed. If not, and the savages capture me, I'd find a way to get free and come and kill first your child, and then you." He laughed throatily. "But first, Margaret June, I'd rape you. I'd have my fun with you, then kill you. I'd delight in sending a knife through that devious heart of yours."

"You can call me devious?" Maggie said, leaning up into his face. "After what you've done to me? You are the most devious, evil man I've ever known."

"The money, Margaret June," Frank said angrily. "Go and get the damn money. That's all I'm interested in. Your savage can have your body. I can return to Kansas City and have any lovely lady I desire."

Maggie spat at his feet. "I pity any woman who allows you to charm her into your bed," she said, then her eyes softened as she gazed down at Sky Eyes. "I'll go and get the money. Just please don't harm my daughter." She gazed up at Frank. "Promise me you won't harm Sky Eyes?"

"It's all up to you," Frank said, his eyes searching her face, touched anew by her loveliness and truly wanting her no less now than he had those many months ago. He might change his plans. He might take her with him. Once she arrived at Kansas City and saw what she had been missing by living in a scroungy tepee, she would change her mind and accept the life that he offered her.

"I won't be long," Maggie said, turning to leave.

"How much is left of the money?" Frank said, causing Maggie to stop and turn his way again.

"Not as much as you'd hope," she said, lifting her chin stubbornly.

"You wench," Frank said, stamping toward her.

Maggie's eyes wavered when she saw how tightly he was holding Sky Eyes, then looked quickly up at him and forced a smile. "I was only jesting, Frank," she said quickly. "There's enough so that you won't ever have to work another day in your life. I . . . hid the money from my husband. He didn't spend a penny of it. I've also hidden it from Falcon Hawk. He doesn't know the money even exists."

She took a step toward him. "Please, Frank," she begged. "Treat my daughter tenderly. That is all she knows in life. Tenderness. Please?"

"Aw, go on," Frank said, easing his hold on Sky Eyes. "I ain't never hurt a child in my life. I sure as hell don't intend to begin now."

"*Hahou,*" Maggie murmured. "*Hahou.*"

"What sort of mumbo-jumbo have you learned in the Indian village?" Frank said, his eyebrows lifting.

"In Arapaho, I just said thank you," Maggie said, moving away from him. She was glad that the strength had returned to her legs. But her heart ached and bled for her daughter!

And just the thought of Soft Voice's role in this made Maggie's blood boil. All the while she was living with Long Hair, it had been a lie! She had not loved Long Hair at all, but instead still wanted Falcon Hawk to herself. Had she gone this far to make room in her life for Falcon Hawk? To hope that Frank would kill both Maggie and the child?

"She's going to pay," Maggie whispered, as her legs grew stronger and her anger built within her. "How could she have done this? Only someone filled with wickedness could go this far to remove obstacles in their lives!"

Her thoughts went to Falcon Hawk. Once he knew about Soft Voice, what would he do? And

Long Hair! Old grandfather. He would be made to look like an old fool!

"No matter what, everyone must know about her," Maggie said, nodding.

Then her thoughts were directed solely to Sky Eyes, and in whose possession she was at this moment. It was up to Maggie to get her child back, unharmed.

The money. The damnable money. She wished now that she had never stolen it. It had not given her any peace or security.

It had only bought her heartache and danger.

When Maggie came to the outskirts of the village, her pulse began to race, realizing that she was not going to be able to enter the village unseen. The smoke was spiraling from the smoke holes in the lodges. She could hear voices coming from the circle of the village, where the usual outdoor fire was being fed fresh wood. She could hear children laughing and playing. She could feel eyes on her, even now!

Maggie stopped and turned quickly. Her gaze met the fear in Soft Voice's from where Soft Voice stood partially concealed in the shadows in back of Long Hair's tepee.

For a moment, time seemed to stand still as Maggie and Soft Voice stared at one another. The air was tight with tension. Their breaths were coming raspily—Maggie's from a pure hate that only one other person had ever stirred within her heart. Frank, and now Soft Voice.

Maggie took short, slow steps toward Soft Voice while Soft Voice took stumbling steps away from her.

"How could you have done this to me and my child?" Maggie said, taking quicker steps now to keep up with Soft Voice, who was stumbling more quickly away from her. "Never did I realize that you were *this* wicked."

Soft Voice's heart pounded like a hundred drums within her chest. She had not thought that Maggie would ever be allowed to return to the village. She had thought that she was finally rid of the white woman.

But here she was, larger than life.

Now everyone would know! It did not matter so much to her now that Falcon Hawk should hate her. But for this child that she was carrying within the cocoon of her womb, she could hardly bear for Long Hair to cast her from his life *and* from her dearly beloved village of Arapaho.

"He let you go?" Soft Voice uttered. "Why did he?" She looked at Maggie's vacant arms, then looked jerkily back up at Maggie again. "The child? He kept the child?"

"What do you care about the child?" Maggie said, her voice a low, threatening hiss. "You took my daughter from the safety of her cradle and gave her into the arms of that treacherous, terrible man."

A flash seemed to start going off and on within Maggie's brain, like a warning. She realized that she was taking too much precious time talking with Soft Voice.

That could come later! After Sky Eyes was safely in her possession again!

"I'll tend to you later," Maggie said, stopping.

Soft Voice pleaded with her wide, dark eyes.

"Please do not tell," she begged.

"I'll tell," Maggie said over her shoulder as she moved quickly away from Soft Voice. "You can depend on that!"

Soft Voice's eyes filled with tears. She kept moving backward. Then her breath was knocked out of her when she fell over a supporting rope that led to one of the tepees. She fell to the ground clumsily.

Soft Voice was momentarily stunned, then her hands went to her abdomen and she pleaded with the Great Unseen Power that the fall had done no damage to her child. This child was all that remained of her existence now. She had no choice but to flee the wrath of not only Falcon Hawk, but also her dear, sweet Long Hair.

She sat there for a moment, slowly rocking back and forth as she hugged her knees to her chest. "What have I done?" she cried, tears flooding her eyes. "Oh, Great Mystery, what have I done?"

After a while, she rose to her feet. She stared at the back of Long Hair's lodge, then walked away from the village, her head hung. She knew not where to go. She only hoped that one of the neighboring tribes would have mercy on her and take her in with promises not to disclose her whereabouts to Falcon Hawk.

"The Ute," she whispered, wiping sprays of tears from her eyes. "They took in Pure Heart. I am younger. They will see me as someone who can carry much firewood and cook many meals. Yes, I will go to the Ute."

Her hand went to her abdomen again. No blood had come with the last moon. She knew without a doubt that she carried a child in her belly, proud because it was the child of a man whom she loved . . . whom she adored. It was Long Hair's!

She could not help but wonder about her child and its future. In the eyes of the Ute, the child would have no worth, while in the eyes of the Arapaho, it would have been looked at with hopes of greatness.

"Long Hair," she whimpered. "And what of Long Hair? Will he hate me too much?"

Maggie moved on into the village. Hoping they would not see the strain in her smile or the tightness in her gait, Maggie greeted the women as they met on their morning vigils and chores. She gazed at the eagle outside the lodge, its eyes eager while it watched her approach, expecting food.

"I'm sorry, sweet thing," Maggie murmured. "Not now."

With an eager heart to return to Sky Eyes, Maggie went inside her lodge, again recalling in jerky flashes the last time she was there, and how she had struggled with Soft Voice. Soft Voice had thought that this would be the end of Maggie's and Sky Eyes's interference in her life. Never would Soft Voice have guessed that Maggie was not Frank's sole interest—that Maggie would be back inside her lodge to get a satchel of money.

Maggie had to remove Soft Voice from her thoughts and get the money from its hiding place. The last thing Maggie wanted was to get Falcon Hawk mixed up in this. If he arrived and she was forced to tell him everything, she had no idea how this might turn out, or if she could rescue Sky Eyes from Frank. And his threats were etched inside her heart, as fossilized leaves leave their imprint, in time, on stone, and in rocks.

With an anxious heartbeat, Maggie hurried to the rear of the tepee and fell to her knees beside the stack of rolled bundles. With eager fingers she tossed one bundle aside and then another, then lifted the mat away, under which lay, beneath only a few inches of dirt, the satchel of money.

Maggie began to dig and soon uncovered the satchel. It seemed strange to her to actually see it again. So much had happened since she had uncovered it from its hiding place in the chicken house. That seemed an eternity ago, a part of her past that had been forgotten once she had allowed her feelings to blossom for Falcon Hawk.

Leaving the satchel on her lap, Maggie began smoothing the dirt back over the hole that was left by the removal of the satchel. In her eagerness to hide her deceit from Falcon Hawk, she had not heard the horses arriving to the village, nor the following commotion as people clamored around those who had arrived.

Falcon Hawk helped his mother from his horse, smiling broadly while everyone gathered around her and took turns hugging her. His eyes shifted to his lodge, wondering why Maggie had not come outside to greet his return.

He left his mother, whose heart was filled with merriment and love as everyone continued making a fuss over her return, and went to his lodge.

When he stepped inside, he stopped suddenly, wondering why Maggie was smoothing dirt over a hole in the floor.

His gaze shifted, stopping at the black satchel that lay across her lap. He had never seen it before. What was it? And why did it seem so important to Maggie?

"Panther Eyes?" Falcon Hawk said, moving into the lodge.

Maggie's heart seemed to do a somersault when she heard his voice. She clutched at the satchel and gave him an awkward smile which was filled with guilt.

Then fears splashed through her. Falcon Hawk. If he were there—how, oh, how could she go and rescue her daughter?

Again she feared what might happen if she was forced to tell Falcon Hawk everything!

And she knew now that she had no other choice.

Chapter Thirty

Her heart pounding, Maggie felt frozen to the spot. She felt like a child who had just been caught stealing from a cookie jar. She now regretted from the bottom of her heart that she had not told Falcon Hawk about the satchel of money long ago. Now was the worst of times to have to take the time to explain!

Her child was with a man who was surely the devil in disguise!

How utterly stupid she had been, under any circumstance, to have left Sky Eyes with Frank. If he could sink so low as to perform the vile act of rape, could he not also abuse her precious daughter?

That thought sickened her very soul. Yet it also gave her the courage to rise to her feet and speak, although guilty of many faults at this moment.

"Falcon Hawk, please allow me to leave without questioning me," Maggie begged, wanting to take no more time away from her daughter. "Darling, I will explain later. Please . . . let me pass. Our daughter's life is in danger."

Falcon Hawk glanced quickly at the empty cradle, then took a step forward. He clasped his fingers to her shoulders and gazed intensely into her eyes. "Where is our daughter?" he growled. His eyes shifted downward. "And what is that, that you clasp so fiercely to your bosom?"

Tears flooded Maggie's eyes. She knew that she had no choice but to give him an explanation. She silently prayed to her Lord, and to Falcon Hawk's Great Unseen Power, that Frank would be decent toward Sky Eyes. If she had only told him the truth! He would not harm his own flesh and blood—his very own daughter!

"Sky Eyes and I were forced from our beds a short while ago and taken to a man of my past," Maggie said, her words rushing across her lips. "Sky Eyes is being held by this man until I . . . until I . . ."

She moved her eyes to the satchel, silently damning it!

"Until . . . ?" Falcon Hawk said, slightly shaking her to loosen her tongue again. "Tell me everything and then Falcon Hawk will go for Sky Eyes! But I must know everything in order to be able to approach this man without harm coming to our daughter."

"I must return this satchel of money to Frank, and then . . . and then he will give Sky Eyes to me," Maggie blurted out, anxiously searching Falcon Hawk's face to try and know his true feelings about these things that were being revealed to him.

"Money? I have known of no money," Falcon Hawk said, cocking an eyebrow. "You never told me of this money. Why did you keep this from me? Have we not exchanged secrets of our hearts more than once?"

A sob lodged in Maggie's throat, to see the hurt and confusion she was causing Falcon Hawk. "Darling, I'm so sorry," she said, tears almost blinding her now as they filled and rushed from her eyes. "I will try to explain quickly, for, my darling, I must return to the cave and exchange this satchel for our daughter."

"Cave?" Falcon Hawk said, his fingers tightening on Maggie's shoulders. "I know of a cave on the butte that overlooks our village. The man is there? He holds our daughter hostage there?"

"Yes, he and our daughter are there," Maggie said, flinching when he dropped his hands angrily away from her and marched stolidly toward his weapons.

Falcon Hawk's fingers clamped around a rifle, and then he set it aside and picked up his short buffalo bow, doubled-curved, sinew-backed, made of resilient wood.

Determinedly he swung his beaver quiver onto his back, filled with a thick sheaf of arrows, all newly sharpened.

He went back to Maggie. "You can explain the rest of this to your husband later," he grumbled. "I will take many warriors and go for her!"

Maggie dropped the satchel and grabbed for Falcon Hawk's arm, stopping him as he turned to leave. "No!" she cried. "Wait! He promised that he would return Sky Eyes to me, then leave. Please,

Falcon Hawk. Let's not try anything else other than what he says. I so fear for our daughter! He's a most despicable, evil man—capable of crimes I have not yet revealed to you."

"These crimes," Falcon Hawk hissed across his lips. "Perhaps this husband does not want to know the worst of them, for in your eyes you have been his victim more than once. It would cut deep within my soul to know the worst of his ways to victimize you."

Maggie dropped her gaze to the floor, ashamed again that she had not confessed everything to Falcon Hawk. *More* secrets! In the end, after he heard everything, would he even want her for his wife? Or would she be cast aside, having lost everything after all, the same as Soft Voice?

Yet, for as long as she had known Falcon Hawk, she had found him to be understanding and loving. When she told him everything, she hoped that he would take her within his arms and still vow to protect her from any future harm. Except for sweet Sky Eyes, and this child that she was carrying within her womb, Falcon Hawk was her world.

To live without him would mean to live an empty existence.

"You say that he is a vile man, yet you trust his word that he will not harm you or the child once you give him that satchel of money?" Falcon Hawk said. He laughed sardonically. "My woman, you are more naive than this husband ever thought. This man—this man who holds our child as ransom—will not allow you to walk away from him. Either he will kill you and Sky Eyes, or he will force you to go with him."

Falcon Hawk leaned his face down into Maggie's. "This husband and father will allow neither to happen," he said, his teeth clenched.

"But what can you do?" Maggie said, bending to pick up the satchel. "He will see you. Then he will certainly kill me and Sky Eyes."

"You must still be a part of the plan," Falcon Hawk said, taking her gently by the arm and leading her outside. "You will return to the cave with the money. I will gather together many warriors and we will surround the cave without his knowing it. He will be too absorbed in what you have brought him to notice that others have followed."

Maggie's attention was momentarily taken to the crowd of people who were surrounding an Arapaho woman she had never seen before. It came to her quickly that she was gazing at Falcon Hawk's mother, and something soft and sweet flowed through her to know that, indeed, he had found her and that she was safe and very sound of mind.

Falcon Hawk's hand, urging her toward this crowd, drew Maggie back to the problem at hand. Everyone turned and stared when he stepped into the center of his people. Maggie could feel his mother's eyes on her, studying her questioningly.

Maggie did not return the gaze, for this was not the time to hand out smiles and greetings. As each moment passed, Sky Eyes was in mortal danger.

She gazed up at the butte, suddenly fearing that Frank would see that she was with Falcon

Hawk, and that he was now talking to his warriors, giving them instructions. She was relieved when she did not see him there.

She turned her fearful eyes up at Falcon Hawk. "We must hurry," she stammered. "Falcon Hawk, I've been gone too long as it is."

Falcon Hawk nodded. He leaned down, and while everyone mutely watched, he explained what she must do, and what he and his warriors were going to do, to get Sky Eyes away from Frank *and* to save Maggie.

"What if it doesn't work?" Maggie said, her pulse racing. "If he has any suspicions that the cave is being surrounded, he has already told me how I will die. He will kill me with his knife, and then . . . and then he will also kill our daughter."

Falcon Hawk took her suddenly in his arms and cradled her close. "My *h-isei,* my beautiful Panther Eyes, do you not know that your husband will not allow anything to happen to you or our daughter?" he said. "Trust me. Go. Do as you are told."

Maggie clung to him for a moment, the satchel impeding their full embrace, then swung around and rushed through the crowd and from the village. Her eyes were on the butte each step that she took, each of her heartbeats paining her.

Just as she reached the steep incline, she stopped to look over her shoulder, to see if she could see Falcon Hawk and his warriors.

She saw no sign of them. Her knees grew weak at the thought that they might not get to her and Sky Eyes in time. Then she found the strength to climb the steep grade of land and was soon entering the cave, her footsteps not taking her fast enough into the darkness. She was relieved to finally see the golden reflections of the fire against the cave wall, and then her first sight of her daughter since she had been forced to leave her.

Maggie stopped with a start, confused and astonished by what she saw. Frank was sitting beside the fire, oblivious, it seemed, of anyone or anything but this little bundle in his arms as he slowly rocked the child back and forth, softly singing to her.

Maggie teetered and grabbed for the wall beside her, absolutely stunned to see this side of Frank. He had always been such a cold, callous man, who did not seem to have feelings for anyone but himself. And now he was singing to Sky Eyes and rocking her as though he adored her.

As though she belonged to him, Maggie thought, fear clutching at her heart.

Hurrying her steps, Maggie soon stepped into view. She threw the satchel down beside Frank, then held her arms out to him. "Give her to me, Frank," she said. "I've brought you the money. Now give me my child."

"Not so fast," Frank said, rising slowly to his feet, Sky Eyes held in the curve of his left arm. "Open the satchel. Let's see the money."

"The money," Maggie said, stiffening. "Is that all you can think about? Of course, it is. While he was alive, you shamefully cheated my father out of all that you could. And when he was dead, you did the same to me, his daughter."

Her fingers trembling from anger, she knelt

down beside the satchel and threw it open. "There," she fumed, moving quickly to her feet again. "Now are you satisfied?"

"For the most part, it seems to be there," Frank said, mentally counting the bills as he gazed down at the bundles tied neatly together.

He shifted his gaze upward. "What I don't understand is, why didn't you spend it when you married that farmer?" he said, again slowly rocking Sky Eyes back and forth when she started fussing. "You lived so poorly. That money could've built you a mansion."

"The money was tainted," Maggie said, her eyes on Sky Eyes, wondering how she would get her away from Frank before Falcon Hawk arrived. "I've regretted taking it. I am gladly ridding myself of it today."

She paused, then again gestured with open arms toward Frank. "Please, Frank," she said softly. "You promised to give her back to me. Please let me have her."

Frank laughed throatily. "Did you truly believe that I would give you the child and allow you to leave?" he said, his eyes narrowing into hers. "I ought to shoot you both, but instead I've decided to take you both with me to Kansas City. You'd make an awful pretty bride." He cast Sky Eyes a soft look. "And I've grown to like the kid." He looked at Maggie again. "But if she's to live under my roof, as my stepdaughter, I'll damn sure change her name into something less savage."

Desperation was rising within Maggie. Her mind was so muddled that she was finding it hard to think. But one thing was certain—she had to get her child into the safety of her arms, and quickly. Falcon Hawk would soon be there. Sky Eyes must be out of harm's way if arrows or bullets started flying through the air.

"I refuse to go with you," Maggie said, lifting her chin proudly.

"Then you'll have to die," Frank said, shrugging.

"If that's the way it must be, then so be it," Maggie said, her heart hammering at the thought of what might transpire if Falcon Hawk did not hurry.

"You choose death over living with me?" Frank said, sounding disbelieving. "Did my touching you repel you so much?"

"Utterly," Maggie said, her voice faltering. She shivered as that vile moment danced before her mind's eye.

"Then I guess I don't have any choice but to make sure it don't happen again and make sure no *other* man gets pleasure from you either," Frank said. He gazed down at Sky Eyes. "Little thing, your mama just signed your death papers."

"I doubt that," Maggie said guardedly, knowing that there might be only one way to stop his madness, especially if Falcon Hawk didn't get there soon. "Surely you wouldn't kill your own flesh and blood."

"What's that you say?" Frank said, lifting puzzled eyes to Maggie.

"You appear to have feelings for my child," Maggie said, taking a step closer to Frank. "Did you look closely into her eyes? Did you see anything familiar about her facial features?"

Frank stared at Maggie for a moment, then turned his eyes down to the child. "What am I supposed to see?" he asked, studying Sky Eyes for a moment, then again looking up at Maggie.

"You should be seeing your eyes in hers, and some resemblance to yourself in her facial features," Maggie said somberly. "For you see, Frank, she is your daughter as well as mine. When you raped me, you planted a seed within my womb that formed this lovely child."

Frank's mouth opened and words were lost to him as he gazed down at Sky Eyes again. Taken aback, he half stumbled backwards. He *could* see himself in her face and eyes. He *had* felt a strange closeness—a special bond with her.

"My child . . . ?" he gasped.

As though Sky Eyes was suddenly a hot coal, he thrust her back into Maggie's arms and drew his knife quickly from the leather sheath at his waist. "You're lying," he snarled. "And you're *dead!*"

Falcon Hawk's teeth bared as he threw his body into the bow with a short, savage jab of the left arm. As he loosed the sinew cord, his braves followed his lead. One after another, feathers showed clinging to the bows, then were set free. . . .

Just as Frank took a step toward Maggie, the knife upthrust and ready for its death plunge, Maggie watched, horrified, as many arrows went past her and sank into Frank's chest.

Dropping the knife, Frank had only time to reach a hand toward the child, his eyes begging, before he slumped to the floor, dead.

Staring down at Frank, Maggie stood as though

in a trance. When Falcon Hawk came to her and circled his arms protectively around both Maggie and the child, only then did Maggie's body relax and her mind snap into place. She began crying, her body racked with deep sobs. She closed her eyes and leaned her cheek against Falcon Hawk's chest.

"It is over," Falcon Hawk said, softly stroking her back. "He is dead. You are safe."

"I didn't think that you'd arrive in time," Maggie sobbed.

"We were there, in the darkness of the cave, watching for the right moment," Falcon Hawk said. "Only when he gave you the child could we make a move to stop him."

"He's truly dead?" Maggie asked, shivering at the thought that Frank was perhaps pretending. She could not envision a future of worrying about this man. He *had* to be dead!

"Very dead, my woman," Falcon Hawk said. He eased from her embrace and took Sky Eyes into his arms. He gazed down at the satchel of money. "There is the cause of this man's greed. There is much money. He would have killed to have it."

"He's been searching for me for a long time to have that money," Maggie said, wincing when she herself gazed down at it. "I should have left it for him. It's been of no use to me. None whatsoever."

Then her eyes widened and she turned to Falcon Hawk. "But it doesn't need to be that way," she said, eagerly placing a hand on his arm. "Let's put it to good use. Let's use it for your people. This amount of money could do much to help the plight of your people. Will you take it, darling, as my gift to you? You see, it was my father's money. He worked hard to earn it. It is only right that it be put to good use now."

"Falcon Hawk is not greedy for money," he said in a low rumble.

"It is not greedy to have money if it is gotten and used in the right way," Maggie said determinedly. "It was my father's money. It is rightfully mine now. And so shall it be rightfully the Arapahos'!"

Falcon Hawk's lips lifted into a slow smile. "You have much to explain to me, woman, about this money," he said, then frowned down at her. "And about this man who has touched your past."

"I know," Maggie said, bowing her head. "And I shall explain about all of the secrets that I kept from you and promise that it shall never happen again."

"Secrets are ugly," Falcon Hawk said flatly. "But sometimes things that come from secrets are good. Our relationship will be stronger once you release from your inner soul that which you have held hidden within you."

Maggie nodded, then gazed down at Frank. "Perhaps he has done me a favor after all," she said, wiping fresh tears from her eyes.

Falcon Hawk told one of his warriors to get the satchel of money, but leave the man for the wolves. Then he ushered Maggie from the cave. She closed her eyes to that brief moment when Frank had sat with the child, gazing at her as though he loved her.

That thought was swept quickly aside when she

recalled the knife. His moment of being a caring human being had passed quickly into hatred. If not for Falcon Hawk and his warriors, Frank would have succeeded at taking not only Maggie's life from her, but also his very own daughter's.

After they arrived at their lodge and Sky Eyes had been fed, it was finally time for Maggie to explain everything to Falcon Hawk. Shaken by the ordeal with Frank, she sat beside Falcon Hawk, the warmth of the lodge fire welcome as she began the solemn tale of her sordid rape, of stealing her father's money and fleeing Frank, and of her marriage to her dear, sweet Melvin, that had seemed to save her life from the utter despair caused by Frank.

"The child is not your husband's?" Falcon Hawk breathed, stunned by her story. "This beautiful child is a child born of a vicious rape?"

"Aa," Maggie said softly, nodding. "It is something I did not want to remember, much less share with anyone. Not even you, Falcon Hawk. It was so shameful—the filthy act and being the victim of such a terrible thing. Please understand why I never told you."

"The money was buried in our lodge all this time?" Falcon Hawk said, finding it necessary to drop talk of the rape. There was no need ever to talk about it again. The man who was responsible was dead. And the child was already Falcon Hawk's, in every way important in life.

"I buried it the first chance that I had," Maggie said, sighing.

"And had Frank not shown up to get it?" Falcon Hawk questioned.

"I had almost forgotten that it was there," Maggie said, the truth being that she *had.* "I became so immersed in my happy life with you and our daughter, and with your people, *and* with knowing that we are expecting our very own son, that I never gave the money a thought. It was so unimportant. Why should I talk about it?"

"Did you ever worry about this man finding you and the money?" Falcon Hawk asked.

"At first, yes," Maggie uttered softly. "But later, no."

She then started telling Falcon Hawk the truth about Soft Voice's deception today. He did not have the chance to reply, nor did she have the chance to tell the whole story of Soft Voice's flight, for Long Hair suddenly appeared in the tepee.

Maggie turned her eyes up to Long Hair, her heart sinking at the thought of what knowing about Soft Voice could do to him. She didn't want to break Long Hair's heart, yet he would want to know the truth and not be treated like an old, senile fool.

Long Hair came and stood over Maggie and placed a hand on her shoulder. "It is good that you and the child are safe," he said, nodding. "Your mother, Falcon Hawk, is resting in her lodge. It is good that we kept it for her after my son's death. Its walls, which hold such memories, give her much comfort."

"And you believe that she can accept the loss of her husband now?" Falcon Hawk said, rising to embrace Long Hair.

"Her heart will always ache for her husband, but her thoughts are stronger now," Long Hair said. He stepped away from Falcon Hawk and gave Maggie a wavering stare. "Soft Voice has not come to me this long day. Nor have her parents seen her. Panther Eyes, do you know where she might be? Never has she been absent this long when no one has been witness to her lovely presence."

Maggie swallowed hard. She rose slowly to her feet. She gave Falcon Hawk a nervous look, and then Long Hair.

Falcon Hawk sensed that more was wrong about Soft Voice than Maggie had told him. "My wife, your eyes say what you are not putting into words," he said, turning to Maggie and placing a hand on her shoulder.

"Falcon Hawk, it's so horrible," Maggie said, her voice catching. "But it must be told. Everyone must know. Especially Long Hair."

Long Hair took a step toward her and peered down into her eyes. "Tell me," he said, his voice flat and wary.

"She . . . Soft Voice . . . is gone of her own choosing," Maggie finally blurted out. "But had she not gone of her own volition, she would have been sent away. You, Long Hair, and you, Falcon Hawk, would have banished her from the village."

Long Hair sought answers from Falcon Hawk as he squinted his old eyes into his grandson's. "What does she mean?" he asked weakly. "What has Soft Voice done to earn such condemnation?"

Falcon Hawk stepped up to his grandfather and clasped a hand onto his frail shoulder. "*Nabaciba,* there is much to say that will sadden your heart," he said solemnly. "But it must be said. It is not something that you should deal with later. It should be dealt with and then cast behind you."

Long Hair leaned into Falcon Hawk's face. "You tell your grandfather what needs to be dealt with," he said, yet fearing the answer. "Tell me about Soft Voice. Why is she gone? Where did she go?"

"*Naba-ciba,* Soft Voice betrayed us all today," Falcon Hawk said, dropping his hand from his grandfather's shoulder and turning away from him. He did not want to watch his grandfather's questioning look turn to despair once he knew the truth about this beautiful maiden to whom he had given not only shelter, but also a good portion of his heart. But Falcon Hawk was convinced that it had to be done now. Never should there be any truths kept from the wise one.

"Betrayed?" Long Hair said, feeling a weakness engulfing him the more he heard. "Soft Voice is capable of betrayal? In what way, my grandson? To me she has only shown a gentle side."

"*Haa,* true," Falcon Hawk said, nodding. He turned a slow gaze to his grandfather, then told him quickly what Soft Voice had done not only to Maggie, but also to the child. He also revealed to his grandfather that Soft Voice had left, fearing everyone's wrath once they knew the truth about her.

Thread Woman had heard the seriousness of the voices as she had passed by the lodge and had crept inside to see why. She had stayed in the shadows until now. When she saw the utter despair in Long Hair's eyes and how this caused his shoulders to slump over heavily, she had to go to him.

Falcon Hawk nodded a silent thank-you to Thread Woman, knowing that if anyone could help Long Hair in this, his time of sorrow and betrayal, it was Thread Woman.

Thread Woman placed a gentle hand on Long Hair's arm. "Come," she murmured. "Let me walk you to your lodge. There I will stay with you until you tell me to go."

Long Hair nodded and turned slowly around and went with her. He walked sluggishly beside her until they reached his lodge. When they were inside, she helped him down onto his bed and covered him with a soft blanket.

Then she sat beside his bed and sang to him. When he reached a hand to hers and brought it onto the bed beside him and held it close to him, she sighed.

"Long Hair, I will stay forever with you if you will have me," Thread Woman said, rising to her knees to gaze down onto his solemn face. She cackled out a forced laugh. "Of course, I realize that I am no beauty, nor is my flesh young to the touch. But at night my body could warm yours and yours could warm mine."

She paused and her voice broke. "I have been so lonely since my husband left me to walk the path of his ancestors," she then said. "Long Hair, I have wanted you to want me for so long."

Long Hair's eyes were kind and gentle as he smiled at Thread Woman. "You do not see this old man as foolish for having taken Soft Voice to my bed, only to be made a fool of?" he asked.

"Never could you be a fool in anyone's eyes," Thread Woman said, reaching a hand to his brow and softly caressing it. "Just blinded for a while by the soft, beautiful curves of one who lured you into wanting her."

"She *was* beautiful, wasn't she?" Long Hair said, his voice distant.

"Beautiful, yet very conniving," Thread Woman dared to say.

"She did seem to care," Long Hair said, taking Thread Woman's hands and leading her up onto the bed beside him.

"And I am sure that a part of her did," Thread Woman said, settling down beside Long Hair, feeling as though she were a young girl again. "Who could not care for a man like you?"

"Your body does warm mine quite nicely," Long Hair said, drawing her closer.

Thread Woman smiled and snuggled against him, and they both went to sleep with a contented look on their faces.

Falcon Hawk held Maggie close on their bed. He did not approach her sexually this night. She had been through many fearful moments through the day. Her mind would not be set on pleasures, except those of being safely home, her troubles behind her.

"Tomorrow peyote will be used in ways different than how Soft Voice used this cactus on you," Falcon Hawk said, gently caressing her back as she lay next to him on her side, facing him.

"I don't want even to hear that word spoken again to me," Maggie said, shuddering.

Falcon Hawk placed his hands to her cheeks and drew her eyes to meet his. "Tomorrow your husband will participate in the peyote ceremony," he said. "In part, you will join him."

Maggie paled and leaned up on one elbow to stare at him. "Why should I?" she gasped, recalling how quickly the drug had caused her to become mindless.

"You will not actually eat the peyote yourself," Falcon Hawk quickly corrected. "You will sit with me during the ceremony and make sure food is brought to those who will be with me. You will be there after it is done, to lead me to our bed. There we will make love. The pleasure will be enhanced for your husband by the taking of the peyote into his body. For many hours we will make love."

"Why did it cause me to become unconscious, when you are saying that you will have the ability to make endless love?" Maggie worried aloud.

"It is the amount taken that makes the difference," Falcon Hawk explained. "Soft Voice gave you too much. She apparently knew just how much to give you so that you would be lethargic enough to do as she told you."

He frowned. "She must use peyote herself at times, to know the exact measurements that should be used for certain purposes."

"Why must you do this tomorrow?" Maggie said, wishing that she could talk him out of it.

"The plant is not ordinarily eaten, even by those devoted to it, except during ceremonies which take place at irregular intervals," he explained. "It has now been many months since our last ceremony. It is time for another."

"You have done this before, then?"

"Many times."

"You will be safe?"

"*Haa.*"

"Tell me something about it so that I will know what to expect other than what I experienced while under the influence of the terrible plant."

He held her tight and talked in a monotone, his thoughts remembering the many times he had participated in the ceremony, having always come away from it feeling uplifted and more powerful.

"The peyote affects the heart," Falcon Hawk began explaining. "It has a marked effect on the general feeling of the person, giving the impression of stimulating, especially the intellectual faculties. In most cases it produces visions. Its emotional effect varies greatly, being in some cases depressing or intensely disagreeable. In others, which are the most frequent, it produces quiet but intense exaltation. For Falcon Hawk, it has always produced mental excitement."

He bent his lips to hers. "As it will for me tomorrow," he said huskily. "I shall show you the meaning of lovemaking as never before."

Maggie clung to him, her heart throbbing as he kissed her long and passionately.

Yet she was glad when he did not attempt to arouse her any further. She was so tired from the day's affairs.

She snuggled, trying to think positively about tomorrow. Yet, remembering the terrible effects the peyote had had on her, she feared for her husband's trust in it.

"Hold me," she whispered. "I love you so, Falcon Hawk. I love you so."

He enwrapped her within his arms, not wanting to think about how close he had come to losing her today.

Chapter Thirty-One

The day had been long for Maggie, especially without Falcon Hawk. At daybreak he had left, gathering together all that would be used in the peyote ceremony.

Now, at sunset, he would be erecting the tepee in which the peyote ceremony would be performed, preparing it for the arrival of the twelve warriors who were going to participate in this event with him.

Before he had left, he had explained to Maggie that he was the leader of the ceremony this time and therefore was the sole director of it. He was going to make his ceremony in accordance with those he had participated in before, adding details to suit his own purpose.

Maggie had been preparing food for the ceremony, Falcon Hawk's mother assisting her. At first there had been a strain between Maggie and Pure Heart, but after a while, the tension had broken and they had been able to talk while cooking the assortment of foods for the night's activities.

Now they were sitting beside the fire, occasionally stirring different pots that hung on tripods over the flames, as the light outside waned.

"I see worry in your eyes," Pure Heart said, gazing at Maggie. "There is no need for concern. Your role in the ceremony will be minor."

"I truly want to believe that my concerns are needless," Maggie said. She moved to her knees and busied her hands stirring a long, wooden spoon through the elk stew that was simmering and sending off delicious aromas that wafted through the tepee.

She sat down beside Pure Heart and gave her a worried look. "But I can hardly stand to think about being a witness to my husband partaking in this ceremony, much less watch him take that terrible plant into his body," she said in a rush of words. "Soft Voice ministered it to me by force, and I became unconscious, then mindless upon my awakening. I fear what it might do to Falcon Hawk."

Pure Heart's long, gray hair flowed across her shoulders and down to her waist; her wrinkles seemed to multiply on her face as the shadows of the fire danced into them. She fell silent and looked away from Maggie. She was tormented with thoughts of Soft Voice and what she had proven herself capable of. Through the years, Pure Heart had taken Soft Voice into her life, and arms; yet even then Soft Voice must have been carrying deceit within her heart to turn into the hideous person that she had finally revealed herself to be.

Then Pure Heart turned and gave Maggie a slow smile. "Little beautiful one, do not worry about my son," she said, reaching over to pat Maggie on the arm. "He has proven to be the wisest of us all. Long before you saw it, Falcon Hawk saw Soft Voice's true nature when no one else did. He knows just how much peyote is safe."

Maggie cast a wavering glance at the smoke hole at the apex of the lodge. "It will soon be dark," she said, growing weak in the knees to know that she would soon have to leave the protective cocoon of her lodge—and her daughter—for a full night. Although Pure Heart was going to stay with Sky Eyes, and Many Children Wife would come and feed Sky Eyes when she demanded feeding, Maggie was no less wary of leaving.

And Pure Heart could say all that she wanted to about there being no danger to Falcon Hawk in participating in the peyote ceremony, but Maggie would never relax her concern.

Suddenly something came to her that made her wonder why she had not thought of it earlier. Instead of dreading joining Falcon Hawk in the ceremonial lodge newly constructed by him today, she was glad. She could be with him, perhaps to help him, if he showed signs of needing assistance.

She turned to Pure Heart. "I will gladly join my husband in the ceremonial lodge," she said, anxiety in her eyes. "Perhaps my presence will comfort him in some way."

"It is good to see you accept that which is expected of you," Pure Heart said, again patting Maggie's arm. "You will be the only woman there.

It is best that this woman be my son's wife."

"The only woman there," Maggie said beneath her breath, uneasy again at the thought of it.

"You look beautiful," Pure Heart said, drawing Maggie's gaze back to her. "So radiant. So lovely. Do you approve of the dress that I gave to you to wear? I wore it ofttimes during peyote ceremonies that my husband supervised. The buckskin dress is symbolically painted, meant to be worn only for the ceremony."

"*Aa,* it is lovely," Maggie said, gazing down at it. It was a pale yellow, the beadwork on the dress also predominantly yellow, yet consisting of a mixture of colors. There were bands of different colors encircling stems made of beads. Along the hem were small glass beads that produced sound when she walked. She wore a bracelet made of twisted cord, as would Falcon Hawk and the other men.

Maggie sighed and went to stand over the cradle, her heart becoming soft and warm as she watched her child sleeping. "I am glad that my responsibilities are only to take food to the warriors when it is time for them to eat," she murmured. Pure Heart stepped to her side, also to peer down at the child.

"There is one other thing that will be required of you," Pure Heart said softly.

Maggie's head turned in a jerk, a renewed uneasiness in her eyes. "What else?" she said, her voice weak.

"At midnight you will leave the tepee," Pure Heart said, seeing herself in her mind's eye with her husband those many moons ago during more than one peyote ceremony. Unlike Panther Eyes, fear had never entered Pure Heart's heart at the thought of helping Dreaming Wolf during his partaking in the peyote ceremony.

But Pure Heart realized that this was because she was Arapaho, born into the knowledge of the peyote ceremony.

Panther Eyes was white and only now was learning what she would have known long ago had she been born Arapaho.

Maggie gently touched Pure Heart on the shoulder, realizing that she was at this moment taken away with remembrances. "Pure Heart?" she said. "You were saying?"

Pure Heart blinked her eyes. She laughed softly when she looked at Maggie and realized what had happened. In her mind's eye, she had been reliving wonderful times. That was all she had left of her beloved chieftain husband—memories, beautiful, soaring memories.

"You were saying?" Maggie prodded. "You said that I would leave the peyote lodge at midnight. What would I be expected to do?"

"It is a simple task that will be asked of you," Pure Heart said. "You will go outside and get a jar of water that I will have placed outside the tepee for you. You will take it to your husband and place it before him. Then you will sit beside him again and be attentive to the continuing ceremony."

"That will be simple enough," Maggie said, sighing heavily.

She was reviewing in her mind what she was supposed to do first. As the men swam nude in the river, she would stay in her tepee, as would everyone else in the village. Only after they left the river and were clothed again would she go and stand beside the lodge door. She would wait until the warriors entered and then she would be the last, except for the one who was called the "fire chief." He would be the last to enter, closing the entrance flap behind him.

She nodded. Yes, she thought that she knew what to do. Now she had only a short while left before having to do it.

She returned to the fire with Pure Heart. A silence fell between them, as both women became lost in their own private thoughts, some sweet, some troubled.

The day was fast fading into the shadows of night. Falcon Hawk had chosen a site for the ceremonial lodge that sat away from the village, closer to the river. Dressed in only a breechclout and standing facing westward of where the center of the lodge would be, he raised his right hand and prayed silently to the Great Unseen Power.

After feeling heard and blessed, he busied himself, anxious to build the lodge. He scraped the grass from the ground with a sharp knife, cutting it first from west to east, and then from north to south. The tepee was then put up facing the east. The wood that was to be burned during the night was stacked inside the tent to the south of the door, making sure that small sticks that would burn without sparks would be used.

Falcon Hawk circled rocks in the center of the lodge for the fire pit, then took a blanket outside and gathered reddish brown earth into it. He took this inside his tepee, placing this reddish earth in a semicircle around the fire pit in the middle of the lodge, the center of the crescent toward the back of the tent, opposite the door.

He pulled sage out of a pouch and laid this on the ground around the inside of the tepee. The men sitting on this would stretch forward to reach the semicircle of soil.

Going outside and glancing at the darkening sky, Falcon Hawk concluded that this was the time to place the mescal plants in water to soak. He went back inside the lodge and took several of the peyote plants from a distinctive, buckskin-fringed pouch. The soaking would render them sufficiently soft to be chewed. The liquid would be used also in the ceremony.

Lifting a blanket from the ground, Falcon Hawk walked to the river, where the other warriors, twelve in number, had gathered waiting. After their blankets and breechclouts were laid aside, they entered the water to take the bath that was required before the peyote ceremony.

In the water they made one plunge against, and one with the current of the river. On coming out of the water, they rubbed themselves with sage. Their heads, blankets, and breechclouts were rubbed with scented plants that were chewed.

Without speaking, they dressed in their breech-clouts and wrapped their blankets around their shoulders, then went to the ceremonial lodge. Earlier in the day Falcon Hawk had chosen who would be the fire-tender tonight, who was called *hictana-tca.*

Falcon Hawk took an eagle-wing feather from the ground where he had placed it earlier. He silently pointed his feather at the fire-tender. This feather the fire-tender would use as a fan for the fire during the ceremony.

But now his duty was to go ahead of the others inside the ceremonial lodge to start the fire. Knives and other sharp instruments were left outside the tent, for this ceremony was an occasion of peace and good-feeling.

Falcon Hawk watched the lodge, and when he saw that the fire had begun to be illuminated, he raised his eyes heavenward and prayed in a low voice.

He then nodded to the other worshippers and they began to walk single file into the tent. The fire-tender was outside now, kneeling beside the door with his head bowed, facing the tent.

Maggie had stood back from the lodge in the darkening shadows, waiting for the time for her to make her appearance. After the last warrior had gone into the lodge, she entered. The fire-tender came after her and positioned himself beside the fire.

Maggie sat down with her husband at the middle of the back of the tent, the others sitting on each side of him in a semicircle.

Corn-husk cigarettes were smoked, lighted with a stick taken from the fire by the fire-tender. Then the plants that had been left to soak were taken from the water, which had become brownish. The plants were laid in a cloth. The dirty and very bitter liquid remaining was passed around to the participants, each of whom took two sips.

Falcon Hawk then smoothed out a little space at the middle point of the crescent of reddish earth before him. Breaking eight short stems of sage, he laid them on this spot in the form of two superimposed crosses, the ends of the stems pointing in the cardinal directions. On this sage, the mescal plants were then laid. A head-feather plume was stuck in the ground so that its tip nodded over the plant.

Then, starting from the plant, Falcon Hawk made a crease along the top of the crescent of earth by pressing his thumbs into it, first to the right, then to the left. This was continued at its two ends by the worshippers sitting on each side of Falcon Hawk. The crease represented the path by which the thoughts of the worshippers traveled to the mescal plant, the peyote.

After this altar was completed, Falcon Hawk passed the cloth of soaked plants four times over cedar incense. He took one plant himself, and then gave one to the man on his left. After these were eaten, Falcon Hawk gave each of the participants four plants, first stretching his hand toward the east.

Falcon Hawk took his own into his mouth, finding the taste quite bitter and the plants still quite hard. He ground them between his teeth, one at a time, until they crumbled. He continued to chew until they were fine.

He then made the mass into a round ball by pressing it with his tongue. When it was soft enough, it was easily swallowed.

Falcon Hawk reached behind him and brought out, one at a time, a kettle drum, a gourd rattle filled with pebbles, and a feather fan that represented the birds linking God and man. He passed these four times over the cedar incense. Falcon Hawk kept the rattle and gave the man at his left side the drum.

Maggie was mystified by all of this, having scarcely breathed while she watched each step of the ritual. Her heart soared when Falcon Hawk began to shake the rattle and sing while the man who had the drum began drumming in time with his song. She was seeing a side of her husband that was both mystical and beautiful. She saw no harm—yet—in his taking of the peyote. She could see serenity in his eyes. She could see peace. She hated it when he stopped singing and passed his rattle on to another participant, each one singing and then passing the rattle on, until each man had sung four songs.

Maggie had been so taken by the ceremony that she had not been aware of the passing of time. When Falcon Hawk gazed at her and nodded toward the door, she hopped quickly up, remembering Pure Heart's instructions about the jar of water. She was surprised to find that Falcon Hawk had followed her. She stood silently by as he prayed. Facing the east, he prayed to the morning star. Facing west, he prayed to the peyote, which was in the tent west of him.

Then Maggie followed him back inside the lodge. After he was sitting again, she placed the jar of water before her husband, then resumed her place beside him.

Falcon Hawk sprinkled cedar on the fire to carry his prayers up. The fire-tender scraped the ashes into a crescent shape inside the crescent of earth, then stood and danced.

Falcon Hawk sang and shook his rattle, the man at his left thumped his drum, and a third participant blew a whistle, imitating a bird. At the end of four songs, the fire-tender sat back down, his eyes eagerly on Falcon Hawk.

Falcon Hawk blew on an eagle-bone whistle with which he imitated the cry of an eagle as it would gradually descend from a great height to the ground in search of water. The gradual approach of the bird from a distance was very vividly indicated, ending with a climax of shrill cries. The end of the whistle was then dipped into the water. After this, Falcon Hawk drank from the jar.

The water was then passed about the tent from left to right in regular ceremonial order, and everyone drank four swallows, as the peyote had made them very thirsty.

From that time on, until sunrise, the singing and the drumming went on continuously. Maggie found it hard to stay awake, but she knew that with the sun came her duty to bring food to the participants.

When this time came, she left and reappeared with four dishes of food and drink, which she placed in a row on the ground between the fire and the door.

Soon after her entrance, the last round of singing was completed, the rattle was laid aside, and the fire was allowed to burn out.

The drum was then loosened and taken apart, and each portion of it was passed around the ring of participants. A little of the water still remaining in the jar was drunk by each worshipper, followed by the dishes of food.

After the food had gone around several times and none of the dishes was any longer touched by anyone, the worshippers rose, stretched themselves, shook their blankets, and one behind the other they left the tepee in the same order in which they had entered it the night before.

For the rest of the day the worshippers lay on their blankets beneath an umbrella of trees, Maggie stretched out beside Falcon Hawk, drifting off into sleep, then waking again to the singing of the men, as they shook their rattles softly.

She smiled, enjoying having the opportunity to join this special time with her husband, and laughing to herself when occasionally more than one man would sing a different song at the same time.

She could tell that the effects of the drug were still very strong. The pleasurable effects seemed at their very height. It was then that Falcon Hawk suddenly grabbed her into his arms and carried her away from the others. He did not stop until he entered their lodge, breathing hard, his eyes never leaving Maggie when he felt the presence of his mother and Many Children Wife, who soon scurried away to give their chief and his wife total privacy.

Maggie had not participated in taking the peyote into her body, but she felt as though she had. Falcon Hawk's kisses made her feel drunk and giddy as he laid her across their bed.

Their hands worked in a frenzy at disrobing

each other. Their lips were wildly grinding together in fiery, savage kisses. Their bodies met and twined together, Falcon Hawk entering her in one maddening thrust.

Maggie locked her legs around him and rode him, his hands at her breasts, molding them within his palms. His tongue pressed between her lips. She met his frenzy with her own, her whole being melting as the heat rose and spread within her.

It was easy to forget that she had been up a full night, with only a short nap while Falcon Hawk had laughed and eaten with his friends after the peyote ceremony.

She was feeling revived, the spinning sensation of ecstasy rising and flooding her body. Tremors cascaded down her back as each of Falcon Hawk's strokes within her promised more, assuring fulfillment. Each thrust brought up fresh desire, filling her, drenching her with warmth and sunlight.

She was vaguely aware of someone making soft whimpering sounds, then realized that it was herself as she thrust her pelvis toward her husband, bringing him more deeply within her. His arms wrapped around her and drew her into the warmth of his body. She was overwhelmed with the sweet, painful bliss of this spiraling need that invaded her senses.

And when he slipped his mouth down and his lips found the soft swell of her breasts, fastening on the tight, pink nub, Maggie closed her eyes and threw her head back as the passion rose, burned, spread. . . . She was close to the brink that she hungered for. She wanted it to happen quickly now, for she could hardly stand the pain of waiting.

Falcon Hawk's blood quickened when his tongue found the softness of her breast, then the erect nipple. He flicked his tongue over the nipple, then licked and nibbled it, drawing a blissful sigh from deep within Maggie. He felt as though he was on fire. He pressed endlessly deeper, seeking that place and time when the only thing that he would be aware of was the intense pleasure that came near the end of the lovemaking.

Placing his hands beneath her, anchoring her to him, he moved more quickly into her, this great burning fire raging within him having become both agony and bliss. His lips brushed against her nipples, his tongue now making its way up the column of her throat, and once again he kissed her. A rumbling seemed to begin within him, starting from his toes, moving like a hot, volcanic flow through him, until the sensual shock of release was theirs, shared.

Falcon Hawk placed his lips against Maggie's cheek and groaned as the great shuddering in his loins sent his seed deep within her. As this flood of pleasure swept through Maggie, she strained her hips up at him, crying out as she found fulfillment and joy where she clung wildly to him.

Falcon Hawk's body subsided exhaustedly into Maggie's. He rolled away from her and lay at her side, his eyes closed, his body still feeling the pleasure.

Maggie drew in a ragged, happy breath and ran

her hands up and down his perspiration-drenched chest. "I so love you," she murmured, leaning to kiss the hollow of his throat. She started to say something else but realized that his breathing was now steady and smooth, as it was when he was asleep.

Maggie leaned up on one elbow. "Falcon Hawk?" she whispered, testing to see if he was asleep.

When he did not answer her, she sighed and lay down beside him. Snuggling close to him, she smiled contentedly and allowed sleep to claim her also.

Some time later, when Sky Eyes began whimpering, Maggie crept from the bed and picked up her daughter. She took her back to the bed and placed her daughter's lips to her breast.

"Soon you will have a brother," Maggie whispered, softly caressing her daughter's brow. "I know it will be a boy. I just know it."

Although filled with peace and joy, Maggie found herself frowning, worrying about a future for a son that would include peyote and sun dance ceremonies.

She gazed at the scars on Falcon Hawk's chest and shuddered. Yet she knew that a son who would grow up in the image of his father must suffer to prove his worth and courage. He would not want less, especially if he wanted to follow his father's footsteps and be a great leader of their people.

"And he will be so handsome," Maggie whispered. She gazed down at Sky Eyes. "As you are beautiful."

She felt warm hands tracing the spine in her back and knew that Falcon Hawk was awake again. "My darling," she murmured, her skin rippling with sensuous pleasure in the wake of his touch.

Sky Eyes slipped her mouth from Maggie's breast. She gazed up at Maggie and showed her mother a big smile. Falcon Hawk swung Sky Eyes away from her and laid her on her tummy on his chest, so that they were eye to eye.

"She is you, through and through," Falcon Hawk said. "She will make many men jealous, for she will steal more than one man's heart before she chooses one for marriage."

"There was only one man for me," Maggie said, cuddling close to his side again.

Falcon Hawk said nothing for a moment, his mind recapturing that moment when she had revealed the rape to him. It was good that he had sent that first arrow into the rapist's chest—and the second and the third. The rifle just did not seem the appropriate weapon for the man who had taken his woman's virginity away.

"And this man, your husband, will satisfy you forever?" Falcon Hawk teased back, brushing ugly thoughts from his mind.

"Do you even have to ask?" Maggie said, laughing softly. She gave him a smile that melted his heart.

Chapter Thirty-Two

One Year Later

Maggie was sitting beside her lodge fire, nursing Gold Eagle, her three-month-old son, while Sky Eyes sat on Pure Heart's lap, playing with a string of colorful glass beads. "Will the ceremony last long?" Maggie asked, touched deeply within her heart over what Thread Woman was about to do.

Today Maggie would acquire Thread Woman's sacred bag, which contained the old woman's incense, paint, and implements for marking and sewing which she used in ornamenting buffalo robes and tents. These implements were painted red and kept wrapped. There were six other bags owned by old women in this village, corresponding to seven sacred bags kept by seven old men, which also contained rattles.

"There will be no actual ceremony, and therefore the actual handing over of the sacred bag to you will not be as timely as those in the past,"

Pure Heart said. "Things change in one's lifetime. The ritual for presenting the sacred bag to someone younger and worthy will be done without the usual pomp and circumstance. It will be done without the presence of the other six women who have sacred bags in their possession. It will be private, shared only between you and Thread Woman, mainly because she not only hands over her sacred bag to you today, but also all of her sewing materials."

"I feel so honored that Thread Woman chose me to have her sewing implements and sacred bag," Maggie said, positioning her son at her other breast so that he could also suckle from it. "It is sad that her fingers are not as nimble as they once were."

"It is the curse of the old," Pure Heart said, sighing heavily. "And, daughter, it is best that the bag and sewing equipment should belong to nimble, young fingers, not those that are old, trembling, and stiff."

"I think it is not only because of those things that she has given up the art of embroidery," Maggie said. "Since her marriage to Long Hair, she spends time being attentive to him." She laughed softly. "It warms me so to watch Thread Woman and Long Hair. Inside their hearts, they have become young again. And have you noticed? They never cease to find things to talk about."

"Yes, it does prove their happiness," Pure Heart said, nodding.

Maggie saw a sadness enter Pure Heart's eyes, and she heard it in her voice. Although much time had passed since Pure Heart's husband's passing, the pain of losing him had not truly lessened. But it was good that she found pleasure in other things, which ofttimes took her mind off her husband. As now. Pure Heart seemed in heaven as she held and played with Sky Eyes.

Maggie gazed down at her son, feeling herself transported to heaven by the mere look at this beautiful son born of Falcon Hawk's love. And how wonderful it had been that Gold Eagle had his father's beautiful copper skin and dark eyes. There was even a shock of coal-black hair that would one day be long and flowing.

She could see her son now, in her mind's eye, as he might be as a young man, proudly riding a horse. His hair would fly in the wind. His shoulders would be square and muscled. He would have the look of nobility, this son of hers.

But now he was asleep, Maggie realized, giggling. His lips were no longer moving and his cheek rested contentedly on her milk-filled breast. "And so you are now dreaming of angels?" she said in a purring voice. "If so, will you tell my mother that I said hello?"

"He sleeps as contentedly as Sky Eyes," Pure Heart said, drawing Maggie's eyes to her.

Seeing her daughter asleep, snuggling affectionately against Pure Heart's bosom, made Maggie smile. The bond grew stronger between Pure Heart and Sky Eyes every day, and it could have been just the opposite. The mere fact that Sky Eyes was a white child could have made the difference. In Pure Heart's youth, the white people were looked on as savages in the eyes of the Arapaho. The white people stole not only their land, but also their dignity. Maggie was thankful to have Pure Heart's heartfelt affection. Her skin color could also have made the difference.

But Pure Heart was a compassionate woman filled with spirituality. She loved more than she could ever be capable of hating.

Maggie carried Gold Eagle to the cradle that had at one time belonged to Sky Eyes and placed him on his side on a soft pelt. Pure Heart carried Sky Eyes to a small bed that sat beside the cradle and laid the child on a thick cushion of blankets, covering her with another one.

Maggie bent over the cradle and kissed Gold Eagle as she drew a blanket over him, then went to Sky Eyes and gave her cheek a kiss.

"They are both beautiful children," Pure Heart said, placing an arm around Maggie's waist.

When Maggie turned to Pure Heart, she gave her a fond embrace. "You have brought so much love into my children's lives," she murmured. "Also into mine."

"It is with a fond heart that I share my love and my life with you and the children," Pure Heart said, returning the hug.

Then Pure Heart stepped away and began walking toward the door. "But if I stay any longer, I will be an interference," she said over her shoulder. "Thread Woman should be here soon."

"Come again later," Maggie said, walking Pure Heart on to the door. "Come and share the afternoon with me and the children. And please bring your embroidery work. I will be anxious to use the sewing tools that Thread Woman is so generously giving to me."

"She would not think to give them to anyone else," Pure Heart said, taking Maggie's hands. "My dear, you have become special to all of our Arapaho people. It is only right that you be singled out for such an honor that you receive today."

They embraced again, then Maggie went and sat down beside the lodge fire, her heart thudding as she waited for Thread Woman's arrival. She felt so blessed for so many things. In a sense she could thank Frank for the injustices that he had bestowed upon her. If he hadn't, she would not have been forced to flee Kansas City. She would not have met Falcon Hawk. She would not have had the pleasure of becoming a part of the Arapahos' lives.

"Yes," she whispered. "Frank Harper wanted the worst for me, and I instead have the *best.*"

A shuffling of feet into the lodge drew Maggie's eyes around. She rose and met Thread Woman's approach and helped the elderly lady down onto the cushion of pelts before the fire. Maggie sat down beside her, resting her trembling fingers in her lap, her wide eyes gazing at the sacred bag that Thread Woman had laid on the floor between herself and Maggie.

"Today I relinquish to you what was relinquished to my care many, many moons ago," Thread Woman said, smoothing a fallen gray lock of hair back from her face. "Do you see this robe I wear today?"

"*Aa,*" Maggie murmured. "It is quite beautiful." Her gaze went slowly over the robe, seeing that it was quite old by the faded colors and the dried-up buffalo pelt.

Yet the buffalo robe was still quite beautiful. It had twenty lines of quillwork, mainly yellow, representing buffalo-paths. From the lower end of the robe hung fifty pendants, at the ends of which hung small hooves and loops covered with quillwork.

"It is the first robe sewn by Thread Woman after I received the sacred bag those many moons ago," Thread Woman said, gingerly running her hands down the front of the dress.

She gazed at the bag, then up into Maggie's eyes. "Raven Woman was the owner of my bag before it was transferred to me," she murmured. "This bag was owned successfully by two other women, and then myself. When I was about to obtain this bag, I provided food, clothing and horses to be given away and called all of the old women who then had bags to join me as the bag was given to me."

Maggie paled. "I did not know that I was to provide food, clothing, and horses," she said in a light gasp. "No one told me."

Thread Woman placed a comforting hand on Maggie's arm. "Do not despair, my dear," she said, her smile causing the craters in her face to deepen. "Your gifts to me have been many."

"But not truly," Maggie said softly.

"Your love, sweetness, and giving of yourself are the gifts I speak of," Thread Woman said softly. "Material, worldly things are of no value to this old woman. But feeling needed and loved is of vast importance. That is what you gave so freely to me. That is why I give you what is most valuable to me today." She cackled beneath her breath. "Now that is not entirely so. What is *most* valuable to me is Long Hair."

Maggie smiled at Thread Woman. "Yes, I know, and I am so happy for you," she said. She drew in a quick breath when Thread Woman quickly placed the sacred bag in Maggie's hands.

Maggie stared down at it, knowing the true meaning of having been chosen to have it. In time, she would choose her own inheritor of the bag—in time, when her fingers would also be old and quavering.

"It is without ceremony that I hand over to you the ownership of this sacred bag," Thread Woman said. "Make many robes and dresses. Wear them with love and always remember Thread Woman when you open the bag, for it is with much love that I give this to you."

"It is with much love and gratitude that I accept that which means so much to you," Maggie said, holding the bag as though it were a delicate, precious flower. "I shall make for you a special robe. Would that please you?"

Thread Woman reached her arms around Maggie's neck and gave her a warm hug. "*Aa,* very much," she murmured. Then she drew away and rose slowly to her feet. "Long Hair awaits my return. We take walks each day now. Too soon the cold winds will blow and confine us in our lodges by the fire."

"I, too, have been sure to take walks each day," Maggie said, placing the sacred bag aside and walking Thread Woman to the door. "The children love the sun. I love the soft breezes."

When they stepped outside together, they

noticed two riders coming into the village. One was a woman, one a man. Maggie quickly noticed that the woman bore a cradle board on her back, a child wrapped securely within it.

"Do you recognize them?" Maggie asked Thread Woman. "They are not familiar to me."

Pure Heart stepped to their side, also staring. "I recognize them both," she said, her eyes brightening. "They are Ute! The woman was most kind to me while I was in their camp. She treated me as though I were her mother."

Pure Heart began walking quickly toward the approaching horses. Falcon Hawk came from his grandfather's lodge and, along with other warriors, met those who were arriving.

Maggie and Thread Woman stood on each side of Falcon Hawk, while Pure Heart reached a hand to the woman, greeting her in the Ute tongue.

"Greetings," Falcon Hawk said, clasping Night Bear's hand as he stepped up to the Ute's white steed. "What brings you to the village of the Arapaho?"

Night Bear looked over his shoulder at the woman, then turned his gaze back to Falcon Hawk. "The child," he said solemnly. "I have brought the child to your village to be raised in the lodge of its true father."

Falcon Hawk dropped his hand and took a startled step back from the horse. "What you say puzzles me," he said, raising an eyebrow. "Who is the mother? Who is the father?"

Without responding right away, Night Bear slipped out of his saddle, went to the woman, and helped her to the ground. She turned her back to him, so that he could loosen the cradle board. After he had the cradle board in his arms, he went and stood before Falcon Hawk.

"Take me to Long Hair's lodge," Night Bear said.

"Why Long Hair . . . ?" Falcon Hawk said, seeing his grandfather approaching him from behind, Thread Woman devotedly at his side.

Night Bear caught sight of Long Hair and stepped around Falcon Hawk. He went to Long Hair and held the cradle board out to him. "Your child," he said, his voice low and smooth.

Confused, Long Hair's old eyes widened. "This child is not mine," he said, motioning with a wave of the hand. "How could you say that it is?"

"Did you not take Soft Voice to your bed?" Night Bear said, forcing the cradle board into Long Hair's arms.

"Soft Voice?" everyone seemed to say at the same time in startled, muted gasps.

Long Hair stared down at the child as Night Bear unwrapped the blanket to reveal the boy-child fully to his father.

"Soft Voice sends your son to you to raise in the tradition of the Arapaho," Night Bear said. "She says it is a token of her love. She says please do not hate her for those things that she did. She not only gives her son to you, to prove that her love for you was true, but also hopes that giving up her son to the Arapaho will erase all ugly thoughts of her from their minds."

"A son?" Long Hair said, tears filling his eyes. "She gives me a son?"

"That is so," Night Bear said, nodding. He gave

the Ute woman a look over his shoulder. "On the journey here, Blue Blossom nourished the child with her milk." He gazed Long Hair's way again. "Is there one among you who can nourish the child until he is weaned?"

Maggie had listened to all that was disclosed with utter awe. From what she had known about Soft Voice, and the lengths she had gone to try and manipulate other's lives for her own benefit, it did not seem at all possible that she would give up her son.

Unless it was still a way to manipulate lives. Maggie almost knew for certain that Soft Voice would not do this from the goodness of her heart. She had probably not wanted to be bothered with a child.

But the wonder of it all was that the child made Long Hair look more virile than ever in the eyes of his people. She could see the pride in his eyes as he gazed down at his very own flesh and blood. His pride was running deep, as was his happiness.

Maggie stepped forth quickly. "I have enough milk to feed two children," she said, before anyone else had a chance. She knew that Many Children Wife's breasts were ripe and full again. She would want the honor of nursing this miracle child.

But Maggie wanted to do it, because of her deep-felt love for Long Hair.

Falcon Hawk swept an arm around her waist. She glanced up at him, seeing the pride in the depths of his eyes.

Then she became breathless as the child began

to cry and was taken from the cradle board.

"He is yours to feed," Long Hair said, laying the child in Maggie's arms. He placed an arm around Thread Woman's waist and drew her to his side. He gazed down at her, adoringly. "We have more reason to feel young again."

Maggie rocked the child slowly back and forth while Falcon Hawk talked further with Night Bear, asking him and Blue Blossom to share food and lodging with them for one night.

When Night Bear mounted his horse, Maggie realized that he preferred to resume his travels and return home.

After Night Bear and Blue Blossom were gone, the Arapaho people gathered around and took a close look at this child who was new to them. But when his wails of hunger became more demanding, Maggie took him to her lodge and offered her breast to him beside the comfort of the fire.

Long Hair and Thread Woman sat down close to Maggie while Falcon Hawk sat across the fire from them, his eyes twinkling. In his heart he was singing, grateful to Soft Voice for having brought an added joy to his grandfather's life.

But Falcon Hawk was not blinded by this generous offering. He understood too well the ways of Soft Voice! Her reasons for relinquishing her son to the care of his father might be valid, but he doubted it.

"Is not he a handsome son?" Long Hair said, unable to stop marveling over this gift that had seemed sent from heaven.

"*Aa . . . haa . . .*" everyone seemed to say at once.

"And what will you name him, *naba-ciba?*" Falcon Hawk said, shoving a piece of wood into the flames of the fire.

"Dreaming Wolf," Long Hair said, his voice now low and serious. "Does it not seem as though my first son has returned to me? *Haa,* he will have the name that my first son was given."

"If he walks in my father's shadow, he will one day be a great leader," Falcon Hawk said, remembering his father before he became bitter because of what the white people took from him. *This* son of Long Hair would not experience those defeats known to Falcon Hawk's father, for everything had already been taken from the Arapaho that could possibly be taken.

"Our sons who are of the same age will grow up to be fast friends," Maggie said, smiling at Long Hair.

"*Haa,*" he said, nodding. "After many moons have passed, and they are young men, they will share in the sun dance."

Maggie's smile faded, still dreading this ceremony that scarred a man's body for life.

"But this old father doubts he will be around to see such a marvelous sight," Long Hair said sadly, then added mischievously, "Yet, too, perhaps he *might.*"

Thread Woman slipped a hand into Long Hair's. They exchanged sweet, endearing smiles.

Chapter Thirty-Three

Sixteen Years Later

The berries in the mountains and forests were ripe. It was the time for the sun dance, a great ceremony of renewal and prayer for blessings. The dance was held in the summer, according to pledges made in the course of the preceding year.

Many people of different tribes had traveled for miles to the Arapaho village to witness the ceremony. They had camped in one big circle beside the river. It was a time for horse racing, gambling on dice and hidden-counter games, feasting, boasting, courting, and visiting.

On the fourth day of the ceremony, those participating had refrained from food and water and gazed endlessly towards the sun. Yet a few young men were going to fulfill their vows by doing more. Painted and wreathed, they would suffer themselves to be tied to the sacred pole by ropes ending in wooden skewers thrust through the flesh of the chest.

Blowing eagle-bone whistles and jerking backward against the skewers they would dance until the flesh gave way. In later years, they would wear the scars received this day with pride as an assurance of divine blessing honorably won.

The sun was high in the sky, sending its gilding rays across the land, settling most importantly on the circular skeleton lodge of poles and greenery called *haseiha-wu,* the Sacred Lodge, which had been erected for the sun dance.

The lodge had been set up in a horseshoe shape, open above except for log rafters extending from the walls to a forked cottonwood trunk set in the center. The lodge was open to the east, while at the west end the dancers formed an arc of a circle facing the central, sacred tree, the focal point of the dance.

This tree trunk, as well as all of the other wood, had been stalked as one would spy upon an enemy's camp, felled, and brought home as if they were enemies. To the top of the sacred tree a rawhide figure had been tied.

Maggie sat on a platform that was scattered with lush pelts in this lodge, Falcon Hawk and Sky Eyes beside her on one side and Long Hair on her other. She cast Long Hair a quick glance and smiled. He had lived much longer than anyone would have ever guessed. He was nearing his one-hundredth birthday, yet he still could think clearly and walk, although slowly and shakily.

Not only had Pure Heart passed away, Thread

Woman had passed on to the other side some ten winters ago. But Long Hair was still very much alive, having Dreaming Wolf to sustain him. His son gave him cause to fight the hand that sometimes reached out for him from the heavens, fighting always to live, to see his son mature into adulthood—and to see him participate in the sun dance, the greatest annual religious ceremony of the Arapaho, a time when blood flowed as a sacrifice to the sun god.

Tears of happiness for Long Hair filled Maggie's eyes, for he was proudly observing his son gaining rank among his fellows as having the four virtues—bravery, generosity, fortitude, and integrity. His son's whole life thereafter would be devoted to demonstrating these virtues in all that he did.

As would Gold Eagle, Maggie thought proudly to herself, wiping tears from her eyes with the back of her hand. Although she still dreaded seeing her son's body scarred, as his father's once was by the same ritual, she had grown used to knowing that it was something she would have to accept.

She glanced over at Falcon Hawk. He was dressed in fringed doeskin to match Maggie's doeskin dress that was fancily fringed and beaded. He was still as handsome and noble as the day she had first met him.

For him, Maggie had, and was still, learning to accept all the customs of the Arapaho people, even the scarring of their son.

Maggie could see the pride in Falcon Hawk's eyes as he gazed ahead, waiting for that moment when Gold Eagle would join Dreaming Wolf and others in the last of the sun dance ritual, when they would stand together as skewers were placed into their chests.

She understood the importance of understanding, and the need of this ceremony for their son to become a man in the eyes of their people. She had watched their son grow into a handsome young man of sixteen winters, who already turned the eyes of many young women to him.

Maggie searched through the crowd of people who sat also waiting for the ceremony to begin, stopping when her eyes found White Doe, the pretty and delicate Cheyenne girl whose heart was sweet for Gold Eagle. She had traveled far with her parents to be able to be with Gold Eagle at this special moment in his life.

Gold Eagle traveled often to White Doe's village, to further their courtship. Although it was best for Arapaho warriors to wait until later in life to marry, Maggie did not think that her son would wait until he was in his thirtieth winter to take a wife.

She only hoped that he would at least wait until he was twenty! She wanted him to be sure about the woman he married. Sixteen was still so young, when life still was meant to be carefree. . . .

White Doe had come not only to observe the ceremony, but to assist Gold Eagle. She would stand with Gold Eagle and wipe the blood from his streaming wounds upon wisps of sweet grass which she would afterwards burn as a prayer offering that she might hold the love of this noble warrior.

Maggie's heart skipped when White Doe rose from the crowd and moved through them. It was almost time for the most sacrificial moment of the ritual to begin.

In nervous jerks, she turned her gaze back to those participants in the sun dance. Those who were not going to venture any farther had stepped aside, allowing room for those who were.

A sob lodged in Maggie's throat and she covered her mouth to stifle the sound of it while she watched her son stand and wait, proud-shouldered, for the special moments to begin. Every step of this ceremony was regarded as pure and holy, the aim to secure power and celestial aid. This was being done in the honor of the sun, who, because it was pleased, would grant the prayers of those who submitted to these rites.

Gazing intensely at Gold Eagle, Maggie wiped tears from her eyes. White Doe was standing a short distance from him, her eyes filled with love and pride. It was so easy for Maggie to understand this young maiden's feelings about her son. Maggie could see his handsomeness, the very mirroring of his father. Today he wore a red breechclout made of soft deerskin, a cape of otter fur, two arm bands made of buffalo hair, two ankle bands made of rabbit fur, ornaments of sage, and a bone whistle made from an eagle's wing which hung on a strip of leather around his neck.

Maggie's eyes widened and she snaked a hand over to Falcon Hawk and intertwined her fingers with his. She clung to his hand as the part of the ritual that she had dreaded began.

Gold Eagle and Dreaming Wolf took their places with the other young warriors, lying facedown on robes. A shaman came forth and in an earnest speech extolled the bravery of the young men, recounting each of their noble deeds.

Maggie's eyes were focused only on Gold Eagle when four men went to him and knelt down beside him. Turning him over, they held her son rigid to the ground while a fifth man raised the muscles of Gold Eagle's back so that he was able to pierce the flesh of his chest with a knife, then run wooden skewers through the incisions.

Maggie turned her eyes away, her heart aching to see the torture her son must be feeling, yet not a sound had he uttered.

Again she watched. Gold Eagle was led alongside Dreaming Wolf and the others to the sacred pole, about which they, one by one, threw their arms and prayed, turning then so that the officers of the rite could fasten thongs in the holes through their flesh, securing them in this way to the sacred pole.

Maggie covered a sob behind her hand, fighting against going to her son and embracing him against any more pain that might come to him.

But it was then that Gold Eagle took his bone whistle in his mouth and began playing upon it, as he, along with the others, moved back violently and began dancing, their gazes never leaving the sun.

This went on for several hours. White Doe stayed close enough to Gold Eagle to keep the blood from his flesh. Maggie could see tears rolling down the pretty Cheyenne girl's face, knowing that she too was hurting inside to see Gold Eagle's exhaustion and suffering.

Gold Eagle still gazed at the sun, making one last final heaving jerk against the thongs, until his flesh gave way, releasing the skewers.

When Gold Eagle crumpled to the ground, it took all of Maggie's willpower not to run to him and lift his head onto her lap.

Falcon Hawk had felt Maggie's pain and despair as she had clasped his hand harder and harder. He knew her thoughts—that she wanted to run to Gold Eagle, the mother in her seeing only the pain that he was in, not the glory that Gold Eagle had achieved for himself today in enduring the most crucial rites of the sun dance.

Falcon Hawk had felt his son's pain also, because he could remember how he had silently suffered through the ritual. But he had been a better man for doing this, as his son would now be. Falcon Hawk had become great in the eyes of his people and blessed in many ways by the Great Unseen Power.

One blessing stood out above the others—that he had been led to Maggie that day of her flight from a husband who had died.

Together they had made this magnificent specimen of a son—this son who would beget sons for Falcon Hawk and Maggie to watch grow and also participate in the sun dance rites!

Life was a continuation of sacrifices which always made one's life more complete, more fulfilled.

"The worst is over?" Maggie whispered, leaning close to Falcon Hawk.

"*Haa,* the worst and the best," Falcon Hawk said, turning smiling eyes to Maggie. "And fret not over our son. At this moment, he is filled with pride and a peace within himself that only those who participate in the sun dance ever feel."

Maggie smiled weakly at him, wanting to believe what he said. Yet she would never forget her son's sufferings. Even though he had not uttered one cry to prove his pain, she knew that he had felt it.

His pain was her pain.

That was the way of mothers.

Turning her head back to her son, Maggie saw that she was no longer needed for comforting. White Doe was there, with Gold Eagle's head resting on her lap.

When Maggie saw the smile that Gold Eagle gave White Doe, she knew that what he had gone through, for the reasons that he had, had been right for him.

In his smile was a soft radiance.

Maggie could believe now what Falcon Hawk had said—that her son was filled with pride, peace, and a greatness known only to those like himself who went the limit to prove their worth to their people.

Maggie looked over at Long Hair. Tears were streaming down his ashen, sunken cheeks as he gazed at his son with his squinted old eyes. And she could see that he approved of the young Cheyenne woman who was ministering to Dreaming Wolf, holding his head and wiping the blood from his chest wounds.

"It is with much thanks that this old man has lived to see this day," Long Hair said, looking at Maggie, then past her at Falcon Hawk. "Falcon Hawk, your old grandfather is now ready to take his place on the long road with Thread Woman."

"*Naba-ciba,* do not be so eager to leave us," Falcon Hawk said, reaching over to pat his grandfather's withered arm. "There is much more to see where our sons are concerned."

"Also daughters," Maggie said, watching Sky Eyes as she slipped away from the platform and ran away with a handsome Cheyenne brave toward the forest. She had stopped only long enough to admire the full-grown, majestic eagle that sat proudly on its perch outside Maggie's and Falcon Hawk's lodge. Many years ago, the female eagle had been set free for mating. Falcon Hawk had since had one more female, and now this male, one as loved as the other.

"It seems that the Cheyenne have ways of stealing our children's hearts," Maggie then said with a sigh.

"I believe we must remind our children that they still *are* children," Falcon Hawk said, worrying about Sky Eyes's infatuation with this young Cheyenne warrior. He brought her gifts often. They took long walks together, straying far from the eyes of Maggie and Falcon Hawk. He did not want his daughter to marry this soon.

Yet a wife his daughter's age was revered by her husband. Falcon Hawk knew this to be true, for had not his Panther Eyes been almost the same age as his beautiful, beguiling daughter?

Maggie watched until she could no longer see Sky Eyes. She was concerned about these times shared alone between her daughter and the young, handsome Cheyenne brave. She recalled so very vividly how the first delicious pangs of love felt! It could blind you to everything else but the arms in which you were being held, and those lips which were making you captive!

But Maggie shrugged and smiled, knowing that no one could control one's heart when that perfect person came into one's life.

She scooted closer to Falcon Hawk and smiled adoringly up at him. His mere presence was magical. His name was like music in her heart.

And when they made endearing love, even after seventeen winters of marriage, the savage embers flamed anew within their hearts!

She would make sure that the fires were never allowed to die between them!

Dear Reader:

I hope that you have enjoyed reading *Savage Embers*. My next Leisure book in the continuing *Savage* series will be *Savage Spirit,* to be released six months from now. *Savage Spirit* is about the proud Apache and promises much adventure and passion!

I would love to hear from you all. For a newsletter, please send a legal-sized self-addressed envelope to:

CASSIE EDWARDS
R#3 Box 60
Mattoon, Il. 61938

WARMLY,

Cassie Edwards